DOCTOR WHO – A COMPANION

(An Unofficial Guide To 60 Years Of T. V's Most Iconic Show!)

Text Copyright: Timothy J. Lee 2013/2023

NOTES ON THE 2023 REGENERATION OF THIS BOOK

"Change, my dear. And it seems not a moment too soon."
- The Sixth Doctor on regenerating.

Ah 2013, I was so much older then. It was the 50th anniversary of my favourite show and simultaneously the year I self published my first ever book; the culmination of 4 years' work watching and reviewing every Doctor Who episode and spin-off episode and writing down my two cents. For me nothing has changed much. It's still my favourite show, my writing is still an awkward bluster; limited by my lack of vocabulary or literary skill. But as for the show itself....we've seen 10 years, 3 'main' Doctors, 2 showrunners and some very notable changes to the whole Doctor Who universe. Plus of course the time to rewatch and reevaluate the entire series.

So I thought it was high-time I revisited this book and reappraised what I now think about each serial. I'm surprised my opinion has changed for so many of these stories. Those stories I rated poorly have moved up in my estimations and even some of the stories that I rated so highly have conversely moved down. I think in many ways this is testimony to how multifaceted and diverse this show is. The whole show is amazing; my opinions of it are just that – completely and utterly subjective.

With this in mind, please take my opinions and reviews as one fan's perspective. The motivation of this book is purely to encourage you to consider and share your own opinions; to enjoy this show in your own way. Your opinion will be different from mine – and that's ok!

I hope you enjoy this 60th anniversary edition of my Doctor Who – A Companion, and as an amateur writer, I hope you know how much I appreciate you picking up and dipping into it.

(N.B - Please note that every time I refer to the Doctor as 'he/him,' it is because the majority of this book is pre-Jodie! Wherever possible I will remember to change the pronouns to 'he/him/she/her.' Apologies for where I forget!).

2013 INTRODUCTION

- Why Who?

So, why bother writing a book about Doctor Who?

Like thousands of people, Doctor Who was an essential part of my childhood. I had little idea of what an iconic show it was – just that I loved the idea of a mystical 'mad man in a blue box' that could transport the viewer through all of time and space, to magical worlds or to any time in history.

At the time I first became a fan, the show was reaching its 25th anniversary. I had a foggy memory of the blonde haired, handsome, heroic Doctor (Peter Davison) that my older brother had enjoyed watching, and a bit more of a recent memory of the cantankerous Doctor with the mane of curly hair (Colin Baker). But it wasn't until I saw the small Scottish whirlwind that was Sylvester McCoy burst onto the screen in the late 80's that I was truly hooked. For all his/her strangeness and complexity, this was an alien that kids could relate to – an energetic hero, an adult with a child's enthusiasm who saw the wonder in new adventures. He/she was also a thoroughly moral character, with a strong and impeccable idea of 'right and wrong' and; uniquely for a children's hero, one that would fight for what was right using intellect, rather than fists or swords. An outsider, who was free to go anywhere they chose, but was always ultimately alone. Someone you could relate to, but also a great mystery that would never truly be solved.

With the memories of Davison and C. Baker, I had a basic idea that Sylvester wasn't the 'first' actor to play the Doctor. But, it wasn't until I acquired a 25th Anniversary collector's annual from Marvel comics that I realised just what an institution this programme was.

Whilst I didn't have access to the old episodes, for the first time I could read about these fascinating interpretations of my favourite character – from the scary looking First Doctor, to the daft looking Yetis of the Second Doctor, the Karate-kicking Third Doctor and so on. This book was like a magical looking glass into a mysterious history of the programme.

Unfortunately for my generation, 'our' Doctor, Sylvester McCoy was to be the last for a considerable time. I always kept an interest in the programme, but as the Internet and videos were not accessible, the pipe-dream of discovering these old episodes remained just that.

It wasn't until some 16 years later (not counting the 1996 film starring Paul McGann, which I never got to see at the time) that the series was revamped with Christopher Eccleston; once again bringing the Doctor back into the living room. This 'regeneration' of the series in 2005 had the same effect for most fans (now grown up) like me of reconnecting us with a childhood favourite and reigniting our interest in the enigmatic Doctor. I decided it was way past time to found out more, and explore the classic series from its beginnings. Up until this point I'd never had the resources, but two equally important strikes of luck were to help me.

Firstly, and most importantly, I had friends who were experts in all things 'Who' and who had an impressive collection of the classic series. I couldn't have even started this book without their support and knowledge, and this book is very much dedicated to them.

The second important element which enabled me to access so much of the classic series was the Internet. Thanks to the following sites and streaming services it has been possible to 'fill in the gaps' of existing serials and episodes:

www.youtube.com/user/B.B.C
www.crossingthewhoniverse.com
www.blinkbox.com www.watchseries.eu
BBC Iplayer
BritBox
Netflix

Finally in this introduction, I want to explain that I am by no means an expert, and this is a selection of reviews from the point of view of someone who primarily loves the series. This book will probably have most Who fanatics reaching for their shredders. But it is my hope that it can also be an introduction for fans like me who love the show but want to know a bit more about it, or those who want to relive their favourite episodes and eras of the show.

I hope you will enjoy my naïve but passionate look at 60 years of this iconic show, from its debut in 1963 to the 60th Anniversary special (also including a detailed guide to all the spin-off series and films the show has spawned). I hope it encourages any fan of the show to go back and watch the old shows and to appreciate the brilliance of one of the longest running shows in history.

- Time Is Relative

This journey has taken me around 4 years (for the first edition, about 2 years for the second edition). Obviously, full-time work and other commitments have meant I couldn't watch the show regularly. Difficulties in finding all the episodes has also meant that I haven't watched these serials in the order they were broadcast. I think this has worked in my favour however, and unless you're a stickler for the linear, I wouldn't recommend trying to watch the series from beginning to end in a short space of time. There are a number of ways to approach watching the shows, and of course you've got to find the right way for you. Take it at your own pace (and hopefully this book will help you to discover which are the 'best' ones to start with..at least from my opinion). Which brings me to my next consideration...

- 'Do I Have The Right?'

So, what gives me the right to critique one of the best beloved shows ever? The short answer is - we all have that right – a right to an opinion...and a right to disagree with that opinion. I am primarily a fan. And I hope that this book is read with the intention it is written. I have the deepest respect for the creators, directors and writers. This book is meant as a labour of love for a show I (like countless others) have grown up with. Even when I give the most damning of criticisms, this is done purely to give a balanced review and is never meant to offend or bring derision to the show. But a book of reviews without light and shade would be pretty boring. So please 'enjoy this book responsibly,' and with great respect for all the people who have been involved in its making over an unprecedented 60 years on television (so far!).

- How To Use This Book

This book is written in broadcast order, from the pilot episode in 1963, through to the 60th Anniversary special in 2023. You can either read it in this order, or dip into it when and where you want. Another way to use this book is by checking out the index at the back. This will give you a run-down of all the elements of the show that you might be looking for. So, if you are a big Dalek fan, the index will help you find all the times the psychotic pepper-pots are mentioned. However you use this book,
I hope it's useful and however you enjoy this book, I hope it's enjoyable.

- 'But What About...?'

This book tries wherever possible to give a full guide to 60 years of the programme and its spin-offs. However, as the 'whoniverse' has included many branches which are either not strictly 'canon' or that are distanced in some way from the 'main show,' I have tried to stick to the more conventional televised episodes of the show. This may exclude non- televised stories (audio and written adventures), animated shorts and I may have missed some of the
many 'prequels' and/or 'minisodes' that were popular around the early 2010's. But I still hope this book provides you with one of the most complete guides you will find...infused with a light-hearted review of each of the televised episodes available.

So, let's begin! Buckle up for a ride through space and time.

THE 'CLASSIC ERA' – (1963-1996)

Introduction

As a piece of television, the classic show is fascinating for several reasons. The different actors who have played the Doctor, and the many writers/producers involved in the show mean that no serial is ever really the same. There are few Doctor Who fans who agree on what is a 'good' or 'bad' serial; and this is a good thing - you never really know what you're going to get. If you dislike some of the serials, it just makes you appreciate the ones you do like all the more. This is reflected in my reviews; which range from affection and praise to frustration and disappointment. Quite a testimony to the diverse nature of the show.

How To Watch The 'Classic Era' For The First Time

When you first start watching the 'classic era,' especially if you are used to the 'modern' show, you would be forgiven for finding it quite hard work. There are a couple of things you can do to help you appreciate what an amazing show it was back then. And believe me, it is well worth the effort!

First of all, it is important to remember the practical differences between the 'classic' and 'modern' shows. Back in the original run of the show, the episodes were almost constantly shown each week, and recorded with little time or space for second takes. This meant that it was impractical (and expensive) to show a completely different story each week. 'Serials' were divided usually into four parts, which would be shown on consecutive weeks. Instead of cramming all the action into one 45 minute episode (as usually happens with the modern show), the action needed to be 'dragged out' for as long as possible. This isn't to under-estimate the writers, who mostly did a sterling job at creating truly memorable and effective television. But it is to explain why the pace feels very different when watching the early shows. In fact, slowing down the pace of your viewing expectation does have a certain therapeutic feel when you get into it. It's also important to understand that these episodes were shown in (usually) 25 minute segments each week, and were not designed to watch all in one go. I now find that I can enjoy watching full serials quite easily, but it took a bit of time to get used to this pacing.

Secondly, it's important to take into consideration the budgetary and time restrictions that the producers had to deal with. The teams that worked on Who in the early days had very little money with which to bring the fantastical ideas of the writers to the small screen, and they managed this with a great deal with ingenuity. What might look rather 'dated by today's standards actually took a lot of creativity to achieve with very little resources. One of the first rules of watching the classic series is that the more you suspend your disbelief, the more you will enjoy the experience. You even grow to love the less than spectacular effects – I actually prefer them in a lot of ways to the 'modern,' more highly budgeted visuals.

A good way to start watching the older shows might be to check out the 'best and worst' episodes of each Doctor at the back of this book. Or if you are a fan of some of the classic companions (such as Sarah Jane) or
'monsters,' (such as the Cybermen) you might want to start with episodes that contain them. My own starting point was to borrow one D.V.D of each Doctor from my friend, and see which era I enjoyed the most, and to go from there.

Anyway, enough of this ridiculous hyperbole Chesterton, it's time to meet the First Doctor!

THE FIRST DOCTOR – WILLIAM HARTNELL (1963-1966)

SEASON 1

In season 1 of the show, we are introduced to the character of the Doctor, a mysterious elderly alien who lives in a time machine disguised as a Police Box, his teenage daughter, and her teachers Ian Chesterton and Barbara Wright, who unwittingly stumble upon a new adventure in time and space.

The series starts by alternating between travels in history and science fiction – echoed by the teacher companions' subjects of history and science.

The characters go through many difficulties with each other, before learning to gel as a team.

An Unearthly Child - 8/10

Ian and Barbara, two teachers from a London school are concerned about one of their pupils Susan. She is exceptionally knowledgeable for a girl her age, and is saying some very strange things indeed. They decide to follow her home to try and unearth the mystery (nothing dodgy about that at all is there?!). But home is apparently an abandoned police box in a junk yard...and the Granddad she lives with is definitely not what he seems...

It turns out both Susan and her Grandad are aliens; travelling through time and space in their time machine, the 'T.A.R.D.I.S' ('Time and Relative Dimension in Space'). Her mysterious Grandfather 'The Doctor,' worried that the 1960's isn't ready to know of this technology kidnaps the two teachers and takes them all to the T.A.R.D.I.S's next destination – Prehistoric Britain.

It's great to get to see the first ever Doctor Who serial for the first time and I wasn't disappointed. The first twenty-something minutes are just so iconic, and establish so much of the premise of what was to come. Many of the things we now take for granted - the Doctor, the T.A.R.D.I.S, the idea of travelling through the 4th and 5th dimensions of time and space - they are all here for the first time.

I was surprised how well produced and gripping this first episode was for its time; playing like a sci-fi thriller. The episode also sets up the Doctor as (at first) rather a guarded, almost frightening character who wants to hide away from humanity (afraid that knowledge of his advanced technology to people from 1963 would disturb time itself). (His character does lighten as the doctor experiences more of the human world, and gets to know his new companions. So if you are unsure about this 'harsher' Doctor, keep watching as the series and characters develop)

Hartnell is a very interesting choice to play the titular character. Before getting into acting, he'd had rather a colourful and troubled life himself, which seems to inform some of the characterisation he brings to the Doctor. Born in 1908 to an unmarried single mother (when such things were very much frowned upon), he never found out who his father was. Living in foster care, he left school early with no prospects and he dabbled in petty crime. He trained as a boxer and as a jockey, but ran away. He entered the theatre at 17 as a stage-hand, and met his future actress wife Heather at 21 whilst working on a play (they would remain married until his passing in 1975). He turned up late to his first film role in 1928, and was made to apologise to each of the crew in turn by the filmmaker (Noel Coward) before being publicly fired; an unceremonious beginning to an illustrious career. He joined the tank corps in World War 2, but was invalided back to England after suffering a mental breakdown. By the age of 55 years old, when he was chosen to play the Doctor, he had already made his name playing tough characters, such as the Sergeant Major in 'The Army Game,' or thugs and villains in a series of films. He was hesitant at first to accept the role, but was interested in trying something different (although arguably there is still a lot of the Sergeant Major in his performance, for all its eccentricity). Once he grew into the part, he enjoyed being a children's hero, as he loved kids (he had one daughter of his own and two grandchildren). Hartnell manages to enthuse his Doctor with both an authoritative and whimsical side; making the character very deep, mysterious and 'alien' from the beginning.

The acting and story in this first serial is stronger than I imagined it would be and the feel of the show is far less 'camp' and 'kitsch' than some of those that followed.
The rest of the serial is a serviceable plot about cavemen. But the first episode is essential viewing for any fan of science-fiction, and I would highly recommend everyone watch it.

The Daleks - 9/10

The Doctor and his cohorts travel to the distant planet of Skaro, to find that everything is seemingly dead; wiped out by radiation. The Doctor tricks the others into exploring the nearby city, where they discover the planet isn't as empty as they'd thought. Enter the iconic Daleks - A race of mutated aliens who are encased in metal killing machines. They have no desire other than to destroy anything in their way. The Doctor encounters their long-term enemies, the Thals;

who's pacifist ways have stopped them from taking on the might of their evil metal enemies. It's up to the Doctor and companions to convince them to rise up and defeat their foes before it's too late.

I'm really enjoying these earlier, slightly grittier Doctor Who serials. Although rather old-fashioned by today's standards, they are highly watchable and stand the test of time as classic science fiction television. The producers did all they could to work with the materials they had, and I think the effects are actually less 'cringe worthy' than, say the Jon Pertwee days. Perhaps the black and white (which often covers a multitude of sins) has something to do with this; adding to the suspense and drama. The action (particularly in this serial) is strong, and the main characters all act their parts well - though Susan's constant terror at almost everything she comes into contact with (Daleks, people...lightning!) did start to grate slightly towards the end.

In this story, both the Doctor and the Daleks are quite different from the characters we've come to know. The Daleks seem a lot more philosophical and individually minded; the Doctor seems much more selfish and manipulative, happy to leave most of the heroics to Ian (his companion). However, I didn't feel that these were 'out of keeping' with the rest of franchise. The Doctor is a renegade from the Time Lords and is likely to be quite cagey and wary at this early stage. It is believable that the Doctor softens as he becomes more fond of humans (most likely through watching the noble actions of characters such as Ian and Barbara). The Daleks are in the process of mutating both physically and mentally in this early series, and it is believable that they 'devolve'/'evolve' (depending on your viewpoint) into the relentless amoral killing machines they become.

Another great early story that is full of action, suspense and continues to show the strong seeds of one of the most iconic sci-fi TV series of all time.

The Edge Of Destruction - 7/10

Strange double partner in which the T.A.R.D.I.S malfunctions; leaking its energy into the control room. This causes all sorts of problems, as the crew rapidly seem to lose their minds, becoming suspicious, paranoid and even aggressive towards each other.

This so-called 'bottle' story (because they stay in one set throughout) isn't quite as enjoyable or compelling as the two which preceded it. But it is exciting to see the first exploration of the T.A.R.D.I.S as a temperamental machine with dangerous potential. This isn't a bad story, if you can put up with Susan's ever increasing over-reacting to everything.

Marco Polo - (All 7 Episodes Missing) 7/10

The Doctor and companions become embroiled in the life and battles of Marco Polo in 1289.

It's such a shame many of these early stories from the First and Second Doctor are missing. It seems amazing in the 21st century where media is so accessible, that the B.B.C would consider simply throwing away their recordings, but that's exactly what they did, including the very popular Doctor Who serials of the 1960's.

Thankfully, you can still follow this story on Youtube (and as an abridged version in the extras on the Edge of Destruction D.V.D). What remains of this serial are photos and the audio track. But even with these meagre elements you can tell this is one of the most lavishly made of the Hartnell stories; with beautifully decorated 13th century sets and costumes. The story is intriguing and the characters are memorable.

Whilst I'm not as big a fan of the 'history' plots, my complete ignorance of this period helped me get into the story more. A fun addition to the series that I'd like to have seen in its original complete condition.

The Keys Of Marinus - 6/10

On an alien planet, the team are forced to look for keys to repair a 'justice machine' which will save the inhabitants from the onslaught of the evil 'Yartek' and his 'Voord.'

As it sounds, this is probably the most ambitious story so far, weaving in all sorts of novel ideas. That said, I did find it quite a difficult one to follow and get into and my attention did wane and wander. Perhaps this serial will improve with repeat watching. It's a misguided cliché that the early sets were wobbly and cheap - the sets for serials like this, Marco Polo and The Daleks are very well built for the time and look great. There are also a couple of very interesting scenes on offer in these episodes. But this serial was a lot more taxing than I thought the serials so far have been.

The Aztecs - 9/10

The T.A.R.D.I.S crew are back in Earth's history again, in the time of the Aztecs. Dematerialising inside a closed temple, they cause quite a stir amongst the locals as they walk out into the light. Opinion is divided on the strange visitors, and whilst some view Barbara as a Goddess, others (like the wonderfully sinister High Priest Tlotoxl) are sceptical. She decides to use her new found divinity to try and stop the human sacrifices that are going on. But the Doctor warns her that 'meddling' in time will have catastrophic consequences!

This is one of my favourites of the early 'back-in-time' stories. The sets and costumes are beautiful again. It's also nice to see Barbara take more of a leading role.
Along with Ian, she is fast becoming one of my favourite of the Doctor's companions in the classic era.

The idea of the 'space-time-continuum' is introduced here - that changing time, in however small a way can seriously damage the future. This is something that has been explored a lot in science fiction, and is explained in a very straightforward way for the first time in this show. The Doctor is adamant that key elements of history (or 'fixed points' as they are later called) cannot, and should not by tampered with, even for moral reasons. This is a brave, and ironic premise for a show where the main protagonist's raison d'etre is to travel through time improving things for people.

One of the better of the early stories, and good kid's drama that is well worth a watch for any fan interested in the Hartnell era.

The Sensorites - 6/10

Deep in space, The Doctor finds a human crew that is being brainwashed by the 'Sensorites,' a telepathic alien race. Susan uses her own telepathic abilities to intervene and try to convince the aliens that the humans pose no threat to them and they should be released.

The Doctor takes on his 3rd alien species and his first mind control story (a staple of the series). I really enjoy these early serials and although this isn't quite as 'classic' or memorable as An Unearthly Child or The Daleks, I found it much easier to watch and the pace is much more fluid and cohesive than The Keys of Marinus space story that came before it.

Yet at 6 episodes, it was a little over-long for my liking, although the aliens' use of telepathy to control the crew of a ship is an intriguing one. Rather like The Unearthly Child, this is a serial that starts really strong and then tails off as it goes on. The Sensorites who start off as menacing at the beginning become more and more 'pathetic,' to the point where their weaknesses are rather laughable.

Hartnell seems to be struggling a little with the script in this one, but he holds his own and is still one of my favourite of the Doctors to watch. It's interesting to see the relationship between the Doctor and Susan his Grand-daughter as she starts to go through her teenage rebellion from him. These earliest companions are still some of my favourites.

The Reign Of Terror - (Episodes 4 And 5 Of 6 Missing) - 5/10

The Doctor finds himself in the middle of the French Revolution.

This one is notable for a couple of reasons. It is the first 'location' shooting, outside of the studio (in the countryside) and we see the Doctor's more violent side, as he takes out a particularly nasty slave-driver at the side of the road (who is then shown to be 'snoring' so as not to implicate the Doctor too harshly).

However, for all its originality, this serial doesn't really seem to 'go' anywhere, and doesn't maintain your interest.

An amazing first season goes out on a bit of a damp squib with this underwhelming serial; which is not terrible by any means, but not up to the same standard as The Daleks or The Aztecs.

With this great first series, the seeds are well and truly planted for the show to now grow and develop in exciting new ways, and I can't wait to discover more.

SEASON 2

The first T.A.R.D.I.S team leave, and we meet the Doctor's new companions from the future Vicki and Steven. The Daleks are at the peak of their popularity and we meet the first new member of the Doctor's race (not counting the Doctor himself or Susan of course).

The stories are even more fantastical and experimental, and there are many stand out essential stories in Season 2.

Planet Of Giants - 7/10

The doors to the T.A.R.D.I.S open during 'materialisation' and as a result the crew on board are shrunk to the size of insects.

Everything around them appears to be dead. They discover a plot by a merciless business man to create a new insecticide, which they find will kill not only harmful insects, but everything in its path. And he's prepared to go to any ends, even murdering his colleague to keep the true nature of his new product a secret. The Doctor must find a way of bringing the 'giants' to justice, and restore himself and his companions to the right size again.

A simple idea that works well and has of course been used by other shows and films since ('Honey I Shrunk the Kids' anyone?). This serial is aimed more towards the younger demographic, which of course is no bad thing - this is after all a family show! It reminded me somewhat of the 'Land of Giants' series I used to watch as a kid.

A lot of fun and the giant sets look great, especially considering the budget they were working with at the time.

The Dalek Invasion Of Earth - 8/10

The team arrive in the 22nd Century to see their recent foes the Daleks have taken over the Earth! They must assist the rebels to take back our planet and free humanity.

Susan finds love in one of the young rebels, and decides the time has come to make a life for herself; staying to help and build a new world.

This serial came in answer to the huge popularity of the Daleks, after their first appearance, dubbed 'Dalek- Mania' by the media (echoing the 'Beatles-Mania' of the 'fab four' who were gaining their first huge success at the time).

At 7 episodes long, the action is slightly slower paced, but this is still one of the best of the earlier stories and

something every fan should see. I really liked the dystopian feel, which actually felt quite believable; reminding me somewhat of the classic War of the Worlds in some respects. It's sad to see Susan go, but her departure is done in a nice way, and William
Hartnell's farewell speech is amongst the warmest performances he delivers in the show.

> *"One day, I shall come back. Yes, I shall come back. Until then, there must be no regrets, no tears, no anxieties. Just go forward in all your beliefs and prove to me that I am not mistaken in mine. Goodbye Susan. Goodbye my dear."* (The First Doctor, The Dalek Invasion of Earth, episode 7)

The Rescue – 9/10

A short and sweet story about the Doctor rescuing an orphaned girl from her stranded ship. Landing on an almost deserted planet, the Doctor finds that the surviving 2 members of a murdered crew are being kept prisoner by a monster, and must find a way to try and rescue them both.

A well written 'who done it' style murder mystery. Whilst not the most ground-breaking of the serials so far, this is quite an easy watch, with some good scenes (such as the Doctor and Ian trying to escape the caves through Indiana Jones style traps). I was surprised that I didn't find Vicki (the new companion) half as annoying as I thought I would - she doesn't seem half as 'screamy' as Susan (though saying that, I did still miss Susan a bit in this).

Whilst the effects are a bit on the rubbish side, this is one of my favourite Hartnell stories as it is so character driven and affectionate. Hartnell's approach to the orphan Vicki is such an affectionate, Grandfatherly one (as it had been for Susan), perhaps drawing on his own troubled childhood (see 'An Unearthly Child' notes) for inspiration. This is in such stark contrast to his brusque, at times angry persona.

This is one of the First Doctor's stories I enjoy returning to most frequently. Good, wholesome, rainy day television.

The Romans – 6/10

The Doctor takes his companions for a holiday in Rome at the time of Emperor Nero. But they are soon in trouble again. Ian and Barbara are sold as slaves, and the Doctor is mistaken for a famous lyre player. Whilst Ian and Barbara must free themselves, the Doctor must convince the mighty Nero he is who he thinks he is.

Compared to 'The Reign of Terror' this is much snappier and consistently enjoyable in the first- couple of episodes, tailing off slightly in the second half. The writing is pretty strong and the chemistry between the main characters works well. A good humoured romp that is one of the most fun of the black and white era.

The Web Planet - 1/10

The Doctor faces his strangest challenge yet - tackling an all-out battle of giant wasps and giant ants?

Well, the costumes are lavish - but this is pretty ridiculous even by Who standards, and definitely not the finest hour for the First Doctor.

The Crusade - (Episodes 2 And 4 Of 4 Missing) 5/10

The team land in the midst of the Crusades and have to assist Richard the Lionheart.

I found it difficult to engage with this one; due in part to only 2 out of the 4 episodes existing (although it was nice to see extra recordings made for the video by an older Ian Chesterton, explaining what we have missed).

The serial itself was pretty fast paced and action-packed, but something felt incomplete and I didn't find it as consistently enjoyable as other Season 2 stories.

The Space Museum - 7/10

This is more my cup of tea. The story is a thought-provoking take on determinism - exploring the main characters' reactions to seeing their own future deaths (as they are turned into frozen museum exhibits in the far future); and their attempts to prevent the seemingly inevitable.

Not the best serial, but I liked it. Barbara is great as always, and Ian is *kickass* as the unlikely (yet well played) science-teacher-turned-action-hero. Vicki is a likeable new companion and Hartnell is at his grumpy, bumbling best. The closed studio sets also make for an effectively claustrophobic feel.

The Chase - 5/10

The Daleks develop their own time machine and pursue the Doctor through time and space. After watching the Space Museum, this story seems rather half-hearted and weak. There are some decidedly odd moments throughout, such as footage of The Beatles (who were huge at the time) being broadcast in the T.A.R.D.I.S, causing all onboard to start dancing inanely and the Doctor exclaiming 'oo, those are my favourite Beatles!' - I'm not lying, this scene really happens! Likewise, they land in the middle of a haunted house, complete with robot versions of Frankenstein's Monster, Dracula et al; leaving you feeling less than convinced.

Worth a watch if only for the sad departure of Ian and Barbara (definitely two of my favourite companions) and the introduction of Steven, the new male companion.

The story is all over the place with some decidedly strange moments, but it's a great T.A.R.D.I.S team of First Doctor, Vicki, Ian and Barbara, and there is some fun to be had along the way.

The Time Meddler - 7/10

The Doctor runs into one of his own kind for the first time; a Time Lord (although not described as such until the Troughton finale 'War Games'). 'The Monk,' travels through time like the Doctor, but
'meddles' in history; causing changes that he feels will profit humanity...but more importantly himself. The Doctor, who has already been involved in historical events, once again takes quite a hypocritical approach to the Monk, worried that his tinkering will endanger the fabric of time.

As a huge Carry On fan, it was great to see Peter Butterworth in a very different sort of role; although he wasn't always convincing as the evil Monk (a bad guy with a progress chart?!).

It is also worth watching to see the first appearance of a rival time traveller - who would no doubt inspire the creation of one of the Doctor's most famous adversaries - The Master!

Hartnell doesn't seem as strong in this serial, transgressing from his original grumpy, mysterious character into a strange giggly creature.

The new companions are ok, but I do agree with Vicki - I miss Ian and Barbara!

SEASON 3

The First Doctor's last full season sees the show lose some of its direction, with a revolving door of companions and ideas. It's still incredibly adventurous television; with epic 12-episode stories and highly inventive enemies.

Tragically the B.B.C had to erase a lot of its archive during the time of the 3rd-6th Season, including Doctor Who. This means that the last 2 seasons of the first Doctor and much of the second Doctor's serials are incomplete. Acknowledgement and thanks go to the various 'Whovians' (Doctor Who fans) who have kept the 'missing' serials alive by sharing audio, creating animations and piecing together photo-snaps on media sites such as Youtube and Dailymotion. Without their sterling efforts, these serials would've been a lot more difficult to access and follow.

Galaxy 4 – (Episodes 1, 2 And 4 Of 4 Missing) 6/10

The Doctor lands on a dying planet, to find two civilizations fighting over one remaining spaceship.

It's difficult to fully review a serial that is sadly missing all but one episode and a few minutes of reconstructed footage and animation. But from what I can make out this looks like a fairly fun (if rather run-of-the-mill) space-based story.

Mission To The Unknown – (Episode 1 Of 1 Missing) 6/10

The only story ('Blink' from the new series being the closest) not to feature the Doctor or companions. The one-off episode details one man's attempts to warn Earth of the Dalek's latest plans - an introduction to the epic Dalek's Master Plan later on in the series. Quite dark and full of suspense even for a one-off episode, although it doesn't really hold your attention without the regular cast. This was unfortunately the last serial to involve Verity Lambert, the first producer and a crucial pioneer of the early show. Without her vision and talent, Doctor Who would never have been the success it is today.

If you get chance, track down the superb recreation of this episode, lovingly (and expertly) made by students at the University of Central Lancashire. It is available for free on YouTube.

The Myth Makers – (All 4 Episodes Missing) 4/10

The Doctor travels to ancient Greece, where he finds himself mistaken for Zeus by the locals and caught up in the fall of Troy.

The last appearance of Vicki, who falls in love with a warrior of Troy, and stays behind (passing into legend as 'Cressida'). I have to say I'm quite sad to see Vicki go actually. She seemed to bring out a more fatherly side of William Hartnell's Doctor, after he fostered her as an orphan in The Rescue. Thankfully, she parts in the happiest of circumstances - which is more than can be said for the companion who replaces her (Troy citizen Katarina).

Again, it was difficult to get into this serial, with so little surviving footage, and what I did see didn't really feel like a normal 'Who,' or certainly not the programme at its best. It had the feeling of 'The Aztecs' about it, but didn't stay with me half as much as that far superior serial.

The Daleks' Master Plan – (Episodes 1,3,4,6,7,8,9,11 And 12 Of 12 Missing) 6/10

The Daleks plan to use a 'Time Destructor' to take over the universe.

This is a noteworthy serial for many reasons. Firstly, it's the longest of any serial to date, spanning an epic 12 episodes (13 if you include the 'prequel' one-off episode Mission to the Unknown). Secondly, it introduces the excellent Nicholas Courtney, who will go on to play one of the 3rd Doctor's major aides, the irascible Brigadier (although he plays a much different character here - the rather cowardly Bret).

But, perhaps most importantly, this is the first serial that sees the death of a companion, the short-lived Katrina. The way in which the show deals with this is truly heart-breaking – watching the Doctor's dismay as he sees his charge sucked out of the airlock to her death. I can't imagine how shocking this must've been at the time.

Unfortunately, only three episodes of the 12 now survive (2, 5 and 10), making it difficult to follow cohesively.

The Doctor seems colder and not as connected with his new companions as he was with Susan, Barbara and Ian, or Vicki, and it seems like a real state of 'limbo' for the show. Vicki has left, to be replaced briefly by Katarina, who is then killed off to be replaced even more briefly by Sara Kingdom. This, plus the lengthy running time of the serial must've made it pretty difficult to follow and keep up with. It seems to 'travel' (both literally and in it's narrative) all over the place, with varying results, and I found my interest faltering throughout. However, there are several excellent scenes, such as the tragic deaths of both Katarina, and Sara (who is killed in an equally dramatic way by the aging effects of the time destructor). This epic story really stretches the show in brave new directions, but many fans will struggle to watch it in its entirety.

The Massacre Of St Bartholomew's Eve – (All 4 Episodes Missing) 5/10

The Doctor returns to Paris, only several years before their visit in The Reign of Terror. The Doctor realises he can't change a massacre of 10,000 people by the French Catholic authorities, even though Steven begs him too.

Rather a slow and unremarkable serial. Steven is likeable, but doesn't seem to carry the same 'weight' as some of the earlier companions, at least not on his own. All the acting is fine, and so is the production, but it doesn't stand out as a classic entry into this season. I can't imagine why they would want to return to a similar period in history only a couple of seasons later, and it does feel like the series is retreading old ground here.

The Ark - 6/10

At the end of the last serial, the Doctor returned to 1966, where his next companion, Dorothea "Dodo" Chaplet walked into the T.A.R.D.I.S, uninvited.

In a similar way to the later 'The Ark in Space' (Tom Baker

story), the T.A.R.D.I.S is then drawn to the end of Earth and the survivors of the human race, who have taken to space in a huge spaceship. They co-habit the spaceship with another race who are escaping from a dead planet; the mop-topped cyborg race of the Monoids.

Dodo wastes no time at being pretty useless, managing to infect the crew with her common cold, to which they have no resistance.

The new companions don't really work, and you care much less about them than companions of past, but the story is a provocative one; showing once again the dangers that the Doctor's travels can bring to the people he meets.

The Celestial Toymaker – (Episodes 1,2 And 3 Of 4 Missing) 8/10

The Doctor becomes involved in the games of a crazed and powerful 'puppet-master.' Steven, Dodo and himself are pitted against different challenges at the whim of the dangerous 'Toymaker,' in exchange for their freedom. This involves lots of 'Crystal Maze' style games and crazed clowns (a semi-recurrent terror in Who, including the fourth Doctor 'Kinda' and the seventh Doctor 'Greatest Show in the Galaxy' stories).

I like it when the show takes on a more psychological angle, especially as The Doctor's main weapon of choice is his intellect, and this serial doesn't disappoint in that regard. Creepy and nicely paced, this would have been an effective piece of children's drama. The Toymaker is a great enemy, played excellently by Michael Gough (who you may know as the butler Alfred in the Tim Burton Batman films, or as the Time Lord Councillor Hedin in the fifth Doctor story Arc of Infinity) and it's a shame he passed away before he could reprise his role (he was due to in a cancelled Colin Baker story many years later). I believe it would have made for a great serial in the new series - to see the Doctor take on an aging and ailing Toymaker set on taking the Doctor down with him. But alas, this is one story we'll have to imagine.

The Gunfighters - 4/10

The Doctor gets himself involved in a fight between Cowboys in the old American West.

The idea of 'Doctor Who meets the Wild West' didn't fill me with hope, and although this isn't as painful as the toothache the Doctor is suffering during the first episode, it is a strange addition to the Hartnell years.
Full of singing (for some reason) and more light-hearted than the earlier serials. Fun, but not one of the best, unless the Wild West is your thing.

The Savages – (All 4 Episodes Missing) 7/10

The Doctor intervenes in another oppressive society, in which the 'civilised' harvest the 'life-force' of the 'savages,' and drain them to gain their energy. This incomplete serial reminded me somewhat of the Pertwee story 'The Mutants,' and although it's perhaps not the most original of the stories this season has to offer, I found it highly watchable, especially considering it only exists in audio and tele-snaps. It's quite sad to say goodbye to Steven, who stays behind to help keep the peace at the end of the story. Whilst he wasn't the most notable of companions, he was very likeable and heroic, in a way that made him a worthy replacement to Ian (the first male companion).

The War Machines - 6/10

The T.A.R.D.I.S returns to the swinging 60's for a full

story. A computer with its own independent thought starts to brainwash people and try to take over the world. So, it's the usual Doctor Who scenario then!

It's interesting to see the series representing 'modern life' as it was at the time of broadcast; from hip nightclubs to beehive haircuts. The serial introduces one such 'hipster,' companion, Polly, and a sailor from the time, Ben, into the series and says goodbye to Dodo. Not bad, and a nice snapshot of the era.

SEASON 4

The season with perhaps the most game-changing idea the show has ever produced...the regeneration of its main character. We say goodbye to Hartnell and hello to Troughton. The historical stories are dialled down and even more inventive science fiction ideas and enemies are introduced; although it will take the 2nd Doctor time to settle into his new persona.

The Smugglers – (All 4 Episodes Missing) 6/10

The Doctor takes on 17th Century pirates. Polly and Ben have now joined him after The War Machines, and Dodo has stayed behind. The new companions are likeable enough – though I still pine for Barbara and Ian. Ben and Polly are more effective at portraying their times (the 1960's) than the ill-fated Dodo, and work well as fire (Ben) and water (Polly) to the Doctor's Earth, if you know what I mean..no, oh well. The Smugglers is not particularly memorable or remarkable, but it's fun enough.

The Tenth Planet - (Episode 4 Of 4 Missing) 8/10

The Doctor and companions land in the North Pole in '1986,' where they stumble upon a science expedition. However, they are not the only visitors that the expedition need worry about. Soon an alien planet hones into view...a mythical 'twin' planet of our Earth. Long ago, its people searched for immortality by replacing their own body with cybernetic parts. And now their planet has returned to its solar system to convert our planet into the same as them.

Have you guessed who we're talking about yet? Yes..it's the debut of the legendary Cybermen! They may look very different in this first serial, but they're still just as scary, and they would have scared me rigid as a kid; as 'naff' as they may seem by modern standards.
The strange-intonations in the voices indeed sound like something you could imagine in a computerised mind trying to interact with humans, and to me the cloth masks were pretty creepy looking too.

One of the problems with any science fiction programme/film that sets itself in the not too distant future, is that when that time arrives, it loses most of its credibility and ends up looking rather outmoded. In this last of the First Doctor's stories, we are told it is '1986,' and yet the fashion and technology are very much from the 1960's when it was shot.
This aside, this is a great story; showcasing both a timeless new villain and the kind of 'base under siege' story that would work so well for the next incarnation of the Doctor.

I'm sad to see the first doctor go, and I'm really impressed with how much depth Hartnell brought to the character, which so many others have explored since he lay down the prototype. His time as the Doctor is probably the most diverse and varied collection of any era of the show; from historical comedies to ground-breaking science fiction, from surrealist nightmares to moving character pieces. Yes, Doctor Number 1 be irascible and difficult, but he could also be paternal, kind, funny and eccentric and Hartnell imbibed the character with so many different traits that continue to be explored by so many other actors since.

THE SECOND DOCTOR - PATRICK TROUGHTON (1966- 1969)

SEASON 4 (CONTINUED)

The Power Of The Daleks – (All 6 Episodes Missing) 8/10

A colony on the planet Vulcan (yes, you heard me right) are trying to create 'robot' servants out of machines that have crash landed on their planet, not realising that they are in fact the deadly Daleks! Obviously, the Doctor is more than a little concerned and goes to explore what's going on. It's a real shame that so little of this serial is left, especially as the first 10 minutes or so see a very important precedent being set – the idea of 'regeneration or 'renewal' (as it is called here) of the Doctor from one form to another insured the survival of the show. In other words the show was no longer dependent on the length of time the actor wanted to play the role anymore. Other important elements of regeneration are explored here also, such as the important link the T.A.R.D.I.S plays in the Doctor's safety (apart from the obvious use as transport), and this first episode would be a must-see for any fan of the show, if it could be found (although there is of course the wonderful animated version now available on DVD/Blu-Ray).

Of course, this first difficult transition from Doctor #1 to Doctor #2 would never have worked had the actor who took over from the excellent William Hartnell not been able to play it with enough of a difference to make it interesting; whilst retaining the basics of the character to keep the consistency needed.

Patrick Troughton (who legend has it Hartnell suggested as his replacement) manages this admirably; remaining both eccentric and 'alien' enough to keep a lot of what made the first Doctor special, but also showing new assets to the Doctor's character - including a more action-orientated physicality, and a shrewd use of bluffing his enemy by pretending to know a lot less about the situation than he really does.

Anyway, onto the serial itself. Usually, a Doctor's first story takes second place to their regeneration, making sure the focus is on the change of actor, rather than necessarily on the inclusion of a difficult or taxing narrative ('Robot,' Tom Baker's first story is a good example of this - a fun serial, but not overly- complicated). One of my favourite things about (most) regeneration episodes is the disorientation and confusion it creates in the Doctor, who takes time to settle into his new persona. This can cause many sides of the character to be explored; whether confusion and strange behaviour (such as here - the Doctor making little sense and reaching for his recorder) or a complete breakdown in his usual self, leading to dangerous, even psychotic consequences (as in the Peter Davison/Colin Baker transformation). Conversely though, Troughton's debut is a strong plot, featuring the Doctor's most famous enemies. Perhaps this first regeneration was seen as a risky option, so the writers weren't going to take any risks by focusing heavily on the Doctor's change as the main 'draw?'

All in all, this is probably the most important of the missing serials, so it's a real shame not to be able to see it in its original broadcast condition. Whilst the serial is fairly slow to get going, it picks up nicely towards the middle episodes, with some great creepy scenes. The end of episode 4 for example; where the Daleks begin to multiply to an eerie score and deafening multiple strained voices must've been particularly effective and terrifying to viewers at the time. A good opening story for the second Doctor, and an exciting new era for the show.

The Highlanders – (All 4 Episodes Missing) 6/10

Arriving in 18th Century Scotland, at the defeat of Bonnie Prince Charlie, the Doctor meets his newest companion, a rambunctious Scottish piper called Jamie.

Again, it's a shame to be missing this serial, which introduces, one of the main companions of the 2nd Doctor and one of the most popular and likeable of the series so far. Fun enough, and it's nice to see Jamie in his first story.

The Underwater Menace – (Episodes 1 And 4 Of 4 Missing) 6/10

The Doctor and company discover the lost city of Atlantis and a scientist who plans to raise it from the depths. Flattering the scientist, the Doctor finds out his true evil intention – to bring the water levels down and destroy the Earth by cracking it in two.

The Doctor and companions are attacked by all sides; as the archaic people want to sacrifice them to their God (again with the sacrificing!), and the scientists want to convert them into 'fish people!'

Slightly different idea but not much to comment on. Quite slow in pace, and probably would've made a better 2-parter, as it does seem to drag on a bit, even at 4 episodes long. Worth it alone for the ridiculously over-the-top villain Professor Zaroff ('Nothing can stop me nooooowwww!') and the B-Movie fish people.

The Moonbase – (Episodes 1 And 3 Of 4 Missing) 7/10

The Cybermen return; trying to control the Earth's weather by capturing the moon.

This is a very similar story to 'The Tenth Planet,' but with has some notable differences. The design of the Cybermen has evolved, from creepy cloth masks to an equally scary but more robotic helmet. The music has a wonderfully unnerving feel to it (it would be used again in the superior Cybermen story 'Tomb of the Cybermen' and I would love it if they could incorporate it into a modern era Cyberman story). I liked the sets, and there are some good scenes, but overall the pace is rather sluggish at first, becoming more engaging and exciting towards the end.

I enjoyed the serial, and it is well worth a watch. But I wouldn't say it was quite as memorable as the other Troughton Cybermen stories that came later.

The Macra Terror – (All 4 Episodes Missing) 6/10

The Doctor arrives in a colony where everything seems relaxed and therapeutic. In truth however, this is a society controlled by an all-seeing 'Big Brother' style authority that brainwashes them whilst they sleep. Only one man seems to see the bigger picture and is deemed mad for seeing large crab-like creatures crawling around outside.

It's a strange mixture of Orwellian nightmare, and some sort of B-Movie 'attack of the killer crabs.'

I liked the mind control elements of the story, and the effects such as the giant crab, which was actually quite impressive for its time. But this seems to be two stories conflicting with each other – the 'Nineteen Eighty Four' theme and the 'giant crab' theme. The serial doesn't seem to be overly confident in asserting either, making for a rather confused and badly mixed concoction.

This said, the pace is fluid, even if most of the cliff- hangers are identical. This would have made for a good serial, or two serials, had the two elements been worked on a little more.

The Faceless Ones – (Episodes 2,4,5 And 6 Of 6 Missing) 7/10

The team arrive at Gatwick Airport, to find strange alien activities going on. Creepy alien 'chameleons' are taking human captives and stealing their faces (quite horrific stuff for a kid's show!).

The aliens are targeting teenagers, using a fake '18-30' style holiday scheme; stealing their bodies and faces to replace their own faceless forms.

This felt quite original and different from the last few serials. I enjoyed this story and would definitely watch it again.

At the end, we bid a fond farewell to Ben and Polly, the two companions who have helped the Doctor through his first regeneration.

The Evil Of The Daleks – (Episodes 1,3,4,5,6 And 7 Of 7 Missing) 7/10

The 2nd Doctor takes on the killer pepper pots for the second time. The Daleks have brought their time machine to hide in the bowels of the airport where we left Jamie and the Doctor at the end of the last serial. From here, they are transporting people between Victorian and modern times (though I never quite worked out why). They have kidnapped humans, including Victoria (who will become the Doctor's next companion), and plan to extract the 'human factor' that will help them become more effective in out- thinking their enemies. *However*, it is all a cunning rouse, and what they really hope to do is the opposite; to install their own evil, merciless ways into the minds of humans, enslaving all in the process! Jamie takes an instant shine to Victoria, and goes to rescue her from her alien captors.

Quite original in its way, introducing the idea that Daleks lack the imagination and 'free-thought' it takes to gain the upper-hand in strategic battle. This is something that will be further explored in later episodes, such as the Fourth Doctor story Destiny of the Daleks and the Seventh Doctor story Remembrance of the Daleks.

As is often the case with the longer Doctor Who stories of the time, there is far too much padding and stalling before we get to two very intriguing episodes at the end.

The disturbing 'human factor' Daleks who talk like terrifying children; the war between the new and old Daleks; and addition of the iconic Supreme Dalek Emperor are all excellently executed. The last episode in particular is well worth a watch, and it's such a shame it doesn't exist fully (although there is a great animated version available now).

SEASON 5

Season 5 really capitalises on one of the most successful tropes of the Second Doctor; the 'base under siege' plot. We see the Doctor and companions fend off the Cybermen in a tomb, Robot Yetis in a Monastery and the Ice Warriors in an artic base.

Tomb Of The Cybermen - 10/10

Arriving on the desert-like planet of Telos, the Doctor and companions run into an expedition exploring an ancient tomb. On further inspection, the Doctor becomes concerned that he has seen the markings of the tomb before, and warns the expedition that it should stay unopened at all costs!

This was the first of the classic series I chose to watch since watching Sylvester McCoy episodes as a child, and I'm glad I started here. There are so many superb elements of the 'classic era' in Tomb of the Cybermen that encouraged me want to go back and watch more. In fact, after watching all of the episodes now, I would count it as probably my all-time favourite Doctor Who serial, which is no mean feat. It's not that it's the most original or remarkable, but it just seems to encapsulate all that I love about Who – the fun, the escapism, the great characters, the slight terror, the warmth, and of course the Doctor himself.

Patrick Troughton is excellent; giving just the right amount of oddness, mixed with compassion and world/time weariness to embody all that William Hartnell and all the actors after him have strived to convey. Although in parts it is laughably outdated (the 'cybermats' for example are rather more on the comical than sinister side), the story is very intriguing and kept me wanting to watch all the episodes until the end. The Cybermen themselves are far less complexly designed than what they will become, and in some ways they are more striking for this reason. Their characters (or lack of) are just as creepy and unsettling as they were in the Tenth Planet.

There are two scenes that really stand out for me in this serial, for different reasons. Firstly, there is a very heart-warming scene in which The Doctor consoles Victoria about the loss of her father (who was killed in the last serial The Evil of the Daleks). Troughton had played the character with a certain Charlie Chaplin style eccentricity up until this point, but he shows such a lovely paternal side here, that we've not seen since the Rescue (Hartnell). It is a tribute to Troughton's skills as a character actor that he can enthuse the Doctor with the best qualities of both the 'inquisitive child' and the
'protective adult' that make his Doctor so likeable.

Secondly, there is the memorable scene in which the Cybermen break free from their catacombs. The eerie way in which they slowly come to life really stays in your mind as one of the stand out shots of the original run.
Indeed, Peter Davison (Doctor #5) cited this shot as something he would bring to mind when he needed to compose himself after a fit of giggles; such is its sobering effect.

Originally thought of as 'lost' or incomplete, I'm so glad

this is available in its entirety, as Who doesn't get much better than this.

The Abominable Snowmen – (Episodes 1,3,4,5 And 6 Of 6 Missing) 6/10

The Doctor takes on Yetis in Tibet! They turn out to be actually robots, being controlled by 'The Great Intelligence.'

There is a lot of talking and not much action at first, and the surviving audio is so poor that it's very difficult to keep up with what's going on. The monsters do look about as terrifying as Sweetums from The Muppet Show, but there is something quite charming about them, and the Great Intelligence itself is quite scary. Oh, and we discover Victoria is a real screamer in this one!

The Ice Warriors – (Episodes 2 And 3 Of 6 Missing) 8/10

Continuing the icy theme, the Doctor and companions arrive deep into the Earth's future and the second 'Ice-Age.'

Here we see the first appearance of the wonderfully creepy, whispering Ice Warriors, one of the most successful of the alien races introduced in the second Doctor's run.

The ships of both the Ice Warriors and the humans are stuck in the ice. And as with previous serials, particularly Troughton's era, the over-reliance on computers seems to be holding the humans back and giving the Ice Warriors the upper hand/claw.

Victoria is quite annoying in this one, screaming her way through most of it, as she did in the last serial, and I miss her gutsier (yet equally vulnerable) characterisation in Tomb of the Cybermen.

The story is mostly well paced, with a couple of moments drag here and there; due to the 5 episodes. Overall though, I thought this was a great serial and well worth a watch.

Enemy Of The World – 5/10

The Doctor, Victoria and Jamie land on Earth in 2018, to find a society that is threatened by a Mexican dictator on one side, and equally power-mad rebels on the other. As soon as they arrive, they are attacked; as the Doctor bears a striking resemblance to the dictator
('Salamander') the rebels are trying to overthrow. After the rebels discover the truth, they enlist the Doctor to pose as his evil 'double' to find out more information.

This serial could have been a gripping one, as the Doctor takes on what appears to be an evil version of himself. A similar idea was explored in Colin Baker's 'Trial of a Time Lord' series and the more recent 'Amy's Choice;' where an enemy is created from the dark-side of the Doctor's psyche. Unfortunately, this story doesn't seem to stretch as far, and the mix-up with Salamander and the Doctor is purely a physical one. A wasted idea really, as this could've been a much more satisfying story had they turned out to a genetic parallel for some other reason.

The reason for the idea of the 'two Troughtons' is mostly to give Patrick (a well respected character actor long before playing the Doctor) more roles to try in the show. However, as much as I have the deepest respect for him as an actor, his portrayal of a Mexican dictator is not one of his finest performances - sounding more like 'Juan Sheet' from a popular tissue commercial(!). Actually, perhaps this is a little unfair...there are a few scenes, particularly towards the end where Troughton is superbly menacing and makes an excellent villain...it just takes a while to get used to the accent.

A nice departure from the 'monster' stories into more of a politically fuelled piece. The pace was ok, with a
similar feel to the later 'Invasion,' but with less of the panache of that story. It's nice to see Troughton being given another darker character to play, but I was slightly disappointed by a story that had a lot of misused potential.

The Web Of Fear – (Episode 3 Of 6 Missing) 8/10

The Doctor takes on the Yetis again, this time in the London Underground!

Although the Yetis are hardly scary by today's standards, the strength here is in the cinematography and direction, which creates a claustrophobic, eerie feel to the lurking menace.

Victoria is pretty useless again in this one; screaming herself silly at everything from the monsters themselves to cobwebs on the wall. Whilst I do tire of the 'bolshie' companions of the revamped series, I wouldn't mind seeing a companion with a bit more backbone than this!

The serial sees the debut of the wonderful Brigadier (or Colonel as he is here). Nicholas Courtney did of course previously play 'Bret' in the Dalek Master Plan, but it's great to see him play his more memorable role (the iconic Lethbridge-Stewart) for the first time.

At 6 episodes long, the story does rather repeat itself. But it is definitely one of the most fun of the Troughton serials to watch, and for the most part it had me glued to the screen.

Fury From The Deep – (All 6 Episodes Missing) 8/10

From radio controlled Yetis to brainwashing seaweed?

A strange seaweed-based creature is escaping from an underwater gas line onto a series of rigs out at sea, and is releasing a deadly gas capable of controlling its victim's mind. The Doctor must convince the stubborn head of one of the rigs about the imminent danger to all onboard.

Like the 'terror' of the last serial, the enemy itself is pretty lame. But the direction of the show makes it actually one of the most frightening of all the Troughton era. Ironically, the only remaining clips from this serial are those that were originally *cut* for being too violent or scary to children. Although today's kids are much more desensitised to seeing such things on television, I can totally understand why the acting of evil 'possession' would've created some nightmares, as it's so well realised. The main cast's reaction to the enemy is also something that stays with you. Victoria's screams are particularly harrowing here (so harrowing in fact that they end up being the main weapon against the monster!).

At the end, Victoria finally hangs up her screaming vocal chords and decides enough is enough. Whilst she's not my favourite of companions, she was sweet, and had a real effect on the affections of Jamie, so I am sad to see her go.

Definitely one of the scariest of the early stories, and even at 6 episodes long, it's surprisingly gripping.

The Wheel In Space – (Episodes 1,2,4 And 5 Of 6 Missing) 6/10

The Cybermen (and funny little Cybermats) are back, attacking a space station.

This is the first appearance of another of the 2nd Doctor's main companions. Zoe is undeniably cute, but an insufferable know-it-all, at least at this early stage – 'all brain and no heart' as they say in the 3rd episode.
However, this does lead to some nice dialogue between her and the Doctor; showing the difference between her *knowledge* and his *wisdom*.

> *"logic, my dear Zoe, merely enables one to be wrong with authority." (The Second Doctor, The Wheel in Space, episode 3)*

The Cybermen are on great 'classic' form again, with added 'hypno-rays' that can control the crew. Not my favourite Cyberman story, coming between the excellent 'Tomb' and 'Invasion,' but definitely one to check out.

SEASON 6

The Second Doctor's final season is also perhaps his most inventive; pushing the formula in different ways that will prove both successful (the psychedelic Mind Robber or the Bond like Invasion) and unsuccessful (the underdeveloped Dominators or Space Pirates). We visit the Doctor's home planet for the first time and bid farewell to black and white Who.

The Dominators - 4/10

The Doctor, Jamie and Zoe land on a seemingly peaceful planet for a spot of r&r, but as usual, things are not as they seem. Within the radioactive wastelands are a race of invaders armed with killer robots (so, it's the usual welcoming party then!).

The robots in question, the 'Quarks' were originally meant to be marketed and merchandised, with a hope to make them as popular as The Daleks. They were used as regular enemies in the Doctor Who comic strip of the time for example. Their masters are pretty menacing and their method of murder is quite gruesome (looking like some sort of melting effect for the poor victim). But the Quarks themselves look like a mixture of Lego and Ping-pong balls, with the voice of Mickey Mouse, so they are less than effective when compared with the iconic enemies they are trying to out-do.

The story itself is fun enough and pretty enjoyable. It fits in nicely with serials from the season such as the equally mediocre Krotons, but doesn't stand up next to the highlights of the season, such as the excellent Invasion, The Seeds of Death, or the epic finale The War Games.

The Mind Robber - 8/10

Slightly trippy addition to the series, in which the Doctor 'leaves reality' and encounters all sorts of mythical creatures who have been brought to life by the Master (no, not that one). Supremely silly at times but entertaining and intriguingly different to the rest of the 2nd doctor's stories. You've got to admire the imagination and scope of these early serials, and nowhere is this more evident than in the Mind Robber.

The Invasion - (Episodes 1 And 4 Of 8 Missing) 10/10

An evil business man (Tobias Vaughn) makes a deal with the Cybermen to take over and rule the Earth. But the Cybermen aren't about to share their power, as he soon finds out!

Wow, I wasn't expecting this serial to be as good as it was. This is easily one of the best of the Troughton years, incorporating all the ingredients that make for a great Doctor Who story.

It isn't without its problems though. At 8 episodes long, the pace falters - it takes too long to get going and then the final part wraps it up far too quickly. But in general, the story is captivating.   The direction seems more filmic and expansive than previous instalments; moving out of the studios to army bases and factories. The music, cinematography and acting lends the story a 'James Bond' feel that would be continued by the third Doctor (Jon Pertwee), with his flying cars, kung-fu fighting and secret Government aides. The main support and adversaries to the Doctor in this - the terribly English Brigadier (superbly played once again by Nicholas Courtney) and the megalomaniac Tobias Vaughn certainly have an air of the Bond allies and enemies respectively.

It takes rather a lot of running about factories and hiding from security before we get to the main point of the story - the Cybermen invasion of Earth. The now legendary scenes of the Cybermen walking along the streets of London and on the steps of St. Peters no doubt had countless young children darting behind the sofa for safety.

Two episodes are unfortunately missing, but Cosgrove Hall have painstakingly gone through all the old audio tapes (many of which were recorded and donated by fans) and animated the missing material. They have done an admirable job, and although the gap between the animation and live action episodes is obvious, I believe they have really captured the spirit of the other episodes. And the black and white really adds something to the animation.

The direction, scenes and acting have stood the test of time well, and thank goodness Cosgrove Hall and the B.B.C saw fit to restore this classic story so that further generations can see one of the best examples of early Doctor Who at its best.

The Krotons - 4/10

The Doctor must stop crystalline aliens from draining the energy of their brightest slaves. The story explores notions of oppression and rebellion against insurmountable odds. If only the enemy was a bit less naff and sounded a lot less like small breaded soup accompaniments(!).

The Seeds Of Death - 9/10

The Ice Warriors return; taking advantage of a future in which over-reliance on technology has rendered humans vulnerable to attack. Patrick Troughton is one of my favourite of all the incarnations, and it's serials like this that helped form my opinion. He has just the right amount of 'quirkiness'/oddness and kindness to embody all that makes the doctor 'who' he is (excuse the pun). It lags a little here and there, but is still one of the best of the Troughton era.

The Space Pirates - (Episodes 1,3,4,5 And 6 Of 6 Missing) 3/10

The Doctor and company land on a spaceship, under attack by...you guessed it – space pirates!

Whilst this sounds like one of the most exciting premises for a kid's programme, this is actually one of the poorest of the 'missing' serials, with little redeeming features. I did like the look of the serial, which was quite ahead of its time. But for all its inventiveness, it just doesn't *feel* like 'Who' and falls flat on first viewing. Characters such as a comedy 'space-age-red-neck' don't really work and are more annoying than entertaining. The pace and storyline don't grip you. This is one of the lesser of the Troughton stories and worth skipping for the epic that lies ahead.

The War Games - 8/10

An evil Time Lord, 'The War Chief' is stealing soldiers out of history's greatest battles in order to create a 'super-army.' The Doctor must contact his own people to help him destroy the time-travelling menace. But there is a reason why he's been reluctant to contact them before. We discover for the first time the Time Lords' main raison d'être; which is to monitor time and never to interfere. To them the Doctor himself is a criminal, for travelling through time trying to help others (Gallifrey forbid!). They help The Doctor defeat his foe, but also put him on trial for his own 'misdemeanours;' forcing him to regenerate, lose his companions and be stranded on Earth!

As much as I love Troughton, a 10-parter was always going to be a slog, and over time this descends into a *loop* story or 'capture-escape-capture' that is often the fall-back for longer Who stories. However, the sets are lavish, the script is sharp and the plot is an innovative spin on the 'history' theme that had been employed so many times before. The range of enemies is strong and diverse; from more 'pantomime' bad guys to the restrained terror of the 'War Lord,' played by the always excellent Philip Madoc. It's great to see the debut of the malevolent Time Lords, and to get some back story on the Doctor for the first time; who have been shrouded in mystery up until this point.

Goodbye and thank you Patrick Troughton – for showing that the show could carry on past its original lead actor and develop in new and exciting ways in the future.

THE THIRD DOCTOR
- JON PERTWEE
(1970-1974)

SEASON 7

And so begins a new era of Doctor Who...enter colour, velvet suits, cravats and a kung-fu kicking, dinosaur beating, crazy haired would- be Wurzel-Gummidge - be prepared...for the Pertwee Doctor cometh!

Spearhead From Space - 9/10

After the events of the last season's finale, the Doctor is sentenced to lose his companions, regenerate and be stranded on Earth. Picked up by his old allies U.N.I.T ('Unified Intelligence Taskforce - See 'The Invasion') who have no idea who the strange man claiming to be the Doctor is. But their troubles soon grow much bigger than a case of mistaken identities, when an alien with a hive mind (similar to the Great Intelligence from 'The Abominable Snowmen'/'The Web of Fear') starts controlling plastic dummies (Autons) and setting them against the population. They have to trust that this 'new Doctor' is the only one that can help them.

The show bursts into a new era of colour with a new Doctor, and a very different feel to what has gone before. Gone are the closed sets and shadowy lighting, and in come bright colours and expansive outdoor shots. Out goes the rather childlike 2nd Doctor and in comes a much more serious and action-orientated Doctor. Although in this early serial, Jon's character isn't quite settled, there is an air of arrogance and sombreness about him from the beginning, which makes him less likeable than his predecessor. The idea of the Doctor's character to me is to be more intelligent than the people around him, but to have affection and interest in all people too, rather than talking down to them, and this is where I find Jon's Doctor more difficult to warm to at first. His new companion Liz Shaw is a good choice of companion; an intelligent and useful friend, but not patronising or irritating in any way (as, say Romana I was at times to the fourth Doctor). The show seems to be aiming for more of an older audience; swapping the family feel of Hartnell or Troughton for a 'James Bond' or the 'Man from U.N.C.L.E' style.

This is a strong first story that must've been very exciting for fans at the time. It seems to be quite a departure, and a real injection of originality into the series (which the series needed at the time as it was struggling for ratings at the end of the Troughton era). Along with the new Doctor and companion, the murderous waxwork Autons are introduced. This is something that I know would've really scared me as a kid, and they still come across as quite creepy now.

Overall, it's a good start for the third Doctor, and essential viewing, although I miss Troughton's more light-hearted era.

Doctor Who And The Silurians - 9/10

We are introduced to the Silurians - a race that descended from reptiles and colonised the planet long before humans evolved from apes. They fled underground and hibernated when they thought a small planet (the moon) threatened to destroy the surface.
Now awoken, they decide to take back what they

consider to be theirs - the planet Earth!

This is an interesting twist on the alien stories – here is another indigenous race with as much claim over the planet as humans. This premise allows the serial to delve into more political areas, rather than the usual 'invading aliens that must be stopped' idea that had been explored countless times before. It also works on the strengths of the third, more authoritative Doctor, who must play as mediator between the two warring Earth races.

I can't understand why some of these serials need to be extended to 7 episodes, because although this is a great story, it takes what seems like an age to get started. This is classic 'Who' though; with one of the most inventive monster ideas of the show so far.

The Ambassadors Of Death - 3/10

Now, *this* is why I'm not as big a fan of some of the third Doctor's tenure! This serial takes itself far too seriously and the Doctor is far too stern sounding. I'm not saying Doctor Who should be light-hearted all the time. But whilst Tom Baker got the balance of eccentricity, seriousness and warmth just right for you to want to get behind him, Jon Pertwee's portrayal of the Doctor just doesn't seem to have the same sort of charm (for the most part anyway).

The story, assumingly trying to cash-in on the space-race from its recent history, is set in the near future where a space probe is being sent to Mars. On the way, it is overtaken by psychotic alien astronauts from Mars. Actually, writing this down, it sounds like a damn exciting story! But the way it is produced, acted and presented is as dull as dishwater. One to miss.

Inferno - 8/10

A power surge in the malfunctioning T.A.R.D.I.S sends the Doctor to a parallel universe, where he must take on zombies and witness the terrible consequences of a project that is about to take place in our own universe.

Strange, but intriguing serial, but again over-long and at times tedious. This era of Doctor Who seems obsessed with the dangers of drilling or digging below ground - first of all the Silurians, then this serial in which radiation is released, and later giant maggots in The Green Death. If the Doctor is stranded on Earth, I suppose the only alternative to having aliens invade is to have the 'unseen' Earth rise up to threaten humanity.

Even so, this does make some of the serials of the time seem like they are repeating ideas. That said, the idea of a parallel universe is used for the first time here, and to great effect. Having 'parallel' versions of the characters also creates some scope for the actors to stretch themselves and their parts, and they all excel in this story. Interestingly different, and worth a watch; even with the inevitable padding that comes with this 7 episode format.

SEASON 8

This season is all about the Master; the Doctor's childhood friend turned megalomaniac evil Time Lord.

Terror Of The Autons - 10/10

The Doctor meets his 'Moriarty' for the first time, with the debut of one of the Doctor's most longstanding, important enemies, an evil Time Lord called *The Master;* played by the wonderful Roger Delgado. From his first appearance, he *owns* the character; with real menace and presence. The series takes a big risk with this new enemy; making him the adversary for the whole series, and it pays off thanks to Delgado's unforgettable performance.

This is also the debut of the Doctor's next assistant, Jo Grant. Whilst I will miss Liz Shaw, who I thought was a really good companion for her short stay, Jo is likeable in her first story.

The Autons return, this time inhabiting all sorts of strange plastic shapes and forms. The effects used for this, such as the murderous doll, seem rather dated by today's standards. But, combined with the synth music, I did find these slightly unsettling for Who, and I think had I been a kid at the time, I would have had a few sleepless nights! Whilst pretty ridiculous at times (killer plastic daffodils?!), the idea of an enemy that can inhabit any plastic object and attack from within the home is an amusing one. The pace of this story is much improved - the serial is cut back down from the 7 part format to a more snappy 4 parts. The addition of enemies like the Master and the increased tension and action here is a huge improvement on the last season - some lessons have obviously been learned!

The Mind Of Evil - 6/10

A machine is created that can remove a person's potential for criminality. The Master steals the machine, and finds a way to reverse it, creating a person's worst nightmares through projected hallucinations.

The idea of a psychological machine that draws all negative criminality from people is an interesting one, but this serial failed to really draw me in. The Master is great again, but the flow and direction let the attention drift too much, and what is a great idea falls a little flat.

The Claws Of Axos - 5/10

The Greek statue looking Axons land on Earth in their organically created spaceship. Apparently, they have escaped their planet on the edge of the galaxy, after solar flares have destroyed their people.

In reality they are a parasitic race, roaming the galaxy with the intention of consuming all energy on each planet they visit; via a seductive element called 'axonite.'

This one felt a bit like a return to more Hartnell territory, though the effects are a lot more advanced (at least for the time). I found this serial quite hard-going. This era seems to have too much of a 'serious' approach; people seem to walk around with an air of annoyance for the majority of the time and the Doctor is cold and arrogant. It's trying too hard to be taken seriously for its own good; losing a lot of its humanity and humour along the way. The Master, who is the saviour of this season, takes more of a backseat in this one, and the story itself just seems to plod along, even for a 4 parter.

Colony In Space - 1/10

The Time Lords reinstate the Doctor's ability to travel in space; on a mission to stop the Master getting his hands on a 'Doomsday Device.'

The news that the Third Doctor was finally getting to leave Earth must've been greeted with excitement by fans. But unfortunately this serial does nothing to improve what is already a pretty average few stories. I found this over-long and less than memorable.

The Daemons - 9/10

The Master harnesses an ancient evil power hidden beneath a leafy village as the series goes all-out 'Wicker Man' in the Daemons.

This serial is often cited as an pinnacle of the 'classic series,' and I would definitely say it is one of the best of the Pertwee years; bringing just enough horror to leave a lasting impression on young fans. It's possibly the darkest since The Aztecs (Hartnell); delving into the occult, witch-craft and black magic. This was no doubt influential on some of the more chilling Tom Baker stories that came years later also (Horror of Fang Rock, Brain of Morbius etc..).

John Pertwee still plays the Doctor with an unpleasant

overt authority; belittling his companion Jo whenever possible ("did you fail Latin as well as science?" he sneers at her at one point). This goading of the people around him doesn't make me want to root for him as I had with Troughton or Hartnell, and makes this era more difficult to watch; even with great stories like this.

The Master is once again on top form; with more of a defined focus to his character. However, there is still no back story - we're never told why he hates the Doctor or why he wants control of the Earth so badly. This can sometimes leave the character (even when played so excellently by Delgado) rather one-dimensional when the writing isn't at its best. Thankfully this is not the case here, and this is one of the highlights of the Pertwee years for me.

SEASON 9

This season sees the Third Doctor venture further afield through time and space to play mediator, as well as continuing to assist Unit in protecting the Earth from memorable monsters.

Day Of The Daleks - 6/10

A group of rebels travel back 200 years into the past to assassinate a terrorist that will blow up a world peace conference; causing World War Three and leaving the Earth open to Dalek invasion.

Not bad. Elements such as the Planet of the Apes style aliens, the Ogrons, are a nice addition. Compared with Who at its best however, this is still a pretty run-of-the-mill serial; apart from the action-packed finale. It will also probably be unsatisfying to Dalek fans, as they don't take centre stage as much as you would expect.

The Curse Of Peladon - 7/10

The Doctor is employed as Earth's delegate at an inter-galactic peace treaty in this stony-faced political story that is engaging, but lacking somewhat in action for the first half. It's great to see some inventive aliens (especially the return of the excellent Ice Warriors), even the one-eyed alien with easily the most annoying 'pre-Mel' (see 'Terror of the Vervoids') voice in the series. The script and plot are thoughtful and intelligent, and it's nice to see a more sensitive side to both Jo and the Doctor in this one; showing the potential of the characters to grow through good writing.

The Sea Devils - 8/10

The sequel to The Silurians finds their sea-bound cousins returning to try to retake the Earth. And like their relatives they see this planet as rightfully theirs; not the human 'apes' that have colonised the planet since their hibernation millions of years ago. The Master escapes from jail and sets about helping the 'Sea Devils' to take over the world and eradicate the humans (although it's still not explained *why* he wants to do this – apart from to annoy the Doctor I suppose).

The scene of the Sea Devils rising up from the sea is a vivid memory to many Who fans. I can see why, as up until this point most creatures had appeared from either space or deep within the Earth, and this creates a striking difference.

There are also some great scenes with the Master, added to a nicely realised (if no doubt dated by today's technical standards) alien race. An action packed, fun and highly enjoyable serial, and a definite contender for the best serial of the Pertwee era.

The Mutants - 5/10

The Doctor is embroiled in strife between the natives of Solos and colonising humans who have fled Earth and are looking for a new home. But the natives have even more to worry about, when they realise they are turning into hideous mutants!

This adventure works as a compelling comment on colonisation, but not as an overly gripping serial. The 'mutants' are some of the best creature designs I've seen in Doctor Who so far, even if their characters aren't up to much. A fairly watchable (if unchallenging) story, which felt a bit sub-par after the brilliant Sea Devils.

The Time Monster - 5/10

Wow, Delgado's pretty tough! I can't imagine Ainley knocking out Sergeant Benton!

A ridiculous story, in which Greek Gods really existed, and The Master decides to track down Chronos to help him become ruler of time (at least I think this is what the story is about!).

Without the amazing writing needed to pull off such a far-fetched idea, this story falters; leading to a mediocre ending to the season. I imagine the intention is a return to the educational drive of the original Hartnell blueprint for the show, and fans of the Greek myths may find some entertainment in the last couple of episodes. Plus it's worth the agonising wait for the serial to get going, if only to see the Master getting *jiggy* with the rather *ample* Queen Galleia.

At least it finally seems like the Doctor has started to be a lot warmer towards Jo; something that has made liking this era quite difficult up until now.

SEASON 10

The show reaches its first decade, with Pertwee's penultimate season. We bid a fond farewell to Jo and see a more delicate side to the Third Doctor.

10Th Year Anniversary Special
- The Three Doctors - 8/10

One of the original Time Lords, Omega (the pioneer who helped develop time travel) wants revenge on his people for banishing him to a realm of 'anti-matter' when he got too big for his boots. To defeat him, the Time Lords must enlist not one, but 3 incarnations of the Doctor – breaking the first law of time and dragging 'One,' 'Two' and 'Three' out of their perspective time-lines to combine their efforts.

Taken on its own merits as a story, this isn't the best special you are likely to see. The villain is particularly melodramatic, in the original sense of the word, and the 'monsters' are laughable (not in a good way). It is nice to have a bit of Time Lord history for the first time however, and this does set the ball rolling for more explorations of Omega, Rassilon et al in later series.

The real reason behind this serial however is not to break any boundaries story-wise, but to commemorate the first big milestone for the show – 10 years since it first began.

And to be fair, it manages this in the most fun way imaginable. It's great to see all three actors back; and there is enough of a difference in their portrayals to make it work. Hartnell is clearly unwell, but still manages to steal the show in the few scenes and fewer lines that he says. Troughton, who has already been away from the role for 3 ½ years at this point, slips back into it as if he's never been away. And Pertwee, to his credit as an actor manages to bring an authority that steers proceedings well.

However much I struggle with some of Pertwee's portrayal of the Doctor, I do like him as an actor, and this serial shows just how well he measures up to the two great actors that came before him. The story is certainly not ground-breaking 'Who,' but it is great to see Patrick Troughton and William Hartnell back in the role and this is a light-hearted way to celebrate how far the show has already come in its first 10 years.

Carnival Of Monsters - 5/10

The Doctor and Jo are trapped inside a miniature world/ playground in which they must fight against monsters for the entertainment of punters outside a 'scope.'

Unfortunately a good premise is rendered absurd by the special effects, costumes and acting, which have not dated well. I found some of the supporting cast particularly annoying in this one, and really didn't find much to enjoy here as a whole.

Frontier In Space - 7/10

The Doctor lands himself and Jo in the midst of an erupting war between humans of the 26th Century and the alien 'Draconians;' as both races spread throughout the galaxy, colonising different planets.

I actually quite liked this serial, and found it to be full of action, even for a 6 parter (though obviously there is still some padding). The design of the sets and aliens (particularly the Draconians) is very good for the time, and the plot is well written and scripted.

Frontier is notable as the last appearance of the brilliant Delgado as the original Master. The actor brought an effective dread to the stories he was in, was truly one of the best Doctor Who villains of the show as a whole and remains a main highlight of the Pertwee years for me. It makes you wonder how the actor would have excelled in future serials with Tom Baker; surely a winning combination! A truly sad loss of a great actor and a great man. On a lighter side-note, the serial also features an updated, but short-lived/heard theme tune. I can't say I like the wah-wah synths; but it is worth a listen for novelty sake at least.

The series loses one of its best actors; but it is nice to see his last serial is one of his finest.

Planet Of The Daleks - 6/10

Revisiting Hartnell Territory, the Doctor runs into the Thals and the Daleks again - albeit some centuries later and on a different planet. The writer Terry Nation (who had created the Daleks) has been criticised for treading over old ground with this serial. But whilst it's not original, it does have an exciting pace and enough to keep you interested throughout.

The Green Death - 7/10

A maniacal computer is using a Welsh chemical plant to breed mutated giant maggots!

I sometimes struggle with some of Pertwee's era as the Doctor . Most of his stories can be encapsulated by the name of one of his worst serials - 'Carnival of Monsters.' With a few exceptions (such as Planet of the Spiders or The Silurians), the pantomime monsters over-take the priority for a great story; which is made worse by the contrasting sternness and aloofness of Pertwee's characterisation. I've got nothing against 'monsters' in Doctor Who at all, but in order for them to work they have to be used to underpin a great story. Without the story or the effects needed to warrant them, they just seem kitsch and pointless. The example of both extremes can be found here in The Green Death, and conversely in The Ark in Space. Both had similar monsters and effects, but the latter had much more depth and purpose to carry it off.

Although I do like Jon Pertwee, I much prefer listening to him in interviews; where he is so much more charming and affable than the way he chooses to play the Doctor. His companion Jo also isn't a patch on the best companions such as Sarah Jane (3rd/4th Doctor) or Barbara and Ian (1st Doctor), but it was still quite sad to see her go after a comparatively long time as the Doctor's assistant.

The story is ok, but pretty grim and unpleasant (not in a good way) and at 6 episodes long, it's rather a slog again. It's also quite preachy, which didn't really add anything to the story as far as entertainment is concerned.

Compared with Doctor Who at its best, this is pretty unsatisfying stuff. It is worth skipping to the end for the best scene. We bid a poignant goodbye to Jo in one of Pertwee's most emotional performances; which rates for me as the saddest goodbyes in Who history.

SEASON 11

In Pertwee's swansong season, we meet one of the Doctor's most beloved companions Sarah Jane Smith as they take on dinosaurs, giant spiders and psychotic potato men.

The Time Warrior - 8/10

An alien is abducting scientists and technology from the present through time to the middle-ages to take over the Earth in the past. U.N.I.T send the Doctor on the trail...along with journalist Sarah Jane Smith.

It's so great to see the debut of both the wonderful Sarah Jane *and* the legendary Sontarans. Some 'hammy' acting aside, this is one of the best of the Pertwee serials, and a great way to start his last season.

Invasion Of The Dinosaurs - 5/10

The Doctor and Sarah Jane arrive in an almost deserted London; to find themselves detained by a martial law that has been levelled on the people. It isn't long until they find out why - the dinosaurs are roaming the Earth again! A mad scientist has found a way to bring the dinosaurs back to Earth, and they are on the rampage!

Whilst the story is ahead of its time (predating 'Jurassic Park' by some 20 years), the special effects seem to hark back a lot further - looking about as convincing as a poorly made 1950's 'B-movie.'

As usual with these 6-part Pertwee stories, the serial drags, and it is difficult to give it your full attention. The story has as much padding as possible - even repeating almost exactly the same cliff-hanger for episodes 1 and
2. And after the 3rd or 4th episode it goes off on a complete tangent and I found it even more difficult to follow. Not great.

Death To The Daleks - 4/10

The T.A.R.D.I.S power is drained, leaving it stranded on a remote planet. The Doctor and Sarah Jane run into other unlucky races that have also lost their energy...including the Daleks!

An odd one. Humans, zombie-like creatures, Daleks and hoover attachments go face-to-face in a real mishmash of a story that I found confusing and difficult to connect with. Doctor #3 has really mellowed however, and his relationship with Sarah Jane is a much more genial one; making this at the least watchable. I've read the Target novelisation and enjoyed it more than the televised version I must admit.

The Monster Of Peladon - 5/10

The Doctor returns to Peladon 50 years later (see 'The Curse of Peladon'), to find it rich in a valuable element that has cast it high in the Galactic Federation. It is also at war with 'Galaxy 5' and endangered by a ghostly image of a mythical beast.

The show returns to political territory with this Peladon sequel; taking on two areas of important debate at the time

- trade union disputes and women's liberation. It's always great to see the Ice Warriors, but the story is not a patch on Third Doctor at his best (Silurians, Inferno and so on). The pace is fairly dull and the story is unremarkable. It picks up towards the end, but it's rather 'too little too late.'

Planet Of The Spiders - 9/10

Giant spiders hold people under their control using powerful blue crystals. But the Doctor has unwittingly picked up the last of their crystals on his travels, and they want it back!

As I reach the last of the Pertwee serials, the unthinkable has happened. I can finally say I'm going to miss early 70's Doctor Who! Along with the Colin Baker years; Pertwee's time as the Doctor *was* my least favourite when I started revisiting the classic show. Unlike Hartnell and Troughton's time; the serials seemed drawn out and tiresome, the effects were ludicrous and, most importantly, the Doctor as played by Pertwee seemed arrogant, cold and unlikable. After watching all of the stories, I still believe some of these things; although my opinion has softened a great deal. This is due to some genuinely redeeming features that make at least some of the stories rate highly as classics of the show. The two main highlights for me are *The Brigadier* and *The Master*.

Although Nicholas Courtney had started as the iconic Brigadier in Troughton's time; it wasn't until Pertwee's Doctor was stranded on Earth and forced to work with U.N.I.T that the character was allowed the time to really flourish. The Brigadier's approach of action over common sense created some great scenes and interplay with the Doctor's more pacifistic approach. Courtney played the part excellently; going down in Who history as one of the most memorable of the Doctor's Aides (I can't bring myself to call him a 'companion' as it doesn't do him justice).

We also had Delgado as the original Master. Playing the character as a *Moriarty* to the Doctor's *Sherlock Holmes*; Delgado portrayed a fantastically sinister and menacing enemy. You really did believe that here was a foe every bit as intelligent and powerful as the Doctor; yet Hell-bent on destruction and ultimate power over all things – in short he was the Doctor's worst nightmare.

As well as great characters, there were many monsters/aliens introduced in this time that have become immortalised in the show's history. Ok, so there were the rather terrible Ambassadors, one eyed roller- balls and killer daffodils; but there were also Sontarans, Silurians and Autons. Even the relationship between the Doctor and his companions seemed to soften towards the end; from almost abusive constant put-downs, to a more affectionate side (albeit rather too late in my opinion).

This last Pertwee story is definitely one of my favourites. The direction and acting are tight and the ideas are captivating ones (telekinesis, the occult, spirituality).
The giant spiders are scary, even if pretty rubbish by today's standards. The story is full of action; including hovercraft/ speedboat and helicopter/flying car chases - what's not to like!

I'm glad to see Pertwee go out with a bang in this exciting and excellent story.

Whilst it's less likely to be held up as my favourite years of the show any time soon; there are definitely more things to recommend than I had previously expected; and many of Pertwee's stories are essential viewing for all fans of the show.

THE FOURTH DOCTOR - TOM BAKER (1974-1981)

SEASON 12

Whilst the first story of Season 12 feels like a hangover of the Pertwee time, it doesn't take Tom Baker long to stamp his indelible character over the show and help usher in one of the most beloved eras of the show.

Robot - 8/10

When compared with one of the best of the Jon Pertwee adventures that preceded it, this seems to be a fairly run-of-the-mill adventure, about a 'friendly robot programmed to do bad.'

Yet the story is more of a vehicle to introduce the new Doctor; in the form of the inimitable Tom Baker. From the outset, Tom gets the character so spot on it's as if he's been playing him for years. He really adds a new depth and 3 dimensions to what has already been established three times before him. Whilst at times he seems to veer towards the silly, he quickly balances this with a kind of pathos and introspection that is utterly compelling. All those ranting monologues to himself as he ponders morality and what action to take are great to watch, and you can understand why, to many he is seen as *the* Doctor of all Doctors.

The story itself gets better each time you see it. When I first watched it, I didn't rate it highly, but there is a certain warmth and simplicity that rewards repeat viewings, and a very witty and memorable script. As well as the new Doctor, Sarah Jane shines, as the only friend to the giant robot...in a theme that bears more than a passing resemblance to King Kong.

A good way to introduce a 'new' character to the Doctor, and it's great to see Tom making it his own in such a novel way.

The Ark In Space - 10/10

The last remaining humans are suspended in time, as they wait for Earth to recover from a cataclysmic event thousands of years ago. As they wake from stasis, they find they are not alone - giant parasitic larvae are onboard and are taking over the ship and its inhabitants!

Doctor Who goes all out Star Trek in this futuristic story. The ideas are intriguing ones; reused in the Hitchhiker's Guide to the Galaxy and Red Dwarf series. The sets are some of the best I've seen on Who; taking their influence from Space Odyssey and the aforementioned Star Trek.

Unfortunately, the 'monster' itself (bubble-wrap aliens anyone?) sometimes lets down a fantastic story. Still, the Doctor, his companions and even the supporting cast are great, and it's an excellent addition to the series as a whole; showing an exciting potential for the 'new' Doctor of the time.

The Sontaran Experiment - 7/10

A lone Sontaran devises horrible experiments on humans, to find out their weaknesses for an upcoming invasion.

Short and sweet. I wasn't expecting this to be half the length of a normal story, so in some ways it felt a little lacking in depth. But that said, I do like the Sontarans in these earlier episodes (who are much more menacing than their modern, comedy counterparts), and the story was an interesting one. A nice stop-gap between two epic serials.

Genesis Of The Daleks - 10/10

The Doctor is once again forced to assist his people, the Time Lords. This time their plan is to rid the universe of its biggest threat – the Daleks. They transport the Doctor back to Skaro; to the creation of his greatest enemy. During the original war between the Thals and the Kaleds; An evil Kaled scientist, Davros has found a way to move his rapidly devolving people (affected by years of chemical warfare) into new and deadly cybernetic bodies (the Daleks). The Time Lords want the Doctor to destroy these new creatures before they develop...but he starts to wonder if he really has the right over life and death of a race, no matter how evil.

Once again, Tom Baker proves he was BORN to play the Role in Genesis of the Daleks! He's superb, as with all this season, and this is one of the best serials since Tomb of the Cybermen for me. The story; the production; the acting; the tragedy; the wit; the morality - everything is perfect. The fact that I watched this all in one sitting on my first viewing, shows just how well written and produced it is, and it is quintessential Tom Baker that every fan should see.

Revenge Of The Cybermen - 6/10

The Cybermen attack a planet full of gold; after realising

that the precious element is deadly to them.

This serial is often considered weak by fans, because it ends arguably the best season the show has had. Indeed, judged by the standards of Genesis of the Daleks or The Ark in Space, it does feel pretty subpar. But judged on its own merits, it's not a bad story at all really. It's good to see the Cybermen back after not appearing at all in the third Doctor's time. Although the story takes a while to get off the ground, it builds momentum and is pretty action packed towards the last two episodes.

I liked the Cybermen themselves, who retain their creepy chrome-meets-flesh look; although the voices are less 'cybernised' and I found the electronic tones of the Hartnell/Troughton versions more disturbing. Baker is once again on top form, ending his first season with the same panache as he started it.

An 'O.K' end to an exceptional season.

SEASON 13

Tom continues to push the show into new and exciting arenas in this absolute classic run of stories.

Terror Of The Zygons - 9/10

Shape-shifting aliens who plan to take over the world using the powers of the Loch Ness Monster(?!).

The perfectly creepy, whispering, coral-styled Zygons are so well realised as to mask a pretty stupid story. Its 'behind the sofa' time in this well directed drama, which harks back to the best of Pertwee and even earlier science fiction of the 1950's. The end of episode 1 especially; where we see an alien hand reaching over Sarah Jane's shoulder, is reminiscent of a similar still from War of the Worlds that used to creep me out no end as a kid. And I'm sure this serial would've had the same effect. Another timeless Tom Baker story that is thoroughly enjoyable from start to finish.

Planet Of Evil - 7/10

The Doctor and Sarah travel to a planet that is under attack by an 'Anti-Matter' monster, and a professor that has gotten too close for comfort.

I enjoyed this return to horror territory. Probably the

best teaming of a Doctor and companion (Tom Baker and Elizabeth Sladen as the excellent Sarah Jane) during one of the high peaks of the series. The effects are great for their time, incorporating proto-'Tron' style super-imposing of light effects. Whilst these may look a tad rubbish by today's standards, I think they're some of the best of the show I've seen. The Forbidden Planet style of the serial also works well, and helps lend an agelessness to the story. Very entertaining.

Pyramids Of Mars - 9/10

A scientist in 1911 is taken over by the spirit of an ancient alien God.

All the great mid-70's Doctor Who ingredients are there. Tom Baker is on top form, Sarah Jane (arguably his best companion) is by his side and the story is daft but fun - in other words it's a great serial.

The Android Invasion – 8/10

The Doctor lands on Earth and quickly finds himself attacked by astronaut-looking robots with more than a striking resemblance to those in the Pertwee story The Ambassadors of Death.

An alien race is capable of creating facsimile robot versions of humans, and plans to take over the Earth using their creations (and also a deadly disease) to wipe out the human race.

Although the story might start off looking like Ambassadors of Death, there is a great difference between the two serials. The pace, story and production are all greatly improved, and what is a fairly simple story is a hell of a lot of fun to watch. The aliens (The Kraals) are well designed; looking rather like a *melted* version of a Ferengi from Star Trek Deep Space 9, if you know what I mean.

I enjoyed it and thought certain parts, such as the tearing off of human faces to reveal their robot insides were memorable.

As with every story of this period, the real highlight is the wonderful chemistry between Tom Baker and Elizabeth Sladen, and this is another great serial to watch.

The Brain Of Morbius - 7/10

An evil Time Lord who has been vanquished is now nothing more than a brain. But a mad professor with his own delusions of grandeur believes he can bring him back.

Doctor Who meets Hammer Horror in this partly brilliant turn for the series. Tom Baker is at his wise-cracking best, plus it's great to see the return of Philip Madoc, making his third appearance in Who after The Krotons and the War Games. Madoc always plays a convincing bad guy, and breathes life into the rather cliché role of mad scientist.

Some aspects don't work so well however. Characters such as the Igor/Frankenstein's Monster inspired assistant are pretty embarrassing and pointless, and the story doesn't move too quickly.

As is often the case with Doctor Who, the ideas are too big for the production values to do justice to or to realise effectively. O.K, perhaps I'm being a little harsh here.

The sets aren't bad really, and there has certainly been

a lot of thought into how they were designed. You've got to admire the scope and ingenuity of the writers in trying to continue to push the boundaries of science-fiction television, and this is a good attempt at taking the series in a new direction. But the serial itself is a little hit and miss.

The Seeds Of Doom - 9/10

The Doctor takes on a race of alien killer plant-life after they are reawakened by Arctic botanists. Sounds ridiculous...and it is, but as is often the case with this era of Doctor Who, witty writing and an excellent cast propel it above the sum of its parts.

Tom Baker is on excellent form again. In serials such as this, it is easy to see why he was so liked by the student fraternity. Although a lot older than that demographic, he has intelligence, wit and enough youthful idealism to make him seem dangerous to any staid older professor he comes into contact with. Elizabeth Sladen also shines as the ever reliable Sarah; bolstering herself way above the usual level of screaming companion and becoming more than engaging in her own right.

Although this story will seem unbelievable to most adults watching the programme, it is easy to see how a child would become engrossed in the suspense generated by the writing, acting and overall feel of the serial, which sits in-between other stories that draw from classic horror films. This story in particular brought to mind the original 'Quatermass Xperiment' film and, of course 'The Day of the Triffids.'

A six parter is always going to be difficult, and this does have the odd episode that seems to draw the story on more than it needs to. But overall, this is a strong addition to the series and a fitting end to another excellent season.

SEASON 14

The dark undertones of Season 13 continue as the Doctor is thrown back to who-done-its, evil alien entities and a schizophrenic computer in another arresting season of classic Who.

The Masque Of Mandragora - 3/10

The 'history' and 'alien' narratives meet, as the Doctor brings an alien energy 'stowaway' with him to Renaissance Italy. Once there, the alien decides to start bumping off all the great thinkers of the age, to return the human race to the dark ages.

There's no denying that this is a well produced and well acted story, and it looks great. But I did find this quite dull and tiresome when compared with other Tom Baker stories. It does improve a lot by the last episode, but it feels like a long time to get to the peak. They've done the whole 'mad cult' thing before, in serials such as Planet of the Spiders or The Brain of Morbius, and to much better effect. Although you can't beat the sight of the Doctor sword-fighting!

The Hand Of Fear - 8/10

After the Doctor lands in the middle of an exploding quarry, Sarah Jane unwittingly finds the remnants of an ancient being. Although only a hand, the creature seizes her mind and convinces her to break into a nuclear reactor and restore it to its full strength.

The enemy – an androgynous crystallised alien that feeds off nuclear energy - is well conceived, constructed and acted, and stands up to the test of time well.

I really enjoyed this story, and would count it as one of my favourites from the time. Whilst I do love Tom's nonchalant, dry wit; it's good to see a more sober, serious side to him here; which adds to the effective suspense. The serial might have worked better as a slightly condensed 2 parter - as the middle two episodes are stronger (apart from Sarah's final scene).

It's sad to have to say goodbye to Sarah Jane in this serial. I really have come to love her short tenure as the best companion/Doctor pairing since Barbara, Ian and Susan with the first Doctor. The chemistry is undeniable, and you can tell the friendship between the two is more than just acting.

A great story with a very poignant ending. Well worth watching.

The Deadly Assassin - 9/10

The Master lures the Doctor onto their home planet Gallifrey; where he sets about his revenge. He first tries to frame the Doctor for the murder of the leader of the Time Lords, and then manages to trap the Doctor within the 'Matrix,' using his own crazed mind (take that Keanu Reeves!).

The Time Lords are shown this time as more 'old and bumbling bureaucrats;' rather than the intimidating authoritarians of the 2nd Doctor serial 'The War Games.' This is explained well by the Doctor, who points out that his people are not keen on action and shy away from it; leading to a certain pompous expectation that nothing should be interfered with. This also reminds us of the reason why they are uneasy with the pragmatic, renegade Doctor.

This is the first time we see The Master since the death of Delgado. They show him as a terrifying skeletal man...on his last legs as he comes towards the last of his 'natural' regenerations. Although Delgado is sadly missed, Peter Pratt does a good job of continuing the sinister feel of the character in his emaciated downfall.

This story stands apart as one of the only times the Doctor has been without a companion. Whilst there is definitely a 'Sarah-shaped-hole' in this episode, the story does enough to bridge the companion gap well, and this is a real highlight in an already strong series.

The Face Of Evil - 9/10

The Doctor returns to a planet from a previous (unspecified) travel; to find that a super-computer he programmed with the intention of improving has actually 'evolved' to the point of near-God proportions. The computer has created its own race of 'savages' and 'civilised priests' that are at constant war with one another (using this as an accelerated way to create a race of 'perfect' humans through 'survival of the fittest').

Added to this megalomania, the computer has also developed deranged multiple personalities; including an evil version of the Doctor it has stored in its memory banks from their previous encounter.

The Doctor meets his next companion, a 'savage' named Leela; who has rebelled against her people when she is put on trial for her lack of belief in the computer's divinity.

This is a captivating story and one of the best of another great series. There are some truly disturbing scenes, particularly at the end of episode 3, when the computer screams 'who am I?!' in multiple, strained voices.

There is also an arresting new companion in the form of Louise Jameson's Leela. After watching the show for some time now, I am starting to pick up certain techniques it uses to try and ensure its longevity - some more effective than others. One of the most difficult things for a television programme to do is try to replace a popular character when they leave. The relationship between Sarah Jane and the fourth Doctor is possibly the best of any Doctor and companion, so when she left at the end of The Hand of Fear, producers were left with a very difficult decision. Thankfully they were clever - they didn't try to replace her at all, but go off on a completely different tangent. In introducing Leela as a savage but passionate tribeswoman, the Doctor finds an equally strong, whilst completely different companion. Louise Jameson plays the character with both strength and a certain vulnerability and naivety that makes her utterly likeable. The new more 'pastoral' relationship between the Doctor and his new 'savage' companion was based on Pygmalion/My Fair Lady, and it's great to see his more 'fatherly' side reappear (echoing Doctor #1 and Vicki or Doctor #2 and Victoria).

The Robots Of Death - 9/10

Killer serving droids go on the attack, killing their owners.

The crew don't believe their robots can harm humans, so a 'Who-done-it' ensues, with the strange alien visitor (the Doctor) as the main suspect.

The design of the robots is one of the most beautiful I've seen in a science fiction programme. Their Art Deco style is completely at odds with the stark chrome of previous enemies like the Cybermen, and is all the more striking for it. The costumes and the sets are also gorgeous. But there is also a lot of substance to go with the style; and this is a timeless suspense which rewards repeat viewing.

The Talons Of Weng-Chiang - 5/10

An alien enlists murderous Chinese henchmen to collect victims for his machine which drains essence and prolongs his life.

Whilst this is one of the most beloved stories from the era, I just didn't enjoy it as much as the rest of the series. It seemed very dated and *of its time* as opposed to other stories that were *ahead*. I found the guy who was made to look Chinese particularly antiquated and distasteful. And whilst I know its sacrilege to criticise the most popular of doctors (and one of my favourites!), I didn't think Baker was up to his best on this one either. I seem to be alone in my opinion here, but for me, this was not one of the better Bakers and not a strong way to end another very first-rate season.

SEASON 15

A more mixed season still manages many high points, including a haunted lighthouse, despotic tax collectors and a friendly robot dog making his introduction.

Horror Of Fang Rock - 8/10

The inhabitants of a lighthouse, joined by the stranded crew of a small vessel are 'haunted' by a strange glowing, electrical 'beast.' This particular beast turns out to be a *jellyfish* styled Rutan; the sworn enemy of the Sontarans; on a mission to rebuild its battle scarred race on Earth.

After complaints from parents about violence in the last season's stories (particularly The Deadly Assassin), the new producer Graham Williams takes more of a subtle, brooding, less obvious approach; but manages to lose none of the suspense or scariness of the show. It's a straightforward show that I found it a lot of fun and a great little story to watch.

The Invisible Enemy - 7/10

The Doctor and Leela answer a distress call in space; only to find that there is a virus taking over the crew and all who arrive, turning them into killing machines. The

Doctor becomes infected himself, and the only cure it is to literally transport themselves inside his mind, by cloning a miniature version of himself and attacking the virus within.

The story is engaging, although it does dip at times. I've always liked these 'Inner Space' type stories, and it did not disappoint on any level...erm, apart from the terrible special effects used for the virus itself in the last episode!

The supporting cast are all good, including Michael Sheard; the actor many people 'of a certain age' will remember as the tyrannical Mr. Bronson in Grange Hill. He makes his second appearance here as one of the crew (after starring in The Mind of Evil), and would become somewhat of a 'regular,' with turns with Davison (Castrovalva) and McCoy (Remembrance of the Daleks) amongst others.

Oh, and let's not forget that this is the serial that introduces the much loved K-9, the tin dog who would become many a child's favourite companion of the 4th Doctor.

Image Of The Fendahl - 6/10

A team of scientists unearth the skull of the Fendahl...and bring an ancient enemy of the Time Lords back to life.

I'm rather slow on the uptake, but I don't remember the point at which the beginning of each serial started with an introduction to the supporting cast and the main 'mystery' the Doctor will face when he arrives. In the early days we always seemed to join the Doctor in the T.A.R.D.I.S at the beginning; travelling from one adventure to another. I tend to prefer this, as it doesn't rely on the supporting cast to draw you into a story; giving you instead the sense of being the Doctor's 'unseen companion' as the viewer. Image of the

Fendahl

is one serial that leads me to this conclusion. I found the supporting cast rather irritating - making me less interested in finding out the mystery by the time the Doctor had arrived on the scene.

The story itself is quite a complex and more *adult* one; tackling evolution, the occult and (more in line with other serials) a life-sucking worm-monster! The connection between these things I found rather confusing, and a little much to cram into a four parter. I did like the idea that 'hauntings' and 'apparitions' are actually the product of a slight time 'fissure' or rip in time or reality; causing certain energies and creatures to capitalise by travelling between worlds. This idea has been influential on many a 'NuWho' episode, as well as Torchwood.

I liked the dark feel of the serial, and it is not awful by any means. There are some strong scenes that are worth waiting through the more slow ones for.

The Sunmakers - 5/10

The Doctor and Leela travel to Pluto in the far future to find human inhabitants enslaved by 'the Collector.'

A very mediocre affair, with little to make it stand out as a classic Tom Baker story. The plot is one often explored by Who; rebels take on an oppressive regime. However, this serial takes on more of a politically motivated style; satirising bureaucracy, taxation and strikes - all issues at the front of people's minds in the late 70's.

There are a couple of saving graces. The main villain is suitably slimy and repulsive, and some of the ideas are intriguing ones. But the script and acting is pretty poor and the sets look like rejects from 'Chock-a-Block' in the '80's (showing my age there!).

Certainly not one of the Baker serials I would recommend.

Underworld - 2/10

The Doctor meets one of the least lucky alien races yet, The Minyans. Not only have they almost destroyed themselves using Time Lord technology, but their only salvation lies in 'race banks;' housed in a psychotic super-computer.

I'm glad to eat my words from a couple of reviews back. This serial does indeed start us off with the Doctor in the T.A.R.D.I.S; helping us to access the adventure from the same starting point. From this point on however, it's difficult to find anything particularly positive about this tale. But then there is little to find negative about it either. In other words - this is almost a 'non-story' in the series. It's more of an amalgamation of previous story elements that have been employed before; and with more panache. Maniacal machine with world domination in its diodes...check...enslaved people kept afraid by myth and folklore...check. If you feel you have seen it before, it's probably because you have.

A space filler with nothing to really make it memorable.

The Invasion Of Time - 7/10

The Doctor returns to Gallifrey, to become President elect of the High Council of Time Lords! Whilst I criticised the last serial for being predictable and treading over old ground, the same could never be said for this story!

From the first episode we are introduced to new rooms in the T.A.R.D.I.S and to a complete departure in the character of the Doctor!

One of the Doctor's main characteristics is an unswerving challenge of authoritarian rule and a rejection of any positions of power awarded him. Yet in the first episode we see him return to Gallifrey with the distinct and almost aggressive intention of taking his place as high president of the council of Time Lords! Of course there is always a cunning rouse behind every uncharacteristic action. Yet the writing is good enough to not make the 'whys' or the 'wherefores' easy to estimate.

The elements of the story do seem slightly disconnected at times...is this a story about the Time Lords, The Sontarans or the weird 'tin foil aliens?' However, it is nice to see more of the Doctor's home planet again, and this makes a good companion story to the Deadly Assassin (take note box set makers!). Even though it is a six parter, the pace doesn't drag, and this is notable ending to the season. It's also a nice ending for another of my favourite companions; the lovely Leela.

SEASON 16 – 'THE KEY TO TIME'

The first season to have a formal 'arc' sees the Doctor paired up with a young Time Lady and be flung into a mission to stop a mysterious 'Black Guardian' from destroying the very fabric of time.

The Ribos Operation - 4/10

The Doctor is contacted by the 'White Guardian,' who enlists him to search for 6 hidden segments of the 'Key to Time;' needed to restore balance and order to the universe. He provides him with a new assistant, young Time Lady Romana to help in his quest. On their first stop, they have to convince a conman on a mediaeval looking planet to part with his possessions.

The show takes a very brave move in producing a series long story arc for the first time (later examples would include the 'Trial of a Time Lord' and more modern examples like the 'Bad Wolf' idea).

It's been argued that the controversial 'Key to Time' series is the worst of Tom Baker's stint as the Doctor. So, why is it considered so bad?

As the central premise of Doctor Who is potentially such a ridiculous one, it only really works when everyone is onboard and really cares about what they're doing. In the late '70's all the ingredients were there; one of the best actors to play the Doctor; a huge fan base; one of the most imaginative science fiction writers of the time (Douglas Adams) as script editor and writer. But the wheels seem to have really fallen off the wagon, and what we are left with is a pale imitation of Who at its best.

The sets, the monsters, the acting – everything seems lacking. Tom Baker doesn't seem to care anymore and has become more of a parody version of his great characterisation of the Doctor. The assistant is pretty arrogant, doing all she can to make one of the greatest minds in science fiction drama into a ridiculous, blundering fool - surely not what any fan wants to see?!

A very disappointing serial that is worth missing, unless you really want to see everything that Tom did.

The Pirate Planet - 5/10

The Doctor and Romana discover that they have landed on a 'pirate planet,' that can transport itself to different areas of the universe and steal the mineral wealth of other planets. The Doctor must stop the crazy Captain before his next stop...Earth!...Oh, and he needs to find the second segment of the key to time whilst he's at it!

I was so disillusioned after seeing The Ribos Operation, that I was probably over-negative about this serial too. In the first 2 episodes the same problems remain - the acting is below par and the assistant is irritatingly smug and obnoxious.

But either my standards have dropped or the serial has

improved (I like to think the latter); but by the end it wasn't too bad at all. It's still not a patch on other Tom Baker stories; but the captain himself is a well designed and fun character, as are the telepathic natives of the planet.

The production has a real pantomime feel to it, and fans of Doctor Who at its most camp and over-blown (such as Happiness Patrol from the Sylvester McCoy days) will no doubt enjoy this. I'm also sure it would be much more enjoyable to young kids too; and let's face it, this who Doctor Who is really aimed at after all!

A huge improvement on the Ribos Operation, but still not up to Doctor Who at its best.

The Stones Of Blood - 5/10

The Doctor and Romana continue their quest for the Key to Time. They return to modern day England, where they find an ancient circle of stones, and a group who worship a Goddess who appears to be coming back to life.

If this was held up to the show as a whole, it would be counted as rather a lackadaisical affair, without much depth or dramatic resonance ('attack of the polystyrene rocks?!'). But weighed against the rest of this particular series; which is not a highpoint for Who, this stands up rather better. Baker is back on form, and Romana seems a lot less irritating in this one. I found it a lot more fun than the previous two (The Ribos Operation was bland and irritating, The Pirate Planet was too pantomime for my liking). And unlike those serials, it made me want to watch the next instalment, instead of not caring less what happened.

The Androids Of Tara - 3/10

Romana is mistaken for a princess, and is kidnapped by an evil lord with an eye on the throne.

Very poor and forgettable; the perfect addition to a pretty lousy season.

The Power Of Kroll - 4/10

The Doctor travels to a marsh moon; where he is once again embroiled in squabbles between the native 'Swampies,' the 'Rohm-Dutt' and the crew of a refinery who are being attacked by a giant sea creature-cum-Swampie-God!

The serial is not terrible, but it's still not particularly extraordinary or memorable either. The Swampies were a noteworthy alien race, but the monster itself was laughably bad.

The Armageddon Factor - 6/10

The Doctor and Romana go in search of the last segment of the Key; on a planet that is in perpetual war with its neighbour. Hot on their tails is the 'Black Guardian;' aiming to get the Key before they do, and plunge the universe into chaos. Only by helping the Princess Astra to save her civilisation can they hope to complete their quest in time.

The last of the Key to Time stories manages to go out on rather a high, and almost redeem the series in this final chapter. The acting and pacing are much better than most of the season; the characters are quite scary for a kid's programme (always a good thing for Who to be!) and the claustrophobic, dank sets are like a more aggressively bleak version of the Ark in Space, which is no bad thing.

I never thought I'd say it, but the first Romana has actually grown on me, and I shall miss Mary Tamm. She was certainly one of the most glamorous of the Doctor's companions, and a very good actress to boot - even if she was beyond annoying in the first two serials of the season.

Baker is getting to the end of a very long stint as the Doctor, and has a couple of scenes in this series where you worry that the magic has gone. Of course, this is Tom Baker, and he'll soon wow you again with another great nonchalant aside that reminds you he's still on the money. The acting of the ensemble cast however is mostly terrible throughout the season, with the odd notable exception.

Overall, I'm glad I sat through the whole thing, and I feel I can call myself a 'real fan' now...whatever that means!

Unless you have a similar desire to sit through some of the worst Doctor Who you are likely to see, I would personally stick with The Stones of Blood and this last story and skip the rest!

SEASON 17

We witness the regeneration of Time Lady Romana, who's second regeneration finds a lot more chemistry with the Doctor. The stories in season 17 veer from the sublime to the ridiculous and back again, but their chemistry is worth sifting through even the poorer stories.

Destiny Of The Daleks - 8/10

The 17th season starts with one of the most controversial scenes in Who history - Romana's regeneration/s. We have been led to believe up until this point (and will continue to be told afterwards) that regeneration is a very sombre, dangerous and, most importantly finite necessity. In other words it is not to be taken lightly or used irresponsibly, but as a last resort when the Doctor needs to save his life or the life of others around him.
Yet in this first scene, Romana appears to flounce her regenerations as if in a game; shifting between bodies in some sort of fashion parade.

Sixteen years of Who mythology and one of the most integral elements of the show; sacrificed for a couple of minutes of comic relief?

Personally, I prefer to think not. Like any defender of an inconsistent show, I ignore the obvious and opt for my own theories to explain away what doesn't fit. I would like to think that the 'bodies' she is 'trying on' are nothing more than projections of options she can make; in the same way as the 2nd Doctor is shown his potential choices at the end of The War Games (but done in true Romana style). I should imagine the Doctor would be pretty annoyed after going through 3 nearly fatal regenerations, to see that his companion was flippantly throwing away her own like dresses.

Anyway, this first scene notwithstanding, it is great to see the new Romana 'II' (Lalla Ward) show a great deal more connection with the Doctor from the outset. Baker and Ward would of course become the first Doctor/Companion actors to marry; so the chemistry obviously spilled over into real-life too!
And whilst I still prefer Sarah Jane and Leela as companions, Lalla does a good job and is instantly likeable in the role.

And now to the Daleks. I know its sacrilege to say this, but although I found the Doctor's most famous foes scary as a young child, as I have grown older I have found them far less threatening than many of the other monsters the Doctor comes up against. I think a lot of this has to do with them becoming a part of the fabric of our culture to such a degree, as to desensitise me to their impact. But with all this said, I found them much nastier and more brutal in this serial; much more effectively threatening. The scene where they first appear, for example; pinning a terrified Romana to the wall, is by far one of the best entrances of any foe since The Tomb of The Cybermen some ten years earlier.

The story itself concerns two mechanised races (yes, I know the Daleks aren't robots, but stick with me here!) - The Daleks and the highly androgynous Movellans. The two have been at war with each other for centuries. But due to their slavish reliance on logic, both have been able to predict the other's next move, prevent it and as such neither has been able to gain the upper hand.

Both races decide to enlist the help of two of the galaxy's strongest strategists to help them find a way to beat their opponents. The Daleks decide to resurrect their creator, the mad scientist Davros (who again is wonderfully sinister and unhinged), the Movellans try to attract, and then force the Doctor to be their aide, pitting the two old enemies into a battle of brilliant minds.

This is a strong Tom Baker Dalek story; probably my second favourite after Genesis. It's a great action story and fun to watch - a real return to form for the show after the last season.

City Of Death - 9/10

An explosion during primordial times fractures an alien's 'being' across history. In modern day Paris, one of these fragments, posing as a human tries to create a time machine to go back and stop the explosion from happening. But, as the Doctor realises the explosion is an important part of the Earth's development, he must stop the alien before unknown damage is done.

The Paris setting is understandably beautiful. The script is shrewd, and the harmony between the Doctor and Romana II continues to blossom. The main highlight of the season for me.

The Creature From The Pit - 5/10

The Doctor arrives on another alien planet...to find hostile inhabitants who capture him. He falls down a pit to a ravaging monster. But is the monster all that it seems?

A pretty forgettable 'Who by the numbers' serial that doesn't really add anything to the season; although I thought Myra Frances was suitably sinister as the main villain of the piece, Lady Adrasta.

Nightmare Of Eden - 5/10

The Doctor must solve the mystery of two spaceships that have materialised and infused together, causing a mismatch of both ships.

Not bad; and more entertaining than the previous serial. But still rather unremarkable.

The Horns Of Nimon - 2/10

The show puts its own science fiction twist on mythology again, as the Doctor must save a race of space-age 'locusts' posing as minotaur-like creatures. A tiresome end to a pretty tame season by Baker standards. Saved only by a nice cameo from Blue Peter presenter Janet Ellis!

Shada - (Unaired) 8/10

The Doctor visits an old Time Lord who has taken residency as a professor at Cambridge University. He finds that a criminal has also tracked down the old Time Lord after escaping from Shada (the Time Lords' prison for vanquished foes) and has stolen an ancient Gallifreyan mystical book of great power from him.
With me so far? Good.

From here on in its pretty classic Who stuff - the Doctor must retrieve the book, keep hold of his brain from levitating spheres that aim to drain it and so on.

The proposed finale to the season was famously unaired due to a B.B.C strike at the time. It languished in the archives, unaired until 1992, when the surviving segments were released on video with narration by Tom Baker to fill in the gaps. It was also later reworked as an audio story for the 8th Doctor (Paul McGann) before finally being released on DVD in 2017 with animated scenes and episodes.

If some of the scenes at the beginning seem
familiar, it's because they were salvaged and used for the fourth Doctor's segments in the 'Five Doctors' special, after Tom Baker declined the offer to join the other incarnations.

It's regrettable that it wasn't aired at the time; as this is a far better offering than most of the rest of the season. It has an enthralling plot, nice locations and sets, a great script and action-packed scenes. A far superior ending to the season and it's a shame it was never seen in its entirety until fairly recently.

SEASON 18

Baker's last season sees the show undergoing a real paradigm shift of both style and substance as a new showrunner brings in the heavy science and loses some of the charm.

The Leisure Hive - 3/10

The Doctor and Romana take a holiday on a distant leisure planet. But their relaxation is short lived, when a machine 'malfunctions,' leaving the Doctor aged and weak, and they realise there is more to this planet and its inhabitants than they first thought.

The feel of the show changes dramatically as we enter Tom Baker's last season. Producer John Nathan-Turner comes in for his first story, and tries hard to make the series much more serious and science-based than the light-hearted style of Douglas Adams. He does rather over-do this intention; and the result is a story that is more earnest than accessible and more sombre than stimulating. The majority of the script alone is impenetrable for most fans I should imagine.

On the plus side, the effects and sets are both great. But unfortunately the show seems to be veering towards a pompous scientific approach that has the effect of alienating half of its audience. There are some good scenes, such as the Doctor's dismemberment and ageing effects. But overall this is not my sort of 'Who.'

Meglos - 6/10

Science and religion go *Mano-a-mano* again, in a culture's search to an explanation for a strange dodecahedron crystal that arrives from space. The religious see it as a gift from their God Ti, the scientific want to use it as a power source. But they are not alone - there is a megalomaniac cactus (no, really!) who wants the power of the crystal too, and can take on humanoid forms to achieve its end. Into this mess comes the Doctor; enlisted to try and solve the rift between the factions. But Meglos (the cactus-like character) takes on the form of the Doctor himself, which causes all sorts of confusion.

This is a good excuse for Baker to show his 'bad-guy' acting credentials; at which he once again excels. It is also great to see the return of a true Who legend, Jacqueline Hill; who had played Barbara, one of the first (and one of my favourite) companions. Here she plays a very different character - the religious leader Lexa; marking the first time a Who companion had come back to play a different character (Nicholas Courtney/The Brigadier as 'Bret' doesn't count, I don't see him as a companion!).

This one is a bit of an acquired taste. It's not brilliant, but it's certainly not terrible either. It's a lot more entertaining than The Leisure Hive. But it still seems to be missing something.

The effects are pretty good for the time, and it's really nice to see both the return of Jacqueline Hill and a different side to Tom Baker. But I doubt this would make any top tens amongst fans any time soon.

Full Circle - 4/10

The Doctor and Romana answer a call from Gallifrey. Following the coordinates however, they find themselves on a completely different planet. Without knowing it, they have managed to travel to another, 'alternative' universe called 'E-Space.' Here they meet up with colonists who have crash landed some time ago and are endeavouring to fix their craft.

Enter Adric; the most irritating companion since Dodo from the first Doctor, and up until Mel of the seventh. Adric is amongst the youngest and brightest of the colonists and I *can* understand what the producers were thinking in casting a younger companion for the target audience to relate to. But not only has he got a plum firmly lodged in his throat, but also the warmth and personality of gazpacho soup. He's arrogant, self- assured and, in short a 'know-it-all.'

Anyway, Adric aside, once we have met the colonists; we're in full on Pertwee territory. We discover the inhabitants are being ravaged by creatures from the swamp; creatures who we then find out are pre-evolved versions of the inhabitants themselves!

Again, like the rest of this series, it's not bad, and the creatures are certainly well designed. But I just find it much more difficult to get enthused about when compared to earlier Baker serials.

State Of Decay – 7/10

Still stranded in 'E-Space,' The Doctor and Romana arrive on an Earth-like planet; to find a civilisation that is in a 'state of decay.' In other words, instead of evolving and moving forwards, they are moving backwards from their origins of space roamers into a more primitive race of kings and peasants. What transpires is a system of *'vampires,'* who are using the blood of the peasants to feed both themselves and a large creature that dwells beneath their spaceship-cum-castle.

A change of style from the last few space-related serials. This has more of a season 13, 'Hammer Horror' feel to it (such as the Brain of Morbius), and it is a much more compelling story than the last few.

The chemistry between Tom Baker and Lalla Ward seems to be growing serial by serial, and you can tell in this one especially that there is more to their relationship than we see onscreen. Adric is still really irritating; but his character is thankfully not as prevalent here. The enemies are creepy and in keeping with iconic vampires of classic films and television.

A welcome return to form.

Warriors' Gate - 4/10

The Doctor and Romana find themselves on the 'universal rift' between 'E-Space' and 'N-Space' (our universe) in this final part of the 'E-Space' trilogy. The lion-like Tharils, once rulers of the 'time winds,' are now enslaved, and the Doctor must free them.

A real mess of a serial that is confusing at best, inaccessible at worst. There are some novel ideas presented, and you get the feeling that had this been directed differently, it could've made for a good serial. But the characters need much more fleshing out, the story is all over the place, and you are left feeling decidedly unsatisfied by the end - particularly with the rushed departure of Romana II and K-9. Whilst I've never been a huge fan of either character, I thought they deserved a better ending than this!

The Keeper Of Traken - 6/10

The Doctor and Adric are summoned to Traken; famous as one of the most peaceful societies in the universe. As you would predict though, this harmony is short lived. A 'living statue' begins to take over the society and 'upturn the apple cart,' as it were.

For inside the statue hides the return of one of the Doctor's most iconic enemies...The Master!

The Doctor's foe returns as the decomposed monster he was in The Deadly Assassin. He takes over a new body at the end of the story from Anthony Ainley's character Tremas (itself an anagram of 'Master'). The re- introduction is done well; with enough suspense and mystery that it's easy to see how exciting it must have been to viewers at the time.

We are also introduced to the next of the Doctor's companions, Nyssa. Whilst Sarah Sutton is undeniably lovely, the character itself was never the most exciting of companions; and it's difficult to get excited about her inclusion in the series.

Overall, this is a much more cohesive serial than Warrior's Gate, and far more easy to watch. As with the rest of the series, it is O.K, but never really earns itself a 'classic' status as a serial. Apart from the great re- introduction of such an important enemy of course!

Logopolis - 7/10

The T.A.R.D.I.S needs a bit of T.L.C, so the Doctor returns to Earth to find and measure a real Police Box. He hopes to take the measurements to Logopolis; where there lives a race of mathematicians who can create matter, and keep the universe together through their equations. The Doctor hopes they can help him repair the dimensions of his ailing ship.

Meanwhile, the Master, having escaped Traken, realises that he can sabotage the work of the Logopolitans, and hold the universe to ransom.

Into the mix bumbles Tegan, an Australian would-be air stewardess, who walks into the T.A.R.D.I.S en route to Logopolis after the Master kills her aunt. Nyssa is also back, having been transported to Logopolis in the hunt for the Master who has taken her father's form.

And finally, watching over all of this is 'the Watcher,' a strange white figure who is following the Doctor; and about to show him that his 4th life is at an end.

Tom Baker bows out, after an unprecedented 7 years as arguably the most popular actor to play the part.
Understandably, towards the end the huge presence of the actor had led to it being a 'one man show' in some ways and to his own admission (in interviews) he had begun to believe his own hype. He was getting more irascible with people on set and more difficult to work with for those around him. This does come across in some of the later shows; where the companions and story seem rather insignificant. It all seems rather too 'clever for its own good,' and lacks some of the simple charm of the earlier show. Whether through the irreverent humour of Douglas Adams (which worked a lot better on the groundbreaking Hitchhiker's Guide to The Galaxy), or his successor John

Nathan-Turner's drive to take the series in new directions; these last few seasons didn't have the same exciting feel for me as the peaks of 'Genesis of the Daleks,' 'Terror of the Zygons' or 'The Deadly Assassin.'

At this last juncture, the series seems to be slightly uneasy in its transition; and the introduction of a rather *over-ripe* version of the Master does little to improve things. From the outset, Ainley plays the character as a *pantomime baddy*; lacking the menace of Delgado or the more recent portrayal by John Simm. He's not awful by any means; but he doesn't really have the same gravitas to make the character as interesting for me.

Whilst it is really sad to see Tom step down; I can see why this was a good time to pass on the torch, and inject some renewed energy into the series (how's that for mixed metaphors?!). His era is easily one of the most exciting of any of the show, and at its best it is difficult to better Baker! But as we step firmly into the '80's, the show is already changing dramatically; and a new era, for better or for worse, is just around the corner.

Goodbye and a HUGE thank you to Baker for really solidifying the importance of the series and for taking it in new and brilliant directions that have never really been surpassed since.
Now...bring on the Davison!

THE FIFTH DOCTOR
- PETER DAVISON
(1981-1984)

SEASON 19

A dashing young Doctor, a crowded TARDIS and some inventive shocks along the way.

Castrovalva - 6/10

As the Doctor gets used to his new regeneration, The Master continues his dastardly schemes by kidnapping Adric and sending the T.A.R.D.I.S back in time to the big bang, where it will be destroyed...if the Doctor can't come to his senses in time!

Whilst the show is still struggling to reach a new high for the new decade, this isn't a bad series opener. I particularly liked the scene in which Davison; struggling to settle into the Doctor's 5th form, does a funny impression of the previous 4 Doctors; and little touches like this work well.

I'm still finding it difficult to take to the 'new' Master. Instead of the great back-story that made John Simm's Master much more believable and deep as a character; Anthony Ainley's Master, whilst fairly effective, is more akin to something from a 1950's adventure series (such as Flash Gordon or Robin Hood), and fails to really capture the essence of what made Delgado's portrayal so memorable.

Production-wise, this story reminded me of the excellent

Hitchhiker's Guide to the Galaxy T.V series; which isn't surprising I suppose, considering that Douglas Adams had not long left the series at the time. The fragmented nature of Castrovalva also works well.

It's worth watching for Davison's first stab at the role. But story-wise, it's underwhelming.

Four To Doomsday - 4/10

Erm...well the sets are good. But the story is poor (a giant toad with God delusions wants to take over Earth and turn everyone into robots?). This, coupled with rather boring companions and a less-than-exciting Doctor (I like Davison, but he's no T.Baker!) make for a unsatisfying serial. Certainly not classic Doctor Who.

Kinda - 9/10

The T.A.R.D.I.S lands on a seemingly peaceful planet that is being assessed for colonisation by a human team; who aim to laud it over the peaceful and harmless inhabitants. The tensions deepen when various people of both sides are possessed by the spirit of the evil snake-like Mara.

This is a very odd, but intriguing story. Sometimes it is odd in a 'good' way (some of the dream sequences are unforgettable), sometimes it's odd in a 'bad' way (what was the point of the stupid jester, and why did the possessed humans have to start acting like toddlers?). I particularly enjoyed the Tegan scenes in which she wanders into an area of the forest that hypnotises her and drags her into a hell of her own making; complete with a Bowie-esque scary mime-artist type creature (Dukkha). This strange and seemingly disjointed story, which is a little bit Avatar, a little bit David

Lynch is definitely an acquired taste. But it's also certainly one of the most captivating of the Davison years and stands apart as a unique highpoint of the era for me.

The Visitation - 8/10

An alien lands on Earth at the time of the Great Plague. Infecting rats with an even deadlier disease, he plans to wipe out humanity without them knowing. He also has a robot that is scaring the locals dressed as the Grim Reaper.

I liked the character design, and both the alien and the android look amazing, even by modern day standards.

The Black Orchid - 8/10

The Doctor and companions travel back to the 1920s, in this mixture of Victorian murder mystery and Phantom of the Opera. After Nyssa is kidnapped, the Doctor must try to uncover a family's dark secret.

Whilst this story may have dragged had it been a full 4 parter; it works well as a 2 parter (the first since The Sontaran Experiment), and the costumes and prosthetics make it a fun addition to the 19th season. Perfect 'rainy day' Doctor Who for me this one.

Earthshock - 8/10

The Cybermen are back, and on the verge of invading 26th Century Earth.

Whilst not my favourite Cyberman story, this was action packed and enjoyable to watch. It's good to see them back again after a bit of a hiatus, but I do prefer the more robotic sounding, emotionless editions from The Tomb of The Cybermen to these more 'Darth Vader' style enemies (maybe they were cashing in a bit?).

Adric is still annoying and whiny, but it is strangely sad to see him go. I'd say he went out with a bang, but that might be rather disrespectful!

This is a well directed and shot story, and not a bad addition to the series. It's nice to see the first tip of the hat to the older series for Doctor #5 (apart from the Master); a desire that would be fully capitalised with the Daleks a couple of series later.

Time-Flight - 5/10

A Concorde flies into the path of the T.A.R.D.I.S as it materialises; forcing the plane to disappear into the time vortex, arriving in prehistoric times (or at least I think this is what happens!). When the T.A.R.D.I.S follows in hot pursuit, it finds there is a crazed conjurer sitting at the end of this time vortex ('like a spider at the end of a web') that can manipulate the perceptions of the passengers and thus control their actions.

Although this premise shows promise, and the supporting cast are strong, the serial started to lose me after this point. The conjurer turns out to be the Master in a zombie mask, doing an embarrassingly cod Chinese accent(?). The plot takes on so many directions as to feel like a 'pick and mix' of half-finished ideas in one, confusing and dissatisfying package. It's very difficult to know what to make of this one, to be honest.

SEASON 20

Some familiar faces return in this season of hits and misses.

Arc Of Infinity - 6/10

Omega is back (having first appeared in the special 'Three Doctors' special 10 years earlier), and he's found a way to join his D.N.A with the Doctor and take over his form. The Time Lords decide that the only way to prevent Omega from taking ultimate power is to sentence the Doctor to death (what is it about the Doctor that makes everyone want to either kill him or sacrifice him to something?!).

The most remarkable part of this serial is its inclusion of an actor who would return to play the Doctor (Colin Baker); here playing a Time Lord Chancellery Guard commander that also tries to kill him(!).

I have my own my daft theory to explain this strange continuity issue. When the fifth Doctor regenerates in The Caves of Androzani ('spoilers!'); it is because he has taken on the poison of his companion Peri and is dying. Therefore his regeneration is from a *sick* body. This explains the irrational and uncharacteristic behaviour he shows in becoming violent towards his companion (see The Twin Dilemma). But I also believe this sickness manifests itself by changing the Doctor into a form he perceives as evil and malevolent - i.e. the guard who has shot him in this serial. Of course, it could just be because they liked Colin Baker's acting, and I may well be reading into this far too much! Either way, Colin certainly does show a great deal of presence in this role, so you can understand why they wanted him to return to the show in a bigger role.

Aside from the joy of seeing Colin make his debut, I found the serial rather difficult to enthuse about. Even though there is a lot of action, it left me slightly cold.

Snakedance - 7/10

Hahahahahahahahaha; look at how young and camp Martin Clunes looks hahahahahahahahaha!

Sorry for that! Being a huge fan of Mr. Clunes I just had to get that out of my system...anyway...

This serial continues from Kinda, one of my favourite of the Davison era, and returns to the story of the Mara, a snake like creature which infects people's minds.

Tegan's mind is still infected with the power of the Mara, and she unwittingly steers the crew of the T.A.R.D.I.S forward 500 years to when the great snake is ready to awaken again.

In its long absence, the Mara has passed into legend and story; becoming more a quaint folktale; paid lip-service in a parade each ten years, rather than given the level of fear and caution it should bring. The Doctor must convince the people of the planet that the threat of its return is very real!

This is a worthy sequel and has some of the same intrigue and originality as Kinda. Clunes, for all his youth is actually really good in this, and the serial is worth watching for its great climactic scene...it's just a shame it takes so long to get to it.

There's something about this period of the show that makes it rarely more than just 'O.K.' Don't get me wrong, It's rarely terrible either, which at least puts it above most of the serials of the next two Doctors. But coming after such a monumental Doctor as Tom Baker, Davison always seems a bit too 'nice;' amiable and likeable, without ever quite possessing the 'bite' of his predecessor.

Mawdryn Undead - 6/10

The Black Guardian catches up with the Doctor, using a carrot-topped schoolboy to try and assassinate the Doctor(?).

It's always great to see the brilliant Brigadier, who returns after a 6 year absence. The schoolboy (Turlough) is an interesting character, at least on paper, and there are a few clues that he is perhaps not what he appears to be. However, the actor doesn't really work in this role; and a potentially promising side-kick doesn't really 'cut it' in my eyes. He has a few moments of brilliance, but it's not consistent enough to make you excited about this mini-story arc ('The Black Guardian Trilogy,' as Mawdryn Undead, Terminus and Enlightenment is referred).

By episode 3 it all gets fairly complicated, and there is a seemingly unconnected story of aliens who have harnessed the power of the Time Lords to regenerate, using a stolen machine, and have trapped themselves in an eternal flux of 'undeath;' needing the Doctor to sacrifice his own regenerations to let them die...

Erm...did I say it was nice to see the Brigadier again?

Terminus - 4/10

The Black Guardian, via Turlough, sabotages the T.A.R.D.I.S; stranding the Doctor and his companions on a ship full of lepers! A ship which also happens to be the centre of the universe and the cause of the big bang(?!).

I'm starting to feel the same creeping annoyance watching the Davison era as I had when I was knee-deep in the Pertwee years. It's not so much an annoyance at the programme itself; but at myself for 'blanket bitching' so many Davison serials. I didn't start writing a book about one of my favourite T.V programmes, just to slag it off. And there is much to be positive about in this time; the Doctor is likeable and heroic (though perhaps not as 'alien' or weird as I would like him to be); the production values are pretty good, and the best stories (such as Resurrection of the Daleks and Kinda) rank amongst the highest of the show as a whole. But there are also far too many lightweight offerings that mar the show.

Take Turlough as another example. I really want to like this companion. But although you get the feeling you'd like the actor if you met him, there seems to be something crucial lacking from the character and the way that he is played.

Take this story as an example of Davison at its worst. This 'Lost in Leper Space' serial could be rechristened *Tedious;* as it just seems to go on forever. There are plenty of action scenes, but still nothing that really engages you.

It's difficult to find anything positive about this one...believe me I'm trying!

Enlightenment - 3/10

Where exactly did Nyssa go? I must've completely missed it!

Anyway, the tedium continues in another lacklustre story of pirates in space (something that sounds a lot more exciting than it is!). The Doctor and companions find themselves on board a Victorian boat. But all is not as it seems; and it turns out that the boat is actually a spaceship, and that those on board are parasitic people who claim the lives of others. At least, I think this is what it was about - I have to admit I completely lost any interest in this terrible serial, which is one of Davison's worst.

The King's Demons - 7/10

The series returns somewhat to form. The Master is back again; taking control of a shape-shifting robot called Kamelion and placing him on the throne as an imposter to King John in 1215. His hope is to stop the king from signing the Magna Carta; thus stunting the development of modern democracy and sending the world into a chaos he can then rule over. With me so far? Good.

This is actually not a bad serial; helped by its short 2- part length to stay fairly tight and well paced. The story is good (though would be more fitting as a Meddling Monk story in my opinion) and the effects, (particularly Kamelion) are very impressive for television at the time. The direction seems to be much improved too, and both Turlough and the Master seem more toned down. This is a slight return to form and much more enjoyable than the rest of the season.

Specials

20Th Year Anniversary Special
- The Five Doctors - 8/10

All 5 incarnations (so far) are pulled out of their respective timelines by a mysterious enemy who wants the powers of the Time Lords; pitting them against a series of dangerous tasks in the 'death zone' on Gallifrey.

First and foremost this feature length show is a celebration of the 20 years of the institution that is
'Doctor Who.' To this end, the producers try to include as many of the Doctors, companions and enemies as possible. However; to do this weaving in of 5 Doctors, 4 companions and 6 nemeses is inevitably at the cost of a coherent or credible plot.

The only way to really enjoy this special is to not take it too seriously. Just sit back and enjoy the spectacle of so many elements that made the classic series so enjoyable being forced inextricably together. Don't expect a great story, but do expect a lot of fun and nostalgia.

It's just a real shame William Hartnell wasn't still alive to join in; although Richard Hurdnall does an admirable job as the first Doctor.

SEASON 21

The final season for the Fifth Doctor sees the return of the Silurians, Sea Devils and The Master. But it's Davison's swansong that really solidifies this Doctor in the memories of the viewers.

Warriors Of The Deep - 6/10

Ghosts of Pertwee past rear their scaly heads; as the Silurians and Sea Devils return to re-conquer 'their world' from the ape-descendants (that's us folks) that have colonised Earth since their hibernation. This time they aim to do this by inciting human war that will kill off the race once and for all.

This 'Cold War' theme has been explored before, and perhaps to better effect, but this is still a good Davison serial that is worth a watch. It hasn't aged quite as well as the Pertwee serials that preceded it. After a slow start however, it does build to a satisfying climax in the final episode, showing both the philosophical as well as action-orientated sides of the Doctor's character.

The Awakening - 5/10

The Doctor and companions land in a remote village

in 1984, to find some battle recreationists have gone mad...well *more mad!* It would appear a demon/alien has created a time field between the 17th and 20th centuries, and is hiding in the wall of the local church.

The supporting cast are much better in this serial than in the last few; and it's a well produced story. It is lacking in any real substance though and feels very much like another series filler, with little to make it memorable.

The only exception would be the creature itself; with its great booming eyes and evil face.

Frontios - 4/10

The Doctor and companions arrive in another militarised community to find they are beset by giant slug monsters arising from the deep. In other words we are in Pertwee territory again. I found this difficult to rave about, and this is certainly not essential Who.

Resurrection Of The Daleks - 8/10

The Daleks have lost the battle against the Movellans (see Destiny of the Daleks), after their enemies released a deadly disease. They return to resurrect their creator Davros to find an antidote.

The series returns to more bleak territory in this thrilling (if a little over-serious) serial. Although not without its faults, this is one of the better of the Davison time. Davros is at his maniacal best and Davison puts in a good performance too (to be honest he's always pretty good, even if it's not one of the most popular portrayals of the character). But the other actors aren't quite up to the same standard, and the companions are some of my least favourite in this. Some notable (if peculiar) cameos from Dirty Den and one of the likely lads don't really add any comic relief to what is quite a grim and unpleasant addition to the series.

I'm usually complaining that the serials aren't taking themselves seriously enough, but this seems to be on the other extreme. The direction is a little dry and in need of some light to go with the dark. As with many Davison serials, it's not at all bad; but it's not quite Doctor Whoat its best. However, the Daleks are much more deep, manipulative characters than in some of their other stories, which is good to see. The plot is a well written way to take the Daleks and Davros forward. Although 'death by shaving foam' was a bit disappointing!

Pretty scary and violent for kids this one, and we are a million miles from the daft and terrible slide Colin Baker and early Sylvestor McCoy era Doctor Who would take.

Planet Of Fire - 7/10

The bikini-clad, cod-American sounding Peri finds a dodgy looking alien artefact on a boat and tries to swim ashore; hoping to sell it as payment to get to Morocco. She proceeds to start drowning, is saved by Turlough and put in the T.A.R.D.I.S to recover; becoming the Doctor's next companion. From here they travel to a 'planet of fire;' an Arabian-styled planet with a super- volcano threatening to erupt at any minute. The Master is back, and manages to connect with the T.A.R.D.I.S via Kamelion.

Just where has Kamelion been since we last saw him in The King's Demons? Sounds like another excuse to come up with one of my daft theories to tie everything together!...Here we go!....

1. The Doctor worries that The Master may have planted

a homing signal on Kamelion to track him down. By de-activating him until they were at a safe distance, he hopes the Master can't catch up. This theory would seem to carry some weight, when the Master does indeed turn up once we see Kamelion again.

2. The Doctor may have been worried that one of his predecessors could commandeer Kamelion for themselves during 'The Five Doctors' - and so he decided to hide him away. This wouldn't explain why Kamelion stayed hidden for the next few stories after this however; unless the Doctor was absent minded and forgot about him.

3. The Doctor may have wanted time to work on Kamelion; to make sure he posed no further threat (he was an ambiguous and susceptible kind of robot; being easily led by the Master when we first met him in The King's Demons).

4. The producers realised their expensive robot was a flop, but thought they'd try to get their money's worth before retiring him.

It is strange to see the Doctor trust and even enthuse about a machine when his own previous incarnations have shown a huge distrust in computers (see the Hartnell serial The War Machines, the Troughton serial The Invasion or the Pertwee serial The Green Death). Although I suppose this attitude was broken by the arrival of K-9 into the series; and Kamelion is a follow on from this?

Whatever the conclusion, Kamelion isn't around for long; being bumped off by Turlough and then used as a channel through which the Master can reappear.

This serial turns out to be not at all bad. Whilst the Davison years don't stand up as the most remarkable period of the show; most of the stories in this last season hold up well. It's nice to see Turlough's character progress, and Davison is excellent in showing many sides to the Doctor's character. The Master is still played as one-dimensional; but his apparent demise in this story is actually quite sad. A worthwhile penultimate story for the 5th Doctor.

The Caves Of Androzani - 10/10

The Doctor and Peri are lethally poisoned. As they search for a cure, they end up in a war between a deformed outlaw and a ruthless businessman. In the end, the Doctor will have to make the ultimate sacrifice for his new companion in this 'Phantom of the Opera' style finale.

From reading the last few seasons; you would be forgiven for thinking I didn't think much of Peter Davison's doctor. I wasn't expecting much when I first started watching Davison in the role...I remembered him more from 'All Creatures Great and Small,' and, in following Tom Baker's highly popular and long-running doctor, he had some big shoes to fill. But I was pleasantly surprised that Davison was able to further diversify the Doctor; adding heroic, compassionate and amiable sides to what had already seemed a fully established character. Traits which would be crucial to the development of David Tennant's more popular portrayal over 20 years later.

One of the biggest problem with some of 1980's Who, is that the three great actors to play the role (Davison, C.Baker and McCoy) are often let down by less than brilliant stories or production; and this is certainly the case with Davison. This is most evident when the better stories show glimmers of brilliance in an otherwise slightly uninspiring era of the show. For Davison these were stories such as Black Orchid, Kinda, Resurrection of the Daleks and; most notably his brilliant 'swan-song' The Caves of Androzani.

Not only is this probably the best Davison serial, it stands up as one of the best of the decade. Yes, it is still unmistakably 80's at times; but the main leads (especially the misunderstood 'villain' of the piece Jek) put on really good performances.

Thankfully a conceivably great doctor gets a suitably poignant ending.

THE SIXTH DOCTOR - COLIN BAKER (1984-1986)

SEASON 21
(CONTINUED)

The Twin Dilemma - 3/10

"I am the Doctor, whether you like it or not." (The Sixth Doctor, The Twin Dilemma, episode 4)

After a difficult regeneration, the Doctor is acting very strangely indeed. He attacks his companion Peri, and then decides to become a hermit on a distant planet. Here he finds two spoilt mathematical boy geniuses who have been kidnapped by a Time Lord, under the influence of a monster.

The first serial for the 6th Doctor is often slated as one of the worst ever. But whilst I wouldn't say it is great by any means, I did find it watchable in parts; which is more than I can say for some of his other serials.

The first serial of any Doctor is always a fascinating one. He is often thrown into mad mood swings or other strange behaviour, as his new mind/body settles down. In the previous regeneration from Tom Baker to Peter Davison; this took on a comedic style. Davison humorously portrayed his four predecessors as they circled around his brain. This time around however, the unsettled Doctor is an unstable and dangerous incarnation; even trying at one point to murder his companion.

Although the change in character was confusing to audiences at the time, I *can* understand why they did it. Davison had played him as a charming and heroic character; leaving only really one direction for the Doctor to go in if he was going to progress in depth and in interest. Colin Baker was given the very difficult task of turning a once likeable and friendly Doctor into a very disagreeable character; and he does this with admirable zeal.

The difficulty however is that to have a hero we all want to enjoy watching, he must at the least be likeable. Colin's Doctor from the outset is obnoxious, arrogant, and very difficult to like. The cantankerous beginnings of the first Doctor worked well, because of his age and the fact that he had never met humans before. When it comes to the 6th Doctor however; it seems rather self-destructive to the programme; which of course it almost was.

I don't want to bad-mouth Colin Baker for the sake of it - he's often derided by fans, and to be fair it's really not his fault. He has the difficult job of taking the Doctor back to his darker roots; and he acts this with a gravitas and authority that most actors would struggle with. He also has moments where he manages to make the Doctor's character completely his own; which is no mean feat when you consider that 5 people had already played him by this point.

Anyway, all of this is of course not telling you whether this is a good story or not. As with most of each Doctor's first stories, the plot takes second priority behind the important task of introducing the Doctor himself. And this serial manages this well, even though the story itself is poor. Slug men versus human fir-cones is the best way I can describe it. A weak story that has none of the fleshing out needed to make it understandable or particularly appealing.

But the main crux of this story is about the change in the Doctor, which makes this a suitable start to a new phase.

SEASON 22

The show struggles to find its feet with its cranky new Doctor and reluctant companion.

Attack Of The Cybermen - 6/10

The Cybermen travel back in time to 1986, to prevent the destruction of their home planet Mondas (see the Tenth Planet). They intend to hijack Halley's comet, and send it on a path to destroy the Earth first.

By relating this story to worthy Cybermen serials The Tenth Planet (first Doctor) and The Tomb of the Cybermen (second Doctor), this serial makes a connection to its own history. However, these references also serve to remind the viewer just what an average instalment this is by comparison.

Another notable connection made here is the 'Chameleon Drive' of the T.A.R.D.I.S, which the Doctor finally manages to fix. The crucial drive changes the appearance of the T.A.R.D.I.S to match its surroundings; and its malfunction is the reason why it has been a Police Box from the first 1963 story onwards. This is a memorable first in this story. But not even a cameo from Brian Glover and Peri's tight-fitting costume can raise this above the run-of-the-mill.

Vengeance On Varos - 9/10

The extremities of reality T.V are the base of the story here; in a future where live torture and execution are televised for the masses. The Doctor must survive the sadistic government, and the even 'slimier' ruthless
'business-slug' Sil to gain precious ore they need to replenish the T.A.R.D.I.S.

I still find this Doctor and his companion difficult to warm to. Yet Sil, a thoroughly vile and grotesque reptilian foe is one of the most effectively realised of the whole era.

The plot really ropes you in. It's intriguing and memorable – which is something that this series had yet to be. The ideas are shrewd and satirical and you really *care* about the story for the first time since Davison.
This is easily the highlight of the Colin Baker years for me, and if I were to pick just one recommendation from his tenure, it would be this one.

(And, on a side note, it's great to see the actor who played King John in the brilliant kid's show Maid Marian and Her Merry Men in a different role here too!)

The Mark Of The Rani - 4/10

The introduction of Kate O'Mara as a renegade Time Lady called The Rani is a curious one. An enemy obsessed with experimenting on what she sees as lesser species (such as humans) was supposed to be a contender for the Master, and as long-running. However, the series is in such dire-straits by this point as to make even a story involving both the Rani AND the Master fall flat and feel tiresome. The

Doctor continues to be irritating (certainly not someone you could imagine kids wanting to idolise). Peri has her heart in the right place and is a good actress, but has the emotional backbone of a wet cabbage. Anthony Ainley continues to play Delgado's sinister creation as a one- note character. And Kate O'Mara, whilst injecting some life into *her* character, isn't too far behind him.

There are, however, some effective ideas. I thought the Rani's plan to remove the chemical that allows sleep; therefore turning humans into violent creatures that could be easily manipulated, showed promise that could've been further explored. But the 45 minute run- time of episodes in season 22 just stretches how watchable these stories are.

It seems the show has run out of energy and is possessing a distinct lack of any real desire to make classic television by this point.

The Two Doctors - 5/10

Doctor #2 (Patrick Troughton) and his companion Jamie are taken out of their time-lines and must work together with Doctor #6 to thwart the plans of an old Time Lord friend whose cannibalistic creation Cheesene has teamed up with the Sontarans to steal the power of vortex travel.

Not dreadful, particularly by mid-80's Who standards. There are a lot of intriguing ingredients put together - the fantastic Patrick Troughton returns as the 2nd Doctor, The Sontarans return as the joint bad guys with a rogue Time Lord, and even Colin Baker's unpleasant Doctor has settled into a more palatable character. But even with all of these elements; there is still something chronically missing again which makes the story (especially at 45 minutes an episode) difficult to care that much about. Another potentially good serial is rendered the worst of the '(insert number here) Doctors' specials. Such a sad waste of the wonderful Troughton.

Timelash - 6/10

The Doctor, Peri and a young H.G Wells (why?) travel into the future, to find a mutated mad scientist has visions of creating a new race like himself. And Peri is to be his first victim!

Whilst this was one of the slightly better Colin Baker stories, it's still not really a 'classic' or particularly memorable. I liked the mutated bad guy; although a name like 'Borad' does unfortunately bring to mind the Sacha Baron Cohen character, which takes some of the sting out of it.

The pacing is fairly good; even if the story seems to jump all over the place. I actually found myself rooting for the 6th Doctor for the first time in a while. Although his usual arrogance and abusive nature towards Peri soon returned my previous attitude unfortunately.

Revelation Of The Daleks - 2/10

Davros has been hiding out at a cryogenic facility; where he has tricked the patients into believing he will heal them...whilst secretly turning them into his new Dalek creations! The Doctor must form an unlikely alliance with the 'old' Daleks to take on their crazy creator before his plans bear fruition.

Growing up with the 1980's Doctors (Davison, Baker and McCoy), I didn't realise just how bad some of these episodes were. It's not until you revisit the Doctor at one of the peaks (such as Hartnell, Troughton and T. Baker, or later in Eccleston, Tenant and Smith) that you realise how embarrassing they can be. Granted, some of the Davison ones aren't too bad; but this was truly awful.

Where to begin? The Doctor is smug, angry and obnoxious. The assistant has a phony accent and has little connection to him. The acting of the other actors is cringeworthy, as are the effects and music. And added to this is Alexi Sayle playing one of the worst Who characters I've seen - 'the D.J' yes, it is as bad as it
sounds!

It's good to see Davros again; and he's at his sinister best once again; but this doesn't save what is a dire addition to the series, and a lacklustre ending to a pretty terrible season.

It's like no one seems to care or want the show to be taken seriously anymore. It's almost as if the show is ridiculing itself and its amazing legacy. A very sad time for the show.

SEASON 23 – 'THE TRIAL OF A TIME LORD'

The Sixth Doctor's 2nd and final season shows a lot more promise; with an overarching theme for the first time since Tom's 'Key to Time' series. The Doctor is pulled out of time and space to face trail for the 'crimes' of interference by his people The Timelords.

The Mysterious Planet - 6/10

The Doctor, suffering from memory loss, is summoned to stand trial for the second time by the Time Lords (see The War Games for the first), for his 'crimes' of interfering in space and time. He is prosecuted by the malevolent 'Valeyard;' who starts to showcase examples of his recent adventures, and the damage he argues the Doctor has done.

In the first of four adventures (the shortest season yet), the Valeyard shows the court the Doctor; arriving on a future Earth that has been dragged across space. Here, he meets a barbaric tribe, led by Queen Katryca (played by the wonderful Joan Sims from the 'Carry On' series). He also meets two conmen, and a dictatorial robot, who's death will set into motion the end of the planet if the Doctor doesn't step in to help.

After the show was put on hiatus for 18 months it looked in real jeopardy of being cancelled altogether. The head of the B.B.C Michael Grade had voiced his dislike of the show and the ratings had been steadily dropping. I was probably a bit harsh in the last review in saying that people didn't care anymore about the show. The show- runner, John Nathan-Turner was crucial in saving the show by doing everything in his power to see it return.

He even commissioned a 'Live Aid' style single called 'Doctor in Distress,' to rally the troops. Yes, it's excruciatingly terrible, but at least the thought was there! Without him and his team, and of course the indignation of the stalwart fans, the show may have ended there and then. Those who loved the show were indefatigable in their protestations that the show be brought back...and after a year and a half of insurmountable odds, it was finally back on our screens.

You can tell there have been a few meetings in the Who camp about motions to try and bring the programme back to its past glory. The Doctor, as played by Colin Baker seems to have mellowed into a much more amiable, funny character than his harsh abrasive side we saw in the last season, and the warmth between him and Peri seems to have grown. The opening shot of an epic spaceship is very impressive, and shows promise of a new level of professionalism and commitment to special effects.

You can tell there is a renewed commitment to make something more consistently engaging and cohesive in the overarching story of the Doctor's re-trial by the Time Lords.
There are also some great cameos, such as the inimitable Joan Sims as Queen Katryca of course, and Lynda Bellingham as the Inquisitor (Time Lord Judge).

It's still not brilliant; but it is a welcome return for the show and a vast improvement on many of the elements it had lacked during the last season.

Mindwarp - 6/10

In the next piece of evidence the Valeyard provides the court, The Doctor and Peri travel to the planet of the 'Mentors' (of which Sil from Vengeance on Varos belongs). Here they meet the Mentor leader who's having his brain 'engineered' by the geneticist Crozier. Unfortunately the brain is growing too big for his head and he decides for some reason that Peri would make a great new host for his gigantic cranium(?). The Doctor is portrayed as slightly 'evil' in this adventure; leaving a barbarian to try to save Peri. Of course, we wonder is this is all just a Valeyard plot to make him look bad!

I'm enjoying the overarching trial scenes, and Michael Jayston is excellent as the Valeyard; seemingly obsessed with showing the Doctor up as a criminal under Time Lord law.

The cameos keep coming. This is no doubt one of the tactics the show employed to try and bolster its ratings again, and it certainly adds interest; especially when it comes to the great bearded one that is Brian Blessed! He appears here in a role designed to really stretch his repertoire - a big bearded barbarian! The less obvious cameo is Mike from The Young ones (Christopher Ryan); playing the hybrid Mentor leader to the villainous Sil. Sil is my favourite of the enemies the Sixth Doctor faced in his short time, so it's great to see back again. However, for the most part, the plot is long and overcomplicated, and feels inconsistent.

Terror Of The Vervoids - 2/10

The Doctor offers the case for his defence. He shows

his positive intervention in stopping a scientific team's experiments, and their mutant plant creatures who are threatening all 'non-plants.'

The Doctor finally shows some compassion for the departed Peri (who seemingly met her end in the last serial). Whilst Peri has never been a favourite companion of mine, the constant berating she puts up with from the 6th Doctor did make me sympathise, and eventually like her. I'm strangely sad to see her go - not in a Sarah Jane or Ace kind of way, but she's still a league above what is about to come.....

Enter Mel! The most terrifyingly awful companion ever. Honesty, she makes Dodo (see, I can get obscure now and everything!) look like a good idea! Now I'm sure Bonnie Langford is a very fine dancer, performer, actor and so on. But her inclusion into Doctor Who has got to be one of the worst ideas of the '80's. She talks to everyone, including the Doctor, as if addressing a pre- school audience. She prances around like a lunatic and at the slightest hint of danger screams like some sort of psychological torture device. In short, she is less than entertaining to watch. And the thought of another 5 serials until Ace takes over is a very daunting one indeed.

The story itself is like a poor man's Seeds of Doom; with male-genital-headed aliens. And Honour Blackman.
That's about all I can say about this one to be honest.

The Ultimate Foe - 8/10

'Spoilers!' - So, the Valeyard turns out to be an amalgamation of the evil parts of the 12th and 13th regenerations of The Doctor; and wants the Doctor to die at the 6th so that he can steal his other lives? This is rather a complicated premise; but at least it's an exciting one. This is more than can be said for the rest of this season (apart from the courtroom scenes).

In a similar way to The Deadly Assassin, the Doctor is forced into a perverse reality of the Valeyard's making; including sand traps and evil desk-clerks.

Although Mel continues to annoy, her part in this serial is relatively brief and painless, and this is a much more entertaining story than the rest of the season.

So departs the 6th Doctor. And as he's probably my least favourite portrayal; I can't say I'm overly gutted. But I do like Colin Baker as an actor and in interviews; and there were certainly glimmers in this season that he could've gone on to be much better, had he been given consistently good stories like Vengeance on Varos and this one.

THE SEVENTH DOCTOR - SYLVESTER MCCOY (1987-1989)

SEASON 24

Unfortunately the demise of the show continues with the debut season of the 7th Doctor being perhaps the worst season the show has ever known. Cannibal grannies, a space-aged Ken Dodd and a clown in Doctor's clothing are all enough to make viewers reach for their remotes. Thankfully, it does get better, I promise!

Time And The Rani - 1/10

The evil Time Lady Rani is back, with another fiendish scheme. This time, her plan is to capture the brains of the universe's greatest thinkers (including the Doctor) to create a huge 'time manipulator,' and take control over all of time and space. She first manages to 'kill' the 6th Doctor, by attacking the T.A.R.D.I.S in space, then impersonates his companion Mel in order to control the newly regenerated, confused 7th Doctor into helping her with her plan. Meanwhile, the 'real' Mel is down on the Rani-ruled planet of Lakertya; taking on bubble traps and 'Tetrap' bat-like aliens.

Oh dear oh dear oh dear! The show by this point has really hit a low. After the relative unpopularity of the last Doctor, the writers appear to be trying to re-address his disagreeable nature by making this 'new show' full of bad jokes and *chirpy* acting. And as much as I love Sylvester McCoy; this really doesn't work. Melanie the companion continues to be excruciating; and it's unclear why the Doctor even considered taking such a liability onboard the T.A.R.D.I.S in the first place!

And most importantly for a regeneration episode, the regeneration into the New Doctor is particularly unsatisfying. Due to the unceremonious way in which Colin was ejected from the show after the last season; he was unwilling to appear in the regeneration scene. So Sylvester McCoy had to don a ginger wig and pretend to be Colin. And of course being a very different height and build to Colin, this is fooling no one. As much as I
wasn't a big fan of Colin's era, I like him as an actor, and I thought he deserved a more dignified send off than this!

So, are there any redeeming qualities? Well, the bubble traps look pretty cool, and I do remember the bat-style creatures being scary as a kid.

Thankfully I've seen Remembrance of the Daleks; so I know this era gets much better. But at this transitional period, the fate of the series, let alone the Doctor, seems to be in the balance. And the balance is decidedly wonky.

Paradise Towers - 1/10

The Doctor and Mel travel to the end of the 21st Century, to a high housing block that has won many awards. However, they find that it isn't quite what it says in the brochure. It is filled with killer cleaning robots, dangerous gangs, and an over-zealous 'caretaker' who is feeding people to a carnivorous monster in the basement.

I had to try to watch this serial at least twice before I could finish it and, had I not wanted to watch all of the Sylvester years I would've avoided it like the plague.
Words cannot describe how truly appalling this is...but

I'll try my best. Where to begin? The acting is atrocious and a little disturbing. I've always loved Richard Briers; but whatever character he has been told to play is embarrassingly beneath him. Also, the teen-gangs acting like toddlers was an especially strange touch. The 'story' is awful and all over the place. Cannibalistic grannies, psychotic hoovers, murderous robot fish and a bureaucratic police state that talk like train spotters; all aspects of the story that don't seem to have any meaningful connection to each other.

I could go on..so I will. The companion is completely dislikeable and the Doctor is portrayed as a comedy character for the most part. To be honest, I simply run out of adjectives to portray what a laughable mess Doctor Who was in at this time. No one seems to be taking it seriously anymore; nobody seems to care. Thank goodness the show recovered enough of its dignity to go out with a bang before its cancellation; so moments like this could be forgotten.

Delta And The Bannermen - 2/10

The Doctor ends up in the middle of an alien battle in a Welsh holiday camp in 1959!

This really is shaping up to be the worst season so far, and this particular serial is a contender for the strangest of the McCoy years; which is up against some stiff competition! A space-age Ken Dodd, a charabanc- shaped 'space-ship' and green soldiers who resemble plastic toys.   no really, these things are all in there!

Please don't waste your time   skip to Remembrance of the Daleks!

Dragonfire - 6/10

The Doctor and Mel land on the trading post of 'Ice World;' to find a dangerous criminal (Kane) has taken power through murder and violence.

The Doctor also meets Ace, a troubled Earth girl from the late 20th Century, who has been inextricably flung through time and space in a 'time storm.' She has had to rely on her own resilience during her difficult past; having never had a family or people to care for her; until the Doctor arrives to show her a new life of adventure.

The awful run of stories thankfully ends, and this isn't bad. There are some good ideas and some scary moments. I particularly liked the character of Kane, who could freeze people to death with his bare hands; and his own demise is pretty spectacular in itself. It is great to see the introduction of the lovely Sophie Aldred as the new companion Ace. Although her clothes and language haven't aged well; her character is much more 3 dimensional than the human scream-machine Mel.
Her relationship with the Doctor is much more fitting, and as a companion she has just the right level of strength and vulnerability to make her the most ideal companion since Sarah Jane Smith.

A huge improvement on the Sylvester stories so far; leading nicely into probably the best in my opinion - Remembrance of the Daleks!

SEASON 25

Whilst a HUGE improvement on the last season, Season 25 is still inconsistent; with absolute essential stories such as Remembrance of the Daleks and The Greatest Show on the Galaxy, but also camp terrors like The Happiness Patrol and Silver Nemesis. The 7th Doctor is starting to find his feet, but is it going to be too little too late?

Remembrance Of The Daleks - 10/10

The Doctor returns to where it all began – 1963 at Coal Hill School. Here he discovers that two splinter groups of Daleks have travelled through a time tunnel to uncover the 'Hand of Omega' stellar manipulator he hid when he first arrived on the planet with Susan (see An Unearthly Child).

I'm sure every Doctor Who fan has a soft spot for whomever was playing the character when they were a child; and Sylvester McCoy played the Doctor from when I was 8 to 10, the perfect Doctor Who age. The fact that I'm still watching it now of course tells you all you need to know about my level of maturity as an adult!

After watching the last Dalek story (*Revelation* of the Daleks), I had almost lost hope in 1980's Doctor Who. The acting was bad, the music and special effects were embarrassing and the Doctor was unlikable. But I held out a tiny vestige of hope that Sylvester McCoy's Doctor; 'my' doctor as it were, could save things.

And thankfully I wasn't disappointed by this Dalek story. Ok, it's very much of its time; the music, the language, the special effects all smack of 1988. But the charm of the programme is back! The dialogue is great; the Doctor, whilst not quite carrying the 'weight' of the Doctor at his peaks still pulls off enough oddball conviction to make the character fun again. And of course, I haven't forgotten the huge crush I used to have on Sophie Aldred (who plays 'Ace'), who is great as the all-action companion again here.

In short, this is a huge return to form for a show that had lost its way in the last season. Great entertainment and, for me highly nostalgic.

The Happiness Patrol - 2/10

The Doctor finds a planet where happiness is compulsory, and sadness is punishable by death...at the hands of a crazed dictator and her robot executioner the 'Kandy Man.'

The show unfortunately nose-dives again. I want to like the Sylvester years, I really do! He was *the* Doctor when I was young, and I really like his madcap portrayal of the character. So there's a bias there that forgives a multitude of sins. And yet, there's no getting around it, stories like Time and The Rani and this are just so dreadful as to almost spoil the whole legacy of the show.

Somewhere along the way, the gritty science fiction drama of the Hartnell years melted away - to leave something that was trying too hard to be *quirky*; to the detriment of a good story. Instead of trying to expand kid's minds; producers often started trying to play down to them. And on occasions like this, it fails miserably.

Thankfully, not all Sylvester stories are rubbish by any means! I loved Remembrance of the Daleks and the upcoming Curse of Fenric; Ghost Light and Battlefield were also great. But unless you're a true completist; I'd steer a wide berth of this and pretend it never happened.

25Th Year Anniversary Special - Silver Nemesis - 3/10

People and Cybermen travel throughout many different times to arrive at the same date...23rd November 1988. The reason? They are all after a living statue with the power of life and death for whoever possesses it.

Of course, the main reason for this choice of date is that it marks the 25th anniversary of the programme. Whilst this is supposed to make us excited about the history of the show; it serves more as a sad indictment as to how far such a great series has 'degenerated' (excuse the pun) throughout the 80's. Hartnell's era was so full of drama, innovation and wonder that carried on well through Troughton, dipped a little (in my opinion) with Pertwee and had a complete new lease of life with Baker. Some of Davison's serials were good, and he wasn't a bad doctor. Colin Baker I found very difficult to warm to as the Doctor (although I like him as an actor), and Sylvester was great, as was Ace - but they just seem really let down by a lack of budget and good stories. They were beset on all sides by difficulties. The B.B.C seemed to want to get rid of what it saw as 'old hat' at the time. The public seemed to be rapidly losing interest. And producers who were trying everything to aide its recovery just didn't seem to have the ability to do so. They brought back the Daleks, and it worked, they brought back the Cybermen, and unfortunately it didn't.

Rather like the Master's fall from sinister Moriarty to pantomime foe; the Doctor's 'third' biggest adversary went from being a sinister villain to a 1-dimensional enemy with none of its former menace by the end of the 80's when the classic series was cancelled. The difference here is very much in the writing. In Remembrance of the Daleks, it worked because the Doctor and his enemy were given the right amount of good writing and production to make the viewer care. In this serial however, the writing goes from being over- complicated (It moved all over the place and I've no idea what any of this story was about to be honest) to ridiculous (the acting is awful in most scenes).

I want to like this era, 'my era' (when I first watched Doctor Who), but I'm finding it increasingly difficult, even with the wonderful Sylvester and Sophie at the helm!

The Greatest Show In The Galaxy - 7/10

Ace and the Doctor arrive on a barren planet where the main attraction is a 'psychic circus.' But they discover the entrance ticket is really an invitation to be killed in front of a ravenous audience!

An odd but attention-grabbing addition to the series; full of sinister clowns and psychotic rapping ringmasters.

The story is confusing but enticing, and although I wouldn't call it a classic from the era, it certainly has enough to make it worth a watch. There are enough creepy scenes and characters to leave an imprint on many a kid's mind (I can certainly remember elements of it from when I saw it as an 8 year old). The main clown

TIMOTHY J. LEE

enemy is superbly frightening and well realised, and there are moments here and there which rival the best of the 7th Doctor's tenure. The 'rapping' segments however are embarrassing, and reminded me of the strange musical introductions to each scene in the Hartnell story 'The Gunfighters.'

It's not consistently great, but it has its moments.

SEASON 26

The Doctor...and unfortunately the show bow out with one of the shortest but most interesting seasons. By this point the awful beginnings of the 7th Doctor's era had been replaced by inventive storytelling and so much potential that it's such a shame it wasn't to get the chance to carry on. It would be a long long wait before we would get to see the iconic show back on our TV screens again.

Battlefield - 6/10

Characters from Arthurian legend come through time to destroy the world invoking the help of the 'Destroyer.'

The characters both main and supporting are good, and it's particularly nice to see the return of the Brigadier, who doesn't disappoint. The other U.N.I.T characters are well played, particularly his female replacement. The effects and costumes are also the best I've seen for a long time.

Unfortunately however, the story itself is pretty ridiculous, and much of the potential is lost. The pacing lags, and unique characters such as the scary 'Destroyer;' whilst having superb effects for the time, are not fully explored. I love McCoy, but he tries to outreach himself a bit here, taking on a darker edge to the character; but lacking the command and authority to really pull it off.

Not one of the better McCoy stories. But there are some great effects, nice cameos and a few good moments along the way.

Ghost Light - 6/10

The Doctor takes Ace back to the place of one of her worst memories; the old eerie house she burned down in her troubled youth. It appears what she felt wasn't just in her head after all. There is an alien presence that has lain dormant in the bottom of the house, and when it awakes, it is ready to take over the Earth.

Pretty odd and incomprehensible, even for Doctor Who. I'm not quite sure what to make of this one, and whether I like it or not. You really feel for Ace in this serial, who goes through quite an emotional journey; once again reminding you how far Sophie pushed the boundaries of the cliché 'screaming companion' into something much more compelling.

There are some original ideas discussed; but there aren't really the production levels needed to realise them. This serial felt like it would make a good contender to be reworked in the new series.

The Curse Of Fenric - 10/10

The Doctor and Ace arrive in World War 2 era England, to find that the ancient Fenric, an evil from the dawn of time is reborn from Viking remains and is summoning a legion of 'haemovore' vampires to rise from the sea.

This is by far one of the best Doctor Who offerings of the '80's and a joint best for the 7th Doctor along with

'Remembrance of the Daleks.'

The story and production itself is strong for the era (the latex vampire-masks still look great, and the acting for the most part is excellent for a seventh Doctor serial).

But it is the relationship between the Doctor and his companion Ace that makes this stand out as something special. Ace is a troubled young woman who is desperate for some sort of focus and faith from someone; and finds it in the shape of the eccentric time traveller. The Doctor becomes both a father figure and best friend to Ace, and helps her to realise she is worth far more than she ever realised. And, as with much great drama, the extent of this relationship is only really felt when it is pushed to its limits. In the final episode; where the Doctor has to convince Ace that he doesn't care about her in order to save her is a truly heartbreaking scene, and shows how well the actors work together. Unlike many other Doctor Who serials from the time, the writers seem to really *care* about what they are doing, and show what a strong format Doctor Who can be when it has the right sorts of people at the helm.

An excellent 4-parter, which would've made a much more suitable ending to the classic series than the final serial that followed it.

Survival - 5/10

Attack of the planet of the killer cats?!

It's a real shame such an iconic show had to bow out (temporarily) on a rather rubbish serial like this. Just what happened? Did the writers run out of stories? Did people stop caring? Did they want the series to end this badly?

For their part, Sylvester McCoy and Sophie Aldred do their darndest to save this. The production level isn't bad either - the costumes are well designed and the effects aren't too bad. But the story...'planet of the cheetah people,' 'cats who can teleport through time and space without any sort of explanation,' Hale and Pace (as much as I loved their comedy series as a kid, what the Hell are they doing in Doctor Who?!). A sad end to a programme that offered, and at its best realised so much potential that no other show came close to. There wouldn't be another series for 16 years, robbing a whole generation of classic science fiction.

Thank goodness this wouldn't turn out to be the complete end.

The only redeeming feature I can think of is the last 30 seconds or so.

Even though it's *only a T.V series*; I found something deeply poignant about watching the Doctor and his companion, walking off together, never to return (not for a long time anyway). It felt as if part of my childhood was going with them.

POST-SEASON 26 – 'THE WILDERNESS YEARS'

Specials

Children In Need Special - Dimensions In Time - 2/10

The Rani kidnaps the Doctor #1 and #2 and places #3,#4,#5#,6 and #7 in a time loop between 1973,1993
and 2013.

On the one hand this Children in Need special has so many inconsistencies, contradictions and plot holes as to make what could have been a fan's dream into a nightmare. Where to begin - the Doctors are much older than they were when they regenerated; they are able to coexist in the same time-line; companions of different Doctors know each other and; most importantly, what the hell are they doing in Eastenders?!

But on the other hand most of these issues are present in all of the specials - from the '3 Doctors,' to the '5 Doctors' to 'the 2 Doctors.' In all of these cases though, there are certain ways in which this nerdy author copes....

Firstly, keep telling yourself - 'this is a kids' show!' and try not to get too upset by how strictly it sticks to its own rules. If this doesn't work, try telling yourself it's not 'strictly canon' with the rest of the show; but more a celebration of the show's history and a way to introduce new and old fans alike to the legacy and history of its cast and characters. And lastly; if this doesn't work I opt for the final get-out clause - that this is all part of some alternative line of continuity. We are in some sort of parallel dimension or time-line; in which all the inconsistencies work . Here the Doctor took much longer to 'die' before regenerating; in which time he re- met his old companions as his new self and vice versa and so on.

But even with all these inconsistencies 'explained away,' there is still no logical reason I can see for the Eastenders tie-in and I'm afraid you're on your own in explaining this one!

Just sit back and try to enjoy it for what it is; a one-off special that has little to do with the series other than to help you appreciate its history. However poor this special is, this cause is surely worthy enough. Just don't expect it to be in your top 10 of Who stories any time soon!

THE EIGHTH DOCTOR - PAUL MCGANN (1996)

Doctor Who (Film) – 6/10

The T.A.R.D.I.S crash lands in San Francisco at the dawn of the millennium. Here the Doctor is shot by gang members and regenerates into his 8 incarnation, who must defeat the Master and his evil scheme to take control of the 'Eye of Harmony' and destroy the Earth!

The third attempt to bring the classic sci-fi television to the big screen, and I'm not quite sure how I feel about this one. I'm not going to criticise it for trying to revive Doctor Who in a new way. The series had been taken off our screens 7 years earlier, and looked unlikely to return. The re-launch was another 9 years away. So I'm glad they tried to bridge the gap and reignite the public's desire for more 'Who.'

The Doctor is well presented - Paul McGann gets the character spot on in the 'one third strange/one third friendly/one third powerful' way I feel it needs to be played. He also manages to bring his own look and character to the Doctor in this very short stint. I also particularly loved the semi- Victorian/semi-medieval look the TARDIS takes in this film.

I can't say the same for Eric Roberts' portrayal of The Master however, which is more of a poor man's 'Terminator,' yet there is also some welcome originality in the portrayal here at least.

So…onto the bad bits…

Most of the continuity is respected, apart from 2 obvious things that really didn't need to change. Firstly, the Doctor is apparently explained to be half human (why?!) and that the centre of the T.A.R.D.I.S, when opened will somehow change the whole molecular balance of the Earth (I'll repeat…WHY?!).

The setting is an obvious ploy at trying to sell the franchise state-side, and it really doesn't work. The acting isn't great for the most part (apart from McGann), and neither is the plot. As a television film, it doesn't really work…and as a continuation to the franchise…it doesn't really work either. What we are left with is a rather disappointing slice of Doctor Who. It does work better than the '60's films, but unfortunately it takes the series off in a direction that loses a lot of its charm.

Thankfully, it didn't take off and we were given a second change in the later series.

To summarise…a good attempt at revitalising the franchise; which unfortunately adds little to the original series except for another interesting Doctor and some good special effects.

THE 'MODERN ERA'
– 2005-PRESENT

Introduction

For 16 long years, one of the greatest shows this country has ever produced was cancelled...a fond memory for older fans; who would have to make do with a
smattering of 'Doctor Who lite' related serials, such as Comic Relief pastiches, Children in Need specials and the failed reboot of the American film. Meanwhile, a whole generation of kids were growing up without ever knowing who the Doctor was, or having chance to see such a dynamic and stalwart hero of the small screen in new adventures.

But the fans never lost hope...clutching to their Doctor Who magazines, new audio adventures and the many rumours that circulated about the show being brought back. Finally, in 2005, they got their wish; thanks to a Doctor Who superfan producer. Already rated for his award winning work on dramas such as 'Queer as Folk,' Russell T. Davies marshalled the troops in Doctor Who's new home of B.B.C Cardiff and started working on a new series.

There would be many changes to the show, the Doctor, the runtime, the production values. But the heart of the show would stay the same. The excitement was palpable...and thankfully well justified. The series was in good hands again, and finally, after all those years in the dark...

The mighty Time Lord hero was ready to take on a new era, and please generations both old and new. The Doctor...had...returned!

THE NINTH DOCTOR - CHRISTOPHER ECCLESTON (2005)

SERIES 1
(SEASON 27)

Although only staying for one season, the Ninth Doctor manages to revitalise the show for a modern era with the help of memorable stories and great Doctor/companion chemistry.

Rose – 8/10

Rose, a department store worker meets a mysterious time-traveller on the trail of mannequins on a killing spree!

So dawns a new age of Doctor Who, after 9 tragic years since the T.V movie and 16 agonising years since the regular series was cancelled. I can still remember the excitement of one of T. V's most iconic shows returning after so long.

There was a new Doctor (number 9!) played by a well-respected dramatic actor, Christopher Eccleston. There was a new producer, Who super-fan Russell T. Davies (equally well respected for his work on Queer as Folk and other successful shows) and a new lease of life for the show. From the very beginning, it is obvious that the show is fresh and exciting, full of hope and potential.

The action is fast and the dialogue is great. There is a real chemistry between the Doctor and his new companion Rose

(Billie Piper), and although the enemy is old (The Autons reappearing for the first time since the Third Doctor), the feel of the show is reinvigorated. Eccleston manages to make the Doctor's character different enough from the others; whilst making him recognisable to old fans of the show. He has a certain child-like wonder for the world and its dangers; but also a kind of Hartnell-inspired pathos and anger that he can switch to unnervingly and without warning. There is a great example of this in the first notable speech of the new show; where he talks about how he feels the moving planets and time as a Time Lord. In short, this is an excellent first episode; which draws in fans both old and new and looks forward to a new era of a classic show.

The End Of The World – 7/10

The Doctor decides to show his new companion Rose the true capability of the T.A.R.D.I.S and flings them into the far future; to the end of the Earth itself.

This is a great excuse to show fans of the new show just what the production team are capable of. We are introduced to a spell-binding array of new alien races and special effects, which all look spectacular. This is also a clever way for the new show to instate that it has respect for its history whilst not being bound to it, and that it has just as many inventive ideas to take the programme in new directions. The chemistry between the Doctor and Rose continues to grow, and the programme continues to present its new venture in style.

The Unquiet Dead – 7/10

Travelling back in time to 1869 Cardiff (the new 'spiritual home of Who,' where the series is now produced), the Doctor meets a rather disillusioned Charles

Dickens, at a turning point in his life and in his writing. There are also some strange goings on - with ghostly figures appearing in a local funeral hall and roaming the streets and theatres. It transpires that these 'apparitions' are actually an alien lifeform known as the Gelf. They have become trapped between a 'rift' or 'fissure' in time and space and are using the gas from decomposing humans as a conduit to travel over to our universe. This idea had first been looked at in Image of the Fendahl (Fourth Doctor)

and would be further explored in the 11th Doctor's first season. Written by the League of Gentlemen's Mark Gatiss, this is another very clever story; with more impressive scenes and special effects. Quite macabre for a kid's programme, and called to mind chilling serials from Tom Baker's time (Brain of Morbius, Planet of Evil and so on).

On a side note, it's also great to see Eve Myles for the first time; who will go on to play an ancestor of this character in the spin-off drama 'Torchwood.'

Aliens Of London/World War Three – 6/10

The Doctor and Rose return to her London home, but end up miscalculating the time and are a year overdue! Her mother Jackie and boyfriend Mickey are understandably rather disgruntled by this, having spent a year searching for her. The tension is soon pierced; when an alien spaceship crashes into Big Ben!

Suspecting that this display is rather 'showy' for any alien visitor, the Doctor goes to inspect. The 'pilot' turns out to be a decoy (a mutated pig); a distraction from the real aliens who have been lying in wait on Earth for some time – The Slitheen - a family of aliens that travel the galaxy trying to make the odd intergalactic buck by turning planets to rubble.

The 8-foot tall monsters have found a way to inhabit specially designed compression suits; taking on the guise of overweight politicians and using the confusion created to plot their attack on the world. Instead of attacking the planet themselves, they hope, through political and social upheaval to entice the powers of the world to fire their nuclear missiles at the sky and destroy the planet – leaving it a molten mass of nuclear energy that can be harvested and sold – with me so far? Good.

The Slitheen are superbly designed and probably the most striking and memorable race of the short Eccleston era. It's great to see U.N.I.T return, but they are sadly not discussed in any great detail (other than the Doctor's nostalgic quip about his old allies).

I didn't find this to be quite as monumental as the rest of the series so far; but it is still an action-packed great piece of kid's drama, with bog-eyed bogie men thrown in for good measure.

Dalek – 8/10

The Doctor and Rose travel to a 'private museum' in the near future, where alien artefacts and remains are housed by the 'owner of the Internet.' What they don't expect however is that down in the depths is the last of a race thought long extinct...a Dalek(!); the only other survivor of the epic 'Time War' that we are told has happened in-between the cancellation and the reboot.

As the Doctor discovers his old nemesis, he shows a new depth of character in possibly the best scene of the series so far. At first he shows fear (something he hasn't shown up until this point), then almost unrestrained anger (again something new) as he taunts his oldest foe.

When Rose meets the Dalek, she is unaware of the

creature's evil past and takes pity on it. Putting a hand out to comfort it, she inadvertently gives it the genetic restorative material it needs. It gains in strength, breaking out of its chains and killing

everything around it. But what the Dalek doesn't know is that Rose's imprint brings with it a humanity that is woven into its own D.N.A as it 'regenerates.' This creates emotions and compassion within the Dalek that it can't cope with and which will ultimately destroy it.

The return of the most historic enemy of the Doctor must've been incredibly exciting to fans of the classic show, and this episode manages to reintroduce the Dalek in quite a novel and unexpected way.

Ironically, for a show centred on one of the Doctor's most evil and *emotionless* foes, the story stands out as being quite a thoughtful and poignant one. It's great to see both the Doctor and his old foe being given some space to develop and grow through a great script.

The Long Game – 6/10

On a space station orbiting the Earth, an alien controls the population through manipulating the media and giving a constant stream of misinformation; stunting the human race's progress by nearly 100 years. The

unwitting crew believe they are awaiting 'promotion' to floor 500, which is actually where the alien resides; living off the essence of its human captives.

It's nice to see Simon Pegg making a cameo as the creepy 'Editor,' and this is a fun, though not overly remarkable addition to the series. The short-lived companion Adam is pretty forgettable and thankfully is seen off in more of a memorable way than he arrives.

Father's Day – 9/10

Realising the power of the T.A.R.D.I.S to travel back in time and potentially change events in history; Rose convinces the Doctor to let them go back to the day her father died to see him one last time. But her hidden purpose is actually to try and save him…little knowing that this altruistic act will unwittingly cause a 'wound in time' that 'Reapers' will feed off.

When the gargoyle-like entities arrive, they start killing everyone within that time wound she has caused. In the end, Rose's dad must sacrifice himself to heal the time wound and restore everything back to how it should be.

It's not often that Who can reduce me to tears – Sarah Jane's departure at the end of the Hand of Fear (Fourth Doctor); The Doctor saving Ace by convincing her he is not the friend she thought he way in the Curse of Fenric (Seventh Doctor), and here, for the first (but not the last) time for the reboot, in this genuinely moving episode. Billie Piper (Rose) shows the best acting I have seen from her so far in the series. I loved how the 'ordinary' and 'everyday' people were shown to be so important to the events of the story. This is something Doctor Who has touched upon before in various ways and does so with great aplomb here. The scene where the Doctor envies the ordinary lives of two of the extra characters for example was particularly touching. The Reapers are also great – perhaps not the best C.G.I in the world; but a good idea that is well designed.

Overall, this is a very emotional and well written story that is certainly one of the best of the first series.

The Empty Child/The Doctor Dances – 10/10

Jack Harness (later to become an evergreen character in his

own right through the Torchwood spin-off series) is a time-travelling con-man; who lures the Doctor and Rose to World War II London, in pursuit of an empty spacecraft he hopes to sell them when it falls to Earth.

What Jack doesn't realise is that the spacecraft bait he has crashed actually houses an invisible contagion which is released into the atmosphere. A contagion which can re-write' human D.N.A and turn everyone into a clone of the first unfortunate boy who it infects.

The Doctor walks around London enquiring about the craft's whereabouts and discovers Nancy; a kind girl who has taken in the homeless children of the street and is helping them to find food and shelter. But there is one child she warns the Doctor to be wary of...the 'Empty Child.' The tragic boy turns out to be her poor brother; the first to become infected. He endlessly searches for
his 'mummy;' converting all he meets by the slightest touch into the walking dead like himself.

In a twist at the end of this superbly written double-parter, we discover the suspected 'contagion' is actually quite the opposite. The craft the Doctor followed was an ambulance; filled with miniscule 'nano-genes' with the power to heal injuries. But in meeting the poor boy first, they build up an idea of what 'healthy humans' should look and act like, and go about 'healing' the rest of humanity, whilst in effect turning everyone into a clone of the same terrified undead boy.

This is the debut serial of Steven Moffat, who has written some of the best stories since the re-launch; becoming the executive producer and lead writer when Russell T. Davies stepped down after series 4. This is possibly my joint favourite of the Ninth Doctor stories, along with the series finale. Well written and as creepy as anything I've seen on Who past or present. 'NuWho' at its best.

Boom Town – 6/10

One of the Slitheen family (Aliens of London/World War Three) lands in Cardiff to wreak revenge on the human race and the Doctor for her defeated siblings. She aims to destroy the planet by placing a nuclear reactor on the site of the damaged 'rift' between this and other universes (which was closed by the Doctor in The Unquiet Dead).

There are some emotionally charged scenes, in this more thoughtful and sombre partner to the action-packed Slitheen stories at the beginning of the season. One scene that sticks out is where the Slitheen bargains for her life by metaphorically holding a mirror up to the Doctor's own past discretions...

> "From what I've seen, your happy -go-lucky little life leaves devastation in its wake." ('Margaret' Slitheen, Boom Town)

...and it is this sort of scene that raises it above the mediocre.

Unfortunately, this isn't enough to make it stand out as a classic episode; especially when compared with the excellent 'Empty Child/The Doctor Dances' that preceded it. Whilst a fun serial, it seems like its treading over old ground when compared to the series at its best.

Bad Wolf – 2/10

100 years on from the events of 'The Long Game,' The Doctor returns to Satellite 5; to find that humans are still competing for their lives. They are forced to play television games for their survival and the entertainment of the

masses, in a kind of updated 'Vengeance on Varos' (6th Doctor). Cue Big Brother, The Weakest Link and even Trinny and Suzanna!

After a strong run of episodes, this seemed lacking somewhat. It's a clever, but rather cheap satire on the pop culture of the time; and as a result seemed much more dated than the rest of the series.

It's well worth waiting until the end however; to discover that the orchestrators of this sick media is none other than the Daleks! This must've been a big shock to fans of the series at the time, who had been led to believe (in 'Dalek') that the race had been wiped out in the 'Great Time War.'

Not only do we get to see the extremely exciting return of the Daleks; but this is done to such a huge scale (hundreds of Dalek ships de-cloaking in space) that it will take away the breath of any Who fan watching. But as this is more a cliff-

hanger to the next (and final 9th Doctor) serial; I can only judge this serial on its own merits...which up until the last 5 minutes, is poor.

The Parting Of The Ways – 10/10

The Dalek emperor has survived the 'Time War' and has lain in the dark silence, rebuilding the Dalek race from the human dead and his own D.N.A. For hundreds of years they have waited; worshipping their Emperor as a God, and plotting their invasion.

The Doctor finds a way to destroy them; by turning Satellite 5 into a huge projector of fatal delta waves. However, this will not only kill the new Dalek race, but also the population of the Earth, and he must make the terrible choice as to whether to let humanity die as humans, or live as Daleks. Before making this choice, the Doctor tricks Rose into the T.A.R.D.I.S, where he transports her (through remote control) to her own time and safety. Rose realises she can't leave him, and

manages to open up the 'heart' of the T.A.R.D.I.S in an attempt to pilot it. Looking into the time vortex at the centre of the time machine; she absorbs its power and is given superhuman, almost God-like power that she uses to return to the Doctor, bring Captain Jack back to life (and immortal...but I'll come back to that!) and wipe out the Dalek threat.

Unfortunately, this power is also far too much for her human form to process, which becomes fatally unable to cope. In a scene that is both romantic and noble; the Doctor sacrifices himself by drawing the power from her with a kiss, and he must again regenerate to survive.

For all that this is an epic Doctor Who 'writ large,' Parting of the Ways also possesses so much heart and emotional impact that marks it as one of the best of any series. Eccleston delivers one of the best performances of any actor to play the role, and Billie Piper and the rest of the cast are all excellent too. If I were to pick just 3 classic Dalek episodes from the whole classic and 'revamped' series; it would be 'The Daleks' (1st Doctor), 'Genesis of the Daleks' (4th Doctor) and this episode...that's how great it is.

A superb finale for a fantastic Doctor and a series that did what every long-awaiting fan had hoped it would...re-energised and 'regenerated' the franchise and once again made it the exemplary example of science fiction at its best.

THE TENTH DOCTOR - DAVID TENNANT (2005-2010)

Specials

Children In Need Special – 5/10

In this 7 minute preview to the new series, we join Rose as she meets the regenerated 10th Doctor, and tries to come to terms with her old friend in a new form. This short film works well as an introduction, though after the poignant farewell of Christopher Eccleston, it did seem twee, and a bit daft.

Christmas Special - The Christmas Invasion – 6/10

This first 10th Doctor serial sees him struggling to regenerate, going into a sort of waking coma (similar to Pertwee in Spearhead from Space). This makes for rather a 'flat' Who story at first, with our main character out of action. But as the Doctor picks up, so does the story.

The alien race (the Sycorax) are pretty cool, creepy customers, who are able to control the blood of 1 third of the human race (the A+ blood types) and they threaten to kill them all if the Earth does not surrender. Through exciting sword fighting and wordplay, the Doctor restores himself, saves the Earth and convinces his companions of his former strength in his new incarnation.

The second series of the 'new' show begins with a new Doctor, the 10th (or 2nd of the 'new' Doctors if you're watching from the re-launch). Out go the slightly grumpy machinations of 'Hartnell-esque' Eccleston; after a superb, if achingly short tenure as the Doctor. In comes a younger, heroic 'Davison-style' heart-throb to fill his boots – David Tennant. And I admit at the time to being slightly disappointed. Eccleston had added a real gravitas to the character that hadn't been seen for a long time, and then was gone far too quickly in just one season. My worry at the time was that the 'new' Doctor would do the same; changing every season, making for a very inconsistent show.

This first serial didn't do much to stop my fears that some of the promise that had been brought by the return of the show would falter at the second hurdle. Preceded by one of the most epic and poignant episodes in recent memory, this is rather a timid affair of 'Doctor saves the Earth from the invasion of the 'one-offs.'

In retrospect of course, we now know that Tennant would become one of the most beloved (and long- lasting) portrayals of the Doctor ever...probably the best since the great Tom Baker himself. Yes, he is a heart- throb hero; but he also possesses just the right amount of eccentricity to pull it off and make the Doctor feel detached and 'alien' enough to be spellbinding.

The main point of any Doctor's first story is to introduce that Doctor, and the story usually takes second place (see 'Robot' or 'The Twin Dilemma' for other examples of this), and in this sense it isn't bad. But coming straight after the 9th Doctor's awesome, emotional swansong, this does seem lacking in depth.

SERIES 2 (SEASON 28)

Possibly the greatest 'love story' between Doctor and companion really takes off in Series 2, against a backdrop of mostly creative, remarkable stories.

New Earth – 5/10

The 'new' Doctor takes Rose far into the future, where they find that the ancestors of cats are cloning humans to imprison as living anti-bodies; infected with a myriad of diseases that can then create cures for the humans on the surface.

Although the sets are beautiful and the scope is large, this is a fairly pedestrian affair. And although Rose is very excited by the Doctor's change, at this point, I was failing to feel the same excitement.

Tooth And Claw – 6/5

After the science fiction futurism of New Earth, we return to a 'history' episode. The Doctor and Rose travel to 1879; to find a werewolf is stalking Queen Victoria. After the Doctor intervenes, the rather ungrateful Queen Victoria has 'Torchwood' set up to protect the British Empire from the 'threat' of the Doctor; creating the seeds of the Torchwood spin-off (but more on that later!).

The feel of the serial is a much-welcomed return to horror, but the poor C.G.I of the creature lets it down. It would've been much more effectively realised by

animatronics wizards such as the Jim Henson's Creature Workshop, which I'm sure the series budget could've managed at the time. It's not terrible, but the series is still struggling to reach the heights of the last series. The highlight for me was the Doctor taking on the alias

'James McCrimmon;' a tip of the hat to the classic series (Jamie McCrimmon being the 2nd Doctor's male companion).

School Reunion – 8/10

The Doctor and company return to the present day, to a school where the teachers are acting very strangely indeed. It turns out they are aliens; using the student's potential to crack a code that will help them rule the universe.

The Doctor isn't the only person looking into these strange goings on, as his former companion Sarah Jane Smith returns to investigate, bringing K-9 with her!

In my opinion, this is where the second series really starts, and shows that it can really deliver. It's so nice to see Sarah Jane return here, after nearly 30 years; and the interplay between the current companion (Rose) and the 'one he left behind' is really worth watching. There is also an insightful analysis of the Doctor's own lifestyle. We are reminded that, as exciting as his life is, he is ultimately someone who must always carry on alone, whilst his loved ones 'wither and die' before him – leading him to keep moving on and leaving those he cares about behind.

The serial itself is quite similar to the Sarah Jane Adventures spin-off that came the year after – more simplistic and child-orientated; but none the worse for it. Once again the overreliance on CGI does ruin some scenes. But the aliens themselves, especially in human form (as brilliantly played by Anthony Stewart Head from Buffy the Vampire Slayer/Little Britain) are suitably threatening, and this is a fun and scary addition to the series.A straightforward story underpins the heart-warming reunion of the Doctor and arguably his finest companion. Essential viewing for old and new fans alike.The Girl in the Fireplace – 10/10Clockwork 'Repair Droids' on a spaceship in the 51st Century harvest the human crew; taking their removed organs and patching them into the workings of the ship to 'fix it.'

Alongside this is the story of Madame de Pompadour, who meets the Doctor as he slips through time and space via a 'magic door' in a fireplace on the spaceship and into her room at different times throughout her life.

Although at first this seems like a separate story, it turns out that the Droids need her brain to power their broken ship, which shares her name; and they are travelling through her timeline to find the ultimate time to take it!
A truly superb serial, which is full of emotion, action and fascinating ideas. The Clockwork Robots, with their 18th Century costumes and eerie masks are inspired, and are easily the classiest monsters since the 'Robots of Death.' What could have been quite a detached group of elements works well through excellent writing, and this
is once again Steven Moffat (who had written 'The Empty Child' from the previous series) at his best.

Tennant has started to really harness both the serious, passionate and more playful sides of the Doctor; and create his unique characterisation that would become a fan favourite. It is nice to see him play opposite Sophia Myles too, his real-life partner at the time; and she also puts in a fantastic performance here.

Whilst the premise is pretty gruesome stuff for a family programme, there is a certain grace and elegance about this serial that makes it work. Possibly the best of the series so far, and definitely worth watching.

Rise Of The Cybermen/The Age Of Steel – 9/10

The Doctor, Rose and Mickey (Rose's long suffering boyfriend) fall through a gap in time and find themselves in London in a parallel universe. They are pleased to discover that in this reality Rose's dad and Mickey's Gran are still alive. But all is not well. Rose's dad is working for 'Cybus Industries' and a crazed Professor Lumic (played by Trigger from Only Fools and Horses), who is hell-bent on stopping his own illness and ensuring his own immortality by creating a 'new human' that feels no pain and never ages – an ageless, emotionless 'Cyberman!' And humans are being harvested and turned into the metal men in the process!

Added to the exciting return of one of the Doctor's most popular foes is an intriguing plot about determinism; as Rose and Mickey must decide whether they want to choose this universe (where their loved ones are still alive) or their own. In the end, Rose decides to return with the Doctor, after finding that her mother and father are quite different in a universe where she was never born. Mickey on the other hand, having never felt accepted or appreciated by Rose or the Doctor, opts to stay and join the resistance against the Cybermen.

If the return of the Daleks really helped the 9th Doctor to show *old* fans what the *new* show could do, then the 10th Doctor's credentials were really set for the 'classic fans' by the return of the Cybermen, in two excellent double- parters that punctuate the season - 'Rise of the Cybermen/The Age of Steel,' and 'Army of Ghosts/Doomsday' (see the end of the series).

It's a truly triumphant return for the Cybermen, whose design is at its most brilliantly realised since their early days of The Invasion and Tomb of the Cybermen. They manage to retain all the menace of the originals, whilst updating the old enemy and bringing it crashing into the consciousness of a new generation.

A thrilling two-parter that really solidifies the importance of the new season.

The Idiot's Lantern – 5/10

The Doctor and Rose travel to 1950's London, arriving at the time of the Coronation of Queen Elizabeth II and the growth in popularity of television. But there is also a parasitic alien that is harnessing the television waves and draining the essence of the viewers!

Maureen Lipman's turn as 'The Wire' (the alien energy beam that takes on the persona of a prim and proper 1950's B.B.C presenter) is superbly menacing. The Mark Gatiss idea is characteristically eerie, with the alien sucking off the faces of its victims in a scene reminiscent of the missing Troughton serial 'The Faceless Ones.' But as scary as the story and the enemy are, there is no hiding the fact that this is a fairly average story. I also found the relationship between the Doctor and Rose increasingly annoying in this serial – they seem to be moving into an irritating 'new love' phase; where they giggle at each other like overwrought adolescents. You half expect them to start doing the 'no, you hang up,' 'no, you hang up,' routine that has many a teenage friend reaching for his or her sick bag!

It's a fun enough serial, but there are not many remarkable points I could say about it really.

The Impossible Planet/The Satan Pit – 6/10

Close to a black hole, a mining ship digs down into a planet, only to find they have awoken a demon older than time itself.

Yes, I know Tennant is everyone's favourite Doctor (he's one of my favourites too!)...yes I know he's a lovable actor and guy...yes I know that at their best, the serials of the 10th Doctor are some of the best ever. I know that to criticise him or his era is sacrilege amongst most Who fans...but...I'm finding his portrayal of the Doctor really annoying for these last couple of serials. He's taken the Hartnell styled world-weariness of Eccleston and turned it into a gurning, over-excited dope; running around declaring his love for everyone and everything. He's far too 'chipper,' too sure of himself for my liking. The scene in which he insists on hugging a guy because of his innate human curiosity looks like some drunken guy at a stag party; shouting 'you're my best mate you are' to anyone who will listen. When I think back to Tom Baker's great 'Homo Sapiens' speech in the Ark in Space, in which the Doctor shows his love for the human race, this seems to really fail in comparison. He does grab it back in the second half - showing a heroism and seriousness that would make him such a greatly loved Doctor - and it is worth the wait to the end. But it's a shame you have to go through all the daftness to get there.

The Doctor aside, this is a good double-parter. The Ood aliens are fantastic and one of my favourite designs of 'NuWho.' Geeks like me will also enjoy some of the references to the 'classic show.' There is the relationship between the Ood and the Sensorites (1st Doctor) and there are also echoes of Katarina in The Dalek Master Plan as we see the sad demise of one of the crew out of the airlock. And of course there are many echoes of the Pertwee episode The Daemons in the climactic 'monster' scenes.

The first half is a bit of a limp fish, but the second half is much more exciting. This 'proper' scary serial will have once again have kids hiding behind the sofa!

Love And Monsters – 6/10

In search of the mysterious 'Doctor' he saw as a child; Elton Pope finds a group of like-minded nerds to help him scour for clues and sightings. They run into Victor Kennedy, an eccentric and over-powering man who becomes their manager; ordering them to increase their efforts in completing their mission. It turns out however that Victor is a grotesque alien they Christen 'the Abzorbaloff.' The hideous beast slowly takes each of the group and consumes them into himself.

There are a few good elements to this serial – the cast of cameos is strong (Peter Kay as the enemy, 'Moaning Mirtle' and that guy from Hustle among others), and it's nice to see an alien that was designed by a Blue Peter competition winner (you've got to admire their imagination!)! But overall it is another disappointing addition to the series and is far too comic and whimsical for my liking. The Doctor plays a very small part, only turning up at the end, and the serial plays more like something out of the awful 'K-9 Adventures' than Who. The only thing that rises it above the average is a witty and poignant script, which rewards repeat viewings.

Fear Her – 5/10

The Doctor and Rose arrive in 2012 in time for the London Olympic Games. Here they find a girl who has the power to capture people in her drawings!

Another in a spate of run-of-the-mill episodes. Thank goodness I know what's coming next!...

Army Of Ghosts/Doomsday – 10/10

The Cybermen are back...having come through a rift from the parallel dimension and into our own! On their trail is the other of the Doctor's oldest opponents...the Daleks!

The Doctor joins forces with Torchwood London in an epic battle between two of his oldest and deadliest enemies!

Wow...that's all I can say! A rather hit and miss season goes out with a HUGE bang in this best serial(/s) since Parting of the Ways.

There are very few serials that can reduce me to a blubbering wreck, and this is one of them. The other notable one would be the end of 'Hand of Fear' (Tom Baker serial); and it is fitting that these are two stories that see the Doctor say goodbye to the two companions he truly loved; or was in love with (a very important difference) – Sarah Jane Smith and Rose Tyler.

Ever since the Doctor returned to our screens, Rose has been the unfaltering, often wonderful (just forget the last few serials!) companion, and her exit is both heart wrenching and compelling; showing that this programme is, and always has been, much more than 'just another sci-fi show.' The 'new' or 'parallel' Cybermen are once again a fan's dream; the most effective since the Troughton days. The plot manages to be all at once epic (the armies of Daleks and Cybermen going into battle are some of the most grandiose I've seen), intimate and groundbreaking.

An excellent double-parter and essential viewing for old and new fans. The ninth/tenth Doctors never really surpassed Rose as a companion, and it's nice to see her get such a fittingly well-written ending.

Specials

Christmas Special - The Runaway Bride – 1/10

Donna, a bride on her wedding day suddenly appears in the T.A.R.D.I.S. Both the Doctor and Donna are very confused about this turn of events, and try to get her home. What they don't know however is that they're both caught up in a giant 'spider' like alien's plans for destroying the planet, and their troubles are just beginning!

The third series of the new show really falls at the first hurdle, as we are introduced to Donna – the most annoying companion since Bonnie Langford's scream- machine in the '80's. Don't get me wrong, I like Catherine Tate and think she's a talented comedian and actress, and there's a good deal of chemistry between her and the Doctor. But the brash, comedic character is, to me, exactly what the series should've been steering away from after the low points of the last series. I'm sure a lot of fans will love the comedy interplay of the new companion and the Doctor, and I'm not adverse to this side of the show (such as the great one-liners between Tom Baker and Liz Sladen in the 4th Doctor's time). But the show is at its worst in my opinion when we lose respect for the central character; when the Doctor is 'sent up' or made to look foolish by their companion. This happened with the case of Romana (I) in Tom Baker's time, and with the aforementioned Langford in Sylvestor McCoy's time, and in both cases helped cause two of the worst series in Who history.

Thankfully, I know a much better (though sadly underrated) companion (Martha Jones) and MUCH better serials (Blink,

Family of Blood etc..) are just around the corner. But this first serial of series 3 is definitely not for me!

SERIES 3 (SEASON 29)

Martha joins the TARDIS team, for a round of fun adventures, poignant stories and surprise returns.

Smith And Jones – 7/10

Martha Jones meets the strange Mr. Smith (The Doctor) whilst training to do her medical degree. Little does she know that this chance meeting will soon change her life beyond recognition. The Judoon are the intergalactic police force from the 'Shadow Proclamation,' in search of an alien perpetrator. With little concern for humans that get in the way, their justice is harsh and immediate. They 'steal' the hospital where Martha is working and transport it wholesale to the moon; hoping to find the criminal that is hiding out there. But in doing so, they jeopardise all of the human staff and patients, and the Doctor must intervene.

The rhino-style Judoon are great fun and I know kids would love them. They are also very convincing; and it's great to see some awesome animatronics reign over some less impressive C.G.I from past episodes.

After the introduction to the irritating Donna in the last episode, I enjoyed the more subtle companion of Martha, and I'm looking forward to watching their chemistry together grow.

The Shakespeare Code – 8/10

Witch-like aliens who can harness the power of *words* for their own 'magic,' travel to Elizabethan England to find the greatest wordsmith there ever was – William Shakespeare. Using the Globe Theatre and the Bard's words, they hope to create a channel to gain power over the universe. The Doctor and companion are much more subtly brilliant now, and the balance between the lighter and darker moments is much more effective.

Whilst this is perhaps not the most memorable of episodes, it was one of my favourite 'history' serials so far, and I thought the ideas were interesting – something that I can imagine a child would come up with...and I mean that in the best possible way.

Gridlock – 6/10

I'm continuing to like this combination of Doctor and companion. I believe Martha is underrated, and is far more a personal favourite of mine than Donna. The tragedy is that she is constantly in the shadow of Rose, yet she is starting to fall in love with the Doctor.
This creates some really sad scenes as the Doctor is blissfully unaware of Martha's feelings, and doesn't reciprocate them (as he is still haunted by the 'ghost of girlfriends past' as it were). This really makes you sympathise and relate to Martha's lovelorn character. Martha is never 'pathetic' or 'needy,' just a little heartbroken at times. If anything, she matches Rose for bravery and strength, and I am growing to like her almost as much.

Anyway, on with the story. The Doctor goes 'back to the future,' (see what I did there?) to the 'New (x15) York' he last saw in 'New Earth.' What he and Martha find is very different from when the Doctor and Rose had visited on

the 10th Doctor's first trip. They arrive not in the affluent riches of the upper-classes as before, but in the smog-ridden dystopia of the working classes; who are destined to spend their lives in an everlasting traffic jam (sound familiar?). In truth, they are unaware that they are being protected from a virus that has wiped out everyone above them in the upper-reaches (physically and metaphorically – we're in Metropolis style sociology here film buffs!).

They are not protected however from a further menace that 'lies beneath;' the giant-crab creatures called 'the

Macra' (first introduced in the missing 2nd Doctor serial 'The Macra Terror'), who are picking off the traffic one by one. Martha is kidnapped, and the Doctor goes to find her by hitching a ride with Dougal from Father Ted dressed as a cat...no really!

Although a bit of a mismatch of different stories all forced together, this is a fun serial to watch. The final scenes are particularly beautiful and poignant; as we see the death of the Face of Boe, which in turn spurs the Doctor to share the truth with Martha about the destruction of Gallifrey and the death of his people, the Time Lords. His description of his home planet and his people will have every Whovian weeping into their Who mugs, and this episode is well worth watching just for these last few minutes.

Daleks In Manhattan/Evolution Of The Daleks – 5/10

The surviving Daleks from the 'Cult of Skaro' (who followed the Dalek Emperor in The Parting of the Ways) have transported to depression-era New York; where they hide in the Empire State Building and are conducting their experiments to 'evolve' the Dalek race. Their leader, Dalek Sec believes that by combining their forms with those of humans, they will harness humanity's capacity for power, hate and war and stop the Daleks from dying out. But by twinning Dalek and humans, the Daleks start to take on their host's emotions, and there is a division in the ranks.

This serial is filmic in every sense. It's Doctor Who writ large – with expansive sets and huge scenes. You can tell the B.B.C has really spent a lot of time and money on this, and it looks and sounds great; showing just how much the B.B.C believes in the 'new' show as it is reaches well into its third season. For an 80's kid like me, who saw the show tragically fall off the radar, this faith is nice to see.

And yet for all the wonder, the extravagance and the scope; something felt weirdly lacking in this double-parter. It looked great, but it just wasn't a patch on Parting of the Ways or the Cybermen double-parters from the last series. The dodgy American accents and over-the-top music and acting reminded me of the last time the Daleks were in New York; in the equally poor Hartnell serial The Chase. I liked the Dalek Sec creature, and I admire the way the series is trying to aim as high as it can; pushing the boundaries of what can be achieved in a science-fiction family programme. But for me, it lacked the heart of serials such as Girl in the Fireplace or Doomsday.

The Lazarus Experiment – 2/10

League of Gentlemen's Mark Gatiss stars as Professor Lazarus; a mad genius who has found a way to reverse the aging process. But by doing so, he invokes a strain of mankind's old evolutionary potential and turns himself into a horrible, man-eating monster...so it's just your usual Doctor Who episode then!

It's great to see Gatiss, the writer of some of the 'new' show's most creepy episodes ('The Unquiet Dead,' 'The Idiot's Lantern,' and later 'Night Terrors') appear as the

villain here, and he does a great job as you would expect. But it's a shame he's only involved in an acting role, as the story and special effects really leave you cold in this one. The C.G.I is the poorest I've seen so far, and the action is very average. The only other high point, apart from Gatiss, is a bit of back-story for Martha, as we revisit her family. But as a whole this serial is certainly not Who at its best, and worth a miss.

42 – 6/10

The Doctor arrives on a spaceship, hurtling towards the sun, and only has 42 minutes to save the crew onboard. Added to this, someone has sabotaged the ship and is killing the personnel off one by one in true Hitchcock style.

Disparate elements of Das Boot, Hitchhiker's Guide to the Galaxy and Red Dwarf. I liked the idea of using the programmes length in 'real time' to create a realistic tension and draw the viewer into the story. It reminded me in story of 'The Edge of Destruction,' one of the earliest episodes of the show in which the crew become trapped in the T.A.R.D.I.S as it self destructs.

On its own, it's a watchable enough romp with a certain amount of suspense. I particularly liked the idea that a sun itself was an intelligent creature that was trying to stop the humans from mining its energy. However, compared with the way the series is about to really take off again, this is a pretty mediocre affair. Worth skipping to get to the really amazing episodes that are coming up!

Human Nature/The Family Of Blood – 10/10

Whilst the last few serials have been reasonable, but not spectacular; the next three serials are testament to the potential this show has to transcend its 'science-fiction kid's show' boundaries and become something truly affecting.

To avoid detection from an alien threat after his life- force ('the Family of Blood'), the Doctor transforms himself into a human. He stores his Time Lord self in a special fob watch that he asks Martha to look after, and takes on the alias of 'Mr. Smith' (the alias the Doctor has always used since the Troughton days); beginning life as a human teacher in a school in 1913. By doing this however, he must lose his memory of who he is. His former self becomes just a recurring dream; known only to Martha (who looks after him in the guise of chambermaid at the school).

Whilst any viewer of the show would love to swap places with the Doctor, to go on mad adventures through time and space, the Doctor himself has always admired the calm everyday life of a human, and at last gets his wish to take on this role. Things get really complicated however as his human form falls in love with Miss Redfern, one of the other teachers.

There are two truly tragic sides to this story. Firstly, Martha becomes completely forgotten, as the one who must always guard the Doctor; but never be known to him. Secondly, we see the Doctor finally able to live an ordinary life and fall in love; only to have to give it all up again when the Family of Blood catch up with him.

Whilst this might not please the more action-centric fans, I found this to be a heart-warming and beautifully written episode. Poignant and unforgettable. Essential viewing for any Doctor Who fan.

Blink – 10/10

Sally Sparrow finds warnings from a mysterious man (the Doctor) cropping up all over the place; on walls and the special features on all her D.V.Ds. They all pertain to 'angels' who can snatch people out of time – throwing them into the past and feasting on the energy created from the transfer. Sally goes to investigate, and loses her best friend to the 'angels;' who capture her and put her in 1920.

The series is really on a roll; following up an unmissable double-parter by introducing one of the most iconic enemies of the new show – the Weeping Angels!

One of the many things that this show has always done well is to capitalise on the everyday, most basic fears of its target audience (8-12 year olds). The idea of something that we come into contact with all the time (a statue), that is able to come to life when we close our eyes and attack us if we blink?...inspired, just inspired.

The episode doesn't really feature the Doctor or companion very prominently; and this is something that has made other serials suffer (Mission to the Unknown for the 1st Doctor, Love and Monsters for the 10th). But this is a very notable exception. The one-off characters carry the episode brilliantly. Carey Mulligan (Sally Sparrow) is particularly lovely; and could've made for a great companion.

My only complaint for this serial is its increasing use of 'dumbed-down' nonsense-speak by the Doctor in this one; such as...

"This is my timey-wimey detector, which helps me

track..stuff." (The Tenth Doctor, Blink)

...I'm sorry Moffatt, but I KNOW you can write better lines than this!! This is the bloomin' Doctor for goodness sake!

Anyway, silly dialogue aside, this is a fantastic episode; showing once again what an amazing show Doctor Who can be.

Utopia/The Sound Of Drums/Last Of The Time Lords – 10/10

Wow, three top scores in a row!

The T.A.R.D.I.S transports The Doctor, Martha and Captain Jack (who has hitched a lift on the side of the T.A.R.D.I.S, in one of the most daft scenes I've seen in a long time) to a trillion years in the future; near the end of time itself. There, they meet up with the last remaining humans, who are sheltering away from Mad Max style cannibals. In hiding, they await a trip on an unfinished rocket to 'Utopia,' with the genius Professor Yana at the controls.

Martha discovers that the Professor has about his person a Time Lord fob watch (the same as the Doctor used in Human Nature/Family of Blood to hide his 'true self'). It appears the Doctor is not the last of his race after all, and that the Professor is not as he seems.....

Unbeknownst to the Doctor and to himself, he is in fact the greatest evil in the universe.....THE MASTER!!

The Professor (played by the renowned Derek Jacobi) remembers his true, evil self and turns on his assistant, before regenerating (after she shoots him) into the new form of John Simm's Master. Whilst the rest of the episode is not overly memorable, these last five minutes are easily the most exciting since the return of the Cybermen last season. Jacobi and Simm are both excellent in their different portrayals of a snarling (Jacobi) and unhinged (Simm) Master and are, to me, the best interpretations I've seen since the late great Delgado introduced the character. The sinister 'James Bond villain' that Delgado created degenerated into a pantomime baddy during the 80's and 90's; and it finally feels like Jacobi and Simm have steered the role (in their different ways) back to its early creepy brilliance again.

Simm adds a real black humour to the character as we head into 'The Sound of Drums.' The Doctor and companions follow the Master to modern day, to find that he has hypnotised Britain into electing him as Prime Minister! We finally get some back story on the Master –apparently he and the Doctor were at the Time Lord Academy together when they were young (ok, we already knew this, but read on!). He was forced by his elders, as a cruel childhood initiation task, to stare into the heart of an 'untempered schism,' a hole through reality, and it drives him insane. As this is described, we get to see the gorgeous landscapes of Gallifrey. We're also reminded of the Time Lords' less than perfect idea of morality, and it's devastating effects. The Doctor also intimates that he may have also been subjected to this test, which may have been when and why he ran away from the Time Lords, stealing the T.A.R.D.I.S on the way. I quite like the idea of an 8 year old Hartnell throwing off the shackles of the academy and escaping in the T.A.R.D.I.S for all his adventures, and this would make a great 50th Anniversary episode!

Anyway, back to the 'Sound of Drums,' which is another amazing and genuinely frightening episode. By the cliff-hanger the Doctor has been aged 100 years and is on death's door (courtesy of the Master's 'lazer screwdriver'), and 1/10 of the population of the world has been massacred by the Master's 'allies' the Toclaphane; who in turn end up being the last of the humans, converted into aliens (the Master having persuaded them to go on his false journey to Utopia with him in the previous episode).

In the final episode 'Last of the Time Lords,' we join the story a year later. The Earth has fallen into the Master's control, the humans are enslaved and the Doctor is imprisoned by his old classmate – pretty bleak stuff.

Martha, who managed to escape in the last episode, is now on a mission to cross the globe, spreading the hope of the Doctor; trying to break the hypnotic power of fear the Master has over them. The Doctor bides his time, waiting for Martha to arrive and put his final battle plan to overthrow the Master into effect.

As much as the Doctor and the Master hold bitterness and contempt for each other; they are the last two remaining Time Lords, and there is a connection between them as close as brothers. The Master is basically the evil mirror image of the Doctor; like a Moriarty to his Holmes, and the two are inexplicably linked, for better or for worse. This is demonstrated in a scene in which the Doctor cradles a dying Master – who, let us not forget is responsible for killing 1/10 of the population of the world – begging him to regenerate and join him as the last of the Time Lords. It takes a great actor and a great character to make you sympathise with a monster, and Simms manages this with great aplomb and through the magical writing of Russell T. Davies.

Yes, there are some supremely daft moments in this three parter; but most of the moments of camp dark humour are done so brilliantly by Simm that you can't help but love it, and this is another fantastic series ender that every fan should see!

Specials

Children In Need Special – Time Crash – 7/10

Leaving Martha on Earth after the events of the last season's epic finale, the Doctor pilots the T.A.R.D.I.S into the path of one of his past selves (his fifth incarnation, played by Peter Davison). Together, they must find a way to separate, before they rip a hole in the very fabric of time and space!

Fans of the new series may be a little confused by this 7 minute Children in Need Special. But fans of the classic series will be beaming to see the return of one of the actors to play the iconic roll. And even though the fifth was never one of my favourite of the Doctors, it is great to see Davison back. Tennant had previously shared a love for the Fifth Doctor, and you can definitely see the influence on his own 'heroic poster-boy' interpretation of the character. There is some great interplay between him and Davison in this short serial.

I also love it whenever there is a tip of the hat to the first Doctor, and Steven Moffat brings together the history and evolution of the character in such a clever and succinct way. He reminds us in this story that, even though the actor is much younger than his forbearer William Hartnell, the character itself is actually a lot older –

> "Back when I first started, at the very beginning, I was always trying to be old and grumpy and important—like you do, when you're young. And then I was you, and it was all dashing about and playing cricket and my voice going all squeaky when I shouted." (The Tenth Doctor, Time Crash)

Yes the story is mad; yes it doesn't make sense (Davison being a lot older than he was when he regenerated and so on). But It's a fun little 'pause' of a story, after the weightiness of the last series' finale and I enjoyed it a lot more than previous Doctor Who Children in Need specials.

Christmas Special - Voyage Of The Damned – 6/10

The Doctor crashes into the 'H.M.S Titanic;' a spaceship mock-up of the famous cruiser. Here, the robot hosts have been programmed to go on the attack.

It's always great to see the wonderful Geoffrey Palmer; here playing the Captain, and it's a fun enough caper. I liked the 'Host Angels' robots, who reminded me slightly of those from 'The Robots of Death.' But unlike that programme, this isn't half as interesting or memorable, and it's all far too pantomime for me. I didn't really warm to the characters, apart from the legendary Bernard Cribbins, making his first appearance as 'Wilf' here.

SERIES 4
(SEASON 30)

Donna returns, as does the comedy interplay between Doctor and reluctant companion. From the sublime to the ridiculous and back again, series 4 is a mixed bag with some seriously stand out highs and some skippable lows.

Partners In Crime – 6/10

Comedy Who is back, in this fun series opener about a pill that makes you thin; but creates a small alien creature (the Adipose) from bonding your living fat together!
Donna, the brash, screaming Cockney has been searching for the Doctor since we last saw her in that The Runaway Bride, and returns at her most loud, obnoxious 'best.'

Along with Donna, Wilf (a character from Voyage of the Damned) is back in this episode, played again by the inimitable Bernard Cribbins. Those of you with a fondness of Who trivia may remember that the actor first appeared in the Doctor Who film 'Daleks – Invasion Earth 2150' back in 1966. We now discover he is Donna's Grandad. Wilf is a lovely character; who will play more of an important role in future stories.

Anyway, back to the serial...There were some great ideas, and I particularly loved the little Adipose creatures. Smaller children and their parents will no doubt love this episode. Personally, I didn't think it was the best series starter ever, but I thought it was a lot of fun and worth a watch.

The Fires Of Pompeii – 7/10

The Doctor and Donna travel to ancient Pompeii...and its 'volcano day!'

The Doctor has to make the decision of whether to save the thousands of people who are destined to die when Mount Vesuvius erupts. To act would effectively change a major event/fixed point in history (not a good idea, as we have seen before in the series). Donna and the Doctor fall out over this decision; with the Doctor reminding her that he is forbidden to change important events in history.

Added to this, the Doctor meets the 'Soothsayers,' a cult of mystical women who worship a rock God within the volcano. The 'God' turns out to be a huge and rather disappointingly dodgy C.G.I rock monster in the depths; bent on converting all humans into similarly dodgy C.G.I rock monsters.

In the end, the Doctor must decide to let the 20,000 people of Pompeii die, in order to save the rest of humanity. A good, dynamic history episode; showcasing once again the awful moral dilemmas that face the Doctor. It brought to mind a similar serial for the first Doctor 'The Massacre of St. Bartholomew's Eve;' where he had to let thousands of people die, rather than tamper with history (to the protest of his companion Stephen at the time), and this story is even more successful at portraying the dangers of living as a time traveller.

It's nice to see 'preview' debuts of two important actors from the future of the show here; appearing as they are as different characters. Firstly, we have the wonderful Karen Gillan playing a Soothsayer. She will of course return as the companion Amy Pond, continuing a Who tradition of returning actors in different guises (Nicholas Courtney, Colin Baker and more recently Freema Ageyeman). And we also get a 'sneak-peak' of the great actor Peter Capaldi, who will of course go on to portray the 12th Doctor. After seeing his performance in 'The Thick of It,' the Torchwood series 'Children of Earth' and here, the excitement for where he would take the character was palpable when it was announced.

Planet Of The Ood – 8/10

The Doctor and Donna travel to the distant future (42nd Century), where the peaceful Ood (first seen in the second series) are again slaves to humans. They are starting to contract a 'red eye' infection and are going loco - killing their masters!

Whilst the Doctor-Donna combination continues to be my least favourite since Sylvester McCoy and Bonnie Langford in the 80's; Donna does show a lot more compassion and character in this serial, and if I had to pick a favourite of her stories, it would be this one.

The best serial of the series so far. I love the peaceful, spiritual Ood and they are easily one of the best
'monsters' of the revamped series so far. I also liked some of the underpinning themes about slavery and freedom, and I thought this was a very well written episode.

The Sontaran Stratagem/The Poison Sky – 8/10

The Doctor answers a distress signal from his old companion Martha. There are some strange goings on at a local boot camp for teenage geniuses.

It turns out that one of the Doctor's old enemies, the Sontarans, are using the aid of a child megalomaniac to install controlling 'sat-navs' into cars all over the world. Their ultimate plan is to then use toxic smoke within the cars to kill the humans and at the same time convert the air to make it a breeding planet for their clones.

It's great to see the return of both U.N.I.T and the Sontarans, who are brilliantly realised. Christopher Ryan (Mike from the Young Ones) returns to Who as the lead Sontaran (having playing a Mentor in one of the 6th Doctor serials), and he is fantastic in the role.

Fictional alien villains tend to exemplify the worst characteristics of human beings; giving a fearful indictment of where we could end up if we're not careful. In the case of the Daleks and Cybermen, it shows what humans would be like with their emotions removed. In the case of the Sontarans, it is man's desire for war and conquest that is shown. And the pompous, comedic aliens with Napoleon complexes have never looked or sounded so good; retaining all the spirit of the originals and evolving into something with a lot more dimensions and depth.

Full on action from beginning to end, and a really electrifying serial for old and new fans alike.

The Doctor's Daughter – 6/10

The Doctor, Donna and Martha arrive in the middle of a war between humans and the fish-like Hath. Both races have been cloning themselves for generations to survive in the endless bloodshed. The Doctor is forced to be cloned on arrival; creating a 'daughter' clone from his
D.N.A (played by the daughter of 5th Doctor Peter Davison,

who will also become the future Mrs. Tennant!).

The pacifist Doctor can't accept his clone daughter, who is bred with an instinct for war like all the clones, and he sees her as no more than an 'echo' of himself. In the end however, he grows to love and accept her; albeit But too late, as she dies trying to protect them, and fails to regenerate...or does she?

Sweet in parts, but really didn't 'do it for me' in the same way as the last couple of serials.

The Unicorn And The Wasp – 5/10

The Doctor meets Agatha Christie as she takes on giant shape-shifter killer wasps. As ridiculous as it sounds and nothing really to write home about.

Silence In The Library/Forest Of The Dead – 10/10

The Doctor and Donna travel to the largest library in the universe...to find it, and the whole planet empty. The cause is a swarm of parasitic micro-organisms, the 'Vashta Nerada,' who create a flesh eating 'shadow' that destroys everything in its wake. The Doctor discovers that when they first spored, the Earth evacuated people through the trans-mats, but were attacked as they were half way to their destination. A dying girl, hooked up to the library computer transported their essences to its own catalogue of books; creating a new life for them, and effectively 'saving' them into the 'cloud.'

The planet has been sealed off for 100 years, but an expedition has finally got through to explore. The Doctor meets River Song of the expedition; a mysterious woman who seems to know everything about him and has memories of travelling with him, although he has no recollection of her.

As we enter the second part, Donna has been snatched from existence and placed in a fake 'modern day life,' where her memory of the Doctor is erased and the library computer carves out a life for her from the scenarios it has on file at the library. The Doctor must convince Donna of her real life, and stop the Vashta Nerada before it's too late.

I liked the mystery of River Song, although she did come across as a bit of a 'stalker' at first. Her character really deepens though as she makes the ultimate sacrifice at the end, and this is something that is even more heartbreaking when you have seen her story in future stories. I thought it an interesting idea to meet a character from the Doctor's future; and considering the non-linear nature of his lifestyle; I'm surprised this hasn't been explored before.

Whilst the first part takes a while to get going, towards the second part it becomes apparent what superb writing and production has gone into this story. Whilst confusing at times, it's highly inventive and intriguing throughout and is really a uniquely brilliant double episode. Again, the strength of the writing is in drawing upon the basic fears of its audience – a child's fear of the dark. Making a 'monster' of the everyday is a sublime
idea, just as it was in 'Blink' in the last series.

Midnight – 7/10

Russell T. Davies goes all out 'Twilight Zone' in this homage to 'Nightmare at 20,000 Feet.'
The Doctor takes a spaceflight through a Bermuda Triangle style galaxy of poisonous but beautiful diamonds...and outside the ship the 'gremlins' are knocking!

I enjoyed this slightly different style of episode, which I found both creepy and highly watchable.

Turn Left – 1/10

Donna meets a fortune teller, who transports her to a life where she never met the Doctor. Just one seemingly unimportant choice (turning left instead of right) creates a completely different reality/time line. Because Donna isn't there to save the Doctor in The Runaway Bride; he isn't there for all the following crises - Judoon on the Moon (so Martha dies), the 'Titanic' spaceship crash-landing into London (killing millions of people), The Sontarans' 'Atmos' poisonous gas, adipose walking the streets and so on.

With all the chaos, England descends into martial law, and Donna and family need to move to ... wait for it ... Leeds! Things must be bad!
As the walls of reality tumble down, Rose returns from the parallel universe where we last left her; to help Donna realise the ultimate sacrifice she must make to bring things back to normal and to save the Doctor.

It's nice once again to see Bernard Cribbins (of Carry On fame for those of us of a certain age!) as her Grandad; but there is far too much Donna and not enough Doctor in this episode for my liking. Donna screams and shouts her way through the whole thing, which is enough by itself for me to steer a wide berth of this one.

Whilst this episode serves as a good introduction to a great finale, it is not a great serial in itself.

The Stolen Earth/Journey's End – 9/10

The Earth is moved to another galaxy by a strange force; placing it within a cluster of over 20 other planets millions of light-years away. The culprit....Davros, creator of the Daleks (who returns for the first time in 20 years)! Harriet Jones, former Prime-Minister, finds a way to reunite all the Doctor's allies to fight the 'reality bomb' that Davros wants to use to destroy all of reality; starting a new universe populated by his crackpot creations!

Much like the old specials of the 'classic' series, such as the 3 Doctors and 5 Doctors, this series finale (excluding the specials) is a celebration of just how far the 'new' series has come since it exploded back onto our screens 3 years earlier. All the companions and spin-offs are brought together in probably the most lavish and certainly the grandest double-parter yet.

It's great to see the characters from Torchwood and the Sarah Jane Adventures, and especially the return of Davros; who is played with a gloriously sinister quality by Julian Bleach. I'd even go so far as to say this is the best portrayal of the genius-cum-psychopath that I've seen – and as a huge fan of the classic series, it takes a lot for me to say that. Sneering and unhinged, Bleach is perfectly cast as one of the Doctors most iconic foes.

The suspense is consistent and both parts are gripping. The end of the first part in particular, where Sarah Jane, Gwen and Ianto all face extermination and the Doctor is on the brink of regeneration is the most exciting cliff- hanger since the return of the Master in the previous series. The end of the second part is both sentimental and exciting; as The Doctor must say goodbye to all his companions once more, in particular Rose, who he leaves with his clone back in the parallel universe (created from the severed hand from the Christmas Invasion episode...you might have to watch the serial for all this to make sense!).

Donna, who joins with the Doctor's regenerative energy when the clone is created, both imparts her own character on the clone and takes on the Doctor's knowledge. And if I thought Donna was annoying, nothing would prepare me for a Donna with the fast talking intellect of the Doctor. To be fair though, when she eventually has to have her memory and knowledge 'wiped' by the Doctor to prevent her human brain from being overwhelmed, the final scene is very tragic. It reminded me of the heartbreaking last scene from the 2nd Doctor's companions Zoe and Jamie, who have all their memories of their adventures wiped at the end of The War Games, and this was just as upsetting, even for a companion I struggled to like. Inevitably the serial goes a little over the top on occasion; and the grand scale of the action makes it difficult to connect with on an intimate level with the characters. You've got to admire the scope of Russell T. Davies for trying though; and this is easily the best of these sorts of celebratory episodes yet (including the 'classic' era). An epic geekfest for any fans of the 'old' or 'new' show.

Specials

Christmas Special – The Next Doctor – 6/10

The Doctor, now on his own, travels to 1851, where he runs into what appears to be a future incarnation of himself. He starts to become suspicious however when 'the Doctor' seems to have no memory of his 'past
incarnation (him)'. It turns out that what has actually happened is that Jackson Lake (the real name of the imposter) has inherited all of the Doctor's knowledge and traits after an 'info-stamp' from a Cyberman backfires into his mind, convincing him that he himself is the Doctor.

Together, 'the doctor' and 'the Doctor' take on the Cybermen and a power-mad Victorian Miss Hartigan who is helping them. Things go from bad to worse when Hartigan is (predictably) double-crossed by the metal men and is converted into the even more dangerous 'Cyber King.'

David Morrissey (the 'imposter Doctor') works quite well. He actually makes for a good Doctor himself, and I was a little disappointed at the time of first watching this that he didn't turn out to be a future incarnation after all.

The Cybermen are great as always, and the one-off 'Cybershades' are an interesting 'animal' variant on the usual 'converted humans' trend. Dervla Kirwan is suitably sinister as the main villain of the piece. Once again the CGI of the 'Cyber King' iron giant does let the finale down a bit; but as with much of Doctor Who, the pleasure comes from a certain amount of wilful suspension of disbelief.

Quite fun and well worth a watch.

Easter Special – Planet Of The Dead – 5/10

The Doctor meets a cat burglar as she escapes from a jewel heist on a London bus (maybe not the best plan in the world?). The Doctor, on the hunt for a 'hole in
reality,' inadvertently leads the bus and all its occupants to a mysterious 'planet of the dead.' He must find a way to get everyone back through the wormhole without turning them into skeletons in the process!

Oh, and they also have giant fly-like humanoids and flying stingrays to contend with!

Another of the 'nearly companions,' Lady De Souza (the cat burglar) was an intriguing character. But I'm not a big fan of this combination and I'm glad it wasn't a lasting one. She is another in a line of female characters (such as Donna) where the writers have mistaken 'bitchiness' for 'wittiness' and ended up with rather an obnoxious character in the process. The idea of a posh rich burglar who steals to get richer isn't the most endearing idea; and as much as I like Michelle Ryan, I really couldn't warm to this character. The Doctor must actually agree, as this is the first time I can remember him refusing to take a companion with him.

Lee Evans also stars as the new scientific advisor for U.N.I.T, with a hero worship for the Doctor, his predecessor. I didn't think I'd like his character, but in contrast to Christina, he was actually quite sweet and fun. I also liked the fly-people, who were a very silly, but fun design.

The story itself didn't really grip me, and this is a pretty substandard serial when compared with the excellent Water of Mars and End of Time.

Autumn Special – The Waters Of Mars – 9/10

The Doctor lands on the first human colony on Mars, 'Bowie Base One (nice!).' Many of the crew contract a water-borne virus whilst creating their own garden on the base – that turns them into 'water zombies!' The water wants not only to infect humans...but to find a way to a planet full of water..Earth! And all it would take is one drop to be taken back and it would infect the whole planet!

The Doctor once again faces a terrible moral decision, when he finds out the death of the historic first Mars colony will inspire humanity's development (through the Captain's granddaughter's future space travel). Once again the Doctor is powerless to intervene; for fear of
shifting an important 'fixed point' in time.

The idea of a water based enemy which can infect and kill is such an arresting one. The crew are all memorable and well written; making you genuinely care as they are picked off one by one. Lindsey Duncan's Captain Brooke is a particularly tragic character, as the audience shares the Doctor's knowledge that she must ultimately sacrifice herself for the sake of humanity. I won't spoil the ending - but there is a superb, if very macabre twist which shows that the Doctor's Time Lord arrogance doesn't always help to better the lives of those around him. This is one of the most thoughtful discourses in the series and definitely worth seeing.

This is quite a scary episode, which might not be suitable for very young children. But it's also a very affecting and absorbing story. I loved it...the best special in ages!

Christmas Special/New Year's Special – The End Of Time – 10/10

As I reach the last of the Tenth Doctor's stories, I'm in contemplative mood. I admit, as much as I like the
Tenth Doctor, I struggled with the whole 'heart-throb Doctor' thing that he seemed to introduce. To me, the Doctor should be much more 'strange' than 'sexy.' Producers never felt the need to make Hartnell or Troughton into poster boys for example. Davison, (the nearest characterisation to Tennant's) suffered a bit from being too much a conventional 'dashing hero' and not quite alien enough; and at first this was something I worried about for Tennant. If it creates more fans for the show, then I'm all for it - but I tend to relate more to the Doctor because he is an oddball, and find it difficult to see him as the object of every girl's desire.

Don't get me wrong, I like Tennant. He's a great actor and can pull off both the sexy and the strange in equal measure. But up until the end of the second series and the beginning of the

DOCTOR WHO: A COMPANION

third, my opinion was divided on this version of the Doctor.

But it's important to remember that whilst this era saw the Doctor become the desirable hero again, it also saw some of the most far-reaching, heart-rending and utterly brilliant serials to match anything the show had produced before...or has since. From the second series we had Army of Ghosts/ Doomsday. From the third we had the wonderful 'Blink,' and the tragic 'Human Nature/The Family of Blood' double parter. In the fourth series preceding these specials we had the Silence in the Library/Forest of the Dead and The Stolen Earth/ Journey's End double parters; both superb. So it's fitting that this Doctor's swansong is both grand and truly memorable. A real celebration of what started (seemingly) as a premature replacement after Eccleston's all-too-brief tenure came to an end...and ended up being possibly the most treasured era of Doctor Who since Tom Baker.

I can now stand amongst the converted, and say that Tennant is an excellent Doctor. Through his extraordinary talents as an actor the whole gamut of different traits of the complex character that is the Doctor were explored. As long as it took to warm to him, I will really miss Doctor Number 10.

So onto Doctor #10's last serial itself. And it's not only one of the best of Tennant, but arguably of the show since its 'regeneration' 5 years earlier.

As we join the first part, people all over Earth are having nightmares of the Master. This is more than odd; as the Master's conquering of Earth was wiped from history by the Doctor at the end of Season 3. Donna's Granddad Wilf has created his own geriatric (and highly comical) group of Doctor fans, who are searching for the legendary hero to help them. And we are in 'Carry On' heaven, as we have not only the great Bernard Cribbins, but also June Whitfield on the team!

Anyway...the Ood summon the Doctor, and tell him a prophesy of the end of time itself.

The Master is reborn, through his followers, who use the essence from his ring to bring him back to life. But his wife, now freed from his mind control, tries to destroy him as he comes back to life. This only serves to create a monster even more dangerous and unhinged – ravenous and even cannibalistic in his half-regenerated/degenerated form.

Another misguided human megalomaniac thinks they can work with the Master, to create an 'Immortality Gate.' True to form, the Master double-crosses him and uses the gate to turn the whole human race into facsimiles of himself – a 'Master race,' of carbon copies. This makes for a cliff-hanger that is not only captivating, but darkly funny to boot.

In this episode, Tennant manages to make the Doctor seem the loneliest we've ever seen him; and his portrayal really pulls at the heart-strings. In contrast, the character of the Master hasn't been this scary since the Deadly Assassin, and this is easily the best portrayal since then.

As we move into the second half of the serial, we are back to the burning remains of the Doctor's home world, Gallifrey, as it lies in ruins at the end of the Time War.

Sat at the head of the Council is Rassilon himself – the founder of Time Lord society.

(N.B - Rassilon has often discussed in the classic series, but is seen here for the first time, and played by Mr. Bond himself, Timothy Dalton)

The Time Lords have been 'locked' by the Doctor in the Time

War, as a way to stop the destruction caused by the ceaseless Dalek/Time Lord battle. The Time Lords come to Earth, using a contact; a signal through the Master that they set up in his infancy. Rassilon takes the Earth; forcing the human race to bow beneath his great power.

Rassilon decides the time has come to destroy time and creation itself, rising him and his race above all. The Doctor is caught between two great evils – the Master and Rassilon.

Unfortunately, in the end nothing can save the Doctor; and he has to sacrifice himself to save Wilf and the rest of humanity. This scene; in which the greatest of all the Time Lords ultimately has to give his life for the life of one human being is beautifully done, and reinforces one of the great moral themes at the heart of the show from its beginnings. Every individual is worth something.

This scene was truly heartbreaking, but so *Doctor Who*. Even more heartbreaking is the next scene. The Doctor, for his last dying wish, visits all of his old companions one last time...to say goodbye...Martha, Mickey, Sarah Jane, Captain Jack, the granddaughter of Joan Redfern (Human Nature), Donna, Wilf and, of course, Rose – who he goes to see in a time before she has even met him back in 2005. I'm not too proud to admit I wept like a baby.

Whilst the plot for this last tenth Doctor story is huge in scope, it also manages to really bring out the best in all it's characters. Through great writing and acting, we are actually made to feel sorry for the Doctor's most evil enemy The Master, and the character is given a much greater depth than has been seen so far. The previously bumbling looking Time Lords are returned to mysterious and corrupt characters. And the Doctor himself is the most heroic we've seen him for a while.

Not only is this a contender for the best special; but this epic, memorable, and thoroughly exciting double parter is essential watching for any fan of the show as a whole.

As one of the main cruxes of the show is *time*, this special serves as a complement; a great testimony to time itself. For whilst time may yield all of life's wonders, in the end all things must pass and time must take its spoils.

'I don't want to go' are Tennant's final words. and as viewers at home, we can't help but agree.

A truly grandiose, heart-warming ending to one of the best Doctors yet.

'Allons-y' Mr. Tennant, and thanks for everything.

THE ELEVENTH DOCTOR - MATT SMITH (2010-2013)

SERIES 5 (SEASON 31)

The youngest actor to take on the mantle of the Doctor shows he can give a timeless quality as a new showrunner (Steven Moffat) returns the show to more of a weekly serial feel in Series 5 with some classic stories.

The Eleventh Hour – 10/10

Geronimo! ...we're flung kicking and screaming into a new era of the show, as the Doctor struggles to land a disintegrating T.A.R.D.I.S after his cataclysmic regeneration.

He crash-lands in the back yard of a young orphan girl, Amy Pond. The Doctor finds that Amy has a crack in her wall through which all of time and space is imploding; a split in the very fabric of reality!

Through this crack comes an escaped criminal alien, Prisoner Zero, hiding out in the house of Amy Pond from the Atraxi, a huge alien eye that is trying to find him, and will stop at nothing to bring him back (including destroying the Earth).

The Doctor promises he will be back to help Amy once he

has taken his T.A.R.D.I.S back into space to repair it...but misjudges the time and instead of 5 minutes later, he ends up returning 12 years into her future. The poor young girl holds out hope that the 'Raggedy Doctor' will return in time to save her...but as the years pass, she loses faith, and gradually grows into a cynical adult, sure that the Doctor she met must have only been a dream.

Amy's story of waiting for the Doctor to return is a really heart-wrenching one. And after the huge scope of the last serial, it is nice to see the show return to the intimate and personal, showing the lasting effect of the Doctor on the life of just one individual.

As with most Doctors in their first episode, I found it hard to warm to Doctor number 11 on first viewing. He seemed to bounce from scene to scene; gurning away like early Sylvester McCoy in Time and the Rani – a pantomime fool in a wise man's clothing. He was also very young...and very *cool*. The 900+ year old alien was now seemingly being played by a 'hipster;' to match the increasing popularity of the show. Out was the older, heroic Doctor, and in was a young tearaway; dating models or turning up at Glastonbury declaring 'yes, it's me,' before jamming with Orbital to the Doctor Who theme tune.

Of course, the increase in popularity is a great thing...it shows that a very old show is in touch with a very modern audience. But to a fan of a cult show, it can feel like you are losing your prized 'secret to the masses.'

The Doctor was never meant to be 'cool' in my book - he's an outsider; an alien with a human look.

Yet, for all these initial concerns, Matt has *so* much range and brings *so* many colours to his characterisation, that he really injects a new and different feel to the show; as each

Doctor should, and it isn't long before you grow to love doctor number 11.

On revisiting this episode, and this Doctor, I believe I made a great misjudgement the first time around.
Once you have gotten used to this era, there is a lot to like about the new portrayal. Matt Smith has a great versatility, especially for such a young actor; effortless traversing between whimsy, erasable energy and then broodiness, often in the space of just one scene. This first story really brings the show 'back to basics,' and in the best possible way. It has a real ageless quality to it, and feels like a classic children's story or a
fairytale – somewhere between 'The Snowman' and 'The Lion, the Witch and the Wardrobe'...or rather 'The Raggedy Doctor' and 'the Girl Who Waited' (read on...this will all make sense later!).

There is also a fantastic scene right at the end of the serial which every fan needs to see. The Atraxi scans the Doctor to see if he poses a threat to it; to see if the Earth is protected. Seeing all that the Doctor has done, the Atraxi ends up fleeing; such is the Doctor's awesome reputation. Watching the scanner move through all the previous incarnations of the Doctor...ending with Matt Smith walking through the projection is a extra special moment, and iterates not only the dept that the new series pays to its history, but also the exciting new direction it's about to take it in.

When I first saw this episode I admit I wasn't sure what to make of it, and I would probably have rated it a lot more harshly. But with the benefit of hindsight, I can see that it is a superb series opener, and an exciting way to start the new Doctor's term.

The Beast Below – 5/10

The Doctor takes Amy into the far future (the 29th Century), to find that the human race has taken to huge 'city' spaceships to escape the solar flares on the Earth below. Here they are judged by the creepy 'Winders' and fed to the 'beast below' if they disagree with their Government.

They discover that the ship in reality has no engine at all, but is strapped to the back of an unfortunate 'Star Whale,' who the crew are torturing to keep them travelling in space.

The feel of the episode was a bit 'over the top' and comedic for me. The 11th Doctor appears to be playing the fool, and whilst this can work at times, in a Troughton sort of way, it can also make him look a bit ridiculous, in an early McCoy sort of way; which is never good for the series.

Whilst having some good scenes and great killer robots this one just doesn't continue the great potential of the first series episode, and is pretty disappointing.

Victory Of The Daleks – 5/10

The Doctor and Amy arrive in Churchill's war office at the time of the 2nd World War. But all is not right. The British have a new weapon, which they christen 'Bracewell's Ironside;' but which the Doctor recognises as something much, much worse...a Dalek!

The inventor Bracewell believes he has created these new weapons; but is actually a robot created by *them*. He is programmed to trap the Doctor with his new inventions, and to signal to the Dalek fleet when the Doctor has arrived. This is all unknown to Bracewell; a 'sleeper agent' who is programmed to believe that he is a living person, with his own memories and life.

In time the Doctor discovers that a handful of Daleks have survived the reality bomb (Journey's End) and are starting to build a new and more powerful Dalek race using a 'progenitor' of Dalek D.N.A.

This is a very far-fetched story, even for Doctor Who...I mean, spaceship Spit-Fires?! But it's a fairly amusing addition to the series. Moments like a 'friendly Dalek' offering cups of tea, or the Doctor trying to convince the Daleks that his jammy dodger is actually a self-destruct button make for silly, but funny moments.

The new Daleks are huge, multi-coloured machines; which look like a cross between Lego and the 60's Daleks of the Peter Cushing films. It's difficult to find them as threatening in this guise, but again they're fun.

This is one of those episodes which remind me of how a lot of enjoyment can be lost when we become 'adults.'

I'm sure had I seen this episode as a child, I would've found the space-age spitfires very exciting indeed. But the adult filter in my brain just sees scenes like this and goes 'what?!!'

This is something that seems to really come across in this series so far – 'fun' over 'feasibility.' But then isn't that one of the hallmarks of the show?

This serial also shows a return to the original remit of introducing kids to history – and Churchill is presented with a great deal of aplomb, which is nice to see.

Not one of my favourite episodes by a long shot, but one that I'm sure younger children would love.

The Time Of Angels/Flesh And Stone – 8/10

The Weeping Angels return in this sci-fi thriller of a serial. Returning too is River Song, on the tail of the Angels. She is under contract from 'militarised clerics,' who are keeping her captive for killing an 'unknown' man (more on that in Series 6!).

They follow an Angel that has been hiding on their spaceship; only to find out they have been lulled into a trap. The angel is leading them into a creepy 'maze of the dead' on an alien planet...full of dormant Weeping Angels who are craving human victims!

Amy discovers to her horror that even an image or recording of an angel can BECOME an angel in its own right! In a very scary scene a video of an Angel comes to life in front of her! She looks into the eyes of her predator and starts to turn into an angel herself. Only by closing her eyes can she stop the Angel from taking over her mind. She has to walk through a forest full of Weeping Angels with her eyes closed – pretty terrifying stuff!

The 'crack in the wall' story arc continues; as it turns out to be a tear in the universe, which will lead to the ultimate destruction of time itself! Time energy is leaking through the crack from one reality to another...and even looking into the light can make you cease to exist! In the end, the Doctor must trick the Angels into being sucked into this crack in space-time before they kill the crew.

The evolution of the Angels as living video monsters was a nice development from their beginnings in Blink. The scale of the story is really 'ramped up' in a way that works extremely well. Overall however, I thought the idea of the Angels worked slightly better in their first story (Blink). This is only because the Angels are such an 'everyday' monster; and work so well in an 'every day' context, rather than in a futuristic one. But having said that, I thought this was a thrilling story, which worked as a kind of mixture between 'Aliens' and 'The Grudge.'

There was only one thing that stifled my enjoyment of this double-parter. I'm sorry, I'm really sorry...but as much as I like Alex Kingston, as much as I like the way she makes 'women of a certain age' sexy on T.V again, I'm really not a fan of River Song as a character. As soon as she enters, she is finding ways to make the Doctor look ridiculous - such as telling Amy that the iconic sound of the T.A.R.D.I.S is 'nothing more than a bad driver who leaves the handbrake on'...yeah, thanks for that! And I don't mean to sound prudish, but her constant flirting with the Doctor just feels too overtly sexual for Doctor Who, and detracts from the feel of the show. It's another example of the re-launched series seemingly unending quest to introduce female characters that belittle and deride the main character at every available opportunity (Donna, Lady De Souza and so on). Just what is this about? Is it so wrong to have a strong, multi-layered, fully rounded male character at the helm of a show in these post-feminist times, that we have to have an obnoxious female companion there to balance him? A kind of 'yes, we know we have an intelligent guy here - but don't worry, the female character will always show she is more capable' sort of thing.

It's not that I am chauvinistic or that I don't like strong female characters in the show. My favourite companions – Sarah Jane, Leela and Ace, could all certainly give River a run for her money. But it's the way that the series is almost *embarrassed* of having a male lead at its centre; and has to find a way of diluting the power of this character by making proto-feminist points at ever juncture(?!).

Even Amy, who I do like, is getting in on the action; showing her true feelings for the Doctor and throwing herself at him at the end. He resists – insisting he is a 'Gandalf' in space. I thought this was a nice touch, making me think of how Hartnell reminded me of a mixture between the wizard and Yoda from Star Wars; and this sits much more comfortably in my head than the 'Doctor-Sex Symbol' thing that had been examined in Tennant's time.

Anyway, rant over. This is a superb suspense story that is really one of the highlights of the series so far and definitely worth a watch...in spite of my misgivings with some of the characters.

The Vampires Of Venice – 7/10

Amy's boyfriend Rory finds out that she has kissed the Doctor (see last episode). To try and make things right again, the Doctor takes the couple for a romantic date together – to the beautiful Venice of 1580. But of course this is Doctor Who...so they soon find themselves battling alien vampires!

This episode looks gorgeous – the costumes, the scenery and of course the city of Venice itself. The 'vampires' (who are actually aliens named Saturnynes), have come through the crack in time (story arc) to escape 'the Silence (more on them next season!).' Only the Queen and the male aliens were strong enough to survive this journey, so she must 'make' her son's new girlfriends through replacing human blood with their own (hence the vampire connection).

It's nice to see the return of Rory as a full-time companion here (having been introduced briefly in the Eleventh Hour). I wasn't sure if I'd like Rory at first. He seemed to be another in a line of unintelligent 'butt-of- all-the-jokes' male companions (see Mickey from the 9th Doctor's time for example). But what Rory has which makes him more than a one-dimensional character, is a Herculean heart. He represents not only the ultimate 'every man,' but has a real humanity that works well as a counter to the Doctor's alien...ness (see, the Series 5 speak dialogue is getting to me!). Yes, he does give us some moments of pure comic relief. But in a way it's his 'ordinariness' we are laughing at rather than his perceived stupidity. Just like a good observational comedian, we laugh at Rory, because we can see in him perhaps how we would really react if faced with all the strange aliens and monsters of the programme. We have a certain amount of admiration for Rory; who transcends his flaws through sheer conviction and strength of character to take on the fearful things that face him for the woman he loves.

Overall, this is a nice gothic horror story that has elements of some of the Tom Baker period. I thoroughly enjoyed it.

Amy's Choice – 8/10

We join a heavily pregnant Amy 5 years into the future, living out a relatively boring existence with Rory in the countryside.

But is it a dream?...They 'wake up' to find themselves back in the T.A.R.D.I.S in the present time. But they've all had the same 'dream...' something's going wrong it would seem.

Again, they fall asleep, to find themselves back in the future. Is this the dream, or is the T.A.R.D.I.S?

It turns out its all the plan of the evil trickster 'The Dream Lord'...a spooky presence that enjoys playing fatalistic games with them. He places them in danger in both 'realities,' placing the choice in their hands. In the 'future' they face alien monsters inhabiting elderly people. In the 'past' they are hurtling towards a 'cold star.' And ultimately it's Amy who must choose what reality she wants to exist in or 'save.' After Rory is tragically killed (in a really moving scene) she chooses the reality where he still lives. In the end, it is this tragic sacrifice that convinces her what she should've know all along...that Rory is the man for her.

The Dream Lord is actually created from all of the darkness inside the Doctor; brought on by an allergy to a strange 'psychic space pollen,' that feasts on the evil nature of people. This idea of an 'evil' Doctor has been explored before in the Ultimate Foe (6th); and it's interesting to see the villainous side to the enigmatic leading man again.

I really like these psychological episodes that mess with your mind and keep you guessing. I loved The Dream Lord, who once again had quite a fairytale element – similar to Rumpelstiltskin from the old German folk tale. He also resembled the character of the Celestial Toymaker from the 1st Doctor story of the same name, and this serial did have a bit of a 'classic series' feel to it.

There are also some sweet scenes between Rory and Amy, and some great twists and turns in the plot. I liked this one, and thought it was a great little detour.

The Hungry Earth/Cold Blood – 10/10

In a small Welsh village the Earth appears to be swallowing people whole(!). In reality, the archaeologists have been digging deep, and have unearthed one of the Doctor's oldest foes – the Silurians!

A quick history lesson for those unfamiliar with the Pertwee era of the show...

The Silurians evolved from reptiles in the same way as we evolved from apes. They progressed much faster than humans, but eventually hibernated after fearing the end of the Earth from a planet on a 'collision course' (which ended up being the alignment of the moon).
Now, millions of years later, they awake to claim what they see as rightfully theirs' from the 'apes' that have colonised the Earth.

When Amy is kidnapped for Silurian experiments, the rest of the team go deep underground in the T.A.R.D.I.S to rescue her. The Doctor offers the small human gang a challenge – to represent the very best of their race in order to broker a deal with the Silurians to share the planet and prevent the inevitable bloodshed.

In the end the Silurian leader agrees to make peace with the humans and go back into hibernation, on the promise they have 1,000 years to make the Earth habitable by both races. With the help of the Doctor, they trick the military arm of the Silurians that there is a virus that will kill them if they don't go back into hibernation. But as one last act of war, the head of the military tries to kill the Doctor; instead killing poor Rory (for a second time). Adding insult to injury, Rory not only dies, but is then consumed by the light of the crack that has been following them (story arc) and 'ceases to exist,' only remembered by The Doctor. A very tragic ending to what is a superb story.

It's so exciting to see the return of one of the classic show's most legendary aliens. The Silurians manage to be both incredibly sinister and also noble; rather like their reptilian ancestors, and they are fantastically realised.

Although their design is totally different (explained by the Doctor by making them a different
'branch of the gene pool'), they look amazing and retain all of the most fascinating elements of the originals.
These are previous inhabitants of Earth, with as much claim to it as the 'ape decedent' humans. It's still a huge twist on the 'alien invasion' idea. It's also puts the Doctor in a very different position: he is the only alien in the equation; not naturally belonging with either 'side.'

Fans of the old and new series will love this serial, which is full of suspense, action and, most importantly a great plot. One of the best aliens of the series' history is back, and the way the serial is written and produced creates a lot to be excited about. In fact, in many ways this is actually an improvement, at least in pace and development than the original story, and that is something I would very rarely say. Essential viewing for fans old and new.

Vincent And The Doctor – 10/10

Amy and the Doctor visit an art gallery in Paris, and Amy is particularly enamoured with the beauty of the Vincent Van Gogh paintings. However, after the Doctor sees what appears to be a monster in the chapel window of one of the great masterpieces, they must travel back in time to meet Vincent and solve the riddle.

On meeting Vincent, they find him to be far from the celebrated artist they imagine. He is ridiculed and hated by his community, who blame his 'madness' (bipolar disorder) for a spate of bad luck the town is facing. It transpires that Vincent's gift for seeing all the beauty and rich colour of life also affords him the power to see what others cannot...in this case a huge invisible alien monster that is murdering the townsfolk! Vincent faces both the tangible monster of the alien and the crippling *monster* of his own depression that proves in the end to be the more fatal.

In the early days of Who, 'history' episodes were separate from the science fiction element, and I got the feeling that this episode would've stood on its own merits as a purely 'history' based story; such was the emotive power of the Van Gogh plot. I did like the idea of an invisible monster (tackled in 'classic' serials such as The Face of Evil), and this is done with some skill; though it felt in some ways an extra bonus to what was already a very strong story.

Written by the great Richard Curtis, this is one of the most tender and emotional episodes in recent memory, and is certainly one of the best written of the 11th Doctor's stories so far. The end scene is particularly affecting. The Doctor takes Vincent forward in time to see just how loved and respected he eventually became after his death. Yet even this cannot dissuade the tortured Vincent from killing himself the same year they return him to. The Doctor consoles Amy with a truly poetic speech about the human condition:

> *"The way I see it, every life is a pile of good things and bad things. The good things don't always soften the bad things; but vice-versa, the bad things don't necessarily spoil the good things or make them unimportant." (The Eleventh Doctor, Vincent and the Doctor)*

For a family programme to approach the issues of mental illness in such a thoughtful and realistic way (rather than treating 'madness' in the stereotypical drama portrayal) is very brave and inspiring. It is a real breath of fresh air, and once again a reminder of how this show at its best can transcend its parameters and create something truly exceptional.

The Lodger – 6/10

The Doctor and Amy are separated when the T.A.R.D.I.S takes off by itself. Stranded in modern day Essex, he must learn to live a 'normal' life with a bloke (that at least looks) his age. Craig, his new housemate is a lonely bachelor, secretly in love with his friend Sophie; unaware that his upper floor is housing a time- consuming alien (hence the T.A.R.D.I.S problems) who is burning up innocent people in an effort to launch its own 'time engine.'

Whilst this is undeniably a 'filler' story; a 'story-lite' before the epic series ender, it is a fun, and heart-warming tale of the Doctor getting to live out a 'human' life whilst his housemate goes through the double anxieties of understanding his strange new friend and not knowing what to do about his love for Sophie.

Whilst this isn't quite in the same league as the Tennant 'human' story 'Human Nature'/'The Family of Blood' (another story in which the Doctor adopts a 'human' life) it is an enjoyable comedy/drama and a nice change in pace from what is to come. Like the series opener ('The Eleventh Hour'), it's nice to see the Doctor's effect on an individual, as well as the larger universe.

The Pandorica Opens/The Big Bang – 5/10

The series story arc of the crack in time finally culminates in the most ambitious story of recent years.
The mysterious 'Pandorica' (similar to the mythical 'Pandoras Box') is fabled to contain the most evil force to ever exist. In reality though, it is a trap for the Doctor;

a prison created by a league of his most feared enemies (Daleks, Cybermen, Sontarans) who foresee that his travels will ultimately destroy the universe.

To assist the Doctor and Amy is River, who tracks them down through space and time. The trap is guarded by Roman Autons, including a robot Rory, who has inexplicably fallen through time, recreated by the subconscious of Amy, who has forgotten him (since he 'ceased to exist' in 'Cold Blood'....come on keep up).

There are some great scenes in this first half, such as the Doctor addressing the 1,000s of spaceships from his oldest and greatest foes. Matt Smith does this with an authority that belies his years, and it's up there with the greatest speeches from the show as a whole.

As the first half closes – the Doctor is imprisoned in the Pandorica, seemingly destroying all of time and space(?). Amy is shot by the unwilling Auton Rory and darkness descends over the universe...as cliff-hangers go, it doesn't get much bigger than this!
As the second half begins, we are now in an alternate reality where history is collapsing, with the Doctor in the middle of the implosion. The stars have gone out and whole races are wiped out. Rory and the Doctor try to resurrect Amy using traces of her D.N.A preserved by the Pandorica (I think this is the plot to be honest, I'm pretty lost at this point!). They put Amy in the Pandorica, where she awakens nearly 2,000 years later to meet her young self (see 'the Eleventh Hour'). Rory stays and guards the box for the full 2,000 years, showing the true extent of his love (aww!).

They all come back together, to see the future Doctor get killed! They have to save him...then the Doctor uses the Pandorica to fly into the heart of the T.A.R.D.I.S, exploding at every point in time, in order to re-boot the whole of time, creating a 'big bang 2' (again, I think this is what happens!), but ultimately writing him out of time, at least long enough for him to go backwards and say goodbye.

In the end, Amy remembers the Doctor at her wedding, and he returns to reality through her memory, and all is restored.

To be honest, whilst I really admire the breadth of this serial, and the writers' aim to stretch the boundaries and possibilities of the show, for me personally it was all a bit too much. I didn't have a clue what was going on for most of the time, and I lost a lot of connection with the story. The whole idea of history being totally rebooted seemed rather far-fetched and over-reaching too; and created all sorts of questions with potentially disappointing answers – does this mean that all the Doctor's adventures have now never happened for example? It does create a nice continuity 'get-out' however, as the show is now operating in a different 'reality' to our own. See – this is what this sort of serial does to my tiny brain!

I have to admit I had to use Wikipedia to understand most of this double-parter, and I'm still pretty sure I've got most of the details wrong, so it might be worth watching this one yourself to make up your own mind!

This is a real shift for the show; taking it in a new and very complex direction that I much less prefer to the whimsical fairy-tale beginnings of the season. This coupled with an annoying River and an increasingly annoying Amy made this a far less satisfying series ender than the previous one. Whilst most fans will no doubt love this, it really wasn't my cup of tea.

As a first series however, I have to commend the writers for introducing the new Doctor with some pretty awesome serials overall (The Eleventh Doctor, Amy's Choice, The Hungry Earth/Cold Blood and Vincent and the Doctor), and it's exciting to see where the show will go next.

Specials

Christmas Special - A Christmas Carol – 8/10

"You know that in nine hundred years of time and space I've never met anybody who wasn't important before." (The Eleventh Doctor, A Christmas Carol)

We're thrown straight into the action, with Rory and Amy onboard a spaceship hurtling towards a planet!

The Doctor lands on the planet to find it inhabited with Victorian styled people, fish (and sharks!) swimming in the foggy air and people who are frozen in time in the vaults of a mean old money lender.

The always excellent Michael Gambon, plays a futuristic 'Scrooge' (Kazran Sardick) in this 'Who' version of the classic 'A Christmas Carol.' The Doctor must persuade the miserly old goat to help the crashing spaceship which is falling through the sky (which he owns). Acting as a 'Ghost of Christmas Past,' the Doctor goes back to Kazran's earlier life, to try and find the heart of the person he once was, and convince him to care about people again. He changes the experiences of the young Kazran, introducing him to the love of his life and her poor family...

For deep in the vaults of the house are encased people frozen in suspended animation. Kazran's evil father lends poor people money, taking and freezing a family member as 'insurance' for their payments. One such person is Abigail (played by the beautiful Welsh opera singer Katherine Jenkins). The Doctor and the young Kazran visit her every Christmas as the years go by, until Kazran falls for her. Unfortunately, she is dying, and this understandably embitters Kazran once more. Only by seeing her one last time is his heart restored and he and Doctor can save the ship from its imminent crash.

As much as I have grown to love Matt Smith's Doctor, the way he flies into the room like a hyperactive toddler who's had too many 'E numbers' is pretty aggravating at times. He is still capable of swinging it back around to sombre territory with dizzying pace though; and he once again delivers some excellent lines in this serial.

Usually, I would find this sort of obvious 'homage'/'rip off' rather lacklustre. But this special is inventive enough to make it different from Dickens, whilst retaining the heart of that great story. Matt's mercurial Doctor fits in perfectly with this sort of fanciful story, and this is certainly one of the best of the Christmas specials, with something to keep all the family interested.

Comic Relief Specials - Space/Time – 3/5

A couple of 'minisodes' aboard the T.A.R.D.I.S. After Rory inadvertently drops a tool into the workings of the T.A.R.D.I.S, it materialises inside itself, in a 'space loop!' In walks a future Amy to help tell them what to do to save themselves.

A fun and funny little story. But from a continuity point of view, I was rather concerned that future versions of characters could meet themselves without there being a tear in the space-time continuum...has no one seen Back to the Future?!!

SERIES 6
(SEASON 32)

Series 6 is perhaps the most ambitious series of the show since it reappeared on our screens. The stories are super complex and confusing, and although impressive will likely turn away the uninitiated.

The Impossible Astronaut/Day
Of The Moon – 7/10

The Doctor is now 1003 years old– meaning he has been gone some time (the last we heard he was 908!). He invites Amy, Rory and River to a particular date, time and space...America, 1969, 'The day the Doctor dies.' An astronaut comes out of the water and shoots the Doctor...twice, killing him before he has time to regenerate.

The Doctor returns...earlier in his time but later in Amy's, Rory's and River's. They all know what is going to happen to the Doctor but him. This sets up the mystery that will form one of the 'story arcs' for the series.

Meanwhile, Amy is seeing mysterious figures, 'The Silence,' and then forgetting all about them. 'The Silence' are a terrifying alien that have been around for a long long time; living in the shadows, making all that see them forget they are there (an excellent attack/defence). A parasitic alien, they steer the human race in whichever way they want. They have been ruling the world since the dawn of mankind with 'post-hypnotic suggestion,' which makes everyone who sees them forget what they have seen. However, the Doctor and companions manage to 'remember' them by installing recordable discs in their hands where they can record their sightings, and also by making marks on their bodies to show how many they have seen.

They meet Canton Everett Delaware III, an ex-F.B.I agent who is summoned by the President (Richard Nixon) to listen to mysterious phone calls he's been getting from an unknown girl asking for his help. The Silence are using the little girl (still unknown); putting her into a spacesuit which sends out a signal to the highest authority on a planet (I.E the President of the United States). She is also the girl who is to shoot the Doctor (against her wishes).

In the end, the Doctor uses The Silence's weapon against them. He broadcasts a video of a Silent saying that the humans should have 'killed them all on sight' across the greatest viewed programme of all time...the moon landing. All humans are therefore subconsciously predisposed to destroy the race as soon as they see them; even if they don't remember what they have done.

Oh, and added to all this Amy is pregnant, but she is unsure whether if her travelling in the T.A.R.D.I.S may have affected her unborn baby. The T.A.R.D.I.S itself shows both positive and negative readings for her pregnancy, which concerns the Doctor enough for him to keep it a secret from her.

This is the first new series to be shown on B.B.C America and there is a very 'Americanised' feel that is no doubt a drive towards conquering the stateside market. The narrative returns to the feel of the Big Bang/The Pandorica Opens; with complex non-linear plots and mysterious characters. Although this is superbly written, all the constant shifting and confusing elements that Moffat brings to this era of the show seem to make it a lot less accessible and watchable...to me at least. I also really dislike the 'sexualising' of the Doctor's character that River Song seems to bring to the show; another taste preference that is just really not for me!

'The Silence' are a wonderful alien, one of the most inventive (and certainly the most frightening) in the series since the Weeping Angels. They also have a creepy whispering voice, much like the Zygons, with a similarly classic delivery of the name 'Doc...tor,' that any great villain needs!

Along with the memorable aliens the series starts in possibly the most intriguing and suspenseful ways; killing off the main character in a 'murder mystery' that leaves the viewer aghast and unsure what is going to happen next.

My opinion overall is mixed. The show really stretches itself in new directions, with an impressive new enemy, new more international locations and a mystery which will grip the viewer and make them want to follow the series. But occasionally, it feels like the show is trying to be 'too clever' for its own good, and is losing some of what connects it with the wider audience in the process.

It's an audacious way to open a series, and definitely one to check out, for all its disarrangement and confusing feel.

The Curse Of The Black Spot – 6/10

The show returns to Pirate territory in this fun romp on the high seas, as the Doctor and company turn up on a 17th Century ship. As soon as anyone gets the tiniest scratch, they are tarred with the 'black spot' and are taken by a 'demon from the deep;' a siren/mermaid who drags them to the next world.

In actuality, she is a 'virtual doctor,' on a far away spaceship with a dead crew. Able to travel between the worlds via reflections, such as water or shining treasure (like the pirates' hoard), she tries to find people to 'care for;' transporting them to the ship and keeping them in stasis.

(N.B - Oh, and Rory dies...again...to be saved...again – how many times can this man die?!).

A fun, swashbuckling serial with a sci-fi twist; which young kids will particularly love. A lot more accessible and cohesive than the last story, but still not quite up to the standards of the great episodes of Series 5 like 'The Eleventh Hour' or 'Vincent and the Doctor.'

The Doctor's Wife – 8/10

The Doctor: "You didn't always take me where I wanted to go." Idris/T.A.R.D.I.S: "No, but I always took you where you needed to go." (The Eleventh Doctor and Idris, The Doctor's Wife)

Written by acclaimed author Neil Gaiman, this is a fantastical episode in which a very key precedent of the show is broken...for the first time in almost 50 years, we get to 'see' the soul of the T.A.R.D.I.S, in a living, breathing person!

Following a floating box/signaller that appears to be from his own all-but-extinct race the Time Lords, the Doctor arrives at a tiny 'pocket' universe attached to the edge of ours'. More specifically, they have landed on a huge living asteroid/space urchin; which absorbs the souls of those it meets. It takes the soul of the T.A.R.D.I.S, placing it in one of its inhabitants, Idris.

Understandably, the T.A.R.D.I.S takes a while to get used to 'living' in its new form.

But the Doctor has even worse problems...he discovers that he isn't the first Time Lord to be lured here...many many Time Lords have been here before him. The urchin has killed them and taken their body parts; making them into his own ragtag inhabitants.
Gaiman is a master of creating strange and wonderful worlds and this is no exception. The sets are like a post- apocalyptic junk yard; full of remnants of all the people the space urchin has dragged there. A very odd, but incredibly creative and different episode which looks amazing. Great writing, as you would expect from a writer like Gaiman, and full of suspense, action and intrigue throughout.

The Rebel Flesh/The Almost People – 8/10

Welcome to the 22nd Century, where workers at a factory use cloned doppelgangers or 'Gangers,' made from 'programmable matter' to work with dangerous acid.

A solar storm strikes, and the living 'flesh' which is grown to create the Gangers become living people themselves – with the desire for a life of their own! To all intents and purposes, they are a living person with the same right to a life as their 'clone fathers and mothers;' sharing as they do the humans' genetic imprint. They are so alike in fact that some of them don't even realise that they are the 'copies' at first.

Opinions and allegiances are divided, as Rory and Doctor sympathise with the Gangers and the others see them as a threat. Things are then further complicated when the Doctor himself is cloned!

The second episode sees the action packed war between the 'originals' and the 'copies' that ensues, with the Doctor playing the mediator between the two.

In the end of the serial, we discover that Amy is also a 'copy' and the real Amy, heavily pregnant has been kidnapped by a mysterious woman with an eye- patch...but more on her in the next episode!

This is another highly inventive serial, with great special effects and some philosophical ideas raised about the 'human condition;' a theme the show has always done really well.

A Good Man Goes To War – 8/10

Rory the Roman goes all badass on a Cyberman ship to find out the location of his bride (kidnapped in the last episode). He finds that their baby, Melody Pond has been born in captivity with her mother, aboard a spaceship of enemies of the Doctor.

Onboard the ship, we meet a group of 'Anglican Marines' who have been convened to find, and destroy the Doctor. Such is his legend, and the mess he has caused to time and space, that he has become a huge threat. Even the term 'Doctor' has become defined as 'Warrior' in this time.

Matt Smith is at the darkest I've seen him so far. Incensed by the kidnap of Amy, he goes on an all-out revenge mission. Lots of space-age fighting follows before we discover a huge twist...the secret of River Song...('spoilers!')

It turns out she is actually Amy and Rory's daughter...Melody Pond ('River Song' being the closest translation from the original 'language of the forest')!

'Melody'/'River' is infused with Time Lord D.N.A; having been conceived in the T.A.R.D.I.S during flight...and the enemy who have kidnapped Amy and Melody are to make the child into a weapon whom will eventually become the programmed young girl who 'kills' the Doctor in the series opener.

Added to all of this are 'Headless Monks,' (a creepy religious order), the Lady Vastra and Jenny, (a Silurian and human detective team), a 'nurse' Sontaran, Judoons and a whole host of other characters old and new. The production is full on Ridley Scott science-fiction, and the sets, costumes and cinematography are all awesome! We are back in 'Pandorica Opens' territory where there are enough elements and 'time streams' to make you dizzy. But this epic serial felt a lot more effective and engaging than that...Doctor Who 'large scale;' in the best way I've seen since 'The End of Time.'

Not the sort of 'Who' I'd want to see every week, and it did lose me here and there. But I found this really impressive in its scope.

Let's Kills Hitler – 2/10

We start off in Amy's childhood, and are introduced to her friend Mels, who persuades the Doctor to go back to the Second World War, where they meet tessellating robots who can mimic human forms. Controlled by shrunken humans, they are on a mission to go back in time and kill history's greatest criminals (in this case the worst evil of them all...Adolf Hitler!).

The twists keep coming, and it's not long before we find out Mels is actually River Song in an earlier regeneration. In the resulting action, Mels is shot and regenerates into River...conditioned and trained by the enemies in the last episode to kill the Doctor. She almost manages...but in discovering the moral nature of the Doctor, she changes allegiances, using her own regenerative powers to restore him.

Whilst it's really sweet to see Amy and Rory's back- story; the rest of this story tries so hard to be cool it's embarrassing. At the same time it also...felt...really...slow, for all its various twists and turns.

I found this opener to the second half of the series very disjointed and quite inaccessible. Quite dissatisfying unfortunately, especially after such a good serial beforehand.

Night Terrors – 6/10

The Doctor answers a distress signal...from a 7 year old child, who is scared of the monsters in his room. The young boy is not what he seems; and turns out to be a 'Tenza' - an alien who can project his imagination into real life creatures. And in this case his worst nightmares are taking the form of horrific killer dolls!

Whilst this seems like a less than deep premise for one of the most thoughtful family programmes to come out of Britain in the last 50 years, it does present quite an intriguing idea. It brings the programme right into the lap of its audience...and the action right to the viewer by making it about them. This must have made for an exceptionally exciting reaction for the legions of young Doctor Who fans - making them think that they too may one day meet their hero!

It's probably not one of the most memorable or striking of recent episodes, but it's still worth a watch. I particularly liked the idea of an alien that can create matter from their own imagination.

The Girl Who Waited – 9/10

The Doctor and company travel to a leisure planet for a spot of R&R. He had tried this before (the 4th Doctor serial 'The Leisure Hive' for example) with disastrous results, but it seems he never learns his lesson!

Within a few minutes he finds himself and his companions in a whole heap of trouble. Amy gets trapped in a different and 'compressed' time-stream from the Doctor and Rory, where she is being chased by maniacal medidroid 'Handbots' bent on 'curing' her (eradicating her alien germs and 'killing her with kindness' in the process).

Poor old Rory and Amy seem destined to do a lot of waiting. It is Amy's turn this time; being caught up in her time stream for over 36 years before the Doctor and Rory can find her again. And, understandably, she has become hardened and embittered from decades of survival against the medidroids that tirelessly pursue her. Rory has to make the tragically difficult choice to either save the Amy he has left behind (the 'older' Amy) or the younger Amy from the alternate time-stream. By saving the younger Amy, who has had none of the hardships of the older Amy, he can save her from a difficult life...but in doing so he will eradicate the Amy he left behind, and deny her the life and the experiences she has had.

Production-wise, the robots are great. Their expressionless, clinical, egg-like heads really add to their scariness. The sterile white environment was how I'd imagine 'Tron' would have looked; had it taken place inside a Nintendo Wii instead of a P.C!

After a couple of rather average episodes, this is a real return to form. It's rare that the companions take such a front seat in a story, and it shows just how effective Amy and Rory have become at holding their own and being crucial in their own right. The story is sweet and tragic; and really brings the actors and their characters up to their full potential. A story with real emotional resonance, which reminds us once more how far above 'average' family drama/science fiction Doctor Who (at its best) can be.

The God Complex – 7/10

The T.A.R.D.I.S arrives in a nightmare hotel, in which each room holds each person's individual fears, personalised and personified. This takes them to the height of their fear before giving them some sort of mental breakdown and converting their wills to the worship of their captor.

It turns out that the 'monster' at large (a distant cousin of the Nimon, first introduced in the Fourth Doctor's tenure) is not feeding on fear, as is first assumed; but on people's underlying faith in whatever they believe will save them (whether religion, luck, experience or faith in each other). To beat this, the Doctor (reminiscent of another very poignant moment from the 7th Doctor serial The Curse of Fenric) must break Amy's faith in him, by tricking her into believing he isn't the hero she thinks he is. This leads to a truly heart-breaking scene, and one which shows the depth of both characters and their relationship.

'Religion' is presented here like a sickness or insanity; and I did find this slightly patronising and offensive to people of different faiths. However, the overall ideas are very original, and this is quite a unique episode.
The hotel setting bears a striking resemblance to Stephen King's 'The Shining,' and the serial had a similarly claustrophobic and creepy feel that worked well.

Night And The Doctor (Minisodes, Available On Series 6 D.v.d) – 5/10

1.   Bad Night

Amy discovers that even at night, the Doctor has a busy time whilst they all sleep.

2.   Good Night

Again, Amy tries to find out what the Doctor skulks off to do in the night. She talks to the Doctor about how messy her life has become since she started travelling with him. He takes her back to her saddest memory...dropping an ice-cream when she was little...so that her older self can give her younger self a new ice- cream(?!).

3.   First Night

The Doctor takes River Song from her prison (Stormcage) on her first night, where she has been incarcerated for 'killing' him. He offers to take her to the starriest sky in history. But in walks another River Song...from another time.

4.   Last Night

The 'future' River is on the run from the Sontarans and walks into the T.A.R.D.I.S. The 'past' River is waiting to be taken on their date. ANOTHER 'future' River walks in...the Doctor is in deep trouble! In the end, he manages to take them all back to their own times.

Fairly fun, but inconsequential 'minisodes' that act as a kind of 'Easter egg' for D.V.D purchasers; rather than any important addition to the show.

Closing Time – 7/10

The Doctor drops in on Craig (played by James Cordon, who we first met in 'The Lodger') for an innocent house- call. They are soon back in trouble again – as power fluctuations start to occur all over the city. These are caused by a stranded Cyberman, who is using Cybermats to harness the power it needs to recover and convert more humans to the Cyber-cause.

As well as returning to a recent story, there are a few different references to the classic series in this episode that are worth noting:

Firstly, as a complete Who geek, it was more than a little pleasurable to see the return of the little Cybermats, who I had not seen since the excellent 'Tomb of the Cybermen' (although they had appeared in a missing serial and a more recent computer game since). And whilst I have to admit, they were always more on the comical than threatening side in 'Tomb,' their modern counterparts are much more sinister and well-realised – all piranha teeth in metal clothing.

Secondly, there is the appearance of the lovely Linda Baron (Open All Hours) in a small role. Fans of the classic series may know that this is actually her 'hat-trick' performance in the show; after playing roles in the first Doctor's 'The Gunslingers' and the fifth Doctor's 'Enlightenment.' Unfortunately for the great actress, neither of these were very good serials, so I'm glad to say she was finally included in a story that is worthy of her.

The final connection of the classic series to this serial is the Doctor's use of the 'powers of persuasion' that he has shown himself capable of utilising in more than one serial before. His use in this story seems rather flippant to me, but it's nice to see a connection with the old series none-the- less.

Whilst I missed Rory and Amy in this episode, it is a surprisingly sweet and effective story, which is straightforward enough to give the viewer a bit of breathing space in a series of weighty dramas.

The Wedding Of River Song – 6/10

We join the Doctor in a very strange situation indeed – the whole of history seems to be occurring at once!
Winston Churchill commands Roman legions, steam trains thunder along tracks coming out of sky-scrapers and cars are carried through the skies by Victorian hot air balloons! It would appear there has been a monumental change in an important event in time that has damaged the fabric of time itself, with potentially catastrophic consequences.

We discover that the key change was the altering of the Doctor's death, orchestrated by River Song (earlier in the series); which has had the knock-on effect of slowly disintegrating time itself. It's up to the Doctor to try and fix this anomaly and heal time before it's too late.

The serial itself feels rather disjointed and inaccessible at times (rather like 'Let's Kill Hitler' had been), and you get the feeling the series is trying to outstretch itself again; making itself more *epic* than *enjoyable*.

There are a few saving graces. It's really poignant to hear of the Brigadier's death in this episode, in a short scene that pays tribute not only to one of the Doctor's greatest and most important aides, but also to the superb actor who played him (the late, great Nicholas Courtney, who sadly passed in February 2011). It's great to see the wonderful Silence back (definitely my favourite alien of this series). And of course the marriage of the Doctor and River Song

DOCTOR WHO: A COMPANION

is sweet...not in a kind of 'Human Nature' standard, but it's still sweet.

But I didn't find this serial half as watchable as some of the other series enders. A decidedly dissatisfying end to a confusing and mixed season which is probably my least favourite of the Matt Smith era. There were moments where it shined brightly and brilliantly, but these were not as consistent as the series which preceded it.

Specials

Doctor Who Confidential Special – Death Is The Only Answer – 5/10

Another Mini episode (or 'minisode') written by children at Oakley Junior School who won a competition for their story to be realised on screen. In it, the Doctor meets an old friend, Albert Einstein (first met in Time and the Rani fact-finders!), who is trying to invent his own time- machine. Drinking a potion, Albert turns into an evil Ood, bent on killing the Doctor. The Doctor throws him into a light beam and he returns to normal...albeit with the crazy hair we associate him with.

Supremely daft and illogical...in the great way in which children write stories. A lot of fun, but hardly classic Who.

Christmas Special - The Doctor, The Widow And The Wardrobe – 6/10

The Doctor decides to cheer up a family who have lost their father in World War II. He follows them as they evacuate to a large country-house, disguising himself as 'the caretaker' and creating a portal to another world (Androzani – a planet which you may or may not remember from the Fifth Doctor's last story 'The Caves of Androzani') through which he hopes the children will escape their own sad lives. However, the planet contains a forest of trees that can change shape, talk to one another and defend themselves. The trees enlist the help of the Doctor and the children to try and defend them against the impending destruction from humans who plan to burn the trees with acid rain and harvest the fuel created.

The Doctor is once again in his most childlike persona. He seems to really emphasise this in the Christmas specials; and of course, this is understandable. The character of the Doctor is basically made up of 3 distinct parts, each representing a different section of the audience – the authoritative adult (for the parents), the eccentric alien (for the student/fanboy/girl fraternity) and the inquisitive, excitable child (for the main target audience of 9-12 year olds). It is the stretching and incorporating of these different elements which gives each actor a different take on the character, whilst retaining the core 'heart' (or should that be 'hearts') of the original blue-print set by Hartnell and Troughton.

Because the first 4-5 actors did such a great job of making the character their own, each actor that has played the part since has woven in these elements to a certain degree. Since the re-launch, Eccleston has played the character as the world-weary loner (in a
Hartnell mould), Tennant as the heroic lady's man (in a Davison mould) and Smith as a jumpy, excitable 'fool' who can turn to a brooding mastermind at the drop of a hat (in a Troughton mould). Of course, this analogy is to do

the newer actors somewhat of a disservice; as each great actor has also managed to weave in their own unique characterisations.

Whilst I took a while to like Matt Smith's portrayal (as brilliant as he is in his execution of the role), it has grown on me greatly. Occasionally though, he will stretch the child-like excitement a bit too far for my liking. In a couple of scenes at the beginning of this serial he bounces around the room describing toys and exclaiming to himself 'humany wumany' when he is impressed by the emotional depth of his human charges. It's difficult to imagine Hartnell being quite so incoherent or illiterate sounding as that. But then after all, this is a Christmas special, so you expect the Doctor to be slightly lighter. It's just not one of the traits that I personally enjoy.

As for the serial itself, it was difficult at times to know what it was trying to be. Was it paying homage to the 'Lion the Witch and the Wardrobe,' in a similar way that last year's special paid homage to 'A Christmas Carol?' Was it an ecological discourse on the way humans are destroying the rainforests? The serial does seem a little incongruent; as fun as it is.

I liked the way the kids played a big part in this Christmas special; and this is a good way for the target audience to feel truly involved in their programme again. The idea of motherhood is the main thrust of this special, which is explored in a powerful and meaningful way - the children's mother has to not only save them, but be infused by the spirit-force of the endangered forest people. She can only do this by the strength of her 'maternal energy;' and again this is something that will strike a chord with the family audience watching at home on Christmas day.

Although the acting, production and special effects were all excellent, this was one of my least favourite of the specials. I think younger kids will love it however.

Blue Peter Special - Good As Gold – 4/10

Following on from the competition winning story 'Death is the Only Answer,' here is another story written by kids at Ashdene School...

Amy is bored of not having had an adventure for a while, so the Doctor sets the T.A.R.D.I.S console to 'adventure setting.' They arrive in the midst of the London 2012 Olympic torch rally, to meet a torchbearer...being followed by a Weeping Angel! The Doctor zaps the Weeping Angel and the Olympic spirit is restored.

A very silly story, as you'd expect. A fun little episode by kids, which even this heartless author can't bring himself to criticise.

Pond Life – 6/10

In the run-up to the new series, this 5 part prequel fills us in on what the Doctor has been up to, and shows us a glimpse into the lives of the Ponds in his year long absence.

Back in the present day, the Ponds continue to live their normal everyday lives. Well, if you can call living with a stray Ood a normal existence. In the end, Rory and Amy separate...which is all a bit sudden and unexpected.

Some nice comedy moments with the Ood, and a shock ending with the breakup – it all seems a very quick...and strange way to introduce the new series.

SERIES 7
(SEASON 33)

We say a sad farewell to Amy and Rory and hello to multiple Claras in this series of less confusing but equally large feeling set of stories.

Asylum Of The Daleks – 7/10

The show returns, after what seems like forever (it's just over 8 and a bit months in reality) and throws up one of the most exciting series openers in a while.

The Doctor is drawn by a distress call to the Dalek's home-planet of Skaro; which turns out to be a trap, made by a Human/Dalek hybrid messenger and puppet of the Daleks. It appears the Daleks actually want to enlist the help of the Doctor! They have created an
'Asylum;' a dumping ground where they allow all the
'reject' and 'faulty' Daleks to reside; believing that their hatred for these 'impure' Daleks will help them grow and develop in their evil intentions. But the Asylum's security field has been breached by a crashing ship, and the Daleks want their greatest 'predator' (the Doctor) to beam down and destroy their 'rejects' before they escape.

Meanwhile, we rejoin Rory and Amy, who have split up and

are in the process of getting a divorce when they are also captured by the Daleks. We discover that Amy has become infertile as a result of what happened to her in 'A Good Man Goes to War,' and blames herself for not being able to give Rory the children he would like to have, and she instead decides to leave him. This is made even more tragic when Amy is 'infected' by the nano-gene robots that are turning all the humans on the asylum planet into the 'Dalek puppets' hybrids.

More meanwhiles...we are introduced to Oswin, a girl seemingly trapped inside the Dalek ship, living out a lonely existence for over a year and planning her escape.

But the truth is far more complicated than that ('spoilers!').

This story is a great excuse to bring back loads of old Daleks; and we are treated to Daleks from throughout the 'classic' and 're-launched' series. Old geeks like me can search the screen for everything from the original 60's Daleks to rarities like the 'Battle Dalek' from 'Remembrance of the Daleks' (although they are a bit hidden under dust and rust, and we don't get to see them in their full glory as much as I'd have liked).

The Amy and Rory side-story is all pretty sad stuff. There are a couple of sweet scenes where we see that the Doctor truly wants to get his companions back together again after their split. As a viewer, it's easy to share this sentiment – it just doesn't feel right those two not being together! Oswin is played by Jenna-Louise Coleman, the actress who will play the Doctor's next companion. In the age of online fandom, poor Jenna-Louise had a great deal of unfair criticism and vitriol aimed at her at first by fans of Amy, who saw her as an unfit 'replacement' for their favourite companion. Not only is it totally unfair to criticise an actress before she's even acted a scene, but it's totally out of keeping with a show that is constantly introducing new companions. So, in my heart I really wanted this companion to work – to show all her naysayers what she is capable of.

Well, the good news is that she really 'owned' all the scenes she was in, showing a real screen presence and skill as an actress. Unfortunately, I really didn't warm to her character, which I found to be far too 'cool for school,' far too cocky and full of herself – the same problems I had with Amy when she first started, and throughout most of River Song's time. Lines like 'save me chin-boy' had me groaning out loud at the television, and really stunted my enjoyment of this character, and the episode as a whole. But thankfully, I seem to be in a minority, and judging on fan's reactions after this episode, Jenna-Louise has quite rightly silenced her critics.

It is a nice twist that Steven Moffat brings the character in early; but its unsure at this point whether she is playing a different character or not and how this will tie- in with the new companion. Will she come back? Will she play an ancestor of herself? Will she be found in the past of her own timeline (as in River Song)? This is another one of Moffat's great twists and turns that keeps you guessing, and more importantly keeps you interested.

(N.B – read to the end of the season to find out!)

I was confused about the location of Skaro in this episode.

I'm pretty sure it was blown up during the 7th Doctor's time, and then all the Daleks 'time-locked' at the end of the 'Time-War' (8th-9th)? I'm guessing this all takes place on a Skaro *before* all of this? Anyway, regardless of this, it is GREAT to see Skaro again for the first time in ages! The Daleks seem much more threatening and 'unhinged' in this episode, which really went someway to making them scary again for me, after their more comical appearance in Victory of the Daleks. I also thought the 'Dalek puppets;' humans with Dalek extras attached, were a nice, creepy addition to the story, and were much better realised than the original 'Robomen' in 'The Dalek Invasion of Earth.'

Overall an impressive and exciting opener to the series.

Dinosaurs On A Space Ship - 2/10

Enlisting the help of a team of different friends throughout time - Queen Nefertiti of Egypt, Victorian explorer John Riddell, Amy, Rory and his Dad (played by the wonderful Mark Williams from the Fast Show/Harry Potter) the Doctor delves into strange goings on aboard a Silurian Ark in space. They find that a bounty hunter (played by David Bradley, also from Harry Potter and later to play the First Doctor) is using robots to kill the Silurian crew and steal all the dinosaurs that are onboard(?!).

My hopes weren't high for the most B-Movie title since 'The Creature from the Pit' (1979), and unfortunately my fears weren't unfounded, in this real mess of an episode.

That's not to say there weren't some great elements. The robots and dinosaurs both looked amazing (it's incredible to think how far the series has come since the awful Pertwee story Invasion of the Dinosaurs) and were a real step up in design for the show. Rory's dad was also a great character, and one whom you liked instantly.

But there were just too many elements forced together in too short a space of time; leading to a story that was difficult to keep up with, or find any connection with. Was this a Silurian story, a 'lost in space' story, a dinosaur story, a history story? It was all of these things...and none of them...for none of the seeds really had chance to bloom.

A really impressive looking episode doesn't manage to

mask the plot. The elements of at least 3 good stories are there, but there is no focus or over- riding point to any of it. This was a real *pick and mix* of ideas that isn't worked on enough to bring them together or make the story work.

A Town Called Mercy – 7/10

The Doctor and company arrive in the Wild West, to find a cyborg from the future haunting the townsfolk, threatening to kill whoever tries to escape the town, as well as a *doctor* of their own, who is hiding a terrible secret.

They discover this doctor, Jek, is an alien scientist (a 'Kahler'), who has been experimenting on his own people in order to create a race of cyborgs that will wipe out the people his race are at war with back home. The terrible experiments have cost the lives of many Kahler, and the cyborg has tracked him down through time and space to wreak his revenge; leaving the townsfolk (and the Doctor and companions) in the crossfire.

To the townsfolk, Jex has been a Godsend, helping them cure the town of cholera and fitting the town with electricity some ten years before it is to be used. But to the Doctor and the cyborg, he is a monster, a murderer of his own people.

In the end, Jek sees that the only way to save the townsfolk and atone for his sins is to blow himself up in his spaceship. The cyborg, realising the extent of which he had potentially harmed the people of the town in his bloodlust for Jek, decides to stay and eternally protect the town as their guardian in recompense. I'm not a huge fan of the Western as a genre, and the only time I can think of that the show has visited this era before this was in the terrible 'Gunslingers' serial from the Hartnell days (as much as I love the Hartnell, it wasn't one of his finest moments!), so my hopes weren't high. Added to this were two mediocre episodes that preceded this one. O.K, Asylum was interesting, but it hadn't really blown me away as I had expected it to. My concerns were unfounded however as this is a lot more cohesive and focused story than the previous two serials, with a straightforward plot which asks strong moral questions, following the tradition of the show in portraying the complex nature of 'good' and 'evil,' 'right' and 'wrong.'

Steven Moffat expressed his wish for series 7 to move away from the 'story arcs' that characterised series 1-6, to create separate, small 'films' in their own right.

Whilst this has sometimes left me as a viewer feeling that too much has been forced into the 45 minute episode format, the writer manages to accomplish this here in this 'Cowboys and Aliens meets the Terminator' mini-film; creating something that is highly watchable, and good family fun.

The scenery and cinematography is lavish and very filmic – like the previous two episodes, and although I couldn't stop thinking of Kryten in the Red Dwarf episode 'Gunmen of the Apocalypse' whenever I saw the cyborg, in the end this didn't detract from what was a nice one-off character. The dialogue and direction were also very good. This isn't yet up there with the peaks of the last two seasons, but it was much more enjoyable and effective than the last two serials and well worth a watch.

The Power Of Three – 7/10

The Shakri are an alien race who were fabled by the Time Lords to be the 'pest-controllers' of the universe; wiping out whole races that they saw as 'contagions.' The Doctor discovers the fairy tale is anything but; as the Shakri start attacking the Earth. They know the future;

of humanity's colonisation of the stars, and go back to destroy what they see as our race's 'infecting' of the universe before it has chance to start.

We only find this out at the end of the serial, after a long drawn out plot involving mysterious cubes. These cubes land on Earth and wait many months to be thought of as harmless and become collected in people's homes. This then gives them time to collect the data they need from their human 'owners' to find their weaknesses and plot their demise.

The mystery of the cubes also gives us time to view the Doctor's attempts at patiently living in Amy and Rory's 'normal' life. This puts a nice twist on the usual run of things (the companions usually have to leave *their* lives behind to follow the Doctor, now it's his turn!). Again, this 'alien in the real world' idea had more of a comic ('The Lodger') than heart-warming ('Human Nature') feel. There are lots of 'trendy' references thrown in (Nintendo Wii, Twitter and so on), which will no doubt make this episode seem as dated as the Big Brother episode of Doctor #9 (Bad Wolf). But it's a nice change to see the Ponds in their 'natural habitat;' as well as seeing the return of the wonderful Mark Williams playing Rory's Dad (probably my favourite character of the series so far, who thankfully gets more of an appearance here than in Dinosaurs in Space). The Ponds seem to have taken more of a backseat over the last few episodes, maybe as a way to emphasise their last serials, and this is a sweet way to reconnect us with their lives both with, and without the Doctor.

The Shakri themselves are such a mysterious and terrifying enemy, that their final unveiling in the last 5 or so minutes of the episode seemed very rushed and unsatisfying.

Along with a great (if fleeting) new enemy, there are some nice 'classic show' references in this episode

– such as a name check for the Zygons and, most importantly, the Brigadier's daughter (a suitably posh, tough cookie like her dad) Kate Stewart making her first appearance as U.N.I.T's representative.

Although this is a far better written episode than Dinosaurs in Space, it did have the same *thrown together* feeling to me...loads of great elements, forced quickly together into 45 minutes. The Shakri, the cubes, the Doctor getting used to 'normal life' and meeting the Brigadier's daughter – all of these things would've made for great episodes...or at least a combined 2-4 parter.

The Angels Take Manhattan – 6/10

The Doctor, Amy and Rory arrive in 1930's New York to find that the Weeping Angels are back, and have inhabited statues all over the iconic city (including the Statue of Liberty herself!). Using clues left in a book written by River Song, they are able to track down the angels and use various time manipulations to see them off. Fans of 'Blink,' will remember that the Angels 'grab' people out of time and throw them back into history; feeding off the 'time energy' created. As the team see Rory as an old man on his deathbed, they realise that the angels must have gotten to him. 'Young' Amy and Rory decide that the only way to stop the Angels is to commit suicide by jumping to their deaths – thus creating a paradox (Rory cannot die old if he dies young?). But they end up being taken by a surviving angel anyway...thus creating a fixed point in time that the Doctor cannot reach them from.

Understand all that? Well you're a better person than me!

What should've been an emotionally charged episode felt like a mess again, and I admit I was left numb by it. Please don't get me wrong – I like Amy and Rory, a lot. The chemistry Doctor #11 has with both of these companions was one of the best of the 'relaunched' series so far, and all three of them are superb actors. When Matt Smith cries at their demise, you can believe his tears are real; such was their connection on and off the screen. But something about this serial just didn't work for me. I know it should; I know that most Who fans will be crying into their fish fingers and custard...but for some reason it left me cold. I've tried to work out why this would be. And once again, a list came to the rescue(!).

1.   **Over-Hype** – Back when I started the process of writing this book, as huge a fan as I was of the show, I never would've considered scouring various groups on Facebook or Twitter to see what was going to happen. Fast forward a few years and there is very little to be surprised about. Almost every big movement in the show is leaked, and then
scrutinised by the 'fan community.' In the 'Asylum of the Daleks' review for example, I slated fans for being so mean to the next companion without ever seeing her in the show...and this was months prior to that episode. So we've known for quite some time that Amy and Rory were going to leave; we just never knew when and how. All the surprise was taken out of the event, and the event became much more predictable and far less shocking.

2.   **Moffat** – Again, please don't get me wrong – Moffat is one of the finest writers to have *ever* worked on the show, and his episodes often rank amongst my favourite of the 'new' show. However, he seems almost obsessed with taking the idea of the Doctor's ability to change time to its most extreme; chopping and changing the story outcomes and sometimes leaving me (as the viewer) not only confused, but sometimes thoroughly dissatisfied as a result. It's almost like 'cry wolf' - he kills off his characters and brings them back together through 'time
manipulation' so often, that you're not sure when to save the tears and when to shed them. In this episode

alone, Rory dies three times...THREE times!! The poor guy has already died so many times over the last couple of series that we're left wondering whether this is just another clever plot twist, or if we're finally able to grieve for the poor guy. Amy too, has undergone many life-times, such as the Girl Who Waited, 'pre' and 'post' Big Bang Amy etc...that I was left a bit emotionally lacking by the time she finally left for 'real.'

3.   **Hindsight** – Perhaps it's yet to sink in? I still find it hard to think of Doctor #11 without the 'other two;' *so* important was the part they played through most of the last two series.

4.   **'Mini Films'** – As I've discussed, Moffat wanted each series 7 episode to feel like 'mini films;' and he has achieved this beautifully. Each of the episodes feels lavish, and the cinematography is breath-taking. And this episode is no exception; a gorgeous love letter to a beautiful city. But there's

something about this first half of the series that just doesn't 'feel' like 'Who' to me.

Whatever the reason was, I didn't feel half the emotional impact from this farewell as I did from Rose being left in the parallel universe or, going back further, the Doctor leaving Sarah Jane at the end of Hand of Fear. I'm hoping, in time, and with repeat viewings, I will, because the feedback from this episode has mostly been in contrast to mine. I'm glad of this, because I really feel the Ponds deserve a good send off.

Specials

Children In Need Special – The

Great Detective – 8/10

Serving as a prequel/teaser for the Christmas Special, this 5 minute 'mini-episode' finds a strange, self-made 'detective agency' of benign reprobates (a human, a Sontaran and a Silurian; all making a return from 'A Good Man Goes to War') trying to persuade a world- weary Doctor to join them in their investigations in Victorian London.

It's a strange premise, but a funny and intriguing one that really makes you want to watch more. Also interesting is the Doctor's attitude in this short episode. Gone is the usual lust for adventure. The Doctor is once again showing his much broodier self; proclaiming himself as 'retired,' and telling the 'team' to leave him alone. It seems the events of the last serial have really left the poor old Doctor feeling more isolated and lonely than ever. Whilst sad, it's nice to see his character react in this more sombre way. I can't wait to see the Christmas special now!

Christmas Special – The Snowmen – 8/10

The Great Intelligence returns (see the 2nd Doctor stories 'The Abominable Snowmen' and 'Web of Fear') for the *first* time – come on, this is Doctor Who, you must be used to this by now! They are a parasitic race that reflect the mental energy of whomever or whatever they come into contact with. Latching onto a young, well-to-do but bitter boy in Victorian London, they manifest his evil desires, creating terrible forms in the snow – killer snowmen!

The power of the Intelligence grows as the boy does. Now Doctor Simeon (played by the excellent Richard E Grant), the grown boy has become an even more twisted man. Clara, a local young barmaid (who bears a striking resemblance to Oswin from Asylum of the Daleks) becomes intrigued by the spooky goings on, and disguises herself as the Governess of the house to delve into the mystery further.

And she finds that she is not the only one. Enter a rag-tag detective agency, made up of the Lady Vastra (Silurian), Jenny (Human) and Strax (Sontaran). Allies of the Doctor since 'A Good Man Goes to War,' they now help look into odd goings on that are happening on his behalf. For the Doctor; finally weary of all the losses he has suffered has gone into retirement...tired of adventuring after losing his last companions Amy and Rory. After Clara meets the 'magical man in a box' however, she won't take no for an answer, and follows him incessantly until he realises she is the new companion he has been subconsciously looking for. It is seemingly in vain though, as the Great Intelligence creates an Ice Monster that attacks her, making her plummet from the T.A.R.D.I.S to her tragic death.

In a final twist we find that Clara/Oswin is an 'impossible' person; a woman who is seemingly alive in many different times and places, and dying again and again, only to reappear in another time and space. It is a strange phenomenon that the Doctor cannot resist investigating.

From the start, this serial is full of some great Christmas treats. The special starts with awesome new titles and theme tune; including The Doctor's face on the credits for the first time since Sylvester McCoy! For older fans there are Silurians, Sontarans and The Great Intelligence. For younger fans there are creepy snowmen and a whimsical Doctor. And added to this is a space-age new T.A.R.D.I.S interior and a fun new companion. I'm still not entirely sure about Clara, who still seems far too smug for my liking; but she certainly makes a great impression on the show again.

Although this probably won't feel quite as 'Christmassy' as 'A Christmas Carol,' I thought it was a really engaging serial that has a lot to make it remarkable. Matt Smith is at his spell-binding, fairy-tale best once again. I can't think of a Doctor more fitting to the Victorian surroundings or the crooked top hat and long coat he wears...certainly not since the great Troughton that this serial tips its hat at.

It's great to see a return to the 'classic' feel of the show; a feeling which had seemed lacking in the seventh series so far. Overall this is a captivating Christmas Special that shows an equal debt to its past and a new lease of life for its future.

Series 7, Part 2 Prequel – 7/10

A nice scene in which a young girl meets the Doctor and asks him questions. A young girl who turns out to be Clara Oswin #3 as a child. It appears that wherever the Doctor goes, this strange 'impossible companion' follows him.

This acts as a reminder of the story arc that was started in Asylum of the Daleks and which continued in the Christmas Special. It's also a reminder of the 'Raggedy Doctor' that Matt Smith has made us love. He has lost none of the timeless Brothers Grimm style that makes him so fun to watch for kids and older fans of the show alike.

SERIES 7 (SEASON 33) (CONTINUED)

The Bells Of St. John – 7/10

The Great Intelligence is back, and using Wifi to 'upload people's souls' to the 'cloud.' The Doctor meets the grown up Clara Oswin #3 after being lulled back from another self-enforced exile as a 13th Century monk, and together they must take on the puppets of the Great Intelligence and the 'Spoonhead' robot 'servers' that are trapping people inside the Internet(!).

Steven Moffat is in the writer's chair again, and plays to one of his main strengths – making us afraid of the 'everyday.' This time around it is society's reliance on social media and the Internet that is used as it's enemy, and this is done with a great deal of aplomb...though perhaps not in the same groundbreaking way as the Weeping Angels made us all scared of statues, or the Vashta Nerada our shadows.

The human 'puppets' of the Great Intelligence were a nice mixture of incompetent and sinister; and Celia Diana Savile Imrie (Acorn Antiques, Dinner Ladies etc..) is great as the next in a long line of evil middle-class, middle-aged women that modern Who does so well.
Her character in particular shows even more

dimensions after the tragic twist at the end.

The show continues from the Christmas special in feeling more 'kid-centred,' and this is nice to see after some of the over-reaching epics of the 6th and first half of the 7th series. Younger kids will particularly love the 'anti-gravity motorbike,' and its little touches like this that are *so* 'Who' (flying car Pertwee fans?). Smith is still at his most intriguing; and it's fair to say he has returned the character of the Doctor to more of an alien quality which it needed. I've still yet to warm to Clara as a companion, but I found her less annoying in this episode. I'm still loving the other changes, such as the new titles and theme, the Doctor's new outfit and T.A.R.D.I.S interior.

This is unlikely to be in any fan's top ten, but it's a fun romp with some compelling and relevant ideas.

The Rings Of Akhaten – 7/10

The Doctor meets up with Clara #3 and takes her on their first proper 'trip;' into deep space. They journey to Akhaten; the fabled birthplace of the universe. Here they mingle with a myriad of different aliens as they wait for the main event – the annual 'lullaby' that is sung by one chosen 'Queen of Years;' to abate a sleeping 'God' that feeds on the 'souls/life stories' of the planet's inhabitants.

The Doctor and Clara have arrived just in time...as the slumbering God is awaking...and is ready to feast! And Clara meets the nervous young girl who is to be this year's sacrificial lamb. The Doctor tries to sacrifice himself in the place of the young girl; feeding the hundreds of experiences he has had as succour to the insatiable hunger for 'tales' the God needs. But in the end, it is Clara's parents' leaf, symbolic of the love they shared and the experiences that they never got to have when their lives were cut short, that finishes off the ravenous beast.

Once again there is a great deal of both ingenuity and

feeling in this episode. Not since 'The End of the World' (9th Doctor) has such a fantastic array of weird and wonderful aliens been seen. The music is also beautiful, as are the scenery and back-drops. The young girl's predicament brings out the best in Clara (who is more likeable here) and Smith gives one of his most powerhouse speeches (arguably the best since the Pandorica Opens) in his protestation to the 'God'/beast.

This episode seems to have polarised fans, with some loving and some loathing it. Whilst it is quite a sombre serial, it is balanced well by some light-hearted quips from the Doctor and his new companion, and personally, I thought it looked great and had some really thoughtful dialogue. It veers towards over- sentimentality at times (Clara's leaf is said to be 'the most important in the entire universe' because it brought her parents together which is rather over-
egging the pudding I would say!) but still mostly hits its emotional mark. I doubt I will return to this one often, but it is certainly one of the most remarkable of the seventh series so far.

Cold War – 8/10

The Doctor and Clara #3 turn up on a Russian submarine in 1983. Not only does this sub have its finger on the button for a potential World War III, but something even more deadly lurking in its depths...a rapidly thawing Ice Warrior!

It's not long before the Ice Warrior is loose on the ship. Considering it a monster, the crew react to him in a hostile way; triggering its laws of combat (if one is threatened, the whole race is threatened). It declares itself enemy to the entire human race! And this isn't just any Ice Warrior...it is one of the most revered amongst all war generals. We've picked the wrong asthmatic space lizard to mess with this time!

Although it is immensely exciting to see the return of the Ice Warriors for the first time in nearly 40 years, the plot is a well trod one with little surprises – a monster is loose in a contained environment (in this case a submarine), and the crew are picked off one by one. A
kind of 'Alien' meets 'Hunt for Red October.' That said, this simpler story works extremely well. There might not have been the same twists and turns as we've come to expect from 'NuWho,' but in some ways this adds to the timeless charm of the serial. The tension was palpable and consistent throughout, and the Ice Warrior himself was the most sinister I've seen since 'Seeds of Death (Troughton).'

Clara #3 also continued to grow on me in this episode. The cockiness of Oswin/Clara #1 (Asylum of the Daleks) seems to have mellowed, and she seems much more amiable here as she tries to find her feet and test whether she has what it takes to be a companion to the Doctor.

The return of a truly classic Doctor Who 'monster' is done with panache in this unique suspense that will be enjoyed by new and old fans alike.

Hide – 7/10

A psychic/empath and an old war hero are hunting down ghosts in a grand old house in 1974. The psychic feels a strong connection to the 'witch of the well;' a ghost that has been seen for centuries in this one location.

It turns out that the screaming apparition is actually a girl, trapped in a 'pocket universe' and communicating over the centuries (which are only a matter of minutes to her in the different time constraints of her reality). She is on the run from a 'monster' and is crying out for help. The psychic is a 'lantern' between the two universes and hears this cry.

The Doctor uses a blue crystal from Metabelis III (Jon Pertwee serials The Green Death and Planet of Spiders) to amplify the connection and transport him to the pocket universe to save the girl and stop the monster. In the end it turns out the monster is just a lost Romeo; on the lookout for his mate who has been trapped in our world.

Jessica Raine from 'Call the Midwife' plays the psychic in a very sweet way. She will return as the 1st Doctor's companion Barbara for the 50th anniversary docu-drama about the origins of the show, and it's nice to get a preview of her in the Who-world.

The Doctor and Clara's relationship continues to improve. It has progressed from a rather irritating banter of 'one-upmanship' into something much more like *childhood pals; off* to solve a mystery of ghosts and ghouls. Their friendship isn't without its troubles though. The psychic warns Clara that she sees a 'sliver of ice' in his heart/s, and Clara sees this for herself when the Doctor transports them from the beginning to the end of the Earth with seeming disregard about the lives of its inhabitants.

The show returns to the children's serial feel of the 1960's show here, and the mixture of haunted house and science fiction is timeless (if a bit slow). The episode also looks great, with some gorgeous locations (Such as Tyntesfield House near Bristol). There are a few too many twists in the narrative; some of which felt a little contrived and unnecessary. But overall this is a nice mini-story.

Journey To The Centre Of The T.a.r.d.i.s – 5/10

After the Doctor takes the safety settings off the T.A.R.D.I.S in order to let Clara have a go at 'steering,' it is left vulnerable to being stolen by a deep space salvage ship.

This 'abduction' damages the T.A.R.D.I.S severely; leading to all sorts of problems. Time starts to 'leak' inside the Doctor's ship, effectively trapping Clara inside a different environment within. The Doctor forcibly enlists the crew of the salvage ship to rescue Clara from an ever-changing T.A.R.D.I.S interior (which is adapting to fool those it perceives as a threat to it). Oh, and added to that are 'zombie' Clara's that are coming out of the 'eye of harmony' that dwells at the centre of the T.A.R.D.I.S herself.

On paper, this serial is an exciting prospect. I've always loved the potential of the T.A.R.D.I.S to be a whole world of adventure and secrets within itself. The huge scale of a ship that is 'bigger on the inside' means that there are always more mysterious things to discover.
Whilst there are some fun rooms here and there (a library, the old swimming pool, an observatory); nothing really leaves you awe-inspired, and although I do still love the revamped interiors; the overall look isn't too dissimilar to other science-fiction sets such as the Alien films or Star Trek and some of the unique charm is lost.

The supporting cast are forgettable, and unlike other 'bottle' T.A.R.D.I.S stories, such as 'Edge of Destruction;' the characters aren't pushed to new limits by the impending destruction of the ship.

There are echoes of the T.A.R.D.I.S's past, as time begins to leak. You can hear Doctor #9's (Eccleston) voice at one point, which is a nice touch...although it would've been nicer for there to be older clips also included; especially with the 50th anniversary looming. I also couldn't understand how everyone could look into the eye of harmony and be unaffected; when it had such catastrophic effects on Rose?

Anyway...this is not a terrible serial by any means. It's a fun little series filler; with the distinct feeling of wasted potential.

The Crimson Horror – 2/10

A crazy old Victorian lady (played by the legendary Diana Rigg) has discovered a prehistoric parasite from the days of the Silurians, and is aiding it in its plan to lull Northerners into a factory where they are to be made into red goo(!).

The detective team from 'The Snowmen' Christmas special (Silurian Lady Vastra, Strax the Sontaran and the human Jenny) go to investigate, and discover that the Doctor has already been converted. They must restore him, and get to the bottom of the mysterious petrified workforce of the factory before it's too late.

Although the detective agency are fun, and funny to watch, we've had a bit too much of them recently, and it seems far too quick to bring them back again.

Whilst It's nice to see the wonderful Diana Rigg and her real life daughter (the equally talented Rachel Stirling), their characters aren't 'fleshed out' enough to hold together possibly the weakest serial of the series so far.
The plot, the humour and the suspense all fall flat. Worth skipping...bring on the Cybermen!!

Nightmare In Silver – 7/10

The young kids that Clara looks after have found out about her secret travels with the Doctor, and 'blackmail' her into taking them on an adventure. The Doctor takes them all on a 'day out' to the 'greatest theme-park in the galaxy.' But the theme-park has seen better days, and is now closed; hiding a terrible secret in its disused grounds.

The planet was once the scene of bitter wars between humanity and the Cybermen. But it's now 100 years since the Cybermen's whole system was destroyed. And unknown to everyone the tin horrors have lain in wait; constructing a new and updated race of unbeatable warriors that are getting ready to wreak their revenge.

The Cybermen start to convert the planet's inhabitants, including the Doctor himself; who must take on the 'Cyber Planner' for control of his mind in a fatal game of chess.

My excitement was high for this serial. The return of the 'Mondas/Telos' Cybermen, combined with one of the most celebrated fantasy writers to work on the show (Neil Gaiman) meant that the credentials were impressive. But whilst Gaiman's last story (The Doctor's Wife) was easily one of the most unique and memorable of series 6, this episode felt a little disjointed and strange.

The human characters are pretty unremarkable (apart from the wonderful Warwick Davies who plays the reluctant Emperor of the planet). The kids are brattish and annoying. The main characters get a lot more to do however. Matt Smith gets to play both the 'good guy' (the Doctor) and the 'bad guy' (the 'Cyber Planner') and does this with a great deal of camp style. Clara too has more of a role in this episode; leading the resistance against the Cybermen whilst the Doctor battles to save his own soul.

To be honest I love all the different incarnations of the Cybermen, and the new ones look amazing, as do the tiny 'Cybermites' they use to convert their victims. As much as I love the 'Cybus' Cybermen, It's nice to see a return to more of a '60's look; with a slimmed down and more 'human' looking design. They have an eeriness that all Cybermen should have, and there are a few scenes where they are genuinely scary; particularly one in which they advance towards Clara and company.

However, they don't seem to be in enough of the scenes, and the plot is a weird and quirky mixture of story ingredients that don't always sit well together. I think I need to see it a few more times to really appreciate what is once again quite a unique Gaiman vision. It's a lot of fun, with some seriously cool Cybermen, but it didn't quite live up to the amount I'd hyped it in my head.

She Said, He Said (Serial Prequel) – 5/10

We see Clara and the Doctor, both talking to a catatonic version of the other about the mysteries that they are trying to find out. None of this makes much sense, but hopefully it will after next week's episode!

The Name Of The Doctor – 10/10

The Great Intelligence is back; kidnapping Lady Vastra and company in a ploy to lull the Doctor to the one place no Time Lord should ever go...the end of their own time line...their grave. The Doctor knows that should he journey to his own tomb, it will have catastrophic effects on the space-time-continuum. But he also is in debt to the team for their care during his 'lost days' of self-imposed 'retirement' before the events of the Snowmen, and so he goes after them.

The Great Intelligence captures them all on the planet of Trenzalore, where the future Doctor resides in his tomb (the dying T.A.R.D.I.S). He blackmails the Doctor for his greatest secret ('his real name'), which will open the tomb and allow him to steal and alter the Doctor's 'time stream.'

In the end, it is not the Doctor, but a projection of his old wife (River Song; returning here for the first time since The Angels Take Manhattan) that utters the fatal name (unheard to us) and allows the Great Intelligence to enter...and for everyone to live.

The Doctor's aforementioned 'time stream' is housed inside...a collection and portal into all of the Doctor's experiences; combined in a beautiful light within the heart of the T.A.R.D.I.S. The Great Intelligence enacts his plan to enter into the stream...which will ultimately 'kill' him, but scatter him into thousands of constituent pieces; that can then alter each of the Doctor's days; denying him each past victory and causing him pain at every turn.
Clara jumps into the stream after the Great Intelligence...sacrificing herself and fulfilling her destiny (and the story arc started back at the beginning of the series) to become 'the Impossible Girl...' following the Doctor to inconspicuously guide him throughout his many lives and journeys to undo all of the Great Intelligence's wrong doings.

In the final twist, the Doctor commits yet another mortal sin, by jumping into his own time stream to save Clara. He manages to do this...but also runs into an alternative older version of himself (played by none other than John Hurt) as a consequence...one that 'broke a promise (the mystery of which will be revealed in the anniversary special!).'

If this plot seems 'packed tight'...it is. The story moves at a dizzying pace and it's difficult to keep up with all the twists and turns. Unlike some serials however, where this has been confusing and inaccessible; this serial is captivating and spellbinding from the offset.

The scenes right at the beginning (which tie in with those at the end) see Clara travelling through each of the Doctor's times to save or direct them in some way. The production team use special technology to bring back archive footage of the Doctor's from years gone by, to make them appear in the modern show. This is everything a fan of the old show could ever wish for.

Seeing gems such as a colourised image of Hartnell's first steps into the T.A.R.D.I.S made me as giddy as a child on Christmas morning, and they are essential viewing.
The characters all put on sterling performances. The Doctor and Clara are both excellent. The gang of detectives, who I'd previously become tired of in 'The Crimson Horror,' are much more 3-dimensional. The Great Intelligence, taking on the look of Doctor Simeon (Richard E. Grant) from the Snowmen is a great snarling Victorian menace. The 'Whisper Men' he brings with him are also another wonderfully spine-chilling monster to add to the series...mixing the look of the Trickster (the Sarah Jane Adventures) and Jack the Ripper.

The idea of revealing the Doctor's name in this episode was another mischievous ruse by Moffat to get the fans into a fervour about a potentially 'sacred' peace of 'Wholore' being broken. It was all of course a hoax; a trick to get everyone to really pay attention to the end of the series. The name was never audible (only whispered by River Song), and we were comfortably none-the-wiser at the end of the story.

This serial is a fan's dream, wrapped in a non-stop thrill-ride of a plot. The perfect way to end the series; leading us ridiculously excited into the 50th anniversary special!

Specials

Night Of The Doctor (Minisode Prequel) – 10/10

We join the 8th Doctor (Paul McGann) in the midst of the fabled Time War. Such is the damage done to the Time Lords' reputation that a survivor chooses death over rescue when the Doctor tries to save her. The ship crashes on Karn, where the Doctor meets the 'sisterhood' (The Brain of Morbius). They warn him he has but minutes to live, and must choose to be turned (regenerated?) into the 'Warrior Doctor' in order to live; taking a drink from their 'elixir of life.' This turns him into the mysterious John Hurt incarnation we first glimpsed at the end of The Name of the Doctor.

The surprise inclusion of the 8th Doctor (McGann; returning here some 17 years after we last saw him on our screens) seems like a tantalising precursor of more game-changing moments to come next.

The Last Day (Minisode Prequel) – 2/10

A cyborg soldier is put through his paces before the Dalek invasion of Gallifrey. Not half as monumental as Night of the Doctor.

50Th Year Anniversary Special – The Day Of The Doctor – 10/10

Doctors Smith and Tennant meet up with the 'Warrior Doctor' (John Hurt) at a pivotal moment in their combined history – the last day of the Time War between the Time Lords and the Daleks. This is the day when the Doctor will use the ultimate Time Lord weapon ('the Galaxy Eater,' which here takes on the form of Rose Tyler) to wipe out both races, as a last resort to save all of time and space from being destroyed. Along the way they must take on Zygons and aid Elizabeth I and the Brigadier's daughter Kate Stewart; to find a way to right the wrongs of the past.

Moffat had a gargantuan task in penning such an important stage of Doctor Who history, and although this is another 'pick n' mix' of stories shoe-horned together, it is easily the most effective anniversary episode yet, and reaches the perfect level of both entertainment and celebration. This special is a real spectacle and doesn't disappoint. There are treats galore; from the triumphant return of Tennant to the breath taking battles of the Time War; from the gloriously creepy Zygons to the surprise inclusion of Tom Baker and even a split second view of doctor-to-be Peter Capaldi at the end. Hurt is fabulous as the 'War Doctor;' bringing his own brand of both gravitas and humour which places him highly amongst the other incarnations, even in this short stint. It would appear he is one of the 'real' Doctors after all, and not an 'alternative' like the Valeyard or Dream Lord. This confuses things slightly; as it makes him the 'real' 9th; which in turn shifts Eccleston to 10th, Tennant to 11th, Smith to 12th and Capaldi to 13th (potentially the 'last' Doctor). For the sake of continuity and sanity, this book with continue to refer to each as they were; but it will be interesting to see where this shift next takes the story of our main man.

Returning to this story however - it is difficult to imagine how this celebration of the last 50 years could have had more scope and colour, and this serial shows a real labour of love by Moffat for the programme.

Happy birthday to a great British institution which 'all started as a mild curiosity in the junkyard and turned out to be quite an adventure.'

Christmas Special – The Time Of The Doctor – 6/10

The Doctor is drawn to Trenzalore once more (his final resting place according to 'The Name of the Doctor') by a military religious sect who are trying to control the hordes amassing around the planet. They have all been attracted to one thing...an ominous signal which transpires to have come from the Doctor's people the Time Lords. They are trying to come through from distant reality into ours via scar-tissue created from the 'crack in time'/'universe reboot' from series 5 and need the Doctor's name to do so. The Doctor becomes effectively 'stranded' on the planet, growing old in the small village of 'Christmas,' unable to bring forth the Time Lords for fear of another time war, but also needing to protect the people from his oldest and deadliest enemies. He must wait for his 13th incarnation (as we find out Smith's Doctor to now be) to die of old age. In the end, the Time Lords are uncharacteristically generous in sending life-force through the crack in reality to allow the ailing Doctor to continue past his last body. Enter Peter Capaldi as the new 14th Doctor!

On first viewing, I was very confused and mildly disheartened by this ramshackle swansong for Matt Smith that seemed to once again flit from point to point without a discernible focus. Plot components such as the backdrop of a village that is eternally 'Christmas' were a bit shoe-horned and unnecessary. Other elements such as the hordes of Who villains amassing on a single planet look great on paper, but strangely fell flat in the actual offering. A 'rule' of the show is broken, as the Doctor is given the ability to live beyond his 13 incarnations. Of course, we knew this rule would have to be broken to ensure the future of the show, but again this was rushed and it would've been nicer for such an important shift to be ruminated on further or to more dramatic effect.

It's sad to see Matt Smith go; and he has become one of my favourite Doctors after my initial hesitance. Little touches such as his Doctor seeing first companion Amy in his semi-regenerated daydream are a sweet addition to the end of the episode and remind us just how far Matt's doctor has come in his 3 years since he burst onto our screen in 2010. Whilst he is somehow less convincing as an elderly Doctor than say Tennant was in The Last of the Time Lords, he retains his wonderful fairy-tale characterisation of the Doctor throughout and although this isn't the best of his epic stories, he carries the story well and you are left sobbing at his departure.

Although certainly a fun Christmas special, this felt a lot less momentous when compared with the last couple of superb episodes.

It's exciting to see where the great actor Capaldi takes the Doctor into the beginnings of the next half Century of the show.

THE TWELFTH DOCTOR – PETER CAPALDI (2014-2017)

SERIES 8
(SEASON 34)

An older, more irascible Doctor takes charge of the TARDIS and ponders his new character.

Deep Breath – 7/10

"Who frowned me this face?" (The Doctor, Deep Breath)

We join the regenerated 12th ($14^{th}/1^{st}$) Doctor, as the T.A.R.D.I.S is unceremoniously vomited from a T-Rex's throat...a T-Rex who is idly walking through the Victorian central streets of London!... If regeneration wasn't enough to confuse the new Doctor, this beginning certainly will!

He runs into the 'Paternoster gang' (Madame Vastra, Jenny and Strax), who are looking into the strange goings on. It's all part of a plan by the Clockwork Droids from the SS. Antoinette (see Tennant episode 'Girl in the Fireplace'), whose scheme is to harvest organs in order to reach their goal of turning from robots into humans and reaching their 'promised land(?)' After they kill the poor lost dinosaur, The Doctor, incensed by such the pointless death of a magnificent creature, decides to take up the mystery and put an end to their plot. If only he can stabilise his new form and persuade his companions (primarily Clara) that he is the Doctor they know and love.

After what seems like forever (8 months since we glimpsed Capaldi's first moments in 'the Time of the Doctor') the 12th (14th /1st) Doctor gets his first proper airing in this partly brilliant début. Capaldi does an excellent job of acting out the usual 'post-regenerative confusion' episode that each actor must complete.

Each Doctor's first episode usually fulfils 3 important tasks. It gives the actor a chance to show a range of different acting abilities; as the Doctor flits between different emotions whilst settling into their new mind and character. It also gives us time as an audience (through the initial confusion and distrust that the companion shows) to get used to the idea of a new actor playing our favourite role. And finally, from a narrative point of view; it helps bridge the gap between one incarnation and another. The story usually acts more as a simplistic 'back-drop' to the more important aim of introducing a new Doctor.

Deep Breath manages most of these requisites pretty well. Capaldi manages the 'post-regeneration crazees' well; with some great lines and scenes which he pulls off with aplomb. Jenna-Louise Coleman (Clara) is equally as strong at showing a state of confusion and insecurity as her friend changes face. In fact, she really manages to steal the show in this episode; showing a level of character development and emotional range I can't remember seeing from this character for some time. The third requisite (a straightforward 'back-drop' plot) is less effectively realised however. Usually, the plot of a regeneration story is second place to the regeneration itself. This works really well in first stories like 'Robot' (Tom Baker);

where a straightforward story underpins the more important introduction of a new Doctor. Unfortunately however, Moffat falls back on the Series 7 tactic of cramming elements together into a confusing mix. As I watch and review each story from this era, I always have to write in 'pieces;' which I then assemble into a coherent story structure at the end. I'm not criticising this style as such, as it is always done in a very sophisticated way. But I do worry how inaccessible this can sometimes make these stories; particularly for a casual viewer (something that the prime-time show has always needed, as well as the more regular fans). I also worry that this more complicated and 'haphazard' structuring of different elements runs the risk of losing some of the show's 'kid's serial charm,' that I felt early 'classic' Doctor who (Hartnell and Troughton) and early 'modern' Doctor Who (Eccleston) had.

All this considered, you can certainly see some of the magnetism in Capaldi's Doctor, and for all that 'Deep Breath' is a short introduction to a blossoming new Doctor, he manages to make his portrayal a classic one even on his first outing. The supporting cast also do well. As mentioned, this is one of Clara's most emotionally resonant episodes so far. The Paternoster gang are all in fine form too. As entertaining as they are though, I do think it's time for something new in that area and I think they've been used enough in recent stories.

Visually, the episode looks great; particularly the opening shot of the T-Rex, which is one of the most striking openings to a series yet. The Victorian clockwork robots aren't quite as visually memorable as their 17th Century counterparts in 'The Girl in the Fireplace,' but are just as frightening. The sound of the clockwork inner-workings of the androids is particularly creepy and effective.

There are quite a few fan treats to be had in this first new episode. The aforementioned spectacle of the T-Rex in front of Big Ben will no doubt stay with you for some time. There is another lavish title sequence and theme. And at the very end there is a nice cameo from previous Doctor Matt Smith, who calls up Clara from the past to persuade her to trust the Doctor of his future ('timey-wimey' indeed!).

Overall it's an intriguing but fragmented story with some real high points, a potentially great new Doctor and an improved companion. I'm looking forward to where the series goes next.

Into The Dalek – 8/10

The Doctor saves a young pilot from the attack of a Dalek Mothership. But in doing so he becomes unwittingly embroiled with the space marines and their Dalek prisoner. His interest is further peaked when he discovers this particular Dalek has acquired a moral conscience; talking of a change of 'heart' brought on by observing the 'beauty' of watching a star being 'born.' Now this Dalek sees creation as more powerful than destruction, and the extinction of his fellow Daleks as the only remedy.

The Doctor, perplexed by this strangely uncharacteristic side of a former killing machine, decides to volunteer to be shrunken down (or 'nano scaled') and transported inside the Dalek to find out more. Rather predictably, the Dalek soon recovers from its 'radiation sickness' that has caused the personality change, and returns to its usual deadly self; leaving the assembled team fighting for their lives against evil mechanical Dalek antibodies!

The Doctor attempts to appeal to the 'good Dalek' within, by melding his mind with it and showing it the wonders of the universe he has seen. But that isn't all that Dalek sees; and the inner hatred the Doctor holds for his nemeses only persuades the Dalek to continue its path of destruction.

In a separate story, we return to Coal Hill School; where Clara works as a teacher. A fellow teacher (and former soldier) Danny Pink is clearly interested in her, but is struggling to find the courage to ask her out on a date. If rumours are to be believed, Danny is to be the next member of the T.A.R.D.I.S team, and although we don't really get to know him fully in this short story, he seems an amiable and fun potential companion to the new Doctor.

Meeting his most famous foe is like a rite of passage for each new Doctor and a chance for them to really show their mettle; which Capaldi does with the sort of arresting intensity you would expect.

This 'Fantastic Voyage' style story has been done before in the show (Tom Baker's 'The Invisible Enemy' for example) and it is a really fun idea that kids and grown-ups will both love. The idea of the Doctor exploring the inner-workings of his worst enemy is an exciting twist on their usual meetings and makes this second story stand out.

After the rather complicated and inconsistent feel of the last couple of episodes, it's a relief to see a return to more straightforward, enjoyable episodes like this one. And whilst the last episode was almost like a 'Matt Smith' cast off (with many of the same elements we know from that era), this is the first real glimpse we see of the new Doctor and the 'new show.'

I also really liked the look of the episode and the special effects used, which gave a psychedelic and distinct feel.

There are some nice Doctor/Companion moments, including a heart-to-heart where the Doctor questions his own morality in the face of the Dalek's discovery of the hatred he holds inside. Clara's response of 'you try to be good, and that's the point,' is one of those warm moments and connections between the show's main characters, and shows a new depth to their blossoming friendship. The Doctor does still seem rather mercurial and even callous at this early stage, and this is creating some great interplay and interesting character moments, which are intriguing to watch.

The rest of the cast are effective, but less memorable. And whilst this episode still wasn't quite up to 'classic' status, the ingredients are certainly there for a return to form and for series 8 to really 'take off.'

Robot Of Sherwood - 5/10

The Doctor asks Clara to 'take a punt' on where she'd like to go and who she'd like to meet. She picks, erm...Robin Hood. The Doctor assures her he's a made up legend, but they go anyway.

And this being Doctor Who he turns out to be very much real... or at least a robot approximation of reality.

This supremely daft 'Doctor Who meets Horrible Histories' will no doubt appeal to younger fans of the series and you can't really knock it for that.

A less substantial episode but not without its fun moments.

Listen - 8/10

Clara is back to life, back to reality, on a date with teaching colleague Danny Pink. Predictably her fantastical life with the Doctor interferes and she is pulled into his latest investigation. The Doctor is consumed by the 'monster under the bed' nightmare that seems to affect everyone through time. It would appear this nightmare isn't so make-believe after all!

They decide to go back and see if Clara had the same nightmare, using the telepathic interface in the Tardis console to tap into her personal timeline. She is distracted at the thought of Danny however and they go back to his lonely childhood in a children's home instead. Here they stumble across a very real 'bogeyman.'

There are a few notable firsts here, including the (proper) introduction of Danny, the first use of the telepathic interface and a brief visit to the Doctor's own childhood.

Moffat once again plumbs childhood fears for timeless tales, and Capaldi is perfectly placed to play the M.R James style narrator in this suspenseful episode.

Time Heist - 6/10

The Doctor and Clara (along with an augmented human and a mutant) are pulled out of space and forced to rob an Intergalactic Fort Knox operated by an evil bank manager (played by the wonderful Keeley Hawes) and her telepathic mind melting alien.

Time Heist is an action packed and inventive ensemble adventure, but didn't grab me as much as I thought it would... and I'm not entirely sure why. Sorry, that's not a very good review is it?! It's certainly watchable and there's nothing I can criticise it for. But it still manages to feel a little flat at times.

The Caretaker - 6/10

Clara's personal dating life with Danny Pink and life with the Doctor continue to clash and something has to give. She decides to spend some quality time in the 'normal world...' which as you can imagine in this show lasts about 2 minutes.

Enter the Doctor, investigating strange goings on under the disguise of a caretaker. There is a killer robot on the loose after all.

Capaldi once again plays the role of the alien interloper to the hilt with great comedic effect. But the plot is pretty lightweight and inconsequential, only really functioning as a bottle story to progress the main character's (especially Danny who I really like as the kind of 'non-companion,' superbly acted by Samuel Anderson). For that, and Capaldi's great one liners, it's worth a watch.

Kill The Moon - 1/10

Turns out the moon is an egg which is breaking apart and will destroy the planet...oh and it has killer spiders on it...

Another in a row of fairly lacklustre stories culminates in one of the worst, most stupid Doctor Who stories of all time. Quite the statement, but have you actually watched Kill the Moon? How was this even greenlit?

A friend of mine put this better than I ever could when he changed his status after watching this to 'my science hurts.'

Mummy On The Orient Express - 7/10

Passengers on a spaceship recreation of the Orient Express are being picked off one by one after seeing a hideous 'mummy' figure approaching them that no one else can see.

Those who are left are tasked with solving the mystery before there is no one left to save.

Who returns to the more Hammer Horror territory of Tom Baker's middle era with this fun futuristic take on a supernatural murder mystery.

Meanwhile Clara begins her looooong goodbye, with the first of many aborted swan songs and Celebrity superfan Frank Skinner makes a cameo (and is far less annoying than you'd worry he might be).

Not a spectacular episode, but an entertaining sojourn into classic horror with a Doctor Who twist.

Flatline - 10/10

Going into a Doctor Who episode is always a bit of a gamble (which is half the fun of watching it). One week you might get some of the most groundbreaking science fiction imaginable, the next you could end up with *Kill the Moon*.

Every so often the show transcends the usual boundaries or constraints of family entertainment to create something truly visionary, such as the episode Flatline.

In this hugely inventive premise, the enemy is housed in a different physical dimension. Not a parallel universe, but a literal spatial dimension, 2D to our 3D. The programme uses its own technical parameters (we are watching on a 2 dimensional format after all) to bend and shift our perception in a way only Doctor Who can.

The only thing that slightly marrs it for me is the continuing over-focus on Clara, but this is nitpicking what is an essential episode.

Flatline shows that Doctor Who at its very best can still do something unique and spectacular.

In The Forest Of The Night - 4/10

Clara and Danny are taking their class on a field trip to Trafalgar Square when a forest randomly pops up. It transpires that the whole planet has turned into one large jungle because the trees are trying to save humanity from an oncoming solar flare.

If one kid in the TARDIS (Adric) was annoying, imagine a whole class of them!

In the Forest of the Night is a real 'filler' episode and has nothing really to make it remarkable or particularly poor either. The idea of Earth's trees being our 'shield' to protect us is a really nice one, but the writing isn't fleshed out enough to make it work.

Dark Water/Death In Heaven – 8/10

The series 8 finale opens with heartbreaking tragedy as Danny is killed by a car just after Clara tells him she loves him. This was incredibly shocking at the time, and a real loss to the show as Danny was one of the highlights of the series for me. His 'anti-companion' stance against the Doctor was marvellously and sympathetically played by Samuel Anderson and I wish he'd had longer to continue with the character.

To try and convince the Doctor to change time and save Danny, Clara threatens to throw away the keys to the TARDIS. This leads to an exploration of the 'afterlife' to bring him back. In this climax to the series, we finally meet the mysterious 'Missy' who has been teased in each episode. She turns out to be the reincarnation of the Master, with a diabolical scheme to turn dead minds into Cybermen.

Only Doctor Who would be brave enough to do a story like this. It brings to mind other experimental writing from the show such as The Mind Robber (which saw the Doctor leave reality), Warriors Gate (exploration outside of the universe) or the more recent Flatline (fighting the very dimensions we live in).

'Heaven' is ingeniously written as bureaucratic and mundane; a stopgap for lost souls in a gigantic filing system.

I was unsure about the gender change of the Master at first (little did I know what was around the corner), but Missy, as played by the all-kinds-of-awesome Michelle Gomez is so wonderfully unhinged and theatrical from the outset that you instantly engage with her as the perfect foil for Capaldi's Doctor.

This two part series finale keeps you gripped throughout with many great reveals and surprises. Dark Water/Death in Heaven is a must for anyone cherry picking the episodes.

Specials

Last Christmas - 2/10

Father Christmas inexplicably turns up and the Doctor has to see why. Turns out it's all the work of the 'Dream Crabs.'

Oh dear. I admire Doctor Who for taking risks with its ideas, and the previous story shows how this can really pay off. Here however the far fetched idea to shoehorn Father Christmas into the Christmas special is its downfall. I love Nick Frost but he is miscast, and although the ridiculous premise is fairly well explained, this is a poor special I doubt I'll revisit often.

SERIES 9
(SEASON 35)

The Doctor takes on some of his oldest foes in a series of epic, memorable two parters.

The Magician's Apprentice/The Witches Familiar – 8/10

'Davros made the Daleks, but who made Davros?'

The Doctor finds a child, lost on an alien battlefield and in need of rescue. He is prepared to save him, until he realises the young boy is Davros, creator of the Daleks. He has to make the decision whether to leave Davros behind and thus destroy the universe's greatest evil, but become evil himself in the process.

Fast forward to the other end of Davros' life to find him dying and desperate for the Doctor to meet with him one last time. But there is more than a final goodbye on his maniacal mind.

Missy is back, at her psychotic pantomime best, after evading death at the end of the last series finale. When she and Clara eventually find the Doctor, he is in a strange mood; believing that he too is at the end of his life/s and partying like a teenager until the last moment. This leads to some gloriously silly but memorable scenes of Capaldi, guitar in hand, riding a tank into an arena of new friends. Capaldi started his career as singer and guitarist in the punk band The Dream Boys, along with fellow future celebrity Craig Ferguson (yes, him of The Late, Late Show fame) so it's a fanboy's dream to see him play guitar like this in the show, however ridiculous the scene might be.

The rest of this two parter (a theme for this series) is equally daft, but somehow seems to work, with the balance of some truly poignant scenes between Davros and the Doctor to counterbalance the comedic enforced camaraderie of Missy and Clara.

An exciting and worthy series opener.

Under The Lake/Before The Flood - 8/10

The crew aboard an underwater mining facility are being picked off one by one and turned into creepy, eyeless 'ghosts.' The Doctor must go back in time to take on the mysterious 'Kingfisher' and stop him from making everyone into electromagnetic projections of their former selves.
This is another classic 'base under siege' story, which calls to mind the 2nd Doctor tales and more recently the Tennant masterpiece 'Waters of Mars.' Whilst this double parter isn't on the same level as that story, it is genuinely frightening, with some of the most imposing and memorable monsters in recent memory.

Capaldi is once again on top form, relishing the role and stealing the show in every scene. Clara is pivotal without her usual arrogant leanings and the rest of the crew are all well acted and utilised. It was particularly great to see the way the programme presents its first openly deaf character and signer. The director, writer and of course the wonderful acting of Sophie Stone made the inclusion of the disabled character as 'normal' a part of the drama as it should be, without ever trying to make it stand out as 'different' or 'signalling' in any way.

The exploration of 'meddling' in time is explored well in the second episode, though there is a 'tailing off' in pace and I didn't find the closer as enjoyable as the first.

In conclusion however this is a strong, suspenseful story that is definitely worth a watch.

The Girl Who Lived/The Woman Who Died - 4/10

History meets science fiction as Vikings from the past take on robots from the future and the Doctor must help them out against insurmountable odds. Young Ashildr is caught in the crossfire and dies, yet the Doctor manages to save her with alien technology, rendering her immortal.

In the second episode, the Doctor finds Ashildr many centuries later. Bitter and jaded by living through many lifetimes whilst everyone she cares about die around her, she has teamed up with an evil alien and is making a living through thievery whilst she waits for the Doctor to return.

A nice cameo from Maisie Williams (Game of Thrones) and a few poignant scenes don't make up for a paper thin plot and pantomime humour in the first episode or a fairly forgettable story in the second.

The Zygon Invasion/The Zygon Inversion – 9/10

"When you fire that first shot, no matter how right you feel, you have no idea who's going to die. You don't know who's children are going to scream and burn. How many hearts will be broken! How many lives shattered! How much blood will spill until everybody does what they're always going to have to do from the very beginning -- sit down and talk!" (The Doctor)

Since the events of 'The Day of the Doctor' (the 50th Anniversary Special where the classic Zygons returned), Earth's powers have formed a secret peace treaty allowing 20 million shape shifting but peace loving Zygons to live unknown amongst humans. The Doctor leaves a 'last resort' in the shape of a 'big red button' in an 'Osgood Box' if ever war were declared....

'War were declared' (Futurama reference there for you fellow nerds!). Well, I never saw that happening!

Osgood is captured by a Zygon terrorist faction who want to create a war between humans and Zygons. But how can you stop a race who change into the likeness of anyone they like, making them impossible to detect?

It's nice to see Osgood, one of the best of the Doctor's 'not-quite companions' taking more of a lead role here. The Doctor shows his moral aversion to war and violence in some truly memorable speeches. Capaldi again shows the kind of authority and presence that great writing can give him in one of the most politically resonant and suspenseful stories of recent years.

Sleep No More – 6/10

A rescue team in the 38th Century discovers a space station where capitalism has forced people to condense their sleep from a whole night into a 5 minute burst so they can work more hours. But in doing so, they have allowed the 'Morpheus Sleep Machines' to create monsters from the cells of the humans inside.

Another base under siege in space story, Sleep No More wasn't reviewed kindly at the time, but I enjoyed it more than most. I love the use of 'point of view' filming which gives a refreshingly different narrative style to the episode and throws the viewer straight into the action. The monsters are pretty ridiculous (mutated eye mucus?) the plot often misses its mark and the supporting cast manage to be simultaneously forgettable *and* irritating. But it's an imaginative adventure which is worth a watch.

Face The Raven – 5/10

Rigsy, the lad from Flatline, contacts Clara after a tattoo appears on his neck of a number...that is counting down to his death! The Doctor, Clara and Rigsy must solve the puzzle which includes a hidden London street, an order of aliens (of course) and Ashildr/Me. Any crime within the order is punishable by death by 'the Raven' that follows until it enacts your fatal punishment. Will Rigsy or Clara 'face the raven?'

At the time of the episode, it was uncertain whether Clara had really 'died,' which made this much more powerful than it is in retrospect, when we know she will be fine. Herein lies my main niggle with the Moffat era...his use of the 'tease death.' This is where a character seemingly dies...but then is brought back to life. It works as a tense but satisfying payoff...the first time. But after it is done multiple times with the same person, it has the negative effect of denying the emotional closure I need and leaving me flat when I should feel something. For me, this approach ruined the eventual departure of Rory and Amy and here it ruins Clara's supposed exit. How many exits has she had at this point? A quick google found me a 'top 6 Clara' exits, meaning she has left, only to reappear at least this ridiculous amount of times. How are we supposed to feel when she does finally leave 'for real?' I certainly didn't feel the way I felt I should.

Anyway, the story itself is an interesting examination of determinism and death in a mixture of Edgar Allen Poe and JK Rowling science fiction magical horror. It's a nice introduction to the overarching arc of death and dying that will be used to much more poignant effect in the coming episodes, but pales in comparison as a result.

Heaven Sent/Hell Bent – 8/10

The Doctor relives the same moment over and over again, trapped in his 'confession dial' a castle-like world constructed to imprison him by the Time Lords who are trying to force him to reveal the secret of the mythical 'Hybrid.' He must find a way to break the cycle and take on his captors.

Not since 'Bad Wolf/Parting of the Ways' has a finale showed the extremes of the very best and very worst of the show running so closely to each other. In the former example, the penultimate episode (Bad Wolf) was one of Eccleston's worst, followed by one of (if not THE) best of his tenure (Parting of the Ways). In Heaven Sent/Hell Bent the extremes are reversed, with Heaven Sent representing Capaldi's crowning dramatic moment in an outstanding piece of television, followed by arguably his most maligned episode Hell Bent.

So I must first review them in isolation. Every so often the Twelve Doctor's inconsistent era produces something uniquely special. Flatline showed the Doctor taking on the very dimensional medium that the programme exists in, 2D. For Heaven Sent, we are once again treated to a different style than we are used to; a 45 minute monologue carried solely by the main character. In the wrong hands, this could've felt stifled and dull, but through good storytelling and the powerful presence that Capaldi commands, Heaven Sent is truly captivating.

We are then into the finale, Hell Bent. Whilst it's not half as bad as I remember from the first viewing, it is still a fairly flawed episode which suffers from comparison with what has just been.

Firstly, there are several throwaway lines which come across as cheesy and not up to the same level of writing we're used to ('all stories are true,' erm, can you expand on that Doctor?) and throwaway moments, such as the Doctor killing another Time Lord in order to escape. This complete trashing of everything the Doctor stands for, which is used only as a way to introduce the idea that a Time Lord can change sex upon regeneration makes a mockery both of the lineage of the show and of the sombreness of regeneration itself. To be honest, this scene was unforgivable. So too was the end scene, where we see Clara (who is saved from death once again but caught in the last second of her life for eternity) and Me/Asildr fly off in their own TARDIS. Ok, so Clara can pilot a TARDIS now too?!

And finally, we have the 'Hybrid' which has been a central story arc for the series. At first this is explained as a combination of a Dalek and Time Lord that scared the Doctor so much as a kid that he ran away (again, completely screwing up the canon for little to no good reason), then it is Me/Asildr (who was saved by combining her dna with that of the Mire making her a hybrid), and then finally, it's apparently the representation of the close bond between Clara and the Doctor? I don't know, I really didn't get it and it really wasn't explained very well; leaving it as a wasted opportunity rather than any kind of satisfactory conclusion.

There were some great moments on Gallifrey and some nice interactions between the Doctor and his people. But for a finale, and in comparison to its superb predecessor it was a complete mess.

Specials

Christmas Special: The Husbands Of River Song – 5/10

River Song enlists the help of who she believes to be the 'greatest surgeon in the galaxy' to save her husband King Hydroflax. She doesn't realise the person she enlists is the Doctor (unaware of the 'extra regenerations' gifted by the Time Lords).

At this point in their characteristically out of sync timelines, River is an archaeologist, who has married a robot Greg Davies (the famous comedian and Taskmaster presenter) in order to steal a diamond artefact lodged in his brain....yes really.

My continuing issues with River Song remain. Her overtly sexist 'jokes' such as 'stop thinking will you, you're a man, it looks weird' are grating (can you imagine the reaction if that 'joke' was reversed?). However, for all I find this need to belittle the Doctor annoying, I can't help but love Alex Kingston herself and this ridiculous and overly comical special is saved by the touching chemistry her and Peter share. It's a shame they didn't share more screen time together.

As a side note, we also meet our next companion, Nardole (played by another famous comedian Mat Lucas), who adds little in his first appearance, but will grow to become a sweet and memorable companion over the following series.

Christmas Special: The Return Of Doctor Mysterio – 2/10

The Doctor inadvertently turns a young boy into a superhero using a space gem.

12 months without Doctor Who and the return of probably my favourite of the 'modern Doctors' means I should've been really looking forward to this special. Yet the premise of 'Doctor Who meets Marvel' created the fear of a return to the dismal self-parodying early days of McCoy. These fears weren't unjustified, and 'The Return of Doctor Mysterio' is easily the daftest and cringiest special for some time. It's not without its highlights though. Capaldi is at his fairy-tale best in the first few scenes with the young Grant (who will become the superhero). It's also impressive that the show continues to experiment with its format and in crossing genres, and it is a fun and light-hearted break from the 'Christmas Special' norm.

But in trying to please two fanbases, it manages to please neither. I tend to find that when Who (a quintessentially British franchise) tries to 'go American' it can come across as tacky and false and lose a lot of its charm.

At this point it seems that Who is struggling to find its tone or its place; using comedians and 'trendy' references in an attempt to grab viewers, but instead borrowing the very worst of the late 80's decline.

SERIES 10
(SEASON 36)

After some epic story arcs, the show makes a conscious effort at returning to more of a 'serial of the week' style. The Doctor is tasked with housing an 'ancient evil' so is stranded on Earth and becomes a professor. His student Bill starts to suspect her teacher of being more than what he seems.

The Pilot – 7/10

Bill has some serious concerns about the strange new university lecturer, who refers to himself as 'The Doctor.' These concerns will have to wait however as she will need his help to solve the mystery of her strange new crush.

I automatically love Bill. She manages to equal the Doctor in both inquisitiveness and drive, whilst never belittling or trying to 'one-up' him. Their relationship is so natural; the 'mysterious space wizard' and the curious student.

As Series 10 begins, you can tell the showrunners have made a conscious effort to make a fresh new start for the show (spot the double-meaning of the title). Gone are the convoluted over-complicated story arcs and arrogant companions trying to ape the main character constantly. We're back to a more serialised, weekly instalments feel, which is refreshing and much more engaging.

The story in this first instalment takes second place to the introduction of Bill and the Doctor's new friendship and is perhaps understandably less remarkable as a result. But come on, in which other programme would you get a man-eating puddle? You've gotta love this show!

Smile – 6/10

The Doctor and Bill travel to a planet in the far future where 'emoji robots' enforce happiness at all costs. To frown is to die.

Bill's enthusiasm for her first adventure in time and space is infectious, reminding us why we love the show as we travel with her. Of course, the story is highly reminiscent of the McCoy story 'The Happiness Patrol' in which a happy attitude is enforced and sadness is fatal. Smile repeats the idea with much more sheen and higher production values, but is perhaps less memorable. Not a stand out episode by any means, but certainly watchable.

Thin Ice – 8/10

In Victorian London a monster is pulling people through the ice to their deaths.

Whilst the underlying story isn't a particularly momentous one, this is a mature and well written character piece which serves in putting the chemistry of Doctor and companion to the test under the most morally challenging of circumstances. To this end, both Peter Capaldi and Pearl Mackie (Bill) are excellent in conveying a thought provoking and compelling drama.

The topic of historic racism is particularly well written and challenged, as well as the issues of the Victorian class system and poverty. The show's original remit of educating and entertaining through the combination of history and science fiction is perfectly balanced through stellar acting and writing.

Knock Knock – 6/10

Bill moves into a shared student house with her uni friends. But this being Doctor Who, nothing is simple, and her housemates are systematically picked off by the supernatural powers at work in the walls.

Knock Knock is a nice bit of filler, without perhaps the appeal of other 'the Doctor is brought into the human day to day experience' stories like 'The Lodger.'

It's always great to see David Suchet (here playing the creepy landlord) but the rest of the supporting cast are more prosaic.

Oxygen – 9/10

On a space station in the future someone has hacked into the crew's spacesuits and ordered them to kill their wearers. Oxygen must be paid for, and it seems human life has become unprofitable.

This scathing commentary on capitalism's inhuman nature of 'money before man' is presented in the most genuinely frightening and claustrophobic episode I've seen for some time. Gripping, 'watch behind the sofa' stuff.

'The Monks Trilogy' - Extremis/The Pyramid At The End Of The World/ The Lie Of The Land – 9/10

The Veritas is a book kept at the Vatican for safety; because anyone who reads it will die by their own hand.
Missy is also back (in flashback...or is it flashforward...'timey wimey' and all that!), having been locked away and guarded by the Doctor (but only now revealed to be the prisoner in the vault that has been teased over the series so far).

It turns out that the Veritas tells of a demon who has created a simulation planet in order to practise their conquering skills, full of shadow people who think they're real. A powerful alien race has taken this influence to create a 'practise Earth' with all of its history reverted to a 'computer game' to give them a trial run at ruling the planet. For those simulants who find out the truth, it's too much to bear and they are 'deleting themselves from the game.'

As we go into the next episode, a 5,000 year old pyramid has suddenly 'appeared' out of nowhere, lying smack down in the middle of a heavily disputed area on the brink of war. It is all part of the Monks' plan to destabilise the world and bring it to its knees. Can the Doctor, as the de facto 'President of the World' stop it? The Monks require humanity's 'consent' to rule them, and at the end of the episode Bill gives them it, in exchange for the Doctor's restored sight and the saving of the human race from a deadly pathogen.

In the third and final part, the Monks have not only taken over the world, but have retconned humanity's history and convinced us that they have always been our true benevolent leaders. As the giver of consent, Bill is the unwitting 'lynchpin' that is transmitting the Monks' propaganda and keeping humans subservient. The Doctor must enlist the help of Missy to reprogramme the message and eject the Monks from the planet.

Outstanding writing and direction, plus memorably sinister villains make the Monks Trilogy a sophisticated and inventive science fiction drama. Younger Who fans may find this more complex, serious approach less enthralling, but to me it was a real highlight of the series. There are many notable scenes, including one in which the Doctor has to convince Bill that he has joined up with the Monks and persuading her to shoot him in order to draw the Monks off the scent. I found it impossible not to be glued to the screen.

The Monks are probably the most terrifying aliens since the

Silence, and indeed the 'conquer by brainwashing propaganda/ mind altering' is a similar theme to those episodes which is executed in the same, inimitable way. Epic, profound and compelling throughout.

Empress Of Mars – 7/10

Victorian soldiers save an Ice Warrior from his spaceship. They are then tempted by the alien to return with him to Mars where he promises untold riches. It's all a trick however to aid him in awakening the 'Empress of Mars, the Ice Warriors matriarch.

After an epic three-parter, Empress of Mars returns to more of a 'serial of the week' approach with this Troughtonesque bottle story set in a Martian cave.

It's an interesting take on the crimes of colonialism; with the Victorian explorers meeting their match when trying to take on the superior alien race. The Ice Warriors have always been one of my favourites, and it's nice to see their culture and hierarchy getting some more backstory here.

The Eaters Of Light – 6/10

The Doctor (and Nardole) takes Bill back in time to investigate her favourite mystery of a fabled disappearance of a Roman legion. It turns out there is a temporal rift through which alien parasites feed off both sides of the Picts (early celts) and Romans that they find.

Rather like the past historical story Vincent and the Doctor and the upcoming Jodie Whittaker story Rosa, I feel that this episode would've worked as a purely historical story without the need of an alien threat (although of course it gives the warring armies something to focus on). But it's a fun enough, if rather run-of-the-mill episode.

World Enough And Time/The Doctor Falls – 10/10

In the most startling couple of opening scenes, we see the Doctor trying to hold off his regeneration and Bill seemingly killed aboard a gigantic spaceship trying to steer itself out of a black hole.

There are creatures in the depths who need humans to live, so as they ascend, Bill is shot by the ship's janitor to bamboozle them.. It fails however and she is taken to the bottom of the ship, where the medical staff start her conversion into....a Cyberman!

Because of the pull of the black hole, one end of the ship moves much faster in time than the other, and whilst Bill is surrounded by terrifying 'experimental' Cybermen in the making, she must wait for the Doctor to catch up.

At the end of the first part, Bill returns as a converted Cyberman and there is 'double trouble' when the Master (John Simm, returning for the first time since Tennant) turns up and teams up with Missy. It's one of the best cliff-hangers for some time and leads us open mouthed into the next and final episode.

As we rejoin the action, we discover that the Cybermen are brought into existence time and time again, through parallel evolution across the universe. The Doctor gives the previous examples of Mondas (The Tenth Planet'), Telos (Tomb of the Cybermen') and Earth ('Army of Ghosts') and asserts that whilst they remain at the 'slow end' of the ship, at the 'fast end' the Cybermen will continue to develop and adapt into more and more of a dangerous enemy. The Doctor, 'Cyber-Bill' and Nardole must lead one last battle to fend them off once and for all.

Ok, first the 'bad,' of which there is very little. The (Simm)

Master's makeup in the first half is a little on the problematic side; reminding me somewhat of the 'Weng-Chiang' approach to silly disguises. When he reveals himself however I loved the *Delgado* beard, so that made up for it I guess.

The biggest issue I had however was that this wonderful series-ender wasn't Capaldi's final outing. His performance, particularly in the final showdown with the Cybermen in the forest, was so incredibly powerful and poignant that it felt like such a waste to bring him back for the sake of one last special. The scene shows Capaldi's Doctor finally reach the end of his long story arc; becoming the brave hero he had always wanted to be but was afraid he would never become. His "Pity...no stars...I hoped there'd be stars" line floored me, it was so emotional and poetic, the perfect ending to a remarkable Doctor. But it wasn't to be his last, alas.

Now onto the myriad of positives. All of the supporting characters are on top form. Bill is one of my favourite companions and it's a shame she wasn't introduced earlier because I would've loved to see her and the 12th Doctor in more stories. There is a nice focus on the Master/Doctor's dynamic and backstory to their friendship, as well as some funny and intriguing interplay between the Master and him/herself Missy. I do believe this is the first time we've had a 'multiple Master' story, and I'd love to see it happen again; especially if it was done this well.

The original cybermen, whilst comical to many, have always scared the crap out of me since I saw them in the First Doctor story The Tenth Planet. It was the way you could still see some human resemblance, perverted, and warped beneath their mechanical voices and suits.

The level of excitement I felt during this episode was palpable. We have the original Mondassian Cybermen returning with all the sinisterness and screen presence they've been sorely missing of late. We had the 10th Doctor's Master make a comeback. And we had one of the most enthralling, captivating and emotional series send-offs of them all.

Marvellous stuff.

Specials

Twice Upon A Time – 6/10

Following the events of the Tenth Planet (1966), the First Doctor is transported out of his timeline in the moments before his 'renewal'/regeneration. In this limbo he meets the Twelfth Doctor, who is also having a crisis of identity and unwilling to regenerate into his next form.

Into the fray steps a Captain from the 1st World War (an ancestor of Brigadier Lethbridge-Stewart) and a facsimile of Bill. Time itself would appear to be in disarray, and both Doctors must make their change if it is to be fixed.
Bradley returns as the First Doctor and is still as hilariously acerbic and irascible as ever. The interplay between him and Capaldi's Doctor is highly entertaining. However, I thought the writing did somewhat of a disservice to Hartnell's wonderful characterisation of the Doctor; rendering him a sexist, xenophobic dinosaur rather than the twinkly space wizard with a grandfatherly compassion that he was.

It's nice to see the show's past and present meet in such a fun and humorous way. But this is a much less weighty end to the Twelfth Doctor's run and less of an essential watch than its predecessor.

Capaldi was born to play the Doctor, and although he had a mixed run of stories, he imbued the character with such depth that he remains my favourite depiction since the renewal back in 2005.

THE THIRTEENTH DOCTOR – JODIE WHITTAKER (2018-2022)

Specials

New Doctor Teaser Trailer

Content:

I was a bit disappointed with the lack of content to be honest; we get about 30 seconds of action, which is the new companions looking confused and the Doctor smiling. Although I love Jodie's smile, I'd have loved to have seen some upcoming monsters, little snippets of stories etc.. Instead we get a load of characters sitting around a cafe.

Which brings me to my next thoughts...

Characters:

The companions aren't enthusing me at the moment. We get

three of them...and they're all from modern day Earth again. It all feels a bit like a cross between the spin-off 'Class' and the worst elements of Davison. It would be nice to get a companion with a more interesting origin, and to not spread it across three different characters.

But I'm hoping to be proved wrong on this.

I'm still not completely sure about Jodie as the Doctor. Again, she reminds me of Davison, in the fact that she's 'playing' an eccentric, rather than being naturally eccentric like say Tom Baker, or other actors who feel born to play the part (like say Tilda Swinton) who have a peculiar 'otherworldliness' for the part.

That said, she seems to emanate the same kind of verve and joy that Matt Smith did, and he was a Doctor that I grew to love after my initial doubts.

She seems to have a child-like wonder and adventurousness about her which will hopefully bring back more young audiences to the show.

I also quite like that she is starting with brand new companions, because I don't want them to dwell on the whole 'gender change' thing for too long. I want people to love her Doctor for being a great Doctor, rather than because of her gender alone.

Look and Feel of the teaser:

Like the characters, there is a joy, a freshness and 'restart' to the short trailer, which gives me hope that this show is going in a new and positive direction.

SERIES 11 (SEASON 37)

A new Doctor, showrunner and a crowded TARDIS of new companions, along with a mixed bag of stories make this a less than stellar first season for the new Doctor.

The Woman Who Fell To Earth – 7/10

Ryan, his Step-Grandad Graham and old school friend Yasmine run into a mysterious alien called the Doctor. Together they must solve the mystery of a more malignant alien threat before they can depart on a new life of adventure in time and space together.

We enter a new era of the show, with a new Doctor (in their first female incarnation, if you don't count Joanna Lumley in the Rowan Atkinson spoof 'The Curse of Fatal Death') and a new showrunner (Torchwood creator Chris Chibnall).

On first impression I'm getting serious Tennant vibes from Whittaker. The debut had lots of energetic, fast, exciting elements and my hopes are high that it will revitalise the series and engage a lot of new viewers. The tone is suspenseful and already different to the Moffat era (which is positive as each era needs to have its own unique feel). She also seems to be a more overtly compassionate and 'human' feeling Doctor; giving me some echoes of Davison too. Unlike the Davison era however, they seem to be making lots of companions work and I liked them all from the start.

As far as the story went, it was another round of 'attack of the 'one offs,' who were scary but superfluous to the introduction of the new Doctor.

As with many post regeneration stories, the Doctor isn't fully formed or sure of themselves yet. Like Troughton, Baker or Davison before her, this leads to a certain *daftness* in her portrayal; so I'm looking forward to Jodie showing more gravitas and more of a serious, world weary side as the series progresses.

To many fans the Doctor's gender change was a big deal, but I'm glad the show didn't dwell on it... 'I'm a woman?' 'Does it suit me?' ... and then the episode moved on. This is how it should be done.

I've got a feeling Jodie Whittaker and Chris Chibnall will return Doctor Who to more of a kid friendly show. There's been signs of it already in series 10, with a more 'classic' Who feel. I'm also loving the new theme!! It hits more like a heavier electronic 80s version and sounds great!

I've got a sneaking suspicion Jodie is going to 'do a McCoy' by starting off over 'silly' to compensate for the previous seriousness we've seen from Capaldi, and then become darker as her era progresses.

I love Capaldi's Doctor, but his stories have been a bit hit and miss and I really hope Jodie manages to re-engage the casual viewer/fan as well as the long term fans. I have faith she can.

The Ghost Monument – 5/10

The Doctor and her new TARDIS team (who she lovingly refers to as her 'fam') go on their first journey together.. After floating in space, they are 'scooped up' by 2 wondering spaceships and transported to an alien planet where they find themselves in the middle of an intergalactic 'Cannonball Run' to reach 'the Ghost Monument' (which just happens to be the Doctor's lost TARDIS).

There are a few highlights in a fairly mediocre episode, including the Doctor reaffirming her anti-gun stance and showing her pride in Ryan for battling through his difficulties with dyspraxia. We get a new TARDIS interior and the first mention of 'The Timeless Child.' However, I'm finding Jodie's constant hyperactive quick talking a bit irritating; reminding me of the worst traits of Tennant or Smith when they were at their most excitable.

Rosa – 7/10

The Doctor and co travel back in time to Alabama in 1955, where they must make sure a fixed point in time passes without issue. Rosa Park's refusal to give up her seat in a segregated bus was the catalyst which started a chain of events which accumulated with the civil rights movement of the 1960's. But a rogue time agent has other ideas.

'Rosa' is a well acted historical story that shows Doctor Who at its most socially conscious. Some detractors were critical of this agenda; forgetting that the show has always had both an aim to educate and stand up for social change (see Monster of Peladon, Remembrance of the Daleks and many more). It's nice to see the more shameful aspects of American history being addressed, as well as their effects on the present. Doctor Who has always been good at creating an allegory for modern issues, and in the era of the 'Black Lives Matter' movement, stories like this could never be more relevant.

The only criticism I would have of the episode is that its doesn't go 'all the way' in remaining a purely historical story; and the science fiction element is less well executed.

Arachnids In The Uk – 5/10

We are back in Sheffield and meet Yaz's family. Yaz's mum is on her first day working at the hotel of a megalomaniac businessman with ambitions of the presidency (ring any bells?). Into his hotel come giant spiders on the prowl... *your usual Doctor Who script then!*

Another in a line of fairly unremarkable Doctor Who stories in this series. Again there are some great moments, such as the truly touching scenes of Graham talking to his wife (Ryan's grandma who died at the end of the Woman Who Fell to Earth) about how much he misses her, and the official coming together of the 'Fam' TARDIS team at the end. They are a charming bunch who I do enjoy watching; even if the stories they are being given aren't up to much yet.

The Tsuranga Conundrum – 4/10

The Doctor and Fam wake up in a hospital (in space) after being 'blown up' by a sonic mine. Here they find themselves under attack from a tiny but dangerous 'space gremlin' who is eating the ship.

I liked the contrast of the existential danger with the cold clinical environment and the creature is cute and memorable (though it did remind me of 'Nibbler' from Futurama). The supporting cast are pretty bland however and the story is pretty forgettable. Everyone is running around breathless, but I wasn't pulled into the drama.

Oh, and there's a pregnant dude...that's nice.

Demons Of The Punjab – 7/10

We travel back in time to Yaz's Grandparent's formative years. Here she meets her Grandma (a Muslim) as a young woman in a mixed engagement to a Hindu man (confusingly not her Grandad) against the background of the 1947 partition of India and Pakistan by Britain.

Added to these political and religious tensions there is the terror of aliens who have come to 'stand witness' to the casualties of the India/Pakistan wars.

A mature historical story with beautiful scenery, great acting and interesting social and political commentary about brothers fighting on newly divided land they used to share in peace.

It's nice to see a slice of history that is not presented as often as it should be.

Kerblam! – 7/10

The Doctor receives a distress call message in her delivery package from 'Space Amazon.' Her and the team must go and work in their space factory to find out who needs help and why.

A critique/satire on the inhuman cost of mass consumerism through the lens of science fiction, starring Lee Mack and Hayley from Coronation Street(!), Kerblam lambasts online shopping in this futuristic story with shades of Robots of Death and The Sunmakers.

I enjoyed the sinister 'Alexa' style AI generated voice of the delivery bots dolling out the horror (think Al in 2001), and it was interesting to see the twist at the end which I hadn't expected.

I also liked the supporting cast of characters, and Kerblam was an averagely entertaining and intriguing tale, if not the most notable or memorable of episodes.

The Witchfinders – 5/10

The TARDIS returns the team to the 17th Century, where they become embroiled in the witch trials of Pendle Hill in Lancashire and a mysterious parasitic alien who is consuming

TIMOTHY J. LEE

the locals.

The series once again proves it's not afraid to examine the darker sides of history in this fairly scary historical. Guest star Alan Cumming plays King James in the most outrageously pantomime style since Graham Crowden in The Horns of Nimon and the whole thing has the dark comedy feel of a Mark Gatiss episode like The Unquiet Dead (which featured similar aliens who consumed the bodies of the dead) but without the charm of that serial. A couple of stand out scenes, but Cumming's scenery chewing and Jodie's lack of necessary gravitas once again let this episode down for me.

It Takes You Away – 8/10

I'd heard really bad things from friends (one in particular said it was one of the worst episodes he'd ever seen and he'd give it 1/10 at best). My low expectations then helped me appreciate this episode more when it turned out I quite liked it.

The story revolves around a girl who is trying to find her dad; transported to another universe through a portal hidden in a mirror. To get to the other universe, the characters must travel through a dangerous 'antiverse' which bridges the two worlds that will destroy each other if they were to touch.

A weird and nonsensical story for sure. But in some ways, this combination of the fantastical and imaginative is what Doctor Who is all about!

The portal through a mirror to another world felt like a wonderful fairy-tale and I know I would've loved this idea as a kid.

The story itself is well paced and suspenseful, and you've got to admire the crazy ideas thrown into it. It was mad, but unique and most importantly (especially for a series that has seen far too many mediocre episodes) gripping and compelling.

In some ways, for me this was the modern show's

equivalent of 'Warriors' Gate' from the classic era...strange, unexplainable and perhaps too many disparate ideas to fit together cohesively. But just like Warrior's Gate you can't help but admire the scope that was attempted to try something completely different. Not all of it worked of course. You didn't really care about the supporting cast for the most part, and the ending seemed daft and anticlimactic (a space frog?!). But overall this was a quirky, thought provoking story that stands out amongst some other underwhelming stories in this series.

The Battle Of Ranskoor Av Kolos – 6/10

A planet has a psychic effect on its inhabitants and visitors. 'Tim Shaw' from the first episode of the season has been stranded by the Doctor on the planet and has managed to connect his hive mind to the planet, causing everyone to worship him as a God.

Graham has a personal vendetta against Tim Shaw for killing his wife/Ryan's Grandma. This creates a divide between him and the Doctor, who warns him if he kills anyone, he can no longer travel with her and will become as bad as Tim Shaw for becoming a killer.

Another imaginative idea but pretty forgettable. The Doctor delivers some of her most irritating lines (the writer's fault, not her's), such as 'I should've brought wellies...that could've been another precaution...always bring wellies...I love wellies...in fact I think I half-invented them.' Mistaking bumbling quick self-talk for eccentricity just doesn't work for me and comes off as false and forced.

Not a bad episode, with a fair amount of tension and character relationship development, especially with Graham and Ryan. But as a finale, it was an disenchanting end to a mostly underwhelming series.

A disappointing first series for Jodie.

Specials

New Year's Special - Resolution - 7/10

In this New Year's special archaeologists manage to unearth a mutated/advanced 'scout Dalek' that can attach itself to humans and control their minds. It latches itself to Lin, one of the archaeologists and uses her to enact its world domination plan. The Doctor calls on UNIT to help, but they have finally been taken down, not by an alien threat but by red tape and call centres!

Meanwhile Ryan's deadbeat dad returns and tries to reconnect with him, stirring up a lot of hidden feelings.

Resolution is suspenseful, full of heart and quite scary at times. It's an average enough episode from a plot point of view, and if you didn't know it was a 'Special,' it wouldn't necessarily stand apart from any other story.

SERIES 12 (SEASON 38)

A much more consistently strong season sees the Doctor take on a new version of the Master, team up with a new/old version of herself and discover her shocking forgotten origins as the 'Timeless Child.'

Spyfall – 8/10

The Doctor and co are enlisted by MI6 to delve into the mystery of agents turning up with their DNA totally rewritten.

As the case unravels, they discover it is all the plan of the Doctor's oldest frenemy, the Master, returning in a new (or is it old) form....and he has the worst possible news about their home planet Gallifrey.

The first half of this two-parter is essentially a pastiche of the James Bond franchise. Although done with a certain amount of style, this genre hopping has the potential to repeat the silliness of the 'Doctor Mysterio' special a couple of series ago. Thankfully there is enough action and suspense for the story not to fall into this trap, even with the daft spy gadgets and other Bondian tropes.

The first episode reveal of the Master hiding in plain sight (after he has impersonated a scientist that has been helping them) is one of my all-time favourite cliffhangers, and Sacha

Dhawan is so impressive in his debut as to automatically catapult him up the chart of favourite Master portrayals. He plays the part with such a visceral, sociopathic relish that is truly compelling. There is an evil and emotional intensity which you can feel brimming just beneath the surface, ready to explode at any minute.

Jodie also seems much more comfortable in the role as her second season begins. Her performance feels more natural, less forced and commanding a lot more authority.

Orphan 55 – 6/10

A holiday is in order and the team visits the planet 'Tranquillity' for a spot of R&R. Of course, this is Doctor Who, so it's not long before things go awry. When a ferocious creature invades the resort, they discover they are actually on an 'orphan planet' that has been rendered inhabitable by the former natives.

There are a few shades of The Leisure Hive (4th Doctor) in this 'holiday from Hell' episode. Whilst this episode might not present as many interesting ideas as that one, I found it more entertaining and easier to follow. I did find some of the supporting characters particularly irritating though, which marked it down.

A fairly enjoyable episode, but nothing to write a postcard home about.

Nikola Tesla's Night Of Terror – 7/10

The Fam are back in time to the 'gilded age' of New York on the cusp of the 20th Century and pioneering technological innovator Nikola Tesla, who helped pave the groundwork for the alternating current (AC) electricity supply system. He is beset by rival Edison who is far less innovative but far more business savvy.

Soon alien weapons, giant scorpions and electric dudes appear to throw a *spark* into proceedings.

A good solid historical mystery adventure. Unlike the last episode, I found the supporting cast one of the highlights of the episode. Somewhat of a mid-level story which isn't a standout for the series.

Fugitive Of The Judoon – 9/10

We meet Ruth, a gregarious tour guide from Gloucester with a bit of a Judoon problem. It seems they are after an alien fugitive who turns out to be her partner Lee.
In reality, he is just a cover for the biggest surprise of all....Ruth is really another *Doctor*, hidden by a chameleon arch (used previously in stories like Human Nature to hide who the Doctor is from everyone, including themselves).

This complicates things! Why is there another Doctor? Why doesn't the 13th Doctor remember being her? This mystery surely has much larger ramifications? Captain Jack also makes a surprise return, on the lookout for the Doctor/s.

The 'Fugitive Doctor' is awesome, with some proper War Doctor vibes – a great mix of compassion, kindness and crankiness that personifies the role for me. You can truly imagine this is a descendant of William Hartnell's irascible space wizard portrayal; a gravitas I've been missing from Jodie's era so far. Along with Sacha Dhawan's Master, Jo Martin's Doctor is easily one of the highlights of this era for me.

It's nice to see the return of the 'police rhinos from space' and I'm loving the mohawk look. Captain Jack's return doesn't land quite as well, feeling a little more tacked on than the character deserves.

But overall Fugitive of the Judoon is a super exciting highlight of the series so far.

Praxeus – 6/10

The one with the Hitchcock crazy birds and the alien corona virus that turns you into woodchip. It turns out that an alien pathogen is infiltrating the planet's plastic, and as we continue to spoil our world with plastic in the sea and microplastics in our system, the infection on humans and animals continues to grow and grow.

A fair episode again, if a little overly preachy for me. Personally I prefer Doctor Who when it's a bit more subtle in its message...like the attack of giant maggots! Ok, maybe that's not the best example.

Can You Hear Me - 7/10

The Doctor drops off her companions and goes for a solo jaunt, ending up in ancient Syria. Here she finds a monster at large which is attacking people in their dreams. But this isn't an incident restricted to time or location. The Doctor's companions are also experiencing 'psychic incursions' of creepy apparitions.

It turns out to be all part of 'the Eternals' games. Two Gods who have toyed with planets for their amusement, only for one of them to be imprisoned during an uprising. The other God has waited for someone like the Doctor to walk into their trap and release the imprisoned Eternal to wreak their revenge.

I love the idea of these 'Gods' and their relation to other celestial beings from the show's past such as the Black/White Guardians and the Celestial Toymaker. For their part, they are well realised, feeling suitably ancient and threatening.

The characters get a lot of development in this episode too, facing their fears and their pasts. I was a bit disappointed at the Doctor's lack of empathy when Graham opened up to her about his cancer struggles, and I felt this could've been approached in a more characteristic way.

But there is a lot to enjoy about the sinister plot and the touching moments of the episode.

The Haunting Of Villa Diodati - 8/10

We are privy to the social gathering of legendary authors Lord Byron, Percy Shelley and his soon to be wife Mary during the evening that will inspire her to create the horror masterpiece Frankenstein. Only, not everything is as it should be. Percy is mysteriously absent and there is a spooky visitor prowling the grounds, who just so happens to be a lone Cyberman!

A suspenseful horror/sci-fi story that is gripping throughout.

Ascension Of The Cybermen/The Timeless Children - 9/10

Following the events of the last episode, the team follows the lone cyberman to the far future and humanity's final war against the Cybermen

In a seemingly unrelated story, we also follow the life of young coppa Brendon, who manages to inexplicably escape death.

It all culminates in the Master's plan to draw the Doctor back to the decimated Gallifrey, his army of Cyber-Time Lord hybrids and the reveal of the Doctor's biggest secret.

This action packed but controversial series finale has so many twists and turns, surprises and shocks that keep you glued to the screen.

To me, this is where Jodie's era really earns its place in the pantheon of Doctor Who. Her episodes up until this point have had shades of brilliance, but also a great deal of below par stories. For better or for worse, Chris Chibnell creates a 'timeless' axis point at the end of Series 12 with the revelations introduced with the 'Timeless Child' arc.

In arguably the most controversial element of the modern show, the '13th Doctor' is told her shrouded origins by the Master. He reveals the unknown truth. Apparently, the Doctor originally fell through a portal from another universe, where she was discovered to have the power of 'renewal/regeneration' by a scientist who then experimented on the poor child to harness her power and create 'The Time Lords.' We don't know how many Doctors there were before we got to Hartnell's '1st Doctor' as seen in the programme, but in flashback scenes we see 7 depictions of these 'pre Hartnell' Doctors. The aforementioned Brendan was simply a 'metaphor' for the Timeless Child, a story or cover up in the Time Lord's Matrix to hide the true origins of the Doctor.

The idea that Hartnell wasn't the 'original,' understandably divided the fans. It's one thing to change a character's story moving forward, but to retcon nearly 60 years of established lore and change the very essence of the show?...to many this felt like too much.

I'm in two minds to be honest. On the one hand, I dislike the thought of replacing some of the importance of the 'First' Doctor and changing the history of the show for one showrunner's own dramatic ends does feel sacrilege. On the other hand however, it doesn't change the nature of the Doctor's character, and does actually explain a lot of loose ends from previous stories.

Firstly we have the 'Brain of Morbius Doctors' from 1976. In one notorious and contested scene, the Doctor (Tom Baker at this point) goes into a mental battle with evil Time Lord Morbius. The different iterations of the Doctor are projected onto the screen. This stretches back to the '1st Doctor,' but then surprisingly harks back to further incarnations we'd never seen before. These went back through 8 'former Doctors' before Hartnell (played by the crew who made the story!) before the Doctor won out against the rival Time Lord. With a myriad of 'unknown' Doctors, this now makes some sense.

There is also the 'Cartmel Masterplan' that was hinted at the end of the Seventh Doctor's era. In episodes such as the Silver Nemesis and The Curse of Fenric, there are teasing clues that the Doctor is much more than 'just another Time Lord,' and (had the series not been cancelled) was destined to be revealed as a Time Lord 'God,' and one of the great founders of their society (along with Rassilon and Omega). If the Doctor was the first person to gift the Time Lords with their ability to regenerate, this too makes sense with the knowledge of the 'Timeless Child' narrative.

It's a brave move, and one that has turned many fans away, already disappointed with the way the show had been going. It certainly raises more questions than answers. But I have to give it credit for showing a lot more vision than the rest of Jodie's era so far. Dhawan and Whittaker are probably the best they've ever been, and series 12 ends in the most intriguing way imaginable.

Specials

New Year's Day Special - Revolution Of The Daleks - 6/10

Narcissistic business mogul Jack Robertson (Arachnids in the UK) has intercepted some alien technology and adapted it as a security device to court his political allies. The only problem is it looks suspiciously like a Dalek, and the genetic information within is lying dormant, waiting for its rebirth. The Dalek consciousness manipulates Robertson's assistant into creating a 'clone farm' with the goal of overthrowing humanity.

Meanwhile, the Doctor is imprisoned by the Judoon in a

maximum space prison for 3 decades (her time) or 10 months (fam's time) depending on your viewpoint. Either way, it gives the Doctor some time to process the events of the Timeless Children, and the fam some cause for distress. After Captain Jack saves the Doctor, she returns, but finds that all of the fam have given up hope except Yaz, who is preoccupied by her return.

At the end of the serial, we bid farewell to Graham and Ryan. It's sad to see them go, although they rarely had a chance to really shine in the overcrowded TARDIS.

Revolution adds little to the well-trod story of Dalek invasion. It's a watchable, but unremarkable special which acts as a comedown after the momentous series finale.

SOME THOUGHTS BEFORE SEASON 13 – HISTORY REPEATING ITSELF?

For the last ten years I've had a strange sense of deja vu about my favourite TV show Doctor Who.

It's a strange theory but hear me out...the show's 80's era/s are seemingly being played out again.

Let me explain.

In the early 80's, a new showrunner John Nathan-Turner took over the show; towards the end of Tom Baker's unprecedented 7 year run as the Doctor and the beginning of his successor, Peter Davison, the youngest actor so far to take on the role.

Nathan-Turner was passionate about exploring much more complex storylines, based on 'high science' theoretical concepts. The effect on the audience was polarising. Many 'hardcore' fans loved the more opaque, complicated plots, whereas more casual fans found the new style inaccessible and more niche.

....any of this seem familiar from the modern era?

In the early 10's, the most popular Doctor since Tom

Baker (David Tennant) stepped down...to be replaced by the youngest actor to have played the role. New series runner Stephen Moffat wanted to explore more complicated and far reaching story arcs. This was appreciated by many of the hardcore fans, but made for an unsatisfying experience for casual viewers who were left scratching their heads.

Back to the mid 80's, and after the young Davison had brought a youthful 'pleasantness' to the role, the show runners decided to take the show in a darker direction; with a Doctor who was older and less predictable in his portrayal. He would start off 'unhinged,' and over time soften and change into the character we had come to love. Unfortunately the long term plan didn't come to fruition, and after only 2 series, Colin Baker was replaced by the much more amiable, if 'lightweight' portrayal of Sylvester McCoy. The theatrical and clownish portrayal of McCoy's Doctor was unpopular and viewing figures plummeted. The show changed tack one less time, producing a much underrated couple of series with much stronger stories and vision. But unfortunately, it was too little too late, and many viewers had already given up on the show.

The show was quietly cancelled in 1989...not to be seen again properly for another 16 years.

Back to the mid 10's, and after the youngest actor to play the role (Smith), the show moves to a much older, less friendly portrayal in Capaldi's Doctor. He starts off uncertain of his values and whether he is a 'good man' or not. His companion Clara struggles to understand this different, more abrasive incarnation of her friend...but over time he softens and finds love for his companions and the human race.

Casual fans were less convinced by this older, more curmudgeonly Doctor. So in walks a completely new era and feel for the show. Back was an enthusiastic, energetic Doctor in the form of Jodie Whittaker; bouncing around the set and showing less grumpiness, but also a fair deal less gravitas. Viewing figures start strong, but then start to drop off.

As the new series begins, we can see a dramatic improvement on the writing and direction of the show. But unfortunately not enough people are tuning in to see the show develop.

I hope and pray that I'm wrong, and that this new improved series will save the decline in the show, because we've seen how this story plays out already and I can't take another 16 years!

SEASON 13 (SEASON 39) - 'FLUX'

The Doctor must save all of space and time from an evil splinter group called 'the Division' who want to destroy the universe as we know it.

The Halloween Apocalypse - 3/10

The whole universe is in danger as a strange phenomenon 'the Flux' threatens to rip a hole in all of time and space.

We meet Dan, a kind but lonely Liverpudlian, who is kidnapped by an evolved 'dog creature' (seemingly from Lancashire) who wants to protect him from Earth's impending destruction. We also meet a host of other characters throughout the universe, including a Victorian cave builder, Claire from the Doctor's future and Vinder (Grey Worm from Game of Thrones) who patrols an outpost out in the cosmos. There are also the Sontarans, a carnivorous planet-eating cloud and Mr & Mrs. 'Diamond Head,' seemingly from an 'anti-time' organisation called 'The Division' pulling the strings.

Well....that certainly happened. The first episode of the first series-long story since the Trial of a Time Lord in Colin Baker's era is a complete mess. Whilst I understand the need to set up as many of the series' strands as possible, there are too many to make any kind of coherent plot. What tries to be exciting through fast twists and turns ends up feeling utterly unfathomable and a real chore to get through. Not a good start.

War Of The Sontarans - 7/10

The Doctor, Yaz and new guy Dan travel to the Crimean War in the 19th Century. But rather than fighting the Russians, the English are fighting the Sontarans?! It appears the Flux is rewriting time.

The TARDIS team are displaced and thrown throughout time and space, where they meet up with other people from history.

Still not up there with the era's best, but an improvement on the first part, with some nice Sontaran action.

Once, Upon A Time - 5/10

The Doctor must save her companions from the clutches of the Division, by pushing them all into a 'time storm.'

Whilst helping them escape, this has the effect of time shifting and undulating out of sync, causing them all to phase in and out of their own timelines.

We also meet Bel, Vinder's partner who searches for him across space, against the backdrop of the flux in time caused by the Division.

The Flux series continues to overreach itself; presenting some clever ideas but leaving me utterly underwhelmed.

Village Of The Angels - 6/10

The Weeping Angels are working for the Division and lure the Doctor with the mystery of a human pulled out of our time to the late 60's, housing a seemingly rogue Angel in her head.

I wanted to like this one more than I did. The elements are

interesting and, this being a Weeping Angels episode, there were some genuinely suspenseful scenes. But the supporting characters were a mixed bag. Bel continues to search for Vinder, but when they do connect (albeit through a 'space-answer machine'), they lack any of the chemistry I would have liked from their characters; feeling more like siblings than lovers. Professor Jericho (played by the wonderful Kevin McNally) was a really sweet character however, and it was a nice change from recent episodes to see a male supporting character from history with some empathy and kindness rather than the ignorance and cruelty of a fair few examples.

The series continues to feel like a chore to get through, although there are some nice moments here and there.

Survivors Of The Flux - 5/10

We discover the Division is spearheaded by Tecteun, the Doctor's adoptive 'mother' who saved/kidnapped her (depending on your perspective) as a child to experiment on her regenerative powers to create the 'Time Lords' (see 'the Timeless Children'). Her aim (I think) is to destroy our universe in order to kill the Doctor and retain the secrecy of the Division which she will carry over to the next one. Meanwhile, 'Time' is working alongside the Division with its servants Swarm and Azure (Mr and Mrs. Diamond Head) to help destroy the universe as we know it.

Tecteun has also kept hold of a fob-watch containing all of the Doctor's forgotten memories as insurance.

Meanwhile, another member of the Division, the 'Grand Serpent' infiltrates the beginning of UNIT and teams up to help the Sontarans take over the Earth.

Yaz and Dan are also trapped in the early 20th Century for 3 years, waiting for the Doctor.

Erm...Is this series nearly over?

The Vanquishers - 5/10

In the final part of the Flux series, the Doctor discovers Swarm and Azure have been working for 'Time' and are trying to create a 'loop of destruction' in revenge for the Doctor's victory over them in her future.

The Doctor finds a way to team up with herself to beat all the odds.

At its heart, the Flux arc (the battle between the very 'cogs' of the show, 'time' and 'space') is a great idea. But the execution is so convoluted and the elements so seemingly disconnected as to make it almost unwatchable 'fan fiction.'

There are some glimmers of brilliance but not enough to make this engaging sci fi drama. You care little for the supporting cast and Whittaker just doesn't sell the role for me a lot of the time, as bad as I feel for saying that.

The concluding scenes lack any real effect. I had mentally switched off by this point, and it was more of a relief to finish the series than to wonder why the main villain just decided to let the Doctor go without even trying to destroy her; rendering the whole reason for the series arc pointless.

Specials

Eve Of The Daleks - 7/10

It's New Year's Eve and Sarah is lumbered with the festive shift at her storage facility. Her only company is Nick, a lonely customer who spends every New Year's Eve there, trying to build up the courage to tell Sarah about his massive crush on her.

This year, they are not as alone as they would imagine. For deep within the bowels of the building is a Dalek; bent on taking down the Doctor. The only problem it has in its task is that the TARDIS is playing up and the Doctor, Yaz, Dan, Sarah, Nik and the Dalek are all in a perpetuating time loop. The companions and newbies face off against the Daleks time and time again, only to be exterminated and returned to the beginning of the loop. They have to try and work out how to end things in their favour before it closes and the Dalek wins out.

I remember at the time this special received mixed reviews, but I quite liked it. Eve of the Daleks contains something that a lot of Jodie's recent specials have not...notable and likeable supporting characters. I really liked Sarah (played with just the right balance of comedy and drama by comedian Aisling Bea) and Nick (played by newcomer Adjani Salmon) and would have loved to see them in more episodes.

I suppose the only criticism I could level at 'Eve' is that the supporting characters feel more central than the main characters, but I didn't mind this as a one-off approach. It's not a particularly significant special, but it was entertaining, with sweet players and an intriguing plot.

At the end of the story, we discover that Yaz is in love with the Doctor. This kind of hit me for six to be honest, not because it was the first overtly lesbian love interest for the Doctor, but because there really wasn't any kind of allusion to Yaz's feelings. She'd never seemed to have romantic feelings for the Doctor and then all of a sudden she is madly in love with her? And to announce this just a couple of stories before the Doctor's regeneration? It all seems a bit 'tacked on' and I feel like Yaz's character deserved better than that. I'm actually a little gutted that this wasn't hinted at a series or two ago, because Yaz's love of the Doctor is so sweet and could've been such a highlight to Whittaker's era. Oh well, it is what it is.

Legend Of The Sea Devils - 6/10

The Doctor and co are pulled out of history to discover a rogue Sea Devil and his crew are aiming to literally turn the Earth upside down and cause floods to consume and thereby reclaim what they see as rightfully theirs.

Legend of the Sea Devils is a swashbuckling adventure with heaps of heart. The balance feels just right, with the action scenes being fun and engaging and the heartfelt moments between the Doctor and Yaz, which felt rushed in the last episode feeling truly moving in this episode. In fact, one scene in particular was probably the most affectionate and stirring performance I've seen in her era. It reminded me in essence of the wonderfully touching scene between the 2nd Doctor and Victoria in Tomb of the Cybermen in fact.

The Sea Devils look and sound awesome, and although this (ironically) isn't the most groundshifting episode ever, it's an enjoyable and emotional special that is well worth a watch.

Power Of The Doctor - 6/10

The Master brings together the Daleks and the Cybermen ('Cyber Masters') in a scheme to erupt all of the Earth's volcanoes and wipe out humanity, before changing himself into the Doctor so that she will be forever blamed for Earth's destruction....or at least I think this is what the plot is about.

Chibnall throws literally everything possible into Jodie's swansong, including multiple past Doctors, companions and references. Whilst this was exciting to see, it gave me real 'The Five Doctors' vibes, where fan service outweighs any kind of congruent story and elements were shoehorned in at the expense of legitimacy. In the case of the Five Doctors this comes across as cheesy but celebratory. In Power of the Doctor, it's more of a shambles.

We are treated to some seriously cool cameos and throw backs though, which can't be denied. We get Doctor number 1 (again played by David Bradley) 5, 6, 7 and 8 (all played by their original actors Davison, C.Baker, McCoy and McGann). We get references to the 2nd Doctor with the Master sat cross legged playing recorder and we get the more recent Fugitive Doctor. We get sweet interactions between 5 and Tegan ('brave heart Tegan') and 7 and Ace (a stirring speech from McCoy which showed he could slip straight back into the role with ease). We also get to see LOADS of old companions, who are either integral to the story (Ace, Tegan, Graham) or at the end, when Chibnall devises the sweet idea of an 'ex-companions support group.' Here we see amongst others Jo, Mel and (the personal highlight for me) Ian.

I think it says a lot though that I'm 4 paragraphs in and haven't really mentioned Jodie's era yet. She goes out with a fair amount of emotion, mostly between her and Yaz, which was nice to see. But it's indicative of her era that I had to really try to care at this point.

There is one final treat in store for Who fans at the end when Jodie regenerates ('degenerates') into Tennant, who will helm the show for the 60th anniversary in a year's time, before handing the reins to Ncuti Gatwa.

Last time they brought back the 10th Doctor (for the 50th), the show was still arguably at the height of its powers, so it felt like a real bonus. At this point it feels much more an attempt to win back audiences who have been leaving in droves. Don't get me wrong, I like Tennant's Doctor a lot and it's nice to see him back. But rather like the rest of this episode it seems to rely too heavily on the show's past triumphs rather than confidence in its future.

I wanted to like Jodie, I really did. But her portrayal of the Doctor just felt far too 'human' for my liking and the stories varied so much in quality that I found much of her era a real slog to get through. There were highlights for sure. I

loved Sacha Dhawan's Master, the relationship between the Doctor and her companions and many of the stories showed a great deal of imagination and courage in taking the show in different directions. But the lack of an enigmatic Doctor and some poor stories make this my least favourite era since Colin Baker in the mid-80's.

A LOOK FORWARD TO THE 60TH ANNIVERSARY CELEBRATIONS OF DOCTOR WHO

At the time of writing, the 60th Anniversary is a matter of days away. Here are some of the exciting programmes the BBC has got lined up to celebrate!

60TH ANNIVERSARY SPECIALS: THE FOURTEENTH AND FIFTEENTH DOCTOR – DAVID TENNANT AND NCUTI GATWA (2023-)

Tales Of The Tardis

In these minisodes, previous Doctors and Companions reunite to talk about their adventures. This coincides with the classic series being returned to the BBC's streaming service BBCIPlayer, and are used as a sweet entry point into some of the best of the era's stories for newer fans. These included the following episodes and characters:

The Time Meddler - Steven and Vicki
The Mind Robber - Jamie and Zoe
The Three Doctors - Jo and (from The Sarah Jane Adventures) Clyde

Earthshock - The Fifth Doctor and Tegan
Vengeance on Varos - The Sixth Doctor and Peri
The Curse of Fenric - The Seventh Doctor and Ace

14Th/15Th Doctor Specials

There are 3 anniversary specials, a Children in Need minisode and Christmas Special featuring the return of David Tennant and his companion Donna Noble, and the regeneration into a new era of the show with the 15th Doctor Ncuti Gatwe and returning showrunner Russel T. Davies. Here's what we know so far...

Children in Need - This will see the return of David Tennant; this time playing the '14th Doctor.'

The Star Beast - From the looks of the trailer, this is based on an old comic story from the 4th Doctor's tenure, featuring a cute little alien called 'Beep the Meep.'

Wild Blue Yonder - According to tardis.fandom.com, this story will involve the TARDIS transporting the Doctor and Donna to a strange land...and leaving them there!

The Giggle - The last of the three specials will see the return of the Celestial Toymaker (originally played by Michael Gough in the time of the 1st Doctor and now played by Neil Patrick Harris) and the regeneration of the Doctor into their new incarnation!

Christmas Special (as yet unnamed) - There are no details of the special at the time of writing, but it's set to be the first to feature Ncuti Gatwe as the titular hero and to set up a new season beginning in Spring 2024!

With the show about to enter its 61st year, it seems in rude health, with many wonderful stories still to tell about this

enigmatic, iconic character.

THE 'SPIN-OFFS'

Introduction

Such is the stature of television's longest running science fiction show that it has spawned many examples of spin-off media in its first 60 years. There have been 3 'big screen' attempts; celebrating the first big success of the 1960's, and conversely attempting to restart the show in the 1990's when it had dwindled in popularity and left our TV screens. On television the first attempt at a spin-off was the aborted K-9 Adventures in 1981. But it wasn't until the show found a new lease of life with the re-launch of 2005 that television spin-offs really took off. The original target demographic had stretched a lot since the 9-12 year old market in 1963; and 'Torchwood' and 'The Sarah Jane Adventures' helped to capitalise on the adult and younger children audiences respectively. Even a different company (and country) had a go; with a second shot at a K-9 series in 2009. Finally (for now at least) was 'Class,' a less successful attempt to corner the teenage market in 2016.

Added to television and film adaptations, there are hundreds of comic, book and audio adventure spin-offs. As I discuss at the end of this section of the book, I have decided not to review these here, as there is already enough to be getting on with...and there is the ever circling question of canonicity amongst purists to contend with too.

As you would expect from off-shoots, the results are varied and not always up to the same quality as the
'Parent' show. But there are also times when the spin-offs manage to stand on their own as equally superb slices of television. This is testimony to the strength of the original show, and the imagination of the fans who it inspired to expand the universe in new and (mostly) exciting ways.

1960'S FILMS:

Doctor Who And The Daleks (1965) – 6/10

The Doctor makes his cinematic debut in this remake of the second William Hartnell serial. For those of you who haven't seen the story...the Doctor whisks his companions off to a seemingly deserted world; where they become embroiled in a battle between the pacifist Thals and the evil Daleks.

There are a few differences with the television story.
'Doctor Who' is a human inventor here, played with panache by the legendary Peter Cushing. Both Susan and Barbara are his Granddaughters, and
Ian is more bumbling than brave as Barbara's boyfriend. This is the first time colour is used (the T.V show will catch up 5 years later), and the film really makes the most of this; looking bright and vibrant throughout.

It's not a bad attempt to bring the early Doctor Who series to the big screen, and the production is much more lavish and extravagant than the T.V show. This creates a feel which is more akin to American science fiction series of the time, such as the original Star Trek or Lost in Space. I thought the film worked better as a light-hearted kid's action sci-fi film for people unfamiliar with the early series; rather than as a big-screen representation of the show. I think my love for the William Hartnell episodes clouded my enjoyment of the film slightly. Though the plot remains pretty much the same, certain crucial elements are changed to the detriment of the film. This is of course 'nit-picking,' and I'm sure most kids would love this action packed film. Personally though, as much as I found it fun, I prefer the grittier, darker T.V version.

Daleks' Invasion Earth: 2150 A.d. (1966) – 6/10

A haphazard policeman wanders into the T.A.R.D.I.S, and is transported by the Doctor to the far future, where the Daleks have taken over the Earth!

Bernard Cribbins makes his first Doctor Who appearance (returning as Donna's granddad Wilf) as policeman companion to the Doctor, his granddaughter Susan and niece Louise(?).

This second film was much more action packed than the first Cushing film, and stands up quite well as a camp 60's sci-fi action kid's film. Unfortunately, even the huge success of the Daleks in popular culture at the time couldn't help this second film at the box-office, and plans for a third film (based on the Hartnell story 'The Chase') were shelved.

If it was a competition, I still much prefer the T.V series; but these two Sixties films are well worth watching without prejudice, as the great kitsch 'of their time' cult curios they are.

K-9 AND COMPANY (PILOT):

Pilot Episode - 'A Girl's Best Friend' (1981) – 5/10

The opening credits to this pilot are *so* 1980's you half expect them to be sung by Max Headroom. But after the credits roll we're straight into what seems like mid-70's Tom Baker era 'Who;' with the mystery of a small rural village where locals practise Pagan rituals on anyone who disagrees with them. Into this walks Sarah Jane Smith and K-9 to look into the spooky happenings.

It's great to see Sarah Jane again...but I found this one off quite slow; especially if considering the younger audience that I'm guessing this was aimed at. The 'Adric-styled' young side-kick that joins Sarah Jane would've also grated had the series been continued. There seems little potential in this pilot, apart from a funky/cheesy theme-tune and the lovely Liz Sladen. Thankfully, her own spin-off, The Sarah Jane Adventures was to be a lot more successful 25 years later.

TORCHWOOD (2006-2011):

Disclaimer – Because of the target adult audience for this spin-off, content referred to in this section may be unsuitable for young readers of this book. Please skip to the next section if you are under 18.

SERIES 1

Everything Changes – 10/10

Gwen, a Policewoman from Cardiff stumbles upon a top secret organisation, 'Torchwood,' responsible for guarding a rift in time and space along which different alien races are escaping. By capturing these aliens and harvesting their advanced technology, 'Torchwood' aims to equip the human race for future alien invasion (operating much in the same way as U.N.I.T from the classic series; though in Torchwood's case acting 'separately' from the government).

After being given amnesia drugs by the head of the organisation Captain Jack (see 'The Doctor Dances'), Gwen loses all knowledge of Torchwood. But she manages to regain enough of the memory to track down the illusive leader, impressing him enough to make him adopt her into the fold.

And so begins possibly the most successful of all the spin-off series the main show has produced so far; the adult orientated Torchwood. The very fact that a children's drama series could inspire a spin-off series for adults shows how far-reaching the appeal of Doctor Who is, and the first episode shows a great deal of promise to stretch the format towards this new target audience.

Fans of the modern series will have some prior knowledge

both of Torchwood (first talked about in the 1st series of the re-launched Doctor Who series and explored more in the 2nd series) and (Cardiff division)

'Torchwood 3's' leader, the immortal Captain Jack Harkness. The new spin-off programme follows on well from these beginnings.

The cast is strong, with Captain Jack (played by John Barrowman) and Eve Myles as Gwen (the inquisitive policewoman and main focus of the show). The plot, production (especially the first alien we encounter, the creepy 'Weevils') and casting are all excellent, and this first episode really makes you want to watch more.

Day One – 1/10

An alien rock crash lands on Earth, releasing a gas-like parasite that is absorbed into a human host. This particular parasite is rather a nymphomaniac; existing on the energy reached...by bringing people to sexual climax(?!!).

To quote Gwen...

> 'Just to recap, you've travelled here to feed off orgasmic energy?' (Gwen Cooper, Day One)

...Yes Gwen, I can't believe this is the premise of the episode either!

Whilst the first episode had been full of such promise, it really fails to impress with its second. It tries too hard to be 'adult;' to separate and distinguish itself from the younger show, by incorporating cheap elements of what it is to be an adult drama – all sex, drugs and rock n' roll...without the necessary depth to make it as effective a drama as its parent show.

Apart from Gwen, at this early stage I am finding it very difficult to warm to the main characters of the show, who seem too 'hip' for me to relate to as much as the eccentric loner of the Doctor.

This second story seems cheap, shallow and lacking in any real interest for me; particularly when compared with the excellent opening episode.

Ghostmachine – 7/10

Gwen chases down a yob, to discover he's carrying an alien piece of technology - a 'quantum transducer device' which can transport the owner to echoes of emotional events that have happened wherever they happen to be standing. Not only that, but the user can feel the emotional imprint of the people who have experienced these moments first-hand. Owen is particularly effected after he is transported back to witness the rape and murder of a teenager in the '60's.

This is a good way to develop the new characters; particularly medical officer Owen, who had been rather a one-dimensional character ('the misogynist') up until this point; showing a new emotional range in this episode.

Still not up to the standard of the first episode, but it's a big improvement on the second and the show is starting to show that its characters have the potential to stretch and evolve.

Cyberwoman – 2/10

Torchwood's 'go-for' guy Ianto has saved his half converted

girlfriend from the Cyberman battle of Canary Wharf (Rise of the Cybermen – DW Series 2). He enlists the help of a doctor/scientist who promises to convert her back. But unfortunately this doctor has the ulterior motive of wanting her fully converted and under his power. As with most people who meddle with Cybermen/women, the doctor is made short work of by the Cyberwoman; who goes on the rampage within the Torchwood grounds.

Again, a fairly good idea is spoiled by poor acting and production. There are a few nice moments, such as the genuinely terrifying scene where Gwen is almost converted herself, but overall this is another pretty poor episode. Scenes such as a distraught Ianto gurning like Stan Laurel, or one of the greatest enemies of the Doctor being slain by a pterodactyl, are best forgotten.

Small Worlds – 7/10

Jack meets up with an old flame from his youth in the 2nd world war. During his absence, she has been following Fairy-like demons that take a chosen one and protect them at all costs.

A slight return to form; with a nice back story for Captain Jack and some affecting scenes towards the end. The C.G.I is a bit rubbish, and it's still not brilliant as an episode, but I did enjoy it and it's a big improvement on the last few episodes.

Countrycide – 10/10

People are disappearing within a 20 mile radius of the Brecon Beacons. Torchwood set up camp and go on the prowl for the suspect killer. What they find inside a farmhouse is worse than any of them could imagine…a group of cannibals has set up a brutal 'harvest' of humans; stripping the skin and collecting the organs for their sport and food.

Suspenseful, macabre and utterly brilliant. This story (the first not to feature an alien presence) had more in common with C.S.I or Silence of the Lambs than its parent show (Doctor Who). And for the first time since the pilot, it truly stood on its own merits, as a show with its own character. It wasn't simply 'Doctor Who with some rude bits and swear words;' it was truly an excellent adult drama. A huge improvement on the rest of the series since the debut episode, and in one act this has totally restored my faith in Torchwood as being a series worth watching.

Greeks Bearing Gifts – 7/10

Toshiko (Torchwood's technology expert) finally gets her own story in this enjoyable but not overly remarkable story about a highly confident and sexual young woman she meets and falls for. Her new love gives her a pendant that allows her to hear the thoughts of others around her. She takes it back to base, hearing all the secrets of her colleagues, including the affair that has been going on between Gwen and her old flame Owen. She also realises how little she is thought of by the rest of the team (or at least it seems this way) and becomes understandably distraught…and vulnerable to the influence of her new partner; who tricks her way into Torchwood in the search for a transporter that will get her home. Yes you guessed it, her new lover (Mary) is in fact a heart-ripping alien killing machine!

Not a bad episode. Not as great as Countrycide, but certainly a continuation of the return to form. The C.G.I used for the alien is particularly beautiful in a couple of scenes, and it's nice to see Tosh getting some more exciting dialogue and storylines.

> (N.B – Another of this alien race, known here as the Arcateenians (also known as the 'Butterfly People') is seen briefly in the debut Sarah Janes Adventures episode 'Invasion of the Bane,' though thankfully this is a much more benign character, known as the 'Star Poet')

They Keep Killing Suzie – 7/10

The team brings Gwen's predecessor Suzie back to life using a piece of alien technology. Jack killed her in the first episode, after she had become mad and murderous; but now they need her to solve a spate of murders that seem connected to the word 'Torchwood.' Although the technology is only meant to bring people back to life for a matter of seconds, Suzie lives on; draining the life of Gwen. As she becomes stronger and stronger, Gwen grows weaker and nearer to death.

It turns out that it was all her plan to implant the trigger-word 'Torchwood' in the minds of those she had given the amnesia drug to (also given to Gwen in the first episode) and turn them into killers; forcing the team to resurrect her and her plan to be reborn in the shell of her 'replacement.'

Again, quite chilling stuff, and well acted/produced here. You care about the characters; through good dialogue and an engaging storyline.

Random Shoes – 6/10

A geeky man wakes up to see he is witness to his own dead body and none of the investigating Torchwood team can see him.

We flash back through his life. He has been obsessed with aliens since he was a child and received what he was told was an 'alien eye.' His lifelong search for aliens leads him to Torchwood, where he becomes besotted with Gwen. The team tolerate his nerdish following of them until he is run over by the car that leaves him in the predicament we now find him in.

He now wanders as a 'ghost' behind Gwen in her attempt to find out what has happened to her annoying but harmless stalker. As he begins to emotionally connect with Gwen, she starts to feel his presence and then to actually hear part of what he is telling her. It turns out that the 'alien eye' that nobody believed in is in fact just that. It allows the owner to view their past life and actually interact slightly with it.

As the young man manages to save Gwen's life, he realises his life has had some meaning, and finally leaves this mortal coil towards his final resting place.

Whilst quite moving and effective in parts, I didn't feel this episode worked as well as stories such as 'Father's Day' (9th Doctor) which had a similar, but more effectual feel to it. The acting isn't brilliant again, and this felt quite disappointing after a good run of episodes. It isn't too bad when rated on its own merits though.

Out Of Time – 8/10

A plane from 1953 travels through the rift and ends up in the present day. The Torchwood team take in the confused passengers - a middle-aged man, a teenage girl and the female pilot - helping them to acclimatise to the very different modern world they are confronted with.

Owen and the gorgeous trailblazing pilot fall in love; which obviously causes many moral and logical implications (being from different times). Not to mention the triangle caused by his on-off affair with Gwen...How does this man do it?! His love is short lived and the pilot manages to fly her way back through the rift and to her own time; leaving poor Owen heartbroken and distraught. The other two travellers take the two extremes of adapting to modern life (the younger woman) and ended their life completely (the middle- aged man, who can't cope in a world where his family is all dead, apart from his tragic son who is old and suffering from dementia).

This was actually one of my favourites of Series 1, incorporating enough heart and character to make it work as a mature and compelling story.

Combat – 7/10

The brilliantly creepy Weevils from the first episode are back – this time being kidnapped by humans and made to fight dispossessed businessmen in an underground fighting arena. A heartbroken Owen (see the previous episode) is vulnerable to this nihilism, and becomes drawn into the 'club' by its charismatic leader.

Meanwhile, Gwen's dual life finally catches up with her. Not only has Rhys (her long-suffering boyfriend) had enough of the constraints of her new secret life, but she finds out about Owen (who she's been having an on-off affair with since 'Countrycide') and his love for the departed pilot from last week's episode.

Whilst the plot is pretty much lifted wholesale from 'Fight Club,' there is a lot of action and some high octane scenes in this very watchable addition to the series.

Captain Jack Harkness – 8/10

In a reversal of fortunes to 'Out of Time,' Jack and Tosh are 'stolen' out of time and transported back via the rift to 1941, where they meet a pilot by the name of...Captain Jack Harkness!

Obviously 'our Jack' has a lot of explaining to do! It turns out that the 'real' Jack is on his final day before he is to tragically (and bravely) die defending his regiment in an aerial dog-fight. The two Jacks fall in love (hey, its Torchwood, of course they do – everyone falls in love within the hour in this show!) but Jack is unable to save him; fearing the danger that altering the space-time- continuum will do.

Meanwhile, Gwen, on the search for Jack and Tosh, finds the creepy 'Caretaker' (who Jack and Tosh simultaneously meet in 1941). It would appear that he has the means to transport himself between the two times and profit from it somehow.

Ianto and Owen come to blows (and even gunshots) arguing about how to get them back to their own time. Eventually, against Ianto's resistance, Gwen manages to open the rift using alien technology (which looks intriguingly like the centre workings of a T.A.R.D.I.S) and gets Jack and Tosh back. But, as predicted, doing this without necessary knowledge of time travel causes immeasurable damage and chaos, which leads onto the final act of the series!

This episode is really gripping throughout, and loaded

with good ideas and stirring scenes. It's taken nearly a whole series to admit it, but I believe I'm finally becoming converted to Torchwood!

End Of Days – 6/10

After last episode's cataclysmic rift opening, all Hell is breaking loose! Reality and time are splintering; sending all sorts of people from other times and places into our time.

Owen and Jack's relationship is already at boiling point (Jack having saved Owen when he wanted to die after losing his beloved pilot Diane in 'Out of Time' and Owen having saved Jack from 1941 and thus causing the apocalyptic events they are now dealing with). This now boils over, and Owen is ungracefully discharged from the team. Jack tries to reign in the rest of the torn team by clamping down harder with a tough 'my-way-or-the- highway' approach; which eventually causes the whole team to 'mutiny' in favour of the dejected Owen.

They take Owen's advice and reopen the rift again, hoping that it will mend itself...and once again cause even more dangers to erupt. The 'Caretaker' character from the last episode returns; using the chaos to summon an ultimate evil upon the world – a death bringing demon (similar in style and story to the excellent 'The Daemons' Jon Pertwee Doctor Who serial) which will destroy everything in its wake. Only Jack's immortality can save them now!

Once again, a great idea seems to be pushed too far in this episode, and in trying too hard to create the ultimate epic series finale, it shifts from the sublime to the ridiculous at an almost dizzying pace. Whilst emotional in some scenes, it's completely daft in others. I was disappointed with this series ender, after such a strong run of episodes before it.

Series 1 has shown many glimmers of brilliance amongst some fairly mediocre episodes; so I have faith that there is a lot of potential for series 2 to be awesome.

Here goes!...

SERIES 2

Kiss Kiss, Bang Bang – 2/10

Jack is away with the Doctor on another mission (see 'Utopia'/'The Sound of Drums'), and the team are lost without him. He returns to a disgruntled team, to take on the first Torchwood task of the season. One of his former rogue Time Agents ('Captain John') has journeyed through the rift to con his way to a new fortune.

This episode played like a Western, with some dynamic moments. But overall, it was trying far too hard to be stylish for my liking.

I do hope that Torchwood is never inspected; because there seems to be any number of dodgy and circumspect behaviours amongst the ranks. Their leader Jack is particularly unprofessional; seemingly compelled to snog any animal, alien, mineral or vegetable that walks through the door! And don't even get me started on the rest of the team!

A very disappointing start to the new season, and one to skip.

Sleeper – 8/10

A woman discovers she is not at all who she thought she

was. All her memories are implanted *fakes*, and she turns out to be an alien 'sleeper agent,' poised to be activated (against her knowledge) at any time, to call out to the rest of an alien invasion force. And she's not the only one. All over the country, unwitting agents are reactivated and start to attack!

Now this is more like it! An excellent story with a clever plot that is well realised. I liked the disturbing idea that any person at any time could be a sleeper agent; and that they wouldn't even know it was them until the time came. Just the right amount of emotion and action – in other words, a great piece of drama!

To The Last Man – 8/10

A man seems to have existed simultaneously between 1918 and 2006 Torchwood. Bits of 1918 start to 'leak' through; causing damage to time again. He and Tosh fall in love as they meet between the times, and must decide whether to sacrifice themselves to save time itself.

Another great piece of drama that I really enjoyed. It's particularly nice to see Tosh getting a good story again.

Meat – 6/10

One of Rhys' (Gwen's fiancé) employees dies crashing his lorry. The cargo is meat...alien meat. The Torchwood team goes to investigate, and Rhys in turn goes to investigate them.

It transpires that the meat comes from a huge sea creature that has come through the rift and is being harvested alive by a group of opportunistic humans.
Although out of their jurisdiction, Jack, influenced by

Gwen, sets out to save the creature.

The story, a fairly simple one, is mainly there as a way to finally let Rhys in on his wife's secret life, and this is probably the most interesting aspect of the episode. In no way spectacular, but a fun episode to watch.

Adam – 8/10

An alien that feeds off memories infiltrates the team and starts to project new memories on them, changing their characters and convincing them he has been one of them for years. Gwen forgets her fiancé Rhys, Ianto is convinced he was once a murderer, Owen becomes a nerdy incompetent with a mad crush on Tosh who then in turn falls madly in love with the alien.

It's confusing stuff, but it's nice to see some of the actors take on different roles as they are pushed in new directions.

Reset – 2/10

Martha Jones, now working for U.N.I.T, is brought in to help the team investigate a drug that can 'reset'
someone's immune system; curing them of A.I.D.S, cancer and other potentially fatal diseases. But the drug is actually an alien larva, which grows inside them to become a fatal giant mayfly(?!).

The team go to investigate the head of the medical research centre, played by Jim Robinson from Neighbours(!), and find that he isn't going to give up his cure-all discovery without a fight.

Even Doctor Who (a kid's programme) at its daftest wouldn't have used this story without a lot more depth…so it's a bit disappointing that the 'adult' spin-off would.

Not a great addition to the series. The only saving grace is the end of the episode, where Owen appears to die, in a very tragic and heart-warming scene.

Dead Man Walking/A Day In The Death – 7/10

After the death of Owen in the last episode, the team manage to resurrect him via the alien gauntlet they have used before ('Everything Changes'/'They Keep Killing Suzie'). But unlike those cases, where the victim is brought back to life for a fleeting amount of time, Owen appears to be brought back indefinitely, albeit as a
walking 'undead' person. He drifts in limbo between life and death, or 'nothingness,' as he hears the creepy voice of Death calling to him.

He becomes possessed by *Death* itself (or a Death-like creature) and takes on the role of *destroyer* against his will. The gauntlet comes to life (in a scene that is unintentionally hilarious and resembles something out of the Addams Family) making Martha into an emaciated elderly woman. In the end he must take on 'Death' and restore everything to normal.

In the second episode we join Owen as he tries to deal with his waking death. He manages to convince a suicidal woman who has lost her husband to give life another try. He shares his own story of spectacularly losing his position at Torchwood, being demoted to less dangerous tasks (such as making the tea) since his *possession*, but then finding the will to go on and live the extra 'life' he has been given.

It is a poignant two-parter that shows just how much the character of Owen has evolved since the beginning of the first series.

We also say goodbye to Martha after her short stint in

the series. As much as I loved her in the third series of Doctor Who, here she seems out of place and without any real character to add. It's a shame, and a waste of a good companion in my opinion.

Overall it's quite a philosophical story that won't be everybody's cup of tea, but I enjoyed it and would definitely watch it again.

Something Borrowed – 9/10

It's Gwen's hen-night and we meet a load of friends that we've never seen before. This is confusing in itself; considering she hasn't even got time to see her fiancé in most episodes...but anyway...

After being bitten by a shape-shifting alien, she wakes up on her wedding day...heavily pregnant! And that's not the least of her problems. The shape shifter was male, impregnating her with a bite...but she has yet to meet the female; who has an even more grotesque idea of childbirth. She follows Gwen to the wedding; intent on ripping the newborn from poor Gwen's womb...nice!

Alien aside, the wedding of Gwen and Rhys plays out much more like a regular drama, which is a nice change of pace after some quite bleak episodes. This episode is funny, sentimental and *thoroughly* Welsh(!). I enjoyed it immensely.

From Out Of The Rain – 7/10

Escaped 'Night Travellers;' creatures can exist for 'reel' on old celluloid film and travel between realities, feeding on the life-essence of others. Torchwood find that two of these beings have begun to roam Cardiff, killing off innocent random victims for their sport.

It's great to see Julian Bleach, who had recently played Davros in Doctor Who, as the 'ringmaster,' and he once again puts in a wonderfully sinister performance. The ideas are all really curious and nightmarish ones...but it does feel lacking in depth at times, and the scope feels like it could've been a little broader. Appealing enough.

Adrift – 6/10

Gwen and Tosh discover that the rift is not *unidirectional* as they had first thought, but has also got the capability to suck people from this side of reality into itself. When one boy goes missing, Gwen's investigation unearths many hundreds of lost cases, all attributable to the rift's force. Yet she also discovers that Jack has actually been hiding the truth - sometimes people are returned!   But it's often at a great cost to their physical or mental health.

It's great to see Ruth Jones (Little Britain, Gavin and Stacey), who plays the mother of the lost boy, and she is great here as always. This isn't a bad serial by any means. But compared with some of the stronger points of the series, it is undeniably a *'filler'* episode.

There's not much to really make it stand out; apart from the enthralling development of the rift's powers to 'take' as well as 'give,' and some worthy dialogue.

Fragments – 10/10

Whilst the last couple of episodes have been rather pedestrian and not overly memorable, that could never be said about this episode, which is arresting and intense from

the outset. Within the first 10 minutes we see more than half the team (Ianto, Tosh, Owen and Jack) seemingly killed by mass explosions! We are then thrown back in time to when Jack first 'joined'
Torchwood, and from there get a back story of all the main Torchwood characters (apart from Gwen, whose story we had followed in the pilot episode).

The flashbacks start with the immortal Jack. The original Torchwood had been set up to monitor and track the Doctor and other aliens/'phantasmagoria' at the behest of Queen Victoria (at the end of the 10th Doctor story 'Tooth and Claw'), and Jack is being hunted down by the first Cardiff branch over 100 years ago after they discover he has links with the Time Lord. Jack is forced to work for them, when they find out about his immortality; which he continues to do until the present day.

Next we follow Tosh's flashback; and discover that she had been made to steal and assemble a high-tech sonic device (similar to a proto-sonic screwdriver) for a company that is holding her mother prisoner. U.N.I.T manages to break into the company, arrest and detain Tosh for stealing the device. However, Jack becomes interested in her clear talent, and makes a deal with U.N.I.T that she can have her freedom in return for working for him.

Jack's back-story really ties in the 'parent-show' and Torchwood spin-off well. Tosh's back-story is done in a really harrowing and rousing way, which makes the story of Ianto - meeting Jack on a routine break from his London Torchwood assignment before the episode
'Cyberwoman' to track down a Pterodactyl - seem rather lacking in substance. This can't be said for the tragic story of Owen that finishes the flashbacks; showing his former life with his fiancé, who has a strange tumour that turns

out to be an alien parasite. This is again pretty ridiculous, but is handled in a very heartrending way.

All-in-all this is essential viewing for any fan of the show, and really adds to the characters' stories; drawing you in as a viewer. One of the most memorable and important episodes of the series.

Exit Wounds – 2/10

The rather annoying Captain John (Captain Jack's ex boyfriend) is back. It would seem that Jack's young brother (last seen being lost by Jack in 'Adam') has grown up with a hatred of him for having lost him as a child. He is now forcing Captain John (by strapping a bomb to him) to destroy all that Jack loves.

Although this end serial could/should be put together with the penultimate episode, as it precedes it...I just couldn't bring myself to review them as such – they're just so wildly different in quality. The last episode broke new ground for the series; showing new depths to the main characters and showing what a great drama this show can be. But this final episode was extremely weak in comparison; rehashing old ideas and throwing together lots of elements of the show that made for a very unsatisfying stew. Captain John continues to be a pretty rubbish character (though he is greatly improved here than the last time we saw him), and Jack's young brother is even less convincing as the main villain of the piece.

Added to this is the untimely and poorly handled death of two of my favourite characters from the show, Tosh and Owen. There were so many other times when both of them faced a much more dignified death than being sidelined to the last five minutes of one of the poorest serials of the series. However, this was beautifully done by Naoko Mori, who I shall miss terribly in the series, along with Burn Gorman's character Owen.

An even less enjoyable finale than the last series, and made even more disappointing after the excellent serial that came before it.

SERIES 3 – 'CHILDREN OF EARTH'

Day 1 – 10/10

A strange alien race The '456' (named by the Government after the frequency they have been transmitting over) are taking over the minds of children. This starts with the abduction of orphans in the mid-60's (apart from one child who escaped, but we'll come back to him).

We are then forced forward to the present day, where children all over the world are suddenly 'pausing' in time for an elongated period of time; stopping dead-still for no apparent reason. After a couple of pauses, the mystery deepens. The children, in their strange trance- like state, now utter the phrase 'we...are...coming,' in unison.

Torchwood and U.N.I.T originally join forces to look into these strange occurrences; but it soon becomes apparent that the Government have an ulterior motive for keeping an eye on Torchwood. John Frobisher, a Government Secretary to the Home Office (played by the excellent 12th Doctor himself Peter Capaldi!) seems to have some previous knowledge of the aliens, and a vested interest in their return. A new P.A in the ministry office, Lois, becomes intrigued by the strange goings on and unearths not only files on the mysterious Torchwood, but a plot to kill off

Captain Jack Harkness.

To quote an earlier episode, 'everything changes' here. We're into a new season. Instead of the usual episodic 45 minutes, we have a series-long story, broken down into 5 parts, and broadcast over a single week. Two of the main characters have tragically died (Owen and Tosh), leaving Jack, Gwen and Ianto to carry on the team.

The last time the Doctor Who universe had attempted one series long story was in the ill-fated 'Trial of a Time Lord' in the mid-80's; though there have been 'story arcs' throughout the first couple of modern Doctor Who series, starting with 'Bad Wolf' in the first series, and the foretelling of the Torchwood spin-off in the second. This is a brave move, but works well.

From the beginning, the whole feeling of the programme has shifted. It feels less 'cheap' and 'sexed up' and much more chilling. There is great acting all-round, a compelling and enthralling plot, great pacing and shrewd direction throughout. All of these ingredients make this the best series opener since the pilot. Even Ianto, who seemed rather a lost character throughout some of the last couple of series, has greatly improved, both in his acting and the scope of his character.

The cliff-hanger to this first episode is one of the best in a long time. The Government tries to cover their tracks surrounding the '456,' and try to kill off Jack, by implanting a bomb inside him; blowing him and the Torchwood base up. It doesn't get much more exciting than that – we're only an hour in, and the main character and environment of the series have already been destroyed!

A real 'game-changer,' and an enticing opening episode.

Day 2 – 10/10

Day two, and we're thrown straight into the action. The Government is trying to kill off the rest of Torchwood, starting with Gwen. She is pregnant and on the run with Rhys, and they make it as far as London, where Lois manages to track them down to join in their search and find out what is going on.

Jack 'reassembles' himself from his constituted 'bits' in a body bag and wakes up as a heavily burned corpse. This scene is supposed to be horrific, but I think perhaps I've watched too many zombie films as I found it quite comical. There are a lot of complicated plot twists and turns and extra characters to deal with here. But I'm not complaining. In fact, I've often criticised Torchwood for being too 'simplistic' in its narrative, especially for an 'adult' spin-off from the Doctor Who series. It seems that the formula is finally working here, and the writers have created something that stands apart as excellent drama on its own merits.

Rhys also adds much needed comic relief to this new, more serious direction for the show, and the combination of all the elements works really well again.

Day 3 – 8/10

The children of Earth once again go into their trances, this time pointing to the skies. It becomes clear that the aliens are coming...and soon! And come they do! The wonderfully creepy '456,' beam down through the rift to where the Government has created a 'cube' of safe gases for them to breathe.

America and U.N.I.T put in their oar; eager to know why the Government of England are taking control of the communication with the aliens. But it becomes more than any one country or force can handle when the aliens issue their demands...they want 10% of the entire children on the planet!

The Torchwood team are now back together, in hiding, and have to resort to stealing their food and resources. Jack's daughter and Grandson (either I'd forgotten about these characters, or this is a new development!) are kidnapped by the Government and used as a deterrence to stop him getting involved.

It appears Jack has already been involved before...as we discover it was him who first gave the 12 children (apart from the one we now know has escaped) to the aliens in 1965!

The peril is constant, the action is gripping and the plot is really bringing the best out of all the characters.
There are some great suspenseful scenes in this episode in particular, and a great 'War of the Worlds' feel to this series, which I like.

Day 4 – 8/10

In the shock cliff-hanger from the last episode, we learned that Jack had surrendered 12 innocent children to the '456' in the '60's. We now discover why he did it; in order to protect the rest of the human race. He chose 12 orphans because 'they wouldn't be missed' – nice Jack, *real* nice!

We at last see the wonderfully creepy aliens, who look rather like an updated version of the 'Fendahl' (4th Doctor). They give the Governments of the world their demand that they must surrender 10% of the Earth's children in order to save the human race. They start to try and decide which children will be 'least missed.' This leads to some rather gruesome social commentary by the show; as they decide in the end to opt for the 'failing schools' on the education 'league tables.'

It's clear that the Torchwood team must act, and fast, if they are going to stop the Government from giving up the children of the world. They record the Government's meetings (via their inside aide Lois), and use them to blackmail the '456' to show the world their intentions so the human race will rise up against them. In retaliation, the '456' declare war; spreading a virus killing everyone in the building. This doesn't include the Government themselves, but it does include many of their staff. It also, tragically involves Ianto, who unlike the immortal Jack, dies as a result of the virus.

It's a real shame to lose Ianto, as his character was really blossoming in this series. The series delves into quite sinister territory here. This is no
'season 1,' that's for sure! It's great, 'edge of your seat' stuff.

Day 5 – 7/10

The Government offers a fake inoculation to fool the parents of the '10%' who are going to be offered to the aliens; feeding them the lie that it will 'cure' them of their 'alien possession/trance.' We eventually find out that the '456' want chemicals they can harness from the children, that can be used as drugs.

In the end, our heroes save the day, by discovering they can kill the aliens by feed-backing their signal to them using a different frequency and pitch; using the children once more as projectors of the signal (though sadly killing Jack's Grandson in the process).

Jack is so upset by the loss of his Grandson and Ianto, that he decides at the end to break off from Torchwood and Earth, and set off on adventures by himself. This effectively ends the team, and the spin-off itself, leaving the whole show in jeopardy.

I thought the conclusion to the mystery of the '456' was a strange and rather disappointing one. But as the rest of the plot is so well written, I'm not complaining.

Whilst I'm no Mary Whitehouse, and enjoy the harrowing sides of drama, I thought there were some scenes here that were unnecessarily bleak and chilling. In particular the scene where Frobisher, who is told his children are to be sacrificed to the '456' as a sign of goodwill from the Government, decides he will instead kill them...and then himself. The camera pans out from the children's bedroom as we hear 4 shots, 3 for his family, 1 for himself. Scenes like this are very disturbing, and I'm unsure if they are perhaps too dark for a spin-off from Doctor Who...even an 'adult oriented' one.

I also thought the serial, which had started out with, and retained such a great pace and intrigue now seemed slightly to drag in its final act. That said, as a whole this is the most consistently strong season so far. A new benchmark in the quality of the show, and essential watching for Who fans and Torchwood fans alike.

SERIES 4 –
'MIRACLE DAY'

The New World – 6/10

One day no one on planet Earth dies...and then the next, and the next. But is this new 'miracle' a blessing...or a curse?

Within 4 months it is forecast that humanity will not be able to sustain the ever growing population of the world.

Gone are most of the old Torchwood faces (who have died off in the last 2 series), and instead we meet lots of new characters. We have Rex (C.I.A) and Esther (journalist, friend of Rex) who start to delve into the mysterious Torchwood organisation and Vera, a medical doctor who is looking into the strange goings on. On the other side of the coin is Oswald Danes (played by the excellent Bill Pullman); a paedophile killer who is one of the first to be 'saved' by the 'miracle;' escaping his death penalty, and even his sentence through not legally being able to be kept imprisoned after his execution has been carried out.

Rex 'dies' on the way to see Vera, getting impaled in a car crash...but like Oswald and everyone else, he continues to live. Meanwhile, Torchwood are carrying out their own investigation into the mystery. Jack recognises the phenomenon as a 'morphic field'...the immortality is not localised, but is connected throughout the whole world. And in a reversal of fortunes, the only person who now *can* die is Jack himself (who viewers will know is usually the only immortal).

This first episode doesn't fill me with confidence. Torchwood goes all-out American in this new re- branding of the franchise stateside, and it just doesn't feel like 'Who,' or even 'Torchwood' to me. It has abandoned what made it a uniquely different programme, in exchange for a pale imitation of superior American dramas like 'House' or 'Crime Scene Investigation.'

For all I have criticised the early show, I now miss the simple old days of series 1 and 2. The remaining 2 original Torchwood characters no longer feel the main focus, and the new characters don't really develop the show in a positive way. The pace is fairly fast though, and there is plenty to watch, however confusing I found it.

Rendition – 6/10

Poor Gwen is separated from her family as the remaining Torchwood team are extradited to the U.S by the C.I.A, with Rex and another officer as their guards.

The officer escorting Rex and the Torchwood prisoners has orders from 'on high' to dispose of Jack, and poisons him with cyanide. Rex, on finding out, changes allegiances to help out Gwen and Jack, and manages to save him. It turns out Rex is pretty badass!

Although it feels very different as a show from previous seasons, you've got to admire the producers for trying to break new ground. You can certainly tell there has been a lot of money spent to really stretch the appeal of the show across the ocean to an American audience. Again, however, it doesn't seem like Jack or Gwen get much of a central role, behind a more prominent Rex and other new characters. These first episodes act as an introduction to Torchwood for potential American fans. But the new characters (apart from Rex, who is growing on me slightly) don't seem to carry the same sort of weight as those from previous seasons, and they are pretty annoying and forgettable.

Whilst the writers managed to make a 5 part story work really well in series 3, I am less confident about a 10 parter working with the remaining 2 Torchwood characters and these new rather less exciting ones. Even Gwen, who I usually love, is irritating in this particular episode!

Dead Of Night – 2/10

Rex, Jack and Gwen track down the C.I.A chief responsible for the hit put out on them...and discover he has orders from a mysterious, unknown force.

They meet up with Esther and Dr. Vera, and the new team is complete. Together, they unearth a factory full of pain-killers. It seems a company, 'PhiCorp' has known that Miracle Day was going to happen for at least a year previously, and has stockpiled drugs to sell to the new legions of 'undead' people.

Oswald, now a celebrity after publicly asking for forgiveness, is now advertising PhiCorp; urging the Government to give people 'free' access to buy their
drugs. Obviously there is a connection and an unknown plan behind all of this which implicates both PhiCorp and Oswald, but we are unsure what this is at this stage.

All of this is interspersed with some pretty boring dialogue and limp sex scenes. Another pretty unsatisfying episode...something tells me this series is really going to drag!

Escape To L.a – 3/10

The team travels to Venice Beach, California, to follow Oswald, who seems to be at the centre of the PhiCorp mystery.

There is a new campaigner on the scene, Ellis Monroe; spearheading the slogan 'dead is dead,' and urging the people who should've died to be segregated before the world runs out of resources. She is soon taken by mysterious men in black, who bump her off by crushing her in her own car(!).

Her ideas however are already in action...and camps spring up around the world to house the 'undead,' including Gwen's father.

I'm still finding this series slow, with unpleasant effects and dislikeable characters.

The Categories Of Life – 4/10

The 'undead' are being divided into 3 categories. Category 1 are those without 'normal brain function,' who would've died under normal circumstances. Category 2 would've died, but are alive and functioning and now may now be 'healing' (like Rex). Category 3 is 'everyone else.' Category 1 and 2 are forced into what are referred to as 'hospitals,' but which are thinly veiled concentration camps. Gwen flies back to South Wales to attempt to rescue her father when he is put into one of the camps there, whilst Rex and Dr. Vera infiltrate one of the American camps. They find separate 'modules,' where the Category 1 patients are being burned to ashes. Unfortunately for Dr. Vera, she finds this out too late, from the inside, and comes to a smoky and sudden end.

Meanwhile, on the outside of the camps, support for the 'redeemed' killer Oswald grows to almost religious fervour, as he goes on a media campaign to convince people their immortality is the next stage of the evolutionary process (or living 'angels' no less!).

Even with the fickle nature of the 'media mob,' it's difficult to really believe this element of the story, as well acted as it is by Bill Pullman. Although this episode is again much more 'adult' and 'gritty,' it's all a bit *too* grim. When one of the main characters is a murdering paedophile, and the good guys are getting burned to death, it's all a bit overblown for my liking.

...and yet for all the shock and gore that is packed into this episode, it *still* manages to drag!

The Middle Men – 6/10

The team continues their research into PhiCorp. Jack follows Chief Operating Officer Stuart Owens (Winston from Ghostbusters), but discovers he is just a 'middle man' to the mysterious over-seeing protagonists. Esther goes after the head of the camp (another rather slimy middle-man), but similarly draws a blank as to the real people in charge. She is reunited with Rex when he is captured videoing Category 1 people being burned in the hidden camp 'modules.' The head of the camp chains him up and stabs him with his pen (a fitting weapon for a faceless bureaucrat).

Whilst I'm slowly starting to get into the series, Jack and Gwen are hardly in this episode, and it really doesn't feel like Torchwood, certainly not at its best.

Immortal Sins – 1/10

We go back to Jack's past (1927), to find him hooking up with an Italian guy called Angelo. Jack introduces Angelo to his Torchwood work, and together they uncover a group of gangsters that have an alien parasite in a box (just a normal Torchwood day at the office then?). But apparently, these insanity inducing parasites are being used by a higher power to influence powerful historical figures; change important events and feed off the changes caused. The higher power turns out to be the 'Trickster's Brigade' (a nice tip of the hat to the creepy recurring character from Sarah Jane Adventures and the Doctor Who episode 'Turn Left').

Meanwhile, back in the present day, Gwen is contacted by more mysterious bad guys, and told to deliver Jack in exchange for her kidnapped family.

Whilst I have criticised other episodes for sidelining the main Torchwood characters (Gwen and Jack) to almost extras in their own story, this one tries to re-address the balance by taking us off on a complete tangent. You can't blame the spin-off for trying to stretch itself away from its origins. But it has gone so far with this aim as to lose most of its foundation as a programme. This is made obvious in this episode, when Jack mentions his old friend 'The Doctor' for the first time in ages, and it feels completely out of place.

The back-story seems like a pointless aside, at least at first...though the episode does end with Angelo's seeming connection to the kidnappers...and we are left wondering what this is all about.

To be honest, I'm not overly interested, but let's keep going with this!...

End Of The Road – 6/10

A woman who has contacted the team turns out to be Angelo's granddaughter; not directly involved with the mysterious enemy, but searching into it just as they are. It appears that after meeting Jack, Angelo (see last episode) spent his whole life trying to discover the secret of immortality. And he was not alone. Three 'families' drained Jack's blood when he was being attacked in the 1920's and discovered 'the Blessing.' This has got some connection to Miracle Day...at least I think this is what is explained in this episode. It all seems rather complicated and long-winded.

Meanwhile, Oswald finds that his luck has run out – there is a new 'Category 0' for people who are going to be put in the 'ovens' for 'moral' reasons – and his name is on the top of the list. As you can imagine, he's not too happy about this. He beats up his P.R agent Jilly...who then sides with PhiCorp/The 'Three Families.'

The C.I.A catch up with Rex. A corrupt agent who has been given instructions by the mysterious powers and promptly tries to 'off' everyone; only managing to 'kill' one of his fellow agents, Angelo's granddaughter...and himself. Meanwhile, Angelo 'manages' to die in the traditional sense; becoming the first since Miracle Day. This raises a few difficult questions – is this the end of Miracle Day? Is everything back to normal? It turns out there is a transmitter under the floorboards of Angelo's room, which is helping to generate the 'morphic field' through which the immortality of the human race is spread throughout the planet. Jack, worried that this sort of 'future technology' could be lethal if taken by the Government, manages to dismantle it, but is shot as he tries to escape.

Confusing, but full of action, this episode was worth a watch. It still feels nothing like Torchwood though.

The Gathering – 6/10

Two months after the last episode, the world is going through another 'Great Depression.' And the camps are very much open again. Jack and Esther are in hiding in Scotland. Esther believes 'The Families' are after Jack's immortality, so is storing his blood as leverage if they should catch them up. Gwen's family are back in Wales, hiding her 'Category 1' father in the basement. Rex is back at the C.I.A, trying to find the links between Jack and the 'Three Families' that have pursued him since the '20s. Oswald finds Gwen, and asks for Jack, in exchange for the name behind the 'Miracle.' Jack appears, but the name given is another 'red herring' – 'Harry Boscoe' – the name of the process by the C.I.A of filtering news from the public through 'media-friendly' translations of events (dating back to Vietnam). We discover Oswald's P.R agent, Jilly Kitzinger, is now working for the 'Three Families' and has been helping PhiCorp to do just that, on behalf of her charges.

The other recurring term that keeps piquing the interest of all sides is 'the blessing;' which appears to stretch in a line from one side of the planet (Shanghai) to the other (Buenos Aires), where two blood banks have mysteriously been destroyed.

When Gwen's father is finally found and taken to the camp to be burned, she has nothing to lose and vows to put a stop to the whole thing once and for all. Flying to Shanghai, Jack and Gwen (with Oswald in tow) discover that Jack's blood is linked and is pointing them literally in the direction of 'The Blessing' itself.

A lot to take in here; and a slightly more absorbing penultimate episode.

The Blood Line – 8/10

Gwen, Jack and Oswald manage to get into 'The Blessing' lair in Shanghai, with Oswald carrying explosions strapped to his chest. But in Buenos Aires, Esther and Rex are captured by 'The Families.' 'Team Jack' have the advantage, as Jack's blood seems linked to 'The Blessing,' and a stand-off ensues between the
'Families' and 'Torchwood.'

They discover 'The Blessing' is actually a friendly entity that has existed in the centre of the Earth since the dawn of the planet; with a 'morphic link' which ties symbiotically with the whole of mankind. The 'Three Families' have been experimenting on 'The Blessing' for some time, and decided to feed it the blood of an
immortal (Jack). Feeling it was being attacked, 'The Blessing' took the blood and sent out a 'morphic field' to try and protect the human race by making everyone immortal; causing the end of world order by trying to protect it. 'The Families' in turn have been using this chaos to seize power over mankind.

The only way to stop it is for Jack's blood to be fed into 'The Blessing' from both sides of the world simultaneously. Rex, who has foreseen this, transfuses Jack's blood, and both he and Jack sacrifice themselves
to stop the 'Miracle.' Life and death return...and so does Jack's (and therefore Rex's) immortality.

A pretty good end to a pretty dire series. It seems coincidental that a series about people who can't die
feels like purgatory to watch, and I found most episodes

difficult to follow or fathom to be honest. Sure, there are some good ideas and a few good scenes, but it takes far too long to get going, takes you down far too many blind alleys and leaves you feeling frustrated rather than intrigued. Rarely reaching above the mediocre, this is a disappointing end to the programme (as it stands there are no plans to 'resurrect' the show).

I must admit, although it took me a long time to warm to Torchwood as a whole, there are several excellent moments that are essential watching for Doctor Who fans. I think it might take me a lot longer to feel this way about the fourth series however; and this final season is worth a miss unless you're a Torchwood completist.

THE SARAH JANE
ADVENTURES
(2006-2011):

PRE-SEASON 1

Pilot Episode - Invasion Of The Bane – 8/10

We rejoin Sarah Jane Smith, years after her ill-fated K-9 outing in the early 80's. 25 years on, she is living in suburbia; still working as a journalist with more than a passing knowledge of the extra-terrestrial. Into her life stumbles Maria Jackson, a young girl who has moved in across the road.

The first story concerns 'Mrs. Wormwood' and the Bane; an alien race who have lured children into their factory using an addictive soft drink. This drink contains alien D.N.A that will convert whoever drinks it into one of them. They have also created a clone, or 'archetype' of a human boy, woven together from scans of 10,000 human visitors to the factory, in order to better understand and enslave the human race. Sarah Jane and her young companion go looking into the mystery, and free the boy ('Luke') from the Bane. The lonely Sarah Jane befriends Maria and adopts the boy, and a new alien fighting team is born!

With a touch of Roald Dahl about it, this pilot episode cleverly satirises the fear of the 'evil additives' being peddled to kids in their diets. And with one of the largest childhood obesity levels in the world, it is a finger well pointed.

Ok, so this isn't up to the standard of the main show, but

in some ways I don't think it's trying to be. The style is much more light and child-friendly, catering to (but never patronising or playing down to – a crucial difference) the younger section of Who fans. It's great to see Sarah Jane back in her own vehicle, and the young actors also perform well in this first episode.

It's the sort of well constructed children's programme that an adult should be proud to like...rather like Doctor Who itself of course!

SEASON 1

Revenge Of The Slitheen – 8/10

Maria and Luke (the boy who had been created as a clone in the last serial and is now the adopted son of Sarah Jane) start at their new school, and find that their new teachers are acting very strangely. Ok, that's nothing new...but in this case it turns out that their teachers are in fact the infamous Slitheen!

Luke struggles with making friends and trying to fit in; not understanding the finer intricacies of trying to be 'cool.' Eventually however, he and Maria make friends with Clyde. The much 'cooler' Clyde is wary of the two slightly strange kids at first, but then finds out about the secret adventures they have with Sarah Jane and is brought into the fold.

A combination of the excellent Slitheen and the age-old growing pains of the main teenage characters make this another great example of kid's science fiction T.V at its best.

Eye Of The Gorgon – 7/10

Sarah Jane, Luke and Clyde go to investigate the strange goings on at an elderly residential home, where there are reports of a 'Gorgon' and nuns haunting the grounds.

One of the residents gives Luke a necklace, which ends up being of alien origin. It seems there is more to this old lady than meets the eye. For one thing, she seems to have knowledge of Sontarans and other alien races. It is all the work of a creepy Gorgon; an ancient myth that is very much real, though slightly different from the legend
– a parasite from another world who feeds on human hosts or turns its enemies into stone!

Meanwhile, Maria is having problems of a more domestic variety as her mum, recently separated from her boyfriend, moves back into Maria's father's house with them. This leads to her mum becoming concerned about the amount of time Maria is spending with Sarah Jane and Luke.

The episode introduces kids to the Greek myths in a fun and modern way. It's quite scary for a children's programme, but I found it an enjoyable and watchable story.

Warriors Of Kudlak – 6/10

A bug-eyed alien from the horse-head nebula lures children using a 'Laser-Quest' style adventure park. His intention is to take children and train them to be soldiers in his army.

As impressive as the aliens themselves are, the story itself is not really as memorable or exciting as the rest of the series so far.

Whatever Happened To Sarah Jane? – 10/10

Maria manages to open a puzzling box and unwittingly change history! Suddenly Sarah Jane and Luke have 'disappeared' and nobody seems to have any memory of them! There is even a different woman living in Sarah Jane's house and inhabiting Sarah Jane's life...strange goings on indeed!

Maria unearths the fact that the new woman in Sarah Jane's house is actually an old friend of hers; someone who should've died on a tragic day in Sarah's childhood. It turns out the woman has 'swapped places' in their fates by making a deal with a terrible soothsayer; leading to her 'stealing' Sarah Jane's timeline. The mysterious figure, 'the Trickster' is an apparition that 'feeds' on the chaos created by damaged timelines and must be stopped if Sarah Jane is to exist again!

Causality may seem rather deep for a kid's programme, but then this isn't just any kid's programme! Once again, the Sarah Jane Adventures shows what an intelligent and thought-provoking piece of children's drama it can be. The Trickster is a superbly sinister addition to a kid's programme; reminding me more of something out of Pan's Labyrinth or a similar more adult horror.

The story, the creepy enemy, the way the serial doesn't 'play down' to kids, but expands their minds and imaginations (just like Who at its best) – this is definitely the best of the series so far in my opinion and well worth watching for fans of both shows.

The Lost Boy – 10/10

Luke discovers that he is not in fact a creation of the Bane (see the pilot episode) but a missing child on the news. Sarah Jane has to bid a tearful goodbye to her surrogate son and get on with her lonely life once more.

But there are many twists to this seemingly simple story.

Firstly, as expected, Luke isn't in fact the missing boy 'Ashley,' and it's all a cunningly ploy by the returning Slitheen to kidnap him. Secondly, the main protagonist that is paying the Slitheen is none-other than Sarah Jane's alien super-computer, Mr. Smith - who turns out to be a 'Xylok,' a crystal-based life-form who has been plotting to take Luke and harness the telekinetic power of his great brain for a weapon with the capability to destroy worlds. Sarah Jane and the gang must defeat Mr. Smith and the Slitheen and save the Earth once more.

I'm going to say something now that will have many a modern 'Whovian' reaching for their pitchforks...but...I actually really prefer watching the first season of The Sarah Jane Adventures to the first series of Torchwood.

Yes, I realise that in many ways it's 'Tracey Beaker meets Scooby Doo,' and it's a daft, pale imitation of the parent show. But then, to me at least, the first series of Torchwood at its worst presented something a lot worse

– 'oo look, its Doctor Who with boobs!' And out of the two, I would opt for Scooby Doo any day. The show at its best (such as the penultimate and finale stories of this season) presents something that stands apart as great kid's television in its own right. It takes the parent show back to its roots as an uncomplicated, child-centred romp; educating and entertaining children without patronising them. Not since the days of the Doctor's Granddaughter Susan in the very first series of the show has Who presented the growing pains of its target audience with such clarity and realism. Liz Sladen must also be commended for taking the character of Sarah Jane and really evolving it. In this serial in particular, she shows an emotional intensity that I'd not seen from the character since her original exit in The

Hand of Fear.

A thoroughly enjoyable series, that might not be a favourite for older fans, but will hopefully be loved and remembered by younger fans for years to come. And let us not forget that this was the reason the original show was invented(!).

SEASON 2

The Last Sontaran – 6/10

Following the events of the end of The Sontaran Stratagem/ The Poison Sky (DW, Season 4), a solitary Sontaran manages to escape the battle and land his ship on Earth. Hiding in the woods, he decides to take revenge on humanity himself. He possesses the mind of a physicist who has access to a network of satellites which orbit the Earth; with the intention of bringing them all crashing into the planet and wiping it out.

We also say goodbye to Maria, who bids a teary farewell to Sarah and the gang after her dad is given a job in America.

It's nice to see the Sontarans, who are distinctive as always. It's also great to see the inside of a Sontaran spaceship again, which doesn't disappoint. And the serial is worth watching to bid farewell to Maria, who was a fun character in the last series. It's all not quite as engaging as some of the better serials in Series 1, but is still enjoyable.

The Day Of The Clown –7/10

Luke is missing Maria, but Clyde is more interested in the new girl at school, Rani (no, not *that* one Who fans!). That is until he discovers her dad is the strict new headmaster, who he has already managed to get on the wrong side of.

As usual, the teenage angst must wait, as there is another mystery afoot. All around children are going missing; abducted by a creepy clown. The clown has haunted Rani for some time, and now starts to haunt Clyde too. This connection brings Rani into the Sarah Jane team; completing the alien beating squad again.

It turns out the clown is really an alien elemental force that thrives on human emotions – fear in particular. Brought to Earth via a meteorite that landed many centuries ago, it has created myths and legends of terrifying abductors (such as the Pied Piper, or scary clowns in more recent times).

We discover that Sarah Jane was an orphan, who lost her parents as a small child, and that when she was living with her aunt she was haunted by a creepy marionette that appears to be returning in this new form. She must learn to conquer her fear and save the children before they disappear for good. In the end, it is Clyde who saves the day, finding that humour is the only way to banish the fear of the monster.

We are in Circus territory again; a popular children's fear that has been utilised before, both in Doctor Who (Kinda, The Greatest Show in the Galaxy etc..) and Torchwood (From Out of the Rain). Although Bradley Walsh (later to appear as a companion to Whittaker's Doctor) is a well-known comedian, his portrayal as the fear-making element is actually quite unsettling, especially for a children's programme.

I liked a couple of other things about this serial. It's nice to see some back-story for Sarah Jane and for some further development of her character. Also, I liked the conclusion of the story: the idea that humour can help banish fear – a nice life lesson to have in a kid's programme.

It's one of the silliest premises so far in the show, but it works well. This is a fun, and quite scary way to continue the second series.

Secrets Of The Stars – 1/10

A charlatan astronomer gets more than he bargains for when 'the ancient lights,' a power as old as the universe, take control of him via a falling star. With his easily corruptible mind, the lights then use him as a channel to enslave all of humanity via their 'star signs.' Only Luke, who was never 'born' and therefore has no star sign, can stop the chain of mind control and restore things back to normal.

From Bradley Walsh (who played the psychotic clown in the last serial) to Russ Abbot – I spot a pattern emerging! It's very difficult to believe in Russ Abbot as a threat to all humanity – this is the guy I used to laugh myself silly over as a kid! He really doesn't carry the right amount of menace to pull off one of the dumbest scripts of the show so far, and this serial is decidedly sub-par...embarrassingly so in fact. Worth skipping.

The Mark Of The Berserker – 8/10

A boy at the teenagers' school finds a pendant that will make everyone do his will...but will also gradually take over the owner; turning them into a 'berserker.'

Meanwhile, Clyde's dad returns, having left him when he was 9. This understandably causes friction in his family. In an effort to connect with his dad, Clyde shows him Sarah Jane's attic. Clyde's dad turns out to be a bit of a 'rotter' and steals the pendant, becoming more power-mad as he wears it. He even makes Clyde forget about his friends and his mum.

I admit I wasn't expecting much from this story. Sarah Jane is hardly in it, and the story didn't sound brilliant.

However, the main thing that sets this episode apart from the last 3 is the evolution of Clyde's character. Up until this point, Clyde had not been an overly
'fleshed out' character; a loveable rogue; a 'Han' to Luke's...erm... 'Luke' if we were talking about Star Wars. But as we see the return of Clyde's dad in this episode, Daniel Anthony (who plays Clyde) gives much more to his role in some really emotional scenes, which he excels in.

The fact that the show can function pretty well in the absence of its main character (at least temporarily) is testimony to how far it has come. I've yet to see a series 2 serial that 'wows' me like some of series 1 did, but this episode certainly goes some way to redressing the balance.

The Temptation Of Sarah Jane Smith – 8/10

The sinister 'Trickster' is back, lulling Sarah through a 'time fissure' and back to 1951 – to the time where her parents 'abandoned' her. He knows that Sarah Jane, on learning of her parents' death, will try to change a 'fixed point in time' and create an alternate time-line where he can rule over all creation. Sounds complicated – but any fan of Doctor Who will be used to this sort of 'time- meddling' story by now.

In the end, Sarah Jane's parents twig that their existence is the thing causing all the chaos, and decide they must make the ultimate sacrifice and drive to their deaths.

This leads to a very bitter-sweet conclusion, as Sarah Jane discovers she was not 'abandoned,' but 'saved' by her parents, who died in order for her to live.

A very poignant episode, with echoes of 'Father's Day' (9th Doctor). Added to the tragedy and horror, there is just the right amount of comic relief to make it work. I particularly liked the part where Sarah Jane runs up to a police box in 1951, believing that the Doctor has come to help her...only to find that it is just a normal 1950's police box!

Another great example of how this spin-off really strikes the balance between great kid's science fiction and heart-warming drama.

Enemy Of The Bane – 8/10

The squid-like shape-shifters from the pilot episode are back! Mrs. Wormwood, ostracised and hunted by her people, teams up with Commander Kaagh (from 'the Last Sontaran' episode). They are after an alien scroll, which will give them the power to rule the galaxy, and restore their honour with both of their people.

The scroll is located in the 'black archive' of U.N.I.T headquarters, and Sarah Jane must enlist the help of her old retired friend The Brigadier to help her reach it before the enemy do. Mrs. Wormwood captures her 'creation' Luke, and tries to convince him that he should help her; his 'real' mother. Will Luke make the right decision?

It's so great to see the wonderful Nicholas Courtney (The Brigadier) one last time. He was to die 3 years later and this is his last performance in a Doctor Who related programme. It is clear as you watch the story that he has lost none of his charm in this swansong performance.

It's also good to see the series not only tip its hat to its 'parent' programme (by the use of the Brigadier and the Sontarans), but also to take stock of its own history so far (tying thos story in with its own pilot episode).

An enjoyable season finale that is full of action and definitely worth seeing.

Specials

Red Nose Day Special - From Raxacoricofallapatorius With Love – 6/10

Ronnie Corbett plays a Slitheen rogue who beams down to the attic to trick Sarah Jane and her companions....yes, *that* Ronnie Corbett!

In this five minute Comic Relief special, the glorious puns fly back and forth at a rate of knots, and although this mad special doesn't add anything to the series, young kids will love it. Their parents will also no doubt appreciate all of the Two Ronnies references as I did.

> *"That was the most bizarre five minutes of my life.." (Sarah Jane Smith, From Raxacoricofallapatorius with Love)*

Sarah Jane, I completely agree with you!

SEASON 3

Prisoner Of The Judoon – 9/10

The first series saw the show borrowing the Slitheen, the second the Sontarans and now it's the turn of the rhino- like Judoon.

Sarah Jane goes to investigate a laboratory that has created nano-formed microscopic robots with the power to create, but also destroy if controlled by the wrong people.

Meanwhile a Judoon, an intergalactic 'police' officer working for the Shadow Proclamation (see 'Smith and Jones' from series 3 of 'new' Doctor Who) is shipping a highly dangerous criminal, when his ship crash-lands on Earth. As the prisoner escapes (the Judoon in hot pursuit) a deadly game of 'cat and mouse' (or 'rhino and lizard?') ensues; with humans being caught up in the crossfire. The team try to assist the Judoon and put an end to both the danger of the prisoner and the Judoon's threat to any humans that get in the way.

The prisoner certainly is dangerous! A 'veil' life form, he can inhabit, or 'step inside' the bodies of others and control them. He takes over Sarah Jane, and using Mr. Smith (Sarah Jane's computer) goes about using the nano-bots to destroy the Earth. In the end, it is Luke that talks the computer out of obeying the 'evil Sarah Jane,' by quoting its 'prime directive' to save humanity rather than destroying it.

Overall, this is a gripping and highly enjoyable serial. There are some hilarious scenes, as the pompous Judoon attempts to adapt to Earth's customs and those of his Earth contemporaries the Police. Seeing the Judoon flag down a 'boy-racer' with a space age blaster for example, was possibly the funniest scene I've seen from the show and needs to be seen to be believed!

The Mad Woman In The Attic – 8/10

We join Rani in the distant future; lonely, world weary and living as a recluse. A young boy has come to find her and discover the truth about the 'mad old woman' in the attic. She tells him the story of how she got to be the way she is, from all those years ago (our 'present').

We're thrown back to the here and now. Rani is struggling with the feeling that she is living in the shadow of Maria (series 1). After an argument with Sarah Jane, she goes off by herself to investigate a strange phenomenon.

People have been going missing at an abandoned fairground. A 'demon' has been abducting people and forcing them to live out their days as walking catatonic 'puppets.'

In reality, the 'demon' is an alien child refugee called Eve, who has escaped from the Time-War between the Time Lords and Daleks (nice tip-of-the-hat to the parent series), and is capturing people through mind-control to be her 'playmates' to keep her from being lonely. After hearing Rani say she wished Sarah Jane and the others would 'leave her alone;' Eve, who is also able to 'grant wishes,' takes Rani's friends out of existence. Not only is the alien powerful in these ways, she also has the Time Lord power of seeing through time, and uses this to show Rani how a life without Sarah Jane and her friends would leave her as the 'mad old woman' we saw at the beginning of the serial.

Her power has not matured however, and she is quickly killing herself by using it. Rani must help her realise that controlling humans will not fill the loneliness she feels, and she must fix her craft and return home.

I wasn't sure about Rani in the last series, and I admit I missed Maria's character. But she finally comes into her own in this serial, getting much more of a central role.

After the original mystery of Eve, she turns out to be a very sweet character who is well played by Eleanor Tomlinson. Her race's superpowers are potentially pretty formidable, and you can imagine the threat a fully developed alien of her type could cause if they were to take on the Doctor or Torchwood (this would make for a fantastic serial for either show!).

Mysterious, intriguing and pretty frightening for a kid's programme. The design of the alien is excellent, as is the creepy 'magic mirror' computer that assists her in her misguided scheme. A highly inventive serial with a mixture of both scary and sweet moments; with an underlying moral story that we should appreciate what we have...and be careful what we wish for.

The Wedding Of Sarah Jane Smith – 8/10

Sarah Jane finally finds love (in the form of the dashing Mr. Nigel Havers)...only to find out it's another of the Trickster's ploys to persuade her to give up her life defending the Earth in favour of settling down.

The Trickster is a 'Pantheon,' and relies on people's

agreement to gain control. He visits people at the time of their death and offers them the 'deal' of life. But in return he tricks them to be under his spell. He has made a pact with Nigel Haver's character (after he dies) that if he will marry Sarah Jane, he will be given his life back.

Thinking that the Trickster is a benevolent angel, the man gives Sarah Jane a magic engagement ring, not realising that if she says 'I do,' time and space will be up for the Trickster's taking!

All is not lost however. An old friend of Sarah Jane's is about to come to the rescue...the Doctor!! In retaliation, the Trickster manages to trap Sarah Jane in one *second* of time, and the Doctor and her companions in another *second*. They are unable to break out of this, and are effectively trapped forever!

There are some really notable character moments in this story. You really feel for the character of Sarah Jane; who finally gets a chance at love after having never quite been able to live 'a normal life' since her adventures with the Doctor. This only serves to make it all the more tragic when she ultimately has to give up her love to save her friends.

It's always great to see the Trickster, who is at his usual snarling, wonderful self. It's also a real treat to see the (10th) Doctor, appearing for the first time in one of the spin-offs. However, I did find him strangely out of place, and even quite annoying in this one. I choose to see this as testimony to how effectively the spin-off is now able to shine on its own, without the need for reference to the original programme. It's a nice treat for kids who have been watching the spin-off to finally get to see the Doctor in the programme (he will return in his 11th form in the next series), and this gives the show a renewed kudos to have this link...even if this serial would have probably been just as strong without it.

The Eternity Trap – 6/10

The team go to investigate a 'haunted house;' only to find that it is ruled by an alien who has trapped people and forced them to live in the house for hundreds of years.

It's fairly spooky stuff, with some nice scenes. But the supporting characters are pretty irritating in this one, and whilst it's a good watch, it wasn't really a highlight of the series for me.

Mona Lisa's Revenge – 5/10

Thanks to 'alien paint' from 500 years ago, paintings are coming to life in a London gallery. The most famous of all portraits, the Mona Lisa becomes flesh, as a living, breathing and evil northerner(?). She plots to take over the world by bringing her 'brother in paint' to life; a painting banned for its power to drive all who look at it insane.

A mixture between Ghostbusters 2 and A Night at the Museum, this is a pretty strange episode, which didn't really work. Mona Lisa is a fun character, but I'm not quite sure why she was evil, or from Northern England for that matter!

Not one of the better episodes.

The Gift – 6/10

Beware aliens bearing gifts! The 'Blathereen,' another family from Raxicoricofallapatorius, visit Earth under the guise of making peace with humanity after the sins of their planet's worst sons the Slitheen. They offer a gift of 'rakweed,' as recompense, saying that it will end world hunger. It is, of course another trick by the tricksy Raxicoricofallipatorians. The plant reproduces with incredible speed, via spores that put humans into a deep and endless coma. It is all a plot by the Blathereen to turn the Earth into one big rakweed crop (which is addictive to their species) and become super-rich in the process.

A rather lightweight end to another excellent series.

SEASON 4

The Nightmare Man – 7/10

Boy genius Luke takes his A-Levels early and sails through with 4 A*s. Offered a place at Oxford University, he realises he will have to leave his mum and friends behind. This rise in anxiety leads to his first ever nightmares and a creepy alien parasite, 'The Nightmare Man;' who feeds off fear and traps him and his friends in an eternity of their own worst imaginings.

Julian Bleach returns; having previously played Davros in Doctor Who and an evil circus master in Torchwood. Although Bleach is a wonderful actor, I didn't feel this third character was as well realised or effective as his previous incarnations. But there is still something there which will no doubt scare viewers, particularly younger children.

Luke's departure is very emotional, and you can tell there is genuine affection between the cast members. Liz Sladen in particular delivers another very heart- warming performance as Sarah Jane, who has finally found something resembling a normal life with her adopted son Luke...only to have to say good-bye to him again.

The Vault Of Secrets – 6/10

Androvax, the 'veil' alien and destroyer of worlds from

'Prisoner of the Judoon' returns...and he needs Sarah Jane's help! His race is dying out and only Sarah Jane can save him from a bite he has acquired from a 'space snake.'

The team and Androvax are pursued by 'men in black;' androids that wipe the memories of anyone who has run into aliens.

I thought the 'men in black,' was quite a lazy piece of writing – they literally 'ape' the Will Smith film, with the name and purpose (if not the flesh and bone). They also look like a bad mixture of 'T-1000' from Terminator 2 and 'Nasty Nick' from Big Brother; which is less than convincing.

Whilst the episode is well paced, it does feel like it's treading over old ground and presenting us with nothing startling or new.

Death Of The Doctor – 7/10

U.N.I.T turns up on Sarah Jane's doorstep to inform her that the Doctor is dead! 'The Shansheeth' (intergalactic vulture-like undertakers!) return the body for the funeral. Sarah Jane is joined at the wake by another of the Doctor's old companions, Jo Grant (who returns for the first time since The Green Death from 1973). Jo is now a very groovy granny; having travelled the world protesting and fighting for environmental issues since leaving the Doctor. Sarah Jane and Jo hit it off quickly as they realise they have the same sneaky suspicion that the Doctor can't really be dead, and that something decidedly dodgy is going on.

After some snooping, they discover it is all part of the evil Shansheeth's plan to capture the T.A.R.D.I.S. They have a machine that can turn objects from people's memories into physical reality. Lulling the companions to the Doctor's funeral, they hope to create the T.A.R.D.I.S key from his companions' memories.

Of course the Doctor isn't dead, and he manages to travel across the galaxy by 'swapping' bodies with Clyde. He takes on the Shansheeth to reclaim his rickety time machine and restore order!

The Doctor returns to the show, this time in his 11th incarnation (Matt Smith). The chemistry between the Doctor and his companions seems more forced this time around. I feel this is something to do with the difference between the two Doctors. Tennant was a huge fan of the 'classic era' of the show when he was young; giving him a certain natural rapport with Liz Sladen during their scenes together; whereas Matt wasn't born at the time of Sarah Jane or Jo Grant's first appearances in the show, and struggles to add the same level of conviction to his connections.

The vulture-like Shansheeth are a wonderfully fun design, but are more on the comic than sinister side, and they are a less than believable threat to the Doctor's life.

What makes this really stand out as essential viewing, (certainly for fans of the older show) is the back-story we get from many companions we have not heard from since their travels with the Doctor. There is a huge amount of satisfaction in getting closure on what has happened to so many characters. Not only is it great to see Jo Grant again, but we find out about Ian and Barbara (1st Doctor - who became Cambridge University professors together after travelling with the Doctor, and apparently haven't aged since their travels with him!), Ben and Polly (2nd Doctor – Married and working in an orphanage in India), Harry (4th Doctor – working on vaccines and finding cures for many diseases), Tegan (5th Doctor – a fighter for Aboriginal rights in Australia), and Ace (7th Doctor – who has set up 'A Charitable Earth' – A.C.E).

Whilst this isn't an amazing story, the links to Doctor Who's past is well worth checking out.

> *(N.B – Another puzzling development in the episode is that the Doctor mentions that he can change '507' times...now I'm confused! It has always been said that the Doctor has only 13 incarnations?!...<2023 addendum - Could this be an allusion to the 'Timeless Child,' and if so, how does the 11th Doctor know about this?!>).*

The Empty Planet – 9/10

One morning, Clive and Rani wake up to find that everyone has disappeared and they are seemingly the only people left on the whole planet!

Not even Mr. Smith works. There are no signals at all - no mobiles, no Internet...just unnerving silence.

As they search for the answer, they run into one other 'survivor,' a 13 year old orphan called Gavin. The three soon wish they really *were* alone; as into the mix come 2 huge rampaging robots that seem bent on finding and destroying them! In the final twist of events, it turns out that Gavin is actually the long lost heir to the throne of an alien planet. Having never met his father, he is unaware that he holds such a position, or that the robots have removed all humans from the planet as *ransom* for his return.

The only reason that Clive and Rani are spared being kidnapped with the rest of Earth is that they had already been 'grounded' by the Judoon in the previous series and told not to leave the planet. It seems even these huge robots aren't brave enough to go against intergalactic law! So it's up to just Sarah Jane's companions to put things right!

This could be seen as a 'Sarah Jane-lite' episode, as the main character hardly appears. Whilst I did miss Sarah Jane, the fact that the supporting cast could sustain a full episode shows just how far the characters have come. This wouldn't have worked a couple of seasons ago.

The robots look amazing, and it's difficult to imagine another children's programme (apart from Who itself) that could pull off such awesome oddball stories as this. A very novel plot, which is full of action and adventure. Definitely one of the high points for the series.

Lost In Time – 5/10

'The Shopkeeper,' a mysterious magician (possibly a Time Lord?) forcibly enlists the help of Sarah Jane, Rani and Clyde to find three lost segments of a case that will help save the Earth from destruction. The Shopkeeper throws the team into three different times, where each of the elements is stranded. In these three separate times, each of them must face their own peril before finding the element they need and returning home.

Sarah Jane is in 1889, helping a young girl face echoes of a future crime. Rani is in 1553, where she befriends the poor Queen Lady Jane-Grey before she is disposed of and beheaded by the soon-to-be Queen Mary. Clyde is in 1941, fighting invading Nazis on the coast of England with an evacuee.

Whilst this an interesting premise, the three elements felt like smaller stories forced inexplicably together; making engagement in all three more difficult. The Shopkeeper is a fun character, but the lack of back-story or 'modus operandi' which would usually make for an enigmatic character left them feeling incomplete. Likewise, the overall threat to the Earth isn't very well explained; leaving you wondering what all the fuss is about in the first place.

A few good scenes, but overall quite dissatisfying.

Goodbye, Sarah Jane Smith – 8/10

After going to investigate a meteor, the team run into 'another Sarah Jane' (Ruby White) who seems to share all the aspects of the original...an attractive middle-aged woman who possesses alien technology and is an investigator of odd phenomenon. She has been looking into the 'Ealing Triangle' (the name given to the area where the mysteries of the last few series have been happening). Sarah Jane falls ill; showing signs of mental deterioration. This combined with meeting the younger, seemingly more successful version of herself leaves her feeling outmoded and out of place. She starts acting very strangely, giving up on her role and on those closest to her.

In reality, it is all part of 'Ruby's' plan. She turns out to be a parasitic alien that creates extreme emotions in others before feeding off them. She has created the illness in Sarah Jane, draining her of all her excitement and adventure. She swaps places with Sarah Jane, banishing her to her own prison and instating herself in Sarah Jane's place. It's once again up to Clive and Rani (and Luke, who returns) to save the day.

This is quite a sombre end to another great series. The illness Sarah Jane undergoes in this episode tragically echoes real life; as this was the last episode to be broadcast before Liz Sladen died. This made this episode particularly sad to watch, and all the more poignant to the viewer.

SEASON 5

Sky – 7/10

An alien baby lands on Sarah Jane's doorstep. As well as the usual baby behaviour, she has telekinetic powers over electrical devices and can damage her environment if she is distressed. She also grows much quicker than humans; developing 12 years in no time at all.

Hot in pursuit is her equally powerful and dangerous 'Fleshkind' mother and a 'Metalkind' organically metal creature. We discover that the young child (who Sarah Jane christens Sky) has been created by the 'Fleshkind' as a weapon; a ticking time-bomb ready to explode and take down the 'Metalkind' in an ongoing intergalactic war.

The wonderful Liz Sladen sadly passed away during the making of this last series; and this makes watching the final episodes all the more moving. Whilst this is not the most momentous episode, the opening scene where Sarah Jane describes the wonders and terrors of the vast universe that she has travelled is really affecting.

The Curse Of Clyde Langer – 10/10

Sarah Jane and company go to investigate a creepy Totem Pole which is fabled to contain the soul of an evil spirit.

They are very sceptical, until Clyde splinters himself on it and everything starts to change. Waking up the next day, he finds to his horror that whenever his name is mentioned, people take an instant dislike to him. Even those closest to him like Sarah Jane, Rani or his own mother suddenly detest him, and aggressively close him out of their lives.

Cast out into the streets, Clyde becomes homeless. He meets and befriends a homeless girl (Ellie). He sets out trying to both solve his own mystery and improve the sorry lot of his new friend.

I found this episode really sad and sobering for a kid's programme. Daniel Anthony steals the show once again as Clyde, and brings an effective realism and warmth to the character. Sky too, who seemed like a bit of a surplus character in the last episode does a great job here as the only companion not affected by the 'psycho- phonic' curse that makes everyone hate the sound of Clyde's name.

Portraying the upsetting subject of homelessness in a children's programme is a very brave move. This story is an inspirational and thought-provoking one; which shows once again the sort of emotional resonance that this programme is capable of having.

The Man Who Never Was – 8/10

'The Serf Board' is the new laptop on the market, and claims to be the new much needed accessory of everyone on the planet. When the team go to investigate the charismatic Mr. Serf however, they discover him to be a high-tech hologram steered by alien slaves. The slaves are being controlled by a profiteering 'P.A,' using cruel punishments to keep them in line. Sarah Jane and company have to find a way to stop the hologram and its master from hypnotising the Earth, and free the alien slaves so they can return to their home-world.

Some fun ideas, but perhaps not the most momentous story to end the series, or Elizabeth Sladen's amazing career. But of course, no one knew that it would be the last. This last series had to be cut short with the tragic death of one of television's most beloved actresses. It seems so strange and bitter-sweet to see her looking so radiant till the end...still so full of life. Her unique beauty and character shine throughout; showing no signs of the terrible illness she was going through.

Liz Sladen was a truly wonderful human being, who helped not only create one of the most loved eras of one show, but was so effective as Sarah Jane that she helped make this series shine in its own right. Had I not been writing a book about Doctor Who, I may not have had the chance to watch all of these episodes, but I'm so glad that I did. It's a great family series; which re-captures the feeling of Doctor Who in its black and white infancy. And although this programme was made for younger children, there is enough there to entertain fans of all ages.

There is a touching tribute that C.B.B.C showed when Elizabeth died. I recommend you track it down on youtube, as it shows just how loved and admired she was by everyone she worked with. It's really sad to say farewell to a great series that I would probably say was my overall favourite spin-off. This is in no small way due to the wonderful woman at its centre.

Goodbye Sarah Jane, and rest in peace Elizabeth Sladen.

K-9 (SERIES) (2009-2010):

SEASON 1

Regeneration – 4/10

The 25+ years of trying to make a spin-off programme for the small robotic dog companion of the 4th Doctor finally 'succeeds' (relatively speaking) in this Australian/British series that started in 2009.

Here's a quick K-9 history for those interested (thank you Wikipedia!) – The first K-9 (or K-9 Mark I) was last seen staying behind with the 4th Doctor's companion Leela when she decides to assist the people of Gallifrey (the Doctor's home planet). The 4th Doctor then made a Mark II model, which travelled with him for several adventures, before staying in a parallel universe ('E- Space') with another of the Doctor's companions, Romana (II). The Doctor's relationships with his robotic dogs seems to be rather on the flippant and fleeting side, because we are then told in the doomed 'K-9 and company' that the Doctor has created yet another K-9 (Mark III), but has tired of him too; this time palming him off on Sarah Jane in 1981.

Anyway...on with the story.

We rejoin K-9 mark I in 2050 AD; when he is unwillingly transported via a proto-time machine experiment (rather similar in style to the City of Death story of the 4th Doctor) by Professor Gryffen. The era is a treacherous one, being run by a totalitarian government ('The Department') and enforced by Cyborg police...with me so far?

Two teenage freedom fighting 'cyber-hackers' (Starkey and Jorjie) escape the police, to find themselves interrupting and inadvertently damaging the professor's machine. This brings not the planned return of the professor's family, but the arrival of K-9, hotly pursued by some rather nasty looking reptilian aliens. In a last act of bravery, K-9 Mark I sacrifices himself to save his new found friends from the aliens and blows himself up...before 'regenerating' into a new K-9...Yes, you heard me right...he 'regenerates(!).' He actually manages to rebuild himself from his main C.P.U, in an impressive, but head-scratching moment.

Whilst there are some intriguing ideas on paper, this programme looks like a real mess. The ideas of the original series don't seem to permeate this spin-off half as much as the Sarah Jane Adventures or Torchwood.

The aliens look like they would be more at home in a Teenage Mutant Ninja Turtles film rather than the Doctor Who series. As the writers don't possess any of the licences to tie-in with the main show, no reference or connection can be made to Doctor Who or its characters. The series conveniently gets around this by giving the dog a kind of 'computer amnesia,' caused by his renewal.

I don't have anything against the tin-dog per-say. I'm not a huge fan, true, but I can recognise a certain cuteness and charm he would have with younger children. It's just that I can't see how such a relatively minor character can carry a whole series – he's just not a strong enough focal point to base an entire programme around; even if the supporting cast of characters was very strong...which unfortunately it isn't. It's easy t0 forgive as not very good by saying 'it's only a kid's programme;' but as the excellent Sarah Jane

Adventures could also be described as such, it doesn't really seem good enough in my eyes.

Liberation – 4/10

Starkey (The main young male character who K-9 now belongs to) goes on the run from 'The Department' (the totalitarian government's police) and the 'Jixen' (the aliens that followed K-9 though the time-machine), but finds himself caught and imprisoned. His young friend Jorjie (a kind of 'Hermione-lite') and the professor's assistant Darius (who is less enamoured with the young hero of the show) must help rescue Starkey, K-9 and the alien prisoners that have been captured.

I suppose my main question is – with Torchwood AND U.N.I.T around, just how many alien task forces does London need? Anyway, the series continues to be watchable enough, but very mediocre in comparison to the other spin-offs.

The Korven – 6/10

The professor's S.T.M (Space-Time Manipulator) time-machine/portal/whatever continues to be a welcome entrance for every nasty alien that fancies a pop at the Earth (U.N.I.T must love this guy!). In strolls another one; the Korven - a brain-sucking alien from the future.

Pretty pedestrian, but worth a watch.

The Bounty-Hunter – 2/10

The portal 'free-for-all' continues, as a bounty hunter from the future comes looking for K-9. Meanwhile Starkey and K-9 stop a publicity stunt by the Department who place a fake bomb on a ferris wheel.

Awful acting, boring story...all-in-all a bit rubbish.

The Sirens Of Ceres – 6/10

Jorje's rebellion against the police state catches up with her, and she is placed by her mother (June) in a girl's academy for 'troublesome teens.' She discovers that a piece of alien technology has her classmates under a spell and is keeping them in order with the harshest of punishments.

A lot more interesting than the last couple of episodes; but still nothing to write home about.

Fear Itself – 5/10

An alien is able to spread panic and fear across the city; causing riots and other destructive behaviour. The alien 'lives' in a wardrobe, and can only be seen by those who are scared of it. K-9 is immune, as he doesn't have human emotions.

The idea of a fearsome things in the wardrobe created by fear is a similar one to the Doctor Who episode 'Night Terrors' (Series 6), and for once this series can boast to have had the idea first. Though as expected, it's not a patch on its parent-programme.

The Fall Of The House Of Gryffen – 5/10

Wow, K-9 is really getting arrogant! He's cruising for a de-fusing!

The Professor originally built the S.T.M time portal (which

K-9 came through at the beginning of the series) to try and rescue his wife and two children who had died in an accident. And at last it seems he has succeeded, as they reappear...albeit as ghostly apparitions. In reality, they are beings from an astral plane who take on the look of his family in an attempt to steal the real forms of the main characters. The story sounds much more captivating on paper than on the screen, and this is another flat helping of a rather dire show (as I'm sure you'll have guessed by now!).

Jaws Of Orthrus – 6/10

K-9 appears to have gone mad! A warrant for his arrest is given after he appears to shoot at Drake (evil head of police). It all turns out to be the work of Drake himself, and an 'evil' lookalike he has built to incriminate K-9.

Meanwhile, the love triangle continues between the three teenagers, exacerbated by the differing opinions over K-9's innocence. Jorjie is smitten with Starkey, and sides with him in his protestation that his robot dog is innocent. Darius is smitten with Jorjie, and feels abandoned when he doesn't share his friends' easy acceptance of K-9 in light of the evidence.

All the characters seem to progress slightly in this episode, with the Professor also showing a nice paternal side to his three teenage charges.

There's no getting around it however; we're still in pretty substandard territory.

Dream-Eaters – 6/10

All over the city, people are falling asleep and having nightmares. It is the work of the 'Bodach,' a race of aliens who feed off the brainwave energy caused by dreams.

They are then also able to control the dreamers.

Some much more fun ideas...it's a pity the monsters themselves were so badly executed!

The Curse Of Anubis – 6/10

Ancient-Egyptian looking Alien cyborg/dog/men arrive, and proclaim K-9 to be their lost 'liberator,' worshipping him like a God. They quickly brainwash the professor and others (except Darius, whom they banish) and enact their plot to enslave humanity. When the cyborgs promise to return his memory banks to him, he becomes too busy to see what is going on and fails to help. In the end, Darius steals the intruders' spaceship and turns it on them.

I liked the alien design, which reminded me of something out of 'Pyramids of Mars' (Tom Baker's era).

Oroborus – 3/10

The space-time manipulator starts working by itself. The professor and K-9 fix it, but disturbances in time have already been caused. Starkey starts feeling as if he is going mad. Time starts repeating itself, and only Starkey can see it, leading others to blame him for the odd goings on.

In truth, time is being stolen by a 'space snake' which feeds on time (oooo...k!). Only Starkey is not affected, so he is the only one who can offer himself as a sacrifice/bait for the snake; giving it the 'time of his life' so to speak.

Cue terrible C.G.I giant snake and enough plot holes to strain spaghetti.

Alien Avatar – 6/10

Starkey and K-9 find a strange alien corrosive substance on some dead fish. Some weird aliens keep appearing out of nowhere. The whole team (excluding the Professor, who is agoraphobic and can't leave the house) try to track down the source, and discover it has come from an alien craft that has crash-landed nearby.

Jorjie's mum (one of the heads of the fascist 'Department') joins forces with her daughter's friends, after she becomes concerned that her colleague Drake (evil head of security) is after the alien's power to see into other people's lives.

Strangely for a K-9 story, I found this one quite difficult to follow at times. I liked the aliens though, who were quite an original design.

Aeolian – 1/10

An alien race is calling to each other during a mating ritual, but their song is so powerful it is causing earthquakes and hurricanes.

Jorjie becomes trapped in the earthquake, and Darius comes to her rescue. During this, she tells Darius of her feelings for Starkey, and Darius, who had thought she was talking about him, nearly tells her of his feelings for her.

The show is so ineffectual, that when Hyde Park and the Albert Hall are destroyed, you hardly bat an eyelid.
Added to this is one of the most illogical plots I've ever heard of, and terrible English accents that boarder on the offensive.

The 'love triangle' that progresses in this episode between Starkey, Darius and Jorjie at least adds some interest to the characters; but it's not enough to save this from being another very poor episode.

The Last Oak Tree – 1/10

A giant 'space-centipede' steals the last oak tree in existence from a museum, to build a nest in the sewers of London. O......k! Not a lot you can say about that really is there?!

Black Hunger – 5/10

Darius steals what he thinks is an innovative cleaning tool, which will half his duties as 'hired help' to the Professor. Unfortunately, it turns out the machine is full of millions of alien mites that devour everything in their path. It is all a plan by Drake at the Department to threaten the population and keep them in line. It backfires on him however when this is found out and he is demoted...to be replaced by an even bigger psychopath, Inspector Thorne.

The all-devouring nano-swarm idea reminded me of the Vashta Nerada (Silence in the Library) in Doctor Who, but with none of the innovation that made that episode enthralling. Still a slight improvement on the last few episodes though.

The Cambridge Sky – 3/10

Jorjie is sucked into the time portal (the 'S.T.M' – 'Space-Time Manipulator') and flung into 1963 (interestingly enough the year that its parent show Doctor Who started). Here she meets the double of Darius (with an even worse cockney accent), who turns out to be his Granddad Bill. When she is found to be carrying futuristic technology, her and Bill are imprisoned. The Professor must intervene, before the changes in Bill's life-line cause Darius to have never been born!

It's nice to see the show return to explorations of time, but as usual its depiction of England and 'Englishness' are way off. Also, when exactly is the show supposed to be set in the future again? Surely Darius's Granddad wouldn't have been born in the 1960's? Another embarrassingly poor episode.

Lost Library Of Ukko – 6/10

After Drake's disgrace in Black Hunger, there is a new villain on the scene, Inspector Thorne.

Starkey and Darius sneak into the Department headquarters during a 'careers day.' Getting into Inspector Thorne's office, Starkey is sucked into a 'library card,' (no really). The librarian Ukkons 'archive' endangered planets by shrinking them and housing them in tiny electronic cards. And Thorne has tricked Starkey into one such miniature prison.

With half the run-time of the other spin-offs, you've got to admire the ingenuity of the K-9 team to cram in as novel ideas as possible. But the change of writers each week, and the little time to establish and follow a story through makes the series feel inconsistent and incomplete at times.

Mutant Copper – 1/10

The team finds a damaged Cyborg police-man, who is on the run from the Department after they have been experimenting on him. The Cyborg has been imbued with human characteristics, and now has a new love for life (and a very high-pitched squeaky Australian accent to boot).

Whilst Inspector Thorpe is a much more effective enemy

threat in the series than Drake; this is another real damp squib of an episode. The premise is flawed – I don't understand why everyone is so incensed; as the Cyborg police are surely already partly human? And K-9 is particularly arrogant and annoying in this one.

The Custodians – 7/10

Thorne uses a telepathic alien race and his prison department to create a new 'must-have' game for kids and teenagers...that actually brainwashes them into being catatonic 'model citizens.' The alien has other ideas however, and is using his connection with the human kids to turn them into aliens like him.

A fairly curious idea, and not a bad episode to watch.

Taphony And The Time Loop – 8/10

The Department has been experimenting on creating a child who can travel through time. But what they have actually created is a very dangerous 'time blank' girl, Taphony, who can manipulate time and drain the life-lines of others to make her stronger.

The Professor, who was forced to aid the Department in their experiments long ago, feels guilty for his part in creating the girl, and takes her under his wing. She becomes friends with Jorjie; but it soon becomes apparent that her presence in Jorjie's life is draining her of her life. In the end, it is K-9 that makes Taphony realise she is not right for this time; and she surrenders herself into the vortex of the S.T.M.

The series really leaps forward in this one episode. This is easily the most inventive script (even if its slightly nicked from the 'Weeping Angels' episodes of Doctor Who) and the most visually effective story of the series. If you want to watch just one episode of K-9, this would definitely be my recommendation.

Robot Gladiators – 1/10

Professor Gryffen's revolutionary work with robotics has been stolen, and is being used to create robot fighters for the illegal entertainment of punters. K-9 goes undercover to try and stop it, but is made into a 'gladiator' himself. He makes friends with some 'clown robots' that have been taken from their home in the circus.

It's all an elaborate (but rather stupid) plan by Thorne to get K-9 blown up in the ring; so he can steal his regeneration unit.

The robot clowns that were supposed to be 'cute' were creepy as anything. The plot is nonsensical and ridiculous. Even for this show, this is an exceptionally poor episode.

Mind Snap – 4/10

The S.T.M appears to be more connected to K-9 than originally thought. After a fluctuation, it zaps his circuits - causing him to malfunction wildly. The Professor and Starkey attempt to reinstate his recent memory to get him back on track.

This is a dressed up 'best of' story, in which K-9's memory-banks are used to replay what has happened in the series so far. Which, as we're reminded, isn't up to a great deal of quality.

Angel Of The North – 6/10

Inspector Thorne forces the Professor to visit a Korven spaceship stranded in Canada, where the S.T.M was originally found. They are trying to find the temporal stabiliser, which will make the S.T.M work properly, and allow the Department to use the vortex to their own benefit. The Professor manages to thwart them and keep the stabiliser hidden.

Pretty run-of-the-mill stuff again; but better than the last couple of episodes.

The Last Precinct – 6/10

Darius's long estranged father returns. As an old police officer for the Department, he rebelled when his force was replaced with the Cyborg police. After taking over Professor Gryffen's house (which used to be the police headquarters), he starts to take his revenge. He infects the Cyborg police with a virus to make them useless. This back-fires however, and turns the Cyborgs against humanity.

Not bad; and it's nice to see a bit more depth and backstory to the rather one-dimensional character of Darius.

Hound Of The Korven – 7/10

Thorne makes a deal with Darius for K-9's regeneration unit, in exchange for his father's ethical treatment in jail. K-9 agrees to give Thorne what he wants, if he will give him back his memory chip. Thorne complies...but the chip he gives K-9 is really a bomb that will programme K-9 to destroy himself and his companions.

The Jixen return, and turn out to be allies of the human

race after all. Originally, they followed K-9, who had been programmed by the Korven with a warning of an imminent invasion of their enemies on an unsuspecting Earth.

The writing has improved a lot here, and the episode leads nicely into the series finale.

The Eclipse Of The Korven – 7/10

The Korven are on the brink of invasion. Thorne has K-9's regeneration unit, and puts it into his new creation ('Trojan'); a hybrid of all the alien races that the team have faced, making it indestructible. However, it turns out Thorpe is on the side of the Korven, and is using his new weapon to aid, rather than defeat them.

This action-packed serial ends a dire series on somewhat of a high. There are a few touching moments here and there, and although I'm still not a fan of the programme, I thought it ended well (it looks unlikely to return).

If you like K-9, you may find enjoyment in some of the series, and it may be worth watching a few episodes here and there. I found it a real slog to get through this poorest of all the spin-offs, which is definitely on the lowest end of the franchise. You do eventually warm to the characters, especially the likeable Professor, who saves the day at the end, but overall I would say this is a series to avoid. It took me as long to watch one series of this programme as it did to watch five series of the Sarah Jane Adventures...which should tell you everything you need to know.

CLASS (2016):

SEASON 1

For Tonight We Might Die - 7/10

Kids are going missing from Coal Hill Academy (where the first episode of Doctor Who began) as a strange new student and a strict new teacher cause ructions.

It turns out the student is an alien prince from a destroyed race called the Rhodians who is linked with the teacher, really a terrorist/freedom fighter from the opposing race the Quill, and they are trying to escape from their mutual enemy the Shadow Kin.

The Doctor sends them both to Coal Hill to protect them, but the Shadow Kin follows and the Doctor must save them once again.

In the same way that Torchwood was a spin off for adults and Sarah Jane Adventures was for kids, Class sets its sights on a teenage audience; with its 6th formers tackling school proms and detentions as well as alien threats.

Buried online on BBC3 and featuring cliche characters (the preppy one, the posh one, the sarcastic one and so on) it was the first of the spin offs (if we don't count K9, and nobody counts that) to fall short of its mark and vanish after just one series.

It's watchable enough, but less than inspiring.

The Coach With The Dragon Tattoo - 2/10

In the first episode, the Doctor placed the safety of the school (which just happens to house a rift similar to that in Torchwood through which all kinds of alien threats are attracted) in the hands of the ragtag team of teenagers. Their second threat, after taking on the Shadow Kin, is discovering that the football coach has an alien tattoo that kills people. And the Ofsted inspector is evil...but then that's to be expected.

It feels like the writers came up with the terrible pun title and wrote the episode from there. There is some nice character development in the story, but overall it's not great.

Nightvisiting - 5/10

On the two year anniversary of her father's death, Tanya is visited by what seems to be his ghost.

Of course, this being a Who spinoff it's actually an alien tentacle with the power to tap into the souls of the dead.

A bit of nice suspense in another fairly lacklustre story.

Co-Owner Of A Lonely Heart/ Brave-Ish Heart - 7/10

In the first episode, April's heart was fused with that of the leader of the evil Shadow Kin King. The pull between them is getting stronger and her behaviour is getting more erratic.

This is the least of her problems as her alcoholic dad is out of jail after serving time for crippling his mother by drunk driving.

After leaping through a rift, April (with Ram along for the ride) is set on killing the king of the Shadow Kin.

The 'Governors,' a shadowy investigative agency (similar to Torchwood or UNIT but seemingly less legitimate) are investigating the 'space-time cracks' focused on the school and make a deal with Quill to claim the 'ultimate weapon' to take on the carnivorous flower petals.

It feels a bit of a jolt to suddenly be transported to an alien world after all the adventures being set around the school, but the Hellish other realm gives a nice level of drama and foreboding.

The rest of the episode, like the series, is less convincing.

Detained - 4/10

Quill puts all the gang in detention (whilst she goes on a mission) before their classroom is thrown across the Galaxy.

A 'meteor of truth' flies through to them, causing them all to start revealing their innermost feelings and opinions about each other and generally just being brattish.

After an epic 2-parter, Detained is much more of a 'bottle story' and filler.

The Metaphysical Engine, Or What Quill Did - 3/10

We rejoin Quill to find out what she's been up to during the last episode (when the rest of the team were put in 'space detention').

The head of the 'Governors' make Quill another offer; this time her freedom from the 'head slug' in exchange for her help in a metaphysical world of the 'Arn's' heaven.

I think this is what the plot is about anyway. At this point I am unfortunately far from caring. It's an incredibly forgettable episode, even if I do actually like Quill as a character (possibility of a return in the main series?) and she is given more of a focus here.

The Lost - 6/10

In the final episode (in retrospect of course...they weren't to know the first series would be its last) the Shadow Kin are back on Earth to enact their revenge. They begin by killing Ram's dad and Tanya's mum. The team must decide whether to use the 'ultimate weapon' of Charles' cabinet of souls before Shadow Kin can invade the Earth.

The show makes a fairly decent job of culminating all the strands from the series and ends on a respectable high.

Discounting (the loose connection of) the K9 series, I would count Class as the weakest of the spin offs, so I can't say I'm disappointed it wasn't brought back for a second series. But I *can* see what they were trying to do, and it did have some fun, dramatic and suspenseful moments here and there that some viewers might enjoy.

'BUT YOU LEFT OUT...!'

As well as the spin-offs reviewed here, there is a huge list of available Doctor Who media that I haven't mentioned for various reasons; partly time and resources constraints, partly confusion over whether they are classed as 'canon' with the rest of the 'official' Doctor Who 'universe.' If you want to find out more about the 'extended Whoniverse,' I would recommend checking out the following:

1. <u>Big Finish Audio</u> – a superb range of audio adventures, featuring all of the Doctors, past and present.

2. <u>Doctor Who Comic Strips</u> – There have been many hundreds of Doctor Who comic strips since its inception; and this, along with the audio adventures could take up another book!

3. <u>Doctor Who Computer Games</u> – the B.B.C has made some fantastic computer games for various platforms.

4. <u>B.B.V Productions Doctor Who Video Spin-Offs</u> – Professionally produced videos, written by fans, mostly in the dark days of the cancellation (1989-1996). Notable for featuring many actors from the show; as well as fans who would go on to work on

the re-launch (such as writer Mark Gattis and future Dalek voice artist Nicholas Briggs).

5. Doctor Who and the Curse of Fatal Death – A spoof episode of Doctor Who; shown for Comic Relief in 1999. It features a long list of 'Doctors,' with Rowan Atkinson, Richard E Grant, Jim Broadbent, Hugh Grant and Joanna Lumley acting as the 9th, 10th, 11th, 12th and 13th incarnations of the Doctor respectively. Very funny and well worth tracking down.

6. 'Mixed Media' releases - To my knowledge, there are two main 'mixed media releases,' which centre on a story which is split between animations, audio dramas, live experiences, books and comics. Between 2020-2021, the 'Time Lord Victorious' was released, which follows different iterations of the Doctor after the events of the televised story 'The Waters of Mars.' In 2023, the 'Doom's Day' (not to be confused with the televised story 'Doomsday') story followed an intergalactic assassin's race against death and seeking the help of the Doctor in her escape.

7. Animations - There have been a few animated series which have either been released on special webcasts (during the last days of the cancellation) 'Scream of the Shalka' (featuring future Doctor Who villain Richard E. Grant as the Doctor) and on television around the hugely popular time of David Tennant's run - The Infinite Quest and Dreamland.

8. Blu-Ray Announcement Trailers - To announce and promote the release of different Blu-Ray Seasons of the classic run, the BBC created some really fun mini episodes on YouTube, often featuring a return of a classic companion to continue their story. These have become more elaborate and interesting as the releases have gone on, and so far (at time of writing), they include:

- **Season 2: 'The Storyteller'** - We revisit the First Doctor's companion Vicki nearly 60 years on from the events of 'The Mythmakers.' She is still living in Ancient Greece, now with a granddaughter to tell all her stories of her travels with the Doctor. It's such a touching snippet. Vicki is probably my favourite 'single companion' (if we're counting Ian and Barbara as a couple). Maureen O'Brien imbued Vicki with so much humanity, warmth and genuine curiosity that she was perfect for the show, and she falls straight back into the character as if no time has passed.

- **Season 8: 'Jo Grant vs the Autons...Again?!'** - Clifford Jones is still with Jo Grant all these years after she left the Doctor to be with him. He has made a deadly discovery however in the shape of a plastic daffodil, which signals the return of the Autons! Jo makes short work of them, using what the Doctor taught her. More on the comic side this one, with a funny but short confrontation between a classic companion and monster.

- **Season 9: 'Defenders of Earth'** - The intrepid Jo Grant takes on the Sea Devils. A nice nod to the late Liz Sladen and Stewart Bevan (who we recently saw return in the Season 8 announcement trailer as his original character Clifford Johns). We are also treated to baby Sea Devils - what's not to love?!

- **Season 10: 'Jo Grant Returns'** - The only issue with releasing the sets out of chronological order is that there is some inconsistency in the plots. Clifford and Jo are back; this time taking on the giant maggots. Katy Manning is such a wonderfully larger than life personality that you can't help but be swept up in her adventures.

- **Season 12: Trailer** - A much more straightforward trailer, with highlights from the season, with a little reminder by Tom Baker to subscribe to the

YouTube channel.

- **Season 14: 'The Home Assistants of Death?!'** - Louise Jameson has just bought herself a 'Voc Robot' from The Robots of Death. This is a comedy skit set in the real world, so obviously isn't canon, but it's lovely to see Louise showing what she does best.

- **Season 17: 'Davros Rises!'** - A dusty Davros reassembles his Dalek army in this season's teaser.

- **Season 18: Announcement Trailer** - Tom Baker presents a spoof advert to the dangerous locations of the season, with more of a nod to showrunner Douglas Adams.

- **Season 19: 'Safety Video with Tegan Jovanka'** - Another meta-spoof with Tegan giving an in-flight introduction to the boxset.

- **Season 20: 'Tegan's Surprise Reunion'** - Tegan is contacted by Nyssa in what appears to be a sweet reunion, but is actually the effects of the Mara still playing tricks on her. A lot more elaborate and almost an episode in itself.

- **Season 22: 'The Eternal Mystery'** - Peri, now the 'Warrior Queen' mourns her late husband King Yrcanos before she is joined by a guard she convinces to come on some adventures with her and the Doctor.

- **Season 23: 'The Sixth Doctor is on Trial AGAIN!'** - Colin Baker is put on trial for a parking fine in a hilarious meta comedy on the series.

- **Season 24: 'A Business Proposal for Mel!'** - Sixth Doctor companion Melanie Bush is now a successful business owner, playing 'Dragon's Den' to a rogue's gallery of entrepreneurs' ideas which have some shocking themes from Season 24. I particularly loved 'Derek the Tetrap.'

- **Season 26: 'Ace Returns!'** - Ace, now the head of 'A Charitable Earth' recounts her adventures with the Doctor 30 years later.

There will no doubt be something important I've missed off the list, and if so, I apologise. Doctor Who is without doubt one of the most inspirational shows, and has spawned so many tie-ins that there's always something new to discover. I hope this book will inspire you to start your own research into finding out more!

ANALYSIS OF AN ICONIC SHOW

In the final section of this book, I will be adding my own analysis of the show. As with the rest of this book, this is to be treated as a subjective viewpoint; and the reader is of course free to disagree and form their own opinions! My own opinion of my favourite episodes and characters changes as I re-watch episodes, so I may well disagree with some of these myself in a few months time!

There's nothing most Doctor Who fans like more than a list, and I'm no exception! So I'll be sharing my personal favourite things about the show. I will then look more deeply into what I consider to be the crucial elements that make up the character of the Doctor and their companions. And finally, I will take a short look at the huge impact the show has had since it started all those years ago.

1. LISTS

My Favourite Doctors

1. Patrick Troughton (2nd Doctor)
2. William Hartnell (1st Doctor)
3. Tom Baker (4th Doctor)
4. Sylvester McCoy (7th Doctor)
5. Peter Capaldi (12th Doctor)
6. Matt Smith (11th Doctor)
7. David Tennant (10th Doctor)
8. Christopher Eccleston (9th Doctor)
9. Peter Davison (5th Doctor)
10. Jon Pertwee (3rd Doctor)
11. Jo Martin (The Fugitive Doctor)
12. Paul McGann (8th Doctor)
13. John Hurt (The War Doctor)
14. Jodie Whittaker (13th Doctor)
15. Colin Baker (6th Doctor)

My Favourite (And Least Favourite) Serials For Each Doctor

William Hartnell

Favourite –
The Aztecs

Least Favourite –
The Web Planet

Patrick Troughton

Favourite –
Tomb of the Cybermen
Least Favourite –
The Dominators

Jon Pertwee

Favourite –
Terror of the Autons
Least Favourite –
The Ambassadors of Death

Tom Baker

Favourite –
The Ark in Space
Least Favourite –
The Ribos Operation

Peter Davison

Favourite –
Kinda
Least Favourite –
Terminus

Colin Baker

Favourite –
Vengeance on Varos
Least Favourite –
Revelation of the Daleks

Sylvester Mccoy

Favourite –
Remembrance of the Daleks
Least Favourite -
Delta and the Bannermen

Paul Mcgann

Doctor Who (1996 Film)

Christopher Eccleston

Favourite –
Parting of the Ways

Least Favourite –
Bad Wolf

David Tennant

Favourite –
Family of Blood/Human Nature
Least Favourite –
The Runaway Bride

Matt Smith

Favourite –
Vincent and the Doctor
Least Favourite –
Let's Kill Hitler

Peter Capaldi

Favourite -
World Enough and Time/The Doctor Falls
Least Favourite -
Kill the Moon

Jodie Whittaker

Favourite -
The Timeless Children
Least Favourite -
The Tsuranga Conundrum

My Favourite (And Least Favourite) Serials Of The 'Spin-Off' Series

Torchwood

Favourite Episode – Countrycide

Least Favourite Episode –
Kiss, Kiss, Bang, Bang

The Sarah Jane Adventures

Favourite Episode –
Whatever Happened to Sarah Jane?
Least Favourite Episode –
Secrets of the Stars

K-9 (Series)

Favourite Episode –
Taphony and the Timeloop
Least Favourite Episode –
Robot Gladiators

Class

Favourite Episode –
Co-owner of a Lonely Heart/Brave-ish Heart
Least Favourite Episode –
The Coach with the Dragon Tattoo

My Favourite Companions/Allies Of The Doctor

1. Sarah Jane Smith (3rd, 4th, 10th and 11th Doctor)
2. Ian Chesterton (1st Doctor)
3. Barbara Wright (1st Doctor)
4. Brigadier Alistair Lethbridge-Stewart (Doctors 2-7)
5. Ace (7th Doctor)
6. Leela (4th Doctor)
7. Vicki (1st Doctor)

8. Jamie McCrimmon (2nd Doctor)
9. Zoe Herriot (2nd Doctor)
10. Liz Shaw (3rd Doctor)

My Favourite Monsters/Aliens

1. The Cybermen (First seen in The Tenth Planet)
2. The Zygons (First seen in Terror of the Zygons)
3. The Ice Warriors (First seen in The Ice Warriors)
4. The Daleks (First seen in The Daleks)
5. The Weeping Angels (First seen in Blink)
6. Sil (First seen in Vengeance on Varos)
7. The Ood/Sensorites (First seen in The Sensorites/The Impossible Planet)
8. 'The Silence' (First seen in The Impossible Astronaut)
9. The Silurians (First seen in Doctor Who and the Silurians)
10. The Sontarans (First seen in The Time Warrior)

My Favourite Evil Masterminds

1. The Master (Various stories)
2. Davros (Various stories)
3. Tobias Vaughn (The Invasion)
4. Tlotoxl (The Aztecs)
5. The Toymaker (The Celestial Toymaker)
6. The Valeyard ('Trial of a Timelord' Series)
7. Dukkha (Kinda)
8. The Dream Lord (Amy's Choice)
9. Eric Klieg (Tomb of the Cybermen)
10. Doctor Solon (Brain of Morbius)

My Favourite Androids/Robots

1. Sandminer Robots (The Robots of Death)
2. Clockwork Androids (The Girl in the Fireplace)
3. K-1 (Robot)
4. Autons (First seen in Spearhead from Space)
5. Yeti (First seen in The Abominable Snowmen)
6. Winders (The Beast Below)
7. Kamelion (First seen in The King's Demons)
8. Handbots (The Girl Who Waited)
9. 'Android' (The Visitation)
10. K-9 (First seen in The Invisible Enemy)

My Favourite 'Historical' Tie-In Episodes

1. Vincent and the Doctor (11th Doctor)
2. The Aztecs (1st Doctor)
3. The Empty Child/The Doctor Dances (9th Doctor)
4. The Time Meddler (1st Doctor)
5. The Shakespeare Code (10th Doctor)
6. Cold War (11th Doctor)
7. The King's Demons (5th Doctor)
8. The Fires of Pompeii (10th Doctor)
9. The Time Warrior (3rd Doctor)
10. The Massacre of St. Bartholomew's Eve (1st Doctor)

My Favourite Vehicles/Space Ships

1. T.A.R.D.I.S (The Doctor's)

2. Sontaran Battlecraft Pod
3. Space Station Nerva (The Ark in Space)
4. Dalek Mothership
5. Time Lord Space Station ('Trial of a Time Lord' series)
6. 'Bessie'
7. The Whomobile
8. T.A.R.D.I.S (The Master's)
9. The Ark (The Ark)
10. Cyber-Ship (Revenge of the Cybermen)

My Favourite Filming Locations

1. St. Peter's Steps, London (The Invasion)
2. Jodrell Bank, Cheshire (Logopolis)
3. Caerphilly Castle and Cardiff Castle, South Wales (The Rebel Flesh)
4. Cambridge (various locations) (Shada)
5. Tyntesfield House, Bristol (Hide)
6. National Botanical Garden of Wales, Carmarthen (The Waters of Mars)
7. Buckhurst House, Sussex (Black Orchid)
8. Oldbury Power Station, Gloucester (Hand of Fear)
9. Portmeirion, Gwynedd (The Masque of Mandragora)
10. Louvre Museum, Paris, France (City of Death)

I hope this has inspired you to start making your very own Doctor Who lists!

2. THE CHARACTER OF THE DOCTOR (AND HOW TO PLAY THEM?)

Of course, the main reason the show has been so popular for so long is the character of the Doctor themself. As I discussed in the introduction, there is no other hero quite like the Doctor. The strange alien with a sense of morality, who travels the realms of time and space to save people from oppression and invasion, using their intellect rather than their fists to right wrongs and save the day. Though they are so much to so many, they are ultimately alone; travelling the universe with an ever changing companion and a time machine they have little control over.

The blue-print for the character of the Doctor was first laid down by the original writers, producers, and of course the inimitable William Hartnell. Since then, all of the actors to play the Doctor have stretched their personality, whilst retaining the core elements that make the Doctor such a fascinating character. They are both accessible and mysterious at the same time; the ultimate 'everyperson' and the ultimate 'alien' in one role.

I have tried to simplify the character of the Doctor into

what I see as three distinct parts - the 'authoritative adult,' 'the inquisitive child' and the 'eccentric alien.' By understanding how each actor has utilised or restrained these individual elements, I would argue we have a way of measuring their effectiveness at portraying the role and engaging with the audience. This is because I believe these elements are aimed very cleverly at the different sections of the audience at home; the child (who of course is the main demographic the show is aimed at), their family and the student fraternity that have helped make the show into such a 'cult' as well as 'mainstream' success (in the same way as other British television institutions like Monty Python's Flying Circus).

I will now look at the pros and cons of stretching each of these elements in creating a portrayal of the Doctor...

Firstly, we have the 'authoritative adult.' The extremes of this element can be seen in the first Doctor (portrayed by William Hartnell), the third Doctor (as portrayed by Jon Pertwee), the sixth Doctor (Colin Baker), the ninth Doctor (Christopher Eccleston) and the twelve Doctor (Peter Capaldi). The advantage of this element is the trust it gives us that the Doctor's intellect and wisdom will carry us through to a safe conclusion. This helps children to feel a certain security and belief in the Doctor. No matter what the odds, the 'authoritative Doctor' will carry an unspoken control of the situation.

If this element is taken too far however, it can distance the Doctor from his audience; making him seem aloof, cold and dislikeable. For me, the third and sixth Doctor often skated this line. This created some rather unsatisfactory scenes in which the Doctor would chastise their companion and become someone it was difficult to like. This is a crucial error in a television show where the Doctor is the one *constant* in an ever- changing world of monsters and other dangers. When this element threatened to damage the series, the producers would try to employ methods that could soften the Doctor's character and return them to their loveable, more child-like innocence and charms. The first Doctor started out as very distrusting of humans, (which is understandable as the character was on the run from their own kind and lost in a strange new world). This harshness was softened through the qualities of their grand-daughter Susan; who persuaded them to see the best in their human stowaways, Ian and Barbara. Over the course of his time, Hartnell's character went from being rather a cantankerous, even aggressive Doctor (showing a violent side in both the first serial and in the Reign of Terror) to more of a loving grandfatherly figure. In the case of the third and sixth Doctors, the character was softened gradually as they became more caring and concerned about their companions, Jo and Peri respectively. The ninth Doctor was the gnarled survivor of the 'time war,' so returned to more of a tough and authoritative presence. Eccleston really pulled off this hard 'Northern' persona, but worked slightly less effectively when showing the more 'kooky' side of the Doctor's character.

The second element, which of course is a very important one in engaging the children in the audience is that of the 'inquisitive child' persona. This makes the Doctor instantly likeable to children - the idea of an adult character who is as full of the youthful energy and love of life as they are. The advantages and disadvantages of stretching this element can be seen in the second Doctor (Patrick Troughton) and the seventh (Sylvestor McCoy) respectively. After the first Doctor was portrayed so well by William Hartnell, Patrick Troughton wisely decided to take the character off in a new direction, which would include a more youthful and action-orientated approach. Even more wisely perhaps, he decided to also retain certain elements that had made the first Doctor such an intriguing character; such as the huge intellect and ability to out-think his opponent at every turn. By combining the elements of both 'child' and 'adult,' the second Doctor created the skill of the 'fool's bluff.' Whilst Hartnell's Doctor would command authority of a situation as soon as he walked in, Troughton's Doctor was the exact opposite, often being ignored and underestimated by his enemies. He could then use this to his advantage; to fool his enemy into believing he was idiotic and ridiculous, both by the way he presented himself (the 'cosmic hobo') and the way in which he gave the impression he didn't have a clue what was going on. This clever technique then lulled the enemy into a false sense of security and allowed him time and space to plot their downfall. The second Doctor became very adept at utilising this technique; using the element of 'inquisitive child' as a smokescreen for the 'authoritative adult' within, whilst also endearing him to both elements of the audience at the same time.

Unfortunately, the same thought wasn't put into the seventh Doctor's portrayal in his first few serials. At this point in time, the series was already in dire straits. As I've discussed, the sixth Doctor had been played as the 'authoritative adult' in a far too extreme way; creating a Doctor who was distant from the audience. Sylvestor McCoy was given the very difficult job of taking over from this and reaching the programme's young audience again. Understandably, he went for a much more 'child-like' Doctor again, but pushed it too far this time. Basing himself on Charlie Chaplin, he created a Doctor who was laughable and ridiculous. As a result, serials like Time and the Rani and Paradise Towers are embarrassing and difficult to watch.

Realising this mistake (some fans might say too late) the series took a different angle, with the introduction of the troubled companion Ace. By bringing in a companion whom the Doctor could support like a father figure, the balance of adult-child was restored and he became a much more loveable and inspirational character as a result.

Thirdly, there is the element of the 'eccentric alien,' perfectly portrayed by possibly the most popular of all Doctor characterisations, Tom Baker. Tom found a way early on of incorporating the authoritative aspects of Hartnell, the child-like qualities of Troughton and weaving it into a weird alien *bohemian eccentricity* that would endear him not only to the younger and older demographics, but also to the student fraternity, a fairly new audience for the show at the time. He still had his moments of supreme intellect. Cleverly though these were rarely directed at others and he would instead ramble monologues to himself that at once made him seem highly intelligent and just the right amount of 'odd,' to make him intriguing.

Again, as with the other two elements, the actor has to make sure they don't push the eccentricity too far and create a Doctor who is out of touch to the point where they can't interact. The Doctor needs to be 'apart' from their surroundings, but also connected enough to engage with them.

A further, more contentious element to the Doctor is that of the 'romantic hero.' This can be seen mostly in the portrayal of the 5th (Peter Davison), 8th (Paul McGann) and 10th (David Tennant) Doctors. These Doctors were young, dashing and brave; attracting many the affection of the 'fangirls' and 'fanboys' in the audience. The 5th Doctor was admired mostly by 'extra' female characters that came in, rather than his companions. The 8th and 10th Doctors however had romantic (if unfulfilled) connections with their companions for the first time.

The 11th (Matt Smith) Doctor was again desired by his companions, but was much more awkward in his reaction to this sort of attention which added to his 'eccentric alien' traits.

The approach of the dashing hero does have advantages – it makes the Doctor loveable, inspirational and a heroic role model for their audience. However, when stretched too far, it can detract from the 'alien aloofness' that the Doctor needs to make them fascinating as a character. They can lose some of the eccentricity of the character; making them less mysterious. They become more of a conventional hero in this guise, which makes them stand out less from the other science fiction/drama serials around. The 'loco parentis' they have had with previous companions and the clear age difference (at least in years) is compromised when they become a 'sex symbol' to them; and this is something I struggle with at times.

However, when the writing is right, there can be some truly emotive moments created by the amorous tension between the Doctor and their companion. The most obvious example of this is between the 10th Doctor and Rose. I see this as the closest the Doctor has been to being 'in love' since the 4th Doctor and Sarah Jane Smith, and after so many hundreds of years alone, you can hardly begrudge them for that.

So, overall it would appear the perfect portrayal of the Doctor is measured by the amount they balance the elements of 'adult,' 'child' and 'eccentric' (with the occasional hint of the romantic thrown in). This is no easy feat; especially as it needs to be constantly changing and stretching in different directions to keep the character unique. The most popular Doctors (such as Tom Baker and David Tennant) have managed to create a character with great depth and dimensions. But all of the actors who have played the Doctor deserve a huge amount of respect for bringing such a complex role to life with such individual panache.

3. THE COMPANION (AND HOW TO PLAY THEM?)

The second most important portrayal in the series is that of the companion. At its worst, the companion simply serves as someone to get into trouble and to be rescued by the Doctor. At its best however, the companion can serve as the counter-balance by which the crucial elemental shifts we have talked about (from adult to child to eccentric and back again) can be realised. It's about bringing the best out of the Doctor, whether by 'humanising' them (such as Susan, Barbara and Ian's effect on the first Doctor) or in giving them a paternal/grandfather/mother role (in the case of Vicki for the first Doctor or Ace for the seventh). A companion can give them someone to bounce ideas off of, someone to educate or someone to do all the more physical things that could cause them to break their non-violent approach. A good companion acts as a mirror to the Doctor, showing them their strengths and faults and giving them something to strive for.

At their best, the Doctor's companion can also become a dramatic focus in their own right. The best example of this is probably Sarah Jane Smith, as played by the wonderful Elizabeth Sladen. Not only did she have an unmistakable chemistry with Tom Baker, but she was intriguing in her own right; leading scenes that she could sustain without the main character. Her character's appeal was such that she even got her own spin-off series nearly 35 years later. And yet at no point did you feel she was 'aping' or 'competing' for the Doctor's limelight in the scenes they shared. She managed to both be strong and vulnerable, intelligent and yet in awe of the Doctor's mysteries.

Other companions that have effectively combined strength and vulnerability have included Leela and Ace from the 'classic' era. Both were very strong, independent, but flawed individuals, who looked up to the Doctor as the one constant on their unsure path. In the 'modern' era, Rose and Amy have shown both a tenacity and drive, coupled with a love and admiration for the 'mad man in the blue box.'

Some companions have not been able to ride this delicate balance as effectively. They may have seemed too weak willed or not had the strength of character to make them as interesting. An older example of this would be Victoria (2nd Doctor), who was likeable, but who would scream at her own shadow. In the 'modern' show, Martha (10th Doctor) was also an amiable character, but lacked the depth or edge to make her character as memorable as the more popular Rose who preceded her. On the other end of the scale we have companions who are *so* self-assured as to appear arrogant and conceited. Companions such as Romana I (4th Doctor) from the 'classic' era or Clara (11th-12th Doctor) from the 'modern' era appear to condescend and ridicule the Doctor at every opportunity they get. This can lead to some funny moments certainly...but it can also lead us to not believing as strongly in our main character...which I believe is dangerous for the show.

For male companions, the Doctor/companion relationship

can be even more problematic. They need to be broad enough characters to make them watchable and likeable; whilst never stealing the thunder from the main character at the centre of the programme.

The series hasn't had as many male companions, and when it has, it has approached it in different ways. In the case of Ian (1st Doctor), the 'other man' was there as the Doctor's moral compass (he was a lot more 'alien' in his first incarnation, and at first wouldn't always take the most noble approach), and also as 'the muscle,' when the more 'frail' Doctor wasn't able to perform energetic feats of bravery. The 2nd and 3rd Doctor's pacifism was countered by Jamie and the Brigadier respectively; who would charge in with their brawn. This was in stark contrast to the Doctor's more peaceful, cerebral approach.

Occasionally, the Doctor's male companion was the butt of the jokes, and this seemed less effective. This can be seen in the much underrated Harry (4th Doctor) and Rory (11th Doctor). These derided characters only worked by combining a true heart and honourable intent to their comedic traits, through the use of good writing.

Each companion has interacted with the Doctor in their own way, and each fan has their own favourites. Like all actors who have played the Doctor, the many actors and actresses who have walked through the T.A.R.D.I.S doors deserve a great deal of respect for their part in helping us walk alongside the Doctor; asking them all the questions that we wanted to ask at home.

4. ANATOMY OF A DOCTOR WHO SERIAL

The average 'classic' era Doctor Who serial has four parts, each lasting around 25 minutes. At the end of each of the 3 episodes leading up to the finale, there is a 'cliff-hanger' (in the case of Dragonfire this is taken rather too literally!). This creates the necessity to move the story along and towards 3 dramatic events. I have found that often, this seems to take a certain pattern...

Episode 1 - Where are we? Who's this? What do they want?... MONSTER!
Episode 2 - Escape, run around, what are we going to do?... CAPTURE!
Episode 3 - Escape again, think of a plan... CAPTURE!
Episode 4 - Escape again, execute plan, save the day... WHERE Next?

In the 'modern' show, the story usually has to be wrapped up within one 45 minute episode. This means that the pace often seems faster, but also on occasion the epic nature of the story isn't given enough space and time to fully develop. There are pros and cons with both the 'classic' and 'modern' era approach. With the right writers and directors, there is superb utilisation of both run-times. All respect must go to the visionary people who have worked within the time constraints of the 'old' and 'new' show to create truly iconic pieces of television.

5. THE IMPACT OF THE SHOW

Imagine a world without Doctor Who? It's a difficult concept. The impact of the show cannot be overstated. Over 60 years, it has become the longest running science-fiction programme on British television and one of the most iconic shows across the world. Even people who have never seen the show will no doubt have some knowledge of what someone is talking about when they mention 'The T.A.R.D.I.S' or 'The Daleks.' It has been referenced, satirised, borrowed from and paid homage to. It has inspired many generations of children and adults and is a crucial element of popular culture. From a practical viewpoint, the show's history maps an ever- evolving media, and it has often been at the forefront of new ideas. It has helped pioneer technology in vision and sound. From a narrative perspective, the character of the Doctor has presented us with a very different kind of hero. It has helped generations of children to believe not only in a wider universe; but in a peaceful way to interact with it.

It's difficult to imagine a world without Doctor Who, and the immense impression it has left on the public consciousness. A hero, and a show for the ages.

FINAL THOUGHTS AND THANKS

Well, that's it. I've had a blast working my way through 60 years of Doctor Who. It's been hard work at times (most notably through some of the Jon Pertwee, Colin Baker and Jodie Whittaker stories), but it's also been some of the best television I've ever seen or am likely to see, and I can only thank the creators and countless writers and producers who have worked on the show for that. I am hugely thankful to my loving wife Lucy for her belief and encouragement, and to my knowledgeable and generous friends for teaching me so much about the show, for lending me their extensive collections and for being so supportive with me in the making of this book. I hope you have enjoyed reading it and that it will encourage you to revisit your favourite episodes, or discover new ones.

Thank you. Tim.

Printed in Great Britain
by Amazon

37661055R00255